Of Time-Cracked Granite

Book One of
The Odyssea Transmortem

Gaines Post

OF TIME-CRACKED GRANITE

Copyright © 2024 by Gaines Post

An **Otherspect** title

www.otherspect.com

ISBN: 978-1-922739-00-1

Cover art by Gavin Post.

for Fiona

Stories by Gaines Post

THE ODYSSEA TRANSMORTEM

1. Of Time-Cracked Granite

2. Of Rain-Battered Vine (forthcoming)

SHORT STORIES

The Pinnacle

That One Pretty Thing

Of Time-Cracked Granite

Chapter One

Tara had always liked graveyards. On her way to school she would often cut through Willow Cemetery, taking a few extra minutes to meander along its silent lanes or pick a new spot to sit and stare at dates etched in granite. She felt at peace among all those headstones, especially the oldest ones, and liked to imagine who the deceased had been, what they had done while still living, what their dreams and aspirations had been. Sometimes she made up entire lives in her head.

This particular slab was so mossy and weathered its dates were difficult to make out, and the inscription below them impossible. The first year looked to be 1790-something; she decided the second could be either 1813 or 1818.

Finlay MacCarthy.

"What made you end up here, Mr. Finlay MacCarthy?" she mumbled, pondering the various fates that could have put a man of that era into an early grave.

A crow bolted overhead, startling a pair of songbirds from the small cedar across the lane. Tara stood.

The sun was well and truly up now, bringing golden warmth to the late winter morning. Though it had not quite been cold enough to frost, she could still feel the chill through her dark blue hoodie and jeans. She turned to face the burning globe, and for one long peaceful moment, her mind dwelled on nothing but its glorious rays as they touched her skin, blooming red through closed lids.

She checked her phone. 7:36—time to start making her way to school. She had a geometry test that morning and was feeling anxious about it; Mrs. Wagster had already warned her twice about the "very real possibility" of failing eleventh grade. Neck rigid, Tara shouldered her bag and headed off in the direction of the south entrance.

There were areas where the grass had not been mowed in a while and was heavily laden with dew. Careful to keep her shoes dry, she steered clear of these, aiming instead for spots with sparser vegetation or hopping from gravel patch to gravel patch. A very long time ago, her father had taught her how best to walk a path: Keep your weight centered; stick to the flat spots whenever possible; always plan your steps; avoid roots or pointy rocks or anything slippery. Over time, he had explained, this would make for more efficient use of energy, enabling one to hike farther before exhaustion set in....

She could still hear his measured words. He and her mother had given her a tiny backpack to wear, no more than a mini knapsack, really; not too big for an eight-year-old. It was so she could carry her share of the load, they had said, but she thought they'd probably just wanted her to feel useful and involved.

The crow called her out of her reverie. Tara looked up and realized she had somehow gone the wrong way; by now she should be approaching the southern edge of the cemetery, but she apparently was nowhere near it. Glancing around, she was stunned to see the same headstone from earlier, only a few feet to her left.

Finlay MacCarthy.

What the...? She was standing in almost the exact same spot she had been a few minutes before.

Did I make a complete circle?! Stupid idiot.

Clouds were moving in. A strong wind kicked up and dragged at the long, newly budded willow fronds like river water through seaweed, or fingers through hair. Tara shivered.

Scolding herself for being a daydreaming fool, she set off once again toward the cemetery entrance, this time at a faster clip and making sure to pay closer attention to where she was going. As she moved, she casually touched her phone's screen on to see how much time she had wasted. What she saw stopped her dead in her tracks.

7:36.

Surely not.

Am I losing my mind?

She blinked several times in confusion. It had easily been a good three or four minutes at least since she had left this place; she was absolutely certain of it.

Weird. Brow furrowed, she shook her phone and watched the screen until the clock flipped over to 7:37. *Okay, so it's definitely still working, at least.* With a mental shrug, she decided she must have simply looked at her phone wrong the first time. It had been a crap night of sleep, after all, so she was pretty tired. Dumping the phone into her bag, she concentrated on putting one foot in front of the other while doing her level best to ignore the building anxiety. It wasn't just the impending test; she always felt this way before school. Some mornings were worse than others, though, and this one was suddenly beginning to feel like a prime candidate for taking the cake.

Tara strode past the newer and relatively treeless section of tombstones and plaques, around the little clump of young ornamental maples next to the entrance, and under the wrought-iron archway, all the while clinging to the details of her surroundings as though they might escape her and spin her right back around to where she had started. Skirting the barren rose bushes to where the gravel met pavement, she glanced to her left up the road that led out of town and stood still for a moment. Powerlines, strung taut like weighted fishing lines or dog-sleigh lashes, narrowed with the road in a trick of perspective toward a cloudy horizon. There was something magnetic about that spot where the road disappeared into an unseen beyond. To Tara, it felt as though it were pulling at her feet like a drain. Or like a big strong hand tugging at her own, grasping warm and firm, accompanied by some distant voice that kept whispering, *Come on, it's this way, just over the hill; it's just over there.…*

Someday, she'd get to see what the world was like beyond that horizon and all the others. Someday, she would let the road take her.

She got to school eleven minutes before the bell—enough time to sit in the seniors' quad and go over her math notes for a bit. She liked to get here early like this; it gave her a moment to sit quietly and compose herself, let her morning anxiety ebb, and that tended to make the din and chaos around her a bit more bearable. She took out her folder and began to leaf through it.

"Hey, *Reed*. I thought you weren't allowed back at school for like another month or something."

Tara looked up. Nora Childs, in all her immaculately dressed blonde bombshell glory, stood flanked by her two besties-of-the-semester. One of them, Sarah, was making a show of eyeing Tara's far less than name-brand shoes.

"I said not to call me that," Tara said in a low monotone, and then pretended to return her attention to her notes.

The shoe judge snorted. "Yeah, better not, or else she might completely lose it again."

Nora's exaggerated "Ha!" clacked like a dropped plastic plate. She had never used to laugh like that, Tara thought; not back before middle school, when she and Tara had been attached at the hip. "Meh. Come on, let's leave *Reed* to her happy place." The three girls snickered and continued on their way.

The familiar wave of anxiety surged through Tara, threatening to capsize her. She bit the inside of her bottom lip hard enough to taste copper. Heart pounding in her throat, she fought the abrupt urge to punch something or worse. She could literally *feel* the violence; it was right there in her chest, immediate and palpable, less than a hair's breadth from the edge of control. All the muscles in her body yearned to explode into action.

She recognized this feeling. This time, however, instead of letting it possess her, she made a conscious effort to recall her exercises. Taking slow, deep breaths, she fingered the rubber band in her pocket and focused on a speck on the ground while she waited for the adrenaline to subside. The agonizing seconds dragged by. A cold little raindrop touched the back of her hand, and another landed on her neck. Droplets were spotting the concrete. She breathed again.

It was going to be okay; the edge was receding. Very carefully, Tara put her math folder away, all the paper notes neatly tucked in, corners squared with corners and nothing accidentally folded or askew. She then stood, shouldered her bag, and forced her trembling legs in the direction of class.

Only a few minutes in, the test was already going as badly as she had feared. Outside was a complete downpour. The rain pelted sideways at the windows, and it and the double punches of lightning-thunder pummeled the whiplashed trees in a contorted rhythm. Tara was reminded of a storm that had once hit while she and her brother and their parents had been at a car campground out west, years ago, back when her dad was still alive. It had come in the middle of the night, and she could still picture in her mind how the erratic flashes of lightning had illuminated those massive thunderheads like light bulbs, the rumbles growing ever louder and more persistent as the storm made its slow but inevitable way up the valley toward their solitary tent.

Her dad had stood outside for a long time, watching, judging, gauging, a dead-serious look on his face as he counted the seconds between lightning and thunder as the wind whipped up and the pines began to bend. Making an abrupt decision, he'd barked at them to quickly grab their sleeping bags and pillows and double-time it into the minivan. As Tara had dashed from the tent to the sliding van door, barefoot on soft earthy pine needles and arms full of sleeping bag and down jacket and her precious diary, a few big fat raindrops had smacked coldly against her face. She had paused to peer down the valley at the dazzling lightning show. In that moment, she had been able to see quite clearly that all that deadly power and brilliance would soon be upon them. She had also known that she should get to safety without delay. Instead of fear, however, she had felt a profound thrill, deep in her bones.

A little alarm went off inside Tara's mind as she realized she was daydreaming. The storm outside continued to rage, and time was ticking by. She forced herself to concentrate on the test.

Even the tenth-graders finished before she did, and in those last few minutes of grappling wildly with hypotenuses and alternate interior angles and shaded areas, Tara could sense Mrs. Wagster hovering from afar as the clock ticked down and down and down like a bomb fuse. Still, despite the tumult of stress and mortification her brain had become, Tara somehow managed to stumble through the last proof right as the bell rang. Avoiding the teacher's eyes, she slipped her paper into the basket on her way to the door.

"Good job, Miss Yewa," Mrs. Wagster offered quietly as she walked past. Tara gave a polite nod, but kept her eyes glued to her feet, face burning ten shades of red. It had most definitely *not* been a good job, but hopefully a passing one.

Somehow, she made it through the rest of the morning. An optimistic rumor of a tornado watch ended in disappointment as the storm passed and school stayed open. At lunch, some boys got in trouble for throwing saltines into the big hanging fan in the corner of the cafeteria that was missing its front grill. Each time a cracker hit home, it made a funny *bzzzzt* sound. The lunch lady was furious, but it took her a long time to figure out who the culprits were. Everyone got glared at for giggling.

Two more periods, and Tara would be able to escape this unbearable pit. Feeling extremely claustrophobic, she carefully made her way down the hall, sticking to the center to keep from being jostled or slammed into by all the knots of insane teenagers around her.

Someone yanked on her backpack from behind, and she nearly jumped right out of her shoes. She swung around glaring hard, expecting to find yet another annoying boy who thought he was being funny, but grinning up at her was Abby Lewis.

"Hey Tara," the shorter girl chirped. "Sorry! I didn't mean to startle you."

"Oh, it's okay. Hi, Abby." Tara had not known her for very long, but a few weeks before, the two of them had spent the better part of an hour sitting next to each other in the office, each waiting to see the vice principal for different reasons. Since that day, Abby had been trying very hard to be her friend.

Abby hesitated, as though suddenly unsure of how to broach something.

"What's up?" Tara prompted.

"Oh! Not much, really. But… well, me and Daphne are having a beading party after school at her house, and we were wondering if you might wanna come. Do you have to work this afternoon?"

"Beading? Seriously? And no, not until day after tomorrow."

"Cool. And yeah, kinda silly, I know, but we thought it might be fun." Abby shrugged. Then she added in a conspiratorial voice, "Oh, and guess what! I'm pretty sure *Josh* is gonna be there."

"Josh? Barrundia? At a beading party?"

Abby widened her eyes theatrically. "I guess the man likes his beads."

"Yeah, I guess." Tara glanced down the hall in the direction of her next class, wincing inwardly at the angsty jumble of hairdos and backpacks and flying pieces of paper.

"Well? Want to?"

She swallowed and stared at the floor for another agonizing moment, unable to decide. Even if these particular people did seem relatively easy to be around, Tara tended to shy away from others whenever she could. She dreaded the prospect of having to act all "normal" and "centered" in a social situation, especially one at which Josh, the object of her one-time crush, would be present. Cynthia, her psychologist, would of course say she needed to make some friends and get more accustomed to social interaction.

It was one of Tara's biggest problems, this confounding and near total lack of social skills. She never felt confident. She never knew what to say. Besides, she wasn't exactly an arts and crafts person anyway, so a very large part of her was yearning to use that as an excuse to say no. She also felt pretty certain people in general didn't actually want her around, so it always felt simpler just to avoid them.

But Abby was evidently determined to contradict that thought pattern; this wasn't the first time she'd invited Tara to do something after school, so she genuinely seemed to want to be her friend. Also, today was Tuesday, and Nick would be home. The second Tara walked in the door, she'd feel those critical eyes on her and hear that condescending tone as he asked how school had been, whether she had any homework, if she had eaten all of her lunch this time, and so on and so forth. He was like some relentless tyrannical microscope, only one with an invisible shield around him— her mother's adoration—which kept Tara from doing anything but nodding and answering his daily interrogations until she was done getting her afternoon snack from the kitchen and could disappear into her room. On bad days, when Nick was drunk or in a mood or both, she would just ignore her ravenous stomach and head straight there, lock the door, and not reappear until she absolutely had to, at dinner time. By then, however, Mom would be home, and her stepfather would have put his other face on: all friendly fatherly smiles and down-to-earth sensibility.

"He-llo-o… Earth to Tara…."

Tara returned her attention to Abby. She still couldn't fathom why this girl wanted so badly to hang out with her. There were plenty of better choices out there. She shrugged and muttered, "Um, sure. Okay. I guess."

Abby beamed. "Awesome!"

Tara struggled to reciprocate the smile. The best she could manage was an upward skewing of one corner of her mouth. "But I've never been to one and I never actually learned how to bead. What do I bring?"

"Oh, nothing; just bring yourself! Daphne and I'll teach you, don't worry. It's easy. I have everything we need, and she has her mom's car today, so we can just go straight there. You can ride with us."

"Alright, sure then." Tara shrugged, knowing it was technically against her parents' rules, it being a school day with homework to do, but not wanting to appear uncool. She reckoned she could get it done after dinner while pretending to read or something, or in the morning before class.

"Great! This is gonna be fun. Meetcha in the parking lot right after sixth period, okay? I always meet her at the curb when she has the car, right next to the big tree. She'll come pick us up there. Sound good?"

"Sounds good." Tara nodded, waving back awkwardly as Abby turned and bounced off down the hall.

Going back over the conversation in her mind, an intense little panic rippled through her, and Tara immediately regretted the decision. The whole thing was suddenly just too overwhelming. A *beading party?!* With *Josh* there, of all people?! What had she been *thinking?* Shaking her head at herself, she glanced up at the wall clock, pulse racing. Her next class was in the opposite direction, but she figured if she hurried, she might have just enough time to catch up to Abby, apologize for having to back out—she would think of some excuse on the way—and then get to class before the bell rang.

She started down the hall, walking as quickly as she could without it becoming a jog. At the intersection she turned right, but Abby was nowhere to be seen. *Maybe she's in here*, Tara thought, and pushed open the door to the girls' room.

"...dn't even if you frickin paid me. I mean, like, absolutely *no way.*"

"Oh c'mon girl, you know I've seen you staring at his butt!"

Laughter.

Tara hesitated, adrenaline surging. She wasn't sure this was worth it. Steeling herself, she swallowed and took another step forward to have a look, braving the attention of Nora Childs and her flunkeys.

"That's such total b—"

"Well well well. Looky here. What's up, Reed?"

Tara ignored her. "Hey Abby, you in here?"

No answer, but a derisive smirk split Nora's makeup-caked face as she stood up straight from where she'd been leaning, arms folded, against the wall between two of the sinks.

Idiot, Tara cursed herself. Even if Abby were there, in a stall, she would not be so stupid as to reply out loud; no one would, not with this gang of girls occupying the bathroom. She turned to go.

"Ha," Nora fake-chuckled. "Oh hey, that reminds me. You know what I heard? I heard little Reed here's got a thing for girls. Gay as a window, just like her big brother what's-his-name. I guess it must run in the family...."

Tara knew she should just ignore Nora and leave, but the homophobic slight against her brother had her abruptly seething. She stopped and glowered over her shoulder. "Oh yeah? So what if I am? You trying to hit on me or something?

As if anyone would be interested in you. Keep dreaming, you pathetic loser." It was the best she could come up with.

"*Pffft*, keep dreaming yourself, little girl. As if anyone would want a scrawny weirdo like you."

"Whatever." Tara rolled her eyes and reached for the door.

"Heh, check it out; apparently little *wuss* here can dish it but she can't take it," Nora pressed, feeding off the chortles that were bubbling up from her surrounding posse. "Aw, what's wrong, little Reed? Didn't daddy give you enough love before he up and *died* on you?"

Tara froze.

"Or, oh—*OHHH!* I know; maybe he went and 'gave' you a bit *too* much love. Oh yeah, it was that special lovely *daddy* touch he gave you, wasn't it? And lots *of* it, too, I bet." Nora had a hand half covering her mouth in laughter, though there was no laughter at all in her eyes. "Oh yeah, check it! Look at her face! Haha... That's gotta be *it!* That right there's why she's so scared of boys! Poor, poor little Reed. It wasn't actually your uncle who did that shit to you now, was it? It was *daddy*. And you know what, all these years you've been telling everyo—"

Tara saw red. Before she knew it, she had Nora pinned to the bathroom floor and was screaming and mashing her pretty blonde head against the tiles as hard as she could.

"Get off me get off me you *bitch!*" Nora snarled, arms flailing.

Tara continued to yell and tear at her face, intent on making the bully bleed. The bigger girl struggled to get up, but Tara's desperate fury had amplified her strength. A wordless scream erupted from her chest in waves as she slapped Nora again and again. Then several hands were grabbing at her shoulders, and soon Sarah and a couple of the other girls had wrenched her away and were forming a barricade between Tara and their leader.

Hours later, Tara was unable to recall the exact sequence of events, but someone must have run to get Mr. Taylor, because she had a vague memory of him and another teacher leading her briskly down the hall by the arm. She did remember the vice principal's face—a mix of wide-eyed shock and narrow-eyed disappointment as he was told a version of what had happened—as well as a lot of murmuring and shaking of heads among the office ladies. Or perhaps she had imagined the murmuring; she wasn't sure. Anyway, she'd then had to wait under supervision in one of the meeting rooms for her stepfather to arrive.

Now they were in Nick's little Toyota pickup truck, halfway home, and he was making no secret of his annoyance at having had to interrupt his day off to come and get her.

"I mean, you were doing so *well*, Tara. What exactly was it that set you off *this* time?"

She glared out the window at the passing trees and rain-soaked lawns and parked cars, refusing to speak. She felt numb.

Nick cleared his throat. "You know, Tara, it's rude not to answer when someone asks you a question."

Her vision darkened a little, nostrils flaring as she ground her jaw tightly shut. Very carefully, she slipped the rubber band in her pocket around her wrist and began to flick it against her skin, quietly so that he would not notice.

"Well." Nick sighed his sigh and shook his head some more. "You heard what Vice Principal Taylor said. He said they'll have to make this be another long-term suspension, at least until they figure out how best to adjust your crisis action plan or whatever."

Yeah, 'or whatever,' Tara thought bitterly. Nick had never really taken much more than a superficial interest, except of course whenever her mother was present.

"And that means you're going to have to stay home until they get this thing sorted." He wasn't even trying to hide the passive-aggressive resentment in his voice. She ignored it and focused her attention out the window. They were turning onto their street now.

"Did you hear me?"

She flicked her wrist three times, tense enough to explode.

"Tara, look."

She looked. He was glancing at her hands.

"You're way too old to be acting out like this. You know it and I know it."

They were almost home. Her teeth were locked together in a continuous grind. It was taking everything in her to stay in control.

Nick pursed his lips and shook his head slowly. She turned away, but he kept talking. "Yeah, see, you know at some point you're gonna have to grow a thicker skin." He sighed. "Your mother and I have been talking, and we both agree you need to learn not to let your classmates get to you so much. At the new school you're gonna have to—"

Tara whipped back around to face him again. "New school?!"

Nick raised an eyebrow and stuttered, eyes on the road. "Oh, ah, no. What I meant to say was—"

"*What?!* Are we moving?! Where?!" Tara was shaking. A few things she had overheard in the last few months were clicking into place in her mind; though they hadn't made sense out of context, she could suddenly see how they did. A vast hollowness tore open inside of her, and she felt herself tumbling straight into it. The hand she'd been playing nervously through her hair gripped abruptly into a fist, uprooting several strands. She barely felt it.

"No, Tara, I mean—I just meant *if* you had to go to a new school; just *if*, you know? That's all I meant. Just a hypo*thet*ical. I was just trying to… I didn't mean—"

She was already unbuckling her seatbelt and tugging at the door handle as they pulled into the driveway.

"Wait, wait, *wait*, Tara. That's not what I was trying to say!"

Grabbing her backpack, she jumped out before the truck had even stopped moving and stormed across the wet yard toward the front door.

"Damnit Tara, stop! Let me explain!" Nick barked. "*Tara!*"

She ignored him and fumbled with her keys, anxiety dangerously close to peaking again. Her fingers wouldn't work properly; she couldn't seem to hold them steady. She heard Nick close both car doors behind her and knew he was coming up the path from the driveway toward the front door, which still would not fucking open.

"Tara. Just *calm down*."

The keys fell out of her hand. With a shriek of frustration, she flung her backpack violently against the wall. It fell to the porch in a jingle of zippers.

"Tara! Just *stop!* Let me explain what I *meant!*"

She turned away and bolted to the side yard, then skirted around to the back of the house. That door was locked, too. She could still hear Nick hollering after her.

She had to get out of there.

At first, she had no direction or plan; she was just stumbling through the thicket that separated their backyard from the neighbor's. She darted around the fence and across to the sidewalk on the adjacent street, and then kept on running, just wanting to get *away*... from whatever the hell it was Nick and her mother were planning, which he seemed to have let slip; from her anxiety and the rushing sound in her ears; from school; from *everything*. She ran and ran, shoes slapping on wet sidewalks, zigzagging from block to block in what she hoped was a random pattern Nick would not be able to anticipate in case he was already out looking for her in his stupid truck.

Time was a blur, and the angry echoes in her head were not diminishing. They drove her feet forward, locked her eyes on the concrete directly in front of them as she repeatedly flicked the rubber band against her wrist the way Cynthia had taught her. It wasn't working.

A small piece of glass next to the curb caught Tara's eye. She stopped to pick it up. It was very dull, but she would try anyway. In a front yard just off to her left were a pair of very tall, thick juniper bushes. She trudged up the slick muddy slope between them, glanced around to make sure she wasn't in view of any windows, and squatted down. Finding the sharpest edge of the glass—which wasn't saying much—she rubbed it hard across the inside of her forearm, between her elbow and her wrist scars. It didn't break the skin. She rubbed harder, managing to pinch and rupture it a little, but the blood still would not flow. The numbness in her mind persisted, spread. After a few more tries, she succeeded in producing a tiny bit of actual pain, but at length, she gave up; the glass was simply too dull to be of much help. She chucked it aside and peeked back out from between the bushes.

There was no sign of Nick's truck or any pedestrians. She crouched there a minute longer, ears buzzing and knees beginning to stiffen. She had no idea where to go; she only knew that she did not want to go home. *Home.* Was it even still that anymore? Could she have misheard, or perhaps misunderstood? She shook her head. There was no point in lying to herself. Nick had definitely uttered those words: "At the new school"—and the high school Tara currently attended was the only one around for many miles, which meant he and her mother were planning on moving to a new town. Maybe even a different state.

Tara's stomach was in knots. Why would they have kept something like that from her? She felt stunned, betrayed, confused.

She needed to walk.

Scanning to the right, she shuffled back down to the sidewalk and resumed her trajectory along the tree-lined street, head down with swift steps, shrinking inwardly every time a car passed, wishing she could just disappear.

After a while, a distant roaring caught her attention, and she looked up. She wasn't very far from Dee's Park, she realized. Through the still mostly budless trees off to her left, she could just make out the age-darkened brick walls of the hospital where it loomed atop Mirador Hill. The sky was still overcast and threatening more rain. *There probably won't be many people at the park,* she thought. Taking a right at the next corner, she made her way eastward for two more blocks before sprinting across Jefferson Street, shoulders hunched and hands jammed into pockets.

The sound of the waterfall grew louder as she approached. From the park's main entrance, she cut across the big lawn and through a stand of trees, and then down to the river trail, too emotionally spent to care about the mud or wet leaves sticking to her school shoes. A newly asphalted path took her downstream around a large bend, and she soon came to a T-intersection with one path circling back to the right and the other heading left across the river over a rusty old steel bridge. Directly beneath it, enormous green tongues of water raced over a sixty-foot precipice to thunder into a churning, boulder-lined spillway. From there, the river disappeared over a series of cascades into the darkly forested ravine. A gust of wind ripped through the tops of the trees, twisting them so far sideways they looked as though they might snap.

Tara stopped in the middle of the bridge. For a moment, the sight of all that raw power distracted her from the insidious panic that had sent its clawing tendrils into every nook of her chest. The cataract was immense. A random memory from physics class popped into her head: This combination of mass and inertia definitely formed an unstoppable force, she figured. *Unstoppable.* She watched the water plummet, anchoring her gaze to various floating dead leaves or twigs or bits of foam and following them all the way into the maelstrom below. The force of gravity on the river was absolute; everything in it was *in* it, inexorably committed, unable to escape. A person would have no chance.

The thought was comforting. It was clean, simple; the logical two-plus-two of it was the complete opposite of all the messy, distressing complexity of school and people and pressure. There would likely be a horrible burst of pain up front, for sure, but then she would pass out and her lungs would fill with liquid, and all this stupid anxiety, this constant unrelenting agony and stress, this *everything,* would just go away. It would be a release; it would be liberation.

Her adrenaline gradually subsided, and her heart no longer felt about to beat right out of her throat. The air was cool on her face. Soothing, even. Tara climbed over the railing and stood with her back to it. Despite the day's events, and even as she faced the immediacy and nothingness between her feet and the yawning death below, she felt calm.

The nothingness put up no resistance.

The nothingness did not judge or expect or try to convince.

The nothingness was neutral, and therefore could be trusted.

She stared down into it. Her gut said that watery void might actually help; it could take her where she needed to go. Rivers were a bit like roads or train tracks, after all. She could feel the pull, and it felt familiar. She had been here before. Not specifically here, at this spot on this bridge, but she had certainly felt this exact feeling before, several times. This same attraction.

"Oy! Look here, girl, before you go and take that next step—d'you think you'd mind letting me draw you, like?"

The voice was so startling Tara nearly lost her balance. Tightening her grip, she turned to look at its source. A young man was leaning over the railing only a few yards to her right, a mixture of amusement and alarm on his shockingly handsome face. He had dark ringlet bangs and penetrating blue eyes, and wore a brown leather jacket over scruffy jeans. A silver chain around his neck disappeared under a very clean-looking white T-shirt.

"What…?" Tara balked.

"Do you mind if I draw you, I said."

"Draw me?"

"Yes, draw. I like to scribble some. Jaysus, it's fierce windy out here today, so it is." He spoke rapidly and had an accent of some sort—Irish, maybe. Or Scottish. He retrieved a pad of paper from under his coat and flipped it open, pencil in hand, his eyes never leaving hers. Tara glanced around, suddenly feeling very self-conscious and alone. There was no one else in sight.

"Don't worry, I'm not going to murder you and hide your body in the woods or anything like that. Although," he snorted, raising an eyebrow, "let's say I did just that. What would be the difference, really? By all appearances, you were about done with it anyway."

Irish, Tara decided. She peered down to where the waterfall boomed and foamed directly below her feet, and an abrupt wave of dizziness nearly tipped her. She scowled at the guy and wished she could somehow *will* him away. She just wanted to be alone, but was too nervous to say it out loud.

"Look," the young man smirked, arms spread wide in an appeasing gesture. "I promise I'll let you jump *afterward*, if that is indeed what you were planning to do. But just let me draw you first, okay girl? *Pretty please*. With a cherry on top, like, and all that."

Tara flushed, feeling both very annoyed and very exposed at the same time. *Had* she been about to jump? She suddenly wasn't sure. Maybe? But even if she had been, she certainly wasn't going to do it with some random dude here watching.

She crossed her arms. "You're an artist? What, like an art student or something?"

"Yeah, well, more of a wannabe, I suppose. But I could use the practice, that's for sure! What d'you say?"

She took a deep breath and relaxed her shoulders a little. Why *not* let him draw her? His attention might be a good distraction from all the dark thoughts tumbling around the back of her mind. Besides, the guy seemed harmless enough. He had an easy smile and looked to be only a few years her senior, and something about him made her reluctant to say no. Still, there was a look in his eyes—a hunger, or a loneliness, or…. Or perhaps he was just different from guys she was used to, she decided. Still feeling vaguely irritated and embarrassed, she mumbled, "Um, okay, I guess," and began to climb back over the railing, keeping a wary eye on him all the while.

"No, no; just stay there, girl. That's just perfect where you are," he said.

She returned to where she'd been standing, and he began to sketch her. As those intense blue eyes studied her from head to toe, his smile slowly gave way to a look of professional seriousness, and his hand became a blur of rapid movements. Tara tried to be patient, but found herself squirming under his gaze, periodically glancing up and down the trail and back over her shoulder. She wondered what direction this guy had come from. The waterfall was so loud she hadn't heard him approach.

There definitely was something a bit odd about him, now she thought more on it. He looked a little too old to be in high school, but he also wasn't dressed like any college student she'd ever seen. However, it wasn't to do with his clothing so much. There was something different about the way he carried himself. Compared to most guys she knew, even including her very independent and self-assured older brother Ronnie, this one seemed a ton more confident and comfortable with himself.... But that wasn't it, either. She couldn't put her finger on it. Again, perhaps it was simply that he was so unlike guys who had grown up in Forestview. She'd never met anyone from Ireland before, after all.

"So, what," she ventured, "you just sneak around the park like this, making drawings of whatever random people you bump into?"

Without breaking his concentration, he chortled. "Well, I never thought of it as *sneaking* before, but yes; I do like to draw people I happen across. The interesting ones, anyway."

Tara looked away and mumbled, "What makes you think I'm interesting?"

He raised an eyebrow. "What makes you think you're not, girl?"

"Stop calling me 'girl'."

He ignored her, seemingly lost in his work.

Darker clouds were moving in, and she could hear more thunder rumbling in the distance.

"Is it going to take much longer?" She felt long past ready to ditch this rando and head on her way… but for the life of her, she could not think of where she wanted to go. "Well?" She kicked at a twig that was caught between the ends of two of the bridge planks.

"Almost done. And then I'll let you get back to your brooding."

"I wasn't brooding."

He laughed. "Okay, okay. Your *deep philosophical pondering*, then. What's your name, by the way? If you don't mind my asking."

She narrowed her eyes at him. "It's Tara."

"Lovely to meet you, Tara," he said, nodding with a cheerful smile. He then held his drawing pad up vertically, closing one eye and glancing back and forth between it and her.

"Well?" she said after a moment.

"Well what?"

"What's yours."

"Oh, me? My name's Fin."

Chapter Two

Tara blinked at the sudden recollection of the gravestone she'd come across that morning.

Serendipity—!

It fit, though, really. What if not totally whacked had this entire day been, after all? Still, she felt an uneasiness snaking very slowly from the back of her neck around to her collarbone, cold scales on bare skin.

"Okay, all done with my scribbling. You can go ahead and jump now if you want, girl."

"I told you not to call me 'girl'. And I wasn't going to jump." Tara hesitated before taking one last look at the torrent below. Sighing inwardly, she returned to the less precarious side of the railing. *It was a stupid train of thought anyway. Or maybe not. Doesn't matter; I can always come back.*

"Well you are one though, aren't you?"

Tara decided to ignore that. "May I see the picture you drew?"

Fin beamed again, took two steps closer, and held his notebook out with both hands like some eager little kid at show-and-tell.

She stared. The likeness, etched in graphite right down to the smallest detail, was uncanny. It even depicted the stubborn little tangle in her normally springy coils that had been making her hair look all boofy and lopsided ever since her attempts to style it that morning, as well as the faint freckles at the corners of her eyes. The expression in them was forlorn. She looked away.

"What, don't you like it?" Fin asked. Every word out of this boy's mouth seemed to have a teasing lilt to it.

"No, it's fine…. I like it fine."

He made as if to say something in response, but then apparently thought better of it. Instead, he tucked the sketchpad under the arm of his leather jacket, pocketed his pencil, and squinted skyward.

She did, too. The trees above howled, still bending this way and that in the gusts like violent dancers whose limbs could snap at any moment. She glanced over her shoulder again, toward the path. "Okay, well, I should get home, I guess. It was nice meeting you."

His face grew somber. "Oh, yeah, sure. Alright then. It was nice meeting you as well, Tara."

She stepped awkwardly around him and continued over to the homeward side of the bridge, not wanting to go home but having no clue of where else to go. Raindrops began to splotch the planks at her feet and patter against her head and shoulders as she walked up the hill.

"Wait, girl, wait. I mean, *not* girl… sorry! But I mean wait, just… wait one second. Please."

She turned to see Fin trotting to catch up, shrugging against the rain with both hands tucked into his jeans pockets.

"Would you like some company, perhaps? I could walk you home, like."

Not really, she thought. She still felt a strong need to be by herself, though she had to admit there *was* something charming about this person. Despite the stranger danger vibes, imagined or not, she was secretly thrilled the guy seemed to actually want to be around her. She immediately suppressed the stray thought that she could perhaps use him to distract Mom and Nick, keep them at bay; it wouldn't exactly be prudent to let a man she had just met know where she lived. He could be anybody. Besides, it wouldn't be fair to him to use him like that.

"Um… okay, but how about just partway, like to the park entrance? And only so long as you really aren't going to murder me and hide my body on the way there," she said, forcing a friendly smile.

"Promise." He grinned.

As they strode up the river trail together, the sky opened up and let loose, big fat drops pelting down. Fin pointed at a pine tree with dense boughs. "Over there!" he shouted into the wind, darting under them for shelter. Tara shook her head and stuck to the asphalt path, not really minding the rain. Fin called after her a few times before giving up. Half a minute later, he was at her side again, chest heaving and hair dripping sheets. Both sopping wet now, they walked up the hill, across the drenched lawn, and out through the Jefferson Street entrance.

Tara stopped, hands in pockets, and for a minute found herself doing that uncomfortable stand-and-wait-until-it's-goodbye thing. Fin stood facing her, seemingly unable to take the hint and making no motion to leave. The rain pummeled down.

Not wanting to be rude, she tried small talk. "So, do you go to college here?"

"What's that?"

"College. Do you go to college here, as in the university."

"Oh, that. No. Why, do you?" he asked. It seemed an honest question, which just made Tara stare at him all the more incredulously.

"You're being serious? No. I'm in high school."

"Ah," he said, nodding absently. "That must be nice, I imagine. Me, no. I've not been a... student... for quite a while now. Oh, except in the whole 'student of life' sense, like."

It was Tara's turn to say something, she knew, but her lack of conversational skills had her paralyzed as always, and the more conscious of that she became, the harder it was for her to think of anything to say. A vicious cycle. Her face burned. This friendly, handsome guy was standing right in front of her, in the rain, waiting. And in that moment, she knew he must think her a complete and utter idiot. An idiot who was still in high school, at that, and one who evidently was far less intriguing than his own silent thoughts, for his attention seemed suddenly to have wandered to the puddles on the ground, or to his feet, or to something he'd much rather be doing. She frowned in the direction of the old public library at the corner of Jackson and Marigold, and abruptly decided that this was as close as she wanted a total stranger to get to her life.

"Okay, well, I should go." She forced another smile, this time a polite one.

Fin straightened and smiled back at her, looking for all the world like a wet puppy. A cute wet puppy. "Grand. Okay, well, that you should then. May I see you again, Tara?"

She hesitated. "I mean... why?"

"Well, because. Maybe I like your company."

Tara found herself blushing again and quickly dipped her head to cover it up. "I mean, we just met. And I don't know you from Adam."

At this, he laughed. "No, I suppose you don't. Fair enough. Alright, well, you take care of yourself then, *girl*. Perhaps I'll see you around."

"Yeah maybe," she mumbled. "But don't call me that again, little boy." She smirked and gave him a little self-conscious wave, then turned to leave. As she walked away, she heard a soft chuckle behind her, and the smile she smiled to herself was a real one.

At first Tara wondered whether she should take a different route home in case this guy really was some creepy stalker type, but when she turned to peek back over her shoulder at him, she saw that he was striding off at a quick pace in the opposite direction, hands stuffed into jacket pockets, apparently having completely forgotten about her already. She shook her head at herself and continued on her way.

Mirador Hill rose above the trees and telephone poles just a few blocks off to her right. For a short time, she managed to ignore it, but crossing a street placed the hospital squarely in her peripheral vision, forcing her to stop and consider. It had only been two days since she'd last visited, but the possibility of having to move had abruptly put things in a very different perspective. Time might be running out. How many more opportunities to visit would there be? And afterward, how few and far between? The thought frustrated her. Angered her. Surely her mother and stepdad wouldn't be so cold as to just up and abandon....

The rising anxiety made up her mind for her. Turning right at the next street, she made her way to the main entrance. It was a steep slope, and the sidewalk was slippery, so she took her time getting up it until a crack of thunder hastened her steps. Several patients and family members of patients stood or leaned outside the front doors, smoking cigarettes and chatting or staring alone at the iron-gray sky, or into the past, or perhaps toward some hoped-for future. It always seemed to Tara that the folks who hung around outside of hospitals and courtrooms tended to have exaggerated features: a middle-aged woman with a crooked nose and a hunched back; an old man with stick legs and dark splotches on his forehead. A kid in a wheelchair with big ears that stuck way out to either side of his crisp new red paisley bandana. It was as though catastrophe and mishap had brought their characteristics into sharper contrast. Hurrying past, she took the elevator up to the third floor, nodded shyly at the palliative care nurse who said "Hi Tara, how are you today?", and knocked softly on her grandmother's door. She entered without waiting for an answer; Grandma would be either asleep or staring into space, as usual.

"Hi Grandma," Tara said cheerfully in a very loud voice as she dragged one of the hard plastic chairs closer to the side of the hospital bed. "It's me, Tara, your granddaughter."

The old woman's gaze drifted slowly over to Tara's face, but the look in her eyes was one of mild bewilderment and fear; they held no trace of recognition. Tara sat down and gently took her grandmother's bony hand in both of hers. "It's *me*, Grandma. You know, *Tara*. Babatunde's daughter."

"Baba... maghan...." Weakly, her grandmother raised a hand halfway to Tara's face, but let it drop again after a moment, brows knitted in deepening confusion.

"No, paatti, it's Tara. *Not* Baba. I am *Tara*. I'm Baba's *daughter*."

Nothing felt permanent anymore. The feeling had been building for years. Ever since her dad's death, things had been unraveling. It was as if he had been the tape sticking it all together; the twist-tie keeping all the loops from uncoiling and flopping apart. Tara was trying so hard to keep them coiled, tight, and safely in place, but inevitably, something else would happen and one or two of the "loops" would start to loosen and slip out. And as of today, all of a sudden, everything had gotten way worse.

Her grandmother, her *paatti*, had always been a twist-tie, too; an even stronger one than her dad, in fact. At least that was how Tara remembered her, back before the cancer and back before her mind began to slip away through what Tara referred to as "the fade". Now, Grandma was hardly even there anymore. It tore Tara apart every time she visited her. Those milky brown eyes seemed to stare right past her, through her, unaware and unrecognizing. Now and then there would be a glimmer, like the time a few weeks ago when paatti had suddenly perked up and cooed, "Oh, Tara! *There* you are. My little shining star," just like how she always used to call her. But the moment had been fleeting, and more often than not, any half-lucid episodes tended to involve her mistaking Tara for Tara's father—or even her grandmother's own deceased sister or mother—or those brief moments of awareness would simply disintegrate into childlike fear.

Tara did have her grandmother's eyes and nose, or so everyone always told her, though she herself couldn't quite see the nose thing even in the older photos of when her grandmother was younger and growing up in an immigrant household in New Jersey. There was one, a black and white, in which Grandma and her sister had been eleven and twelve years old, respectively, and they and their parents and the dog had all been posing with the family car. A big deal back then, Tara supposed. In the photo, she recalled, her grandmother wore a plain white dress and a naughty smirk, and her sister looked rather put out next to her. Behind them, Tara's great grandmother looked taut and distant, almost like a cardboard cut-out, and her great grandfather next to her looked bent and tired.

"Have you eaten, Grandma?" Tara squeezed her hand and smiled as warmly as she could.

Anxious, her grandmother turned toward the door, as if looking for a nurse to rescue her from this strange young woman she apparently had never seen before. Tara's smile faltered, but she bravely squeezed and grinned again.

"I can get you some cookies if you want, paatti," she said, winking conspiratorially. "Chocolate chip! Your *favorite*."

That seemed to do the trick. Her grandmother's lips parted in a wan smile, the crow's feet at the corners of her eyes stretching. "Oh...." she breathed as a slight hint of recognition relaxed her shoulders.

By the time Tara returned with the packet of cookies, paatti was fast asleep, chest rising and falling beneath the thin gown, her frame and wrinkled neck appearing extremely frail and emaciated. Tara sat back down and tried to open the packet, but her fingers could find no purchase on the slippery plastic. She tried again from a different angle, and then again, to no avail. Everything welled up at once, overwhelming, upending her. She burst into tears, burying her face in her grandmother's arm so that no one would hear. For a long, long time Tara wept and wept and wept, until she was spent and the thunder outside had stopped.

At length, she placed the cookies on the bedside tray where a helpful nurse might find them, kissed her grandmother on the forehead, and left to walk home in the cold and wet.

When she got there, both cars were in the driveway. Sighing a tense sigh through her nose, she wished silently that she could melt away with the raindrops. After another minute of indecisiveness, she clenched her jaw, turned the knob, and pushed the front door open.

The annoying little bell her stepdad had placed at the top of it tinkled, causing the cat to look up wide-eyed from where it had been licking its ass, one leg straight up like a flagpole. The air inside was warm; they had the gas heater pumping.

"Tara! You're okay," her mother said, bolting up from the couch and darting over to her, reaching for a hug.

"I'm fine, Mom," she mumbled into Aileen's auburn curls, only barely touching the worried woman's back with unbending hands. Her mother was still dressed in her work clothes and a half-empty glass of water was on the coffee table next to her phone. The hug felt good, Tara had to admit to herself, and the familiar scent of professional massage oil was vaguely comforting. Over her mother's shoulder, she could see Nick rummaging around in the kitchen, back turned, clearly acting as though nothing had happened and he hadn't heard Tara come in. *Tonight's going to suck.*

"You need to get out of these wet clothes right this minute. What were you *thinking?* You could catch pneumonia," Aileen fretted. "Maybe go take a hot shower, yeah?"

Normally, Tara might protest and point out that she wasn't a little girl anymore and could shower on her own schedule, but in that moment, she just felt empty. Utterly drained. Besides, taking a shower would at least give her an excuse to go into the bathroom and be alone a while longer; anything to avoid having to rehash the incident at school or explain where she'd gone afterward. So she just nodded as casually as she could, murmured an "mmhmm", and headed back toward her room, trying her best not to be too obvious about how desperate she was to leave her mother's (and stepfather's) presence.

"And Tara." Her mother stopped her.

"Yeah?" She turned, already halfway down the hall.

"After you dry off, I'll come back and we can talk about what happened at school today." It wasn't a question.

Tara nodded, eyes down, and continued to her room. She had expected worse, honestly, but it seemed Nick had been told to butt out, which was fine by her.

The shower was very relaxing. She stood in the hot water for a long time, not thinking about anything, just feeling the rivulets shift back and forth across her skin, the steam filling her lungs, the enveloping warm embrace of all that water pressing down on her shoulders and neck and back, constant, steady, unwavering. Until the hot water finally ran out, that is. She marveled that no one had come to bang on the door and yell at her to get out. They didn't usually let her take such long showers. Aileen must be trying very hard not to upset her, she decided.

She dried off and got into a pair of sweatpants and a comfy old sweatshirt that had belonged to her father. When her mother finally came knocking, Tara was sitting on her bed with her back against the pillows and both legs under the covers, flipping through posts and messages on her phone without actually paying any attention to them. Knowing the conversation was inevitable, she had left the door partway open, so her mother came right in and sat on the edge of the bed, just that little bit too close for comfort.

"*So.* It's been quite a day, hey," Aileen began, projecting purposeful kindness through her eyes.

But Tara could see the uncertainty underneath it. She responded by nodding stiffly and placing her phone facedown on the quilt.

"Wanna talk about it?" Her mother put a gentle hand on the lump in the bedding that was Tara's knee.

"Sure, I guess. It's not like I have a choice anyway."

Aileen tilted her head. "You always have a choice, Tara. We don't have to talk about it right now if you really don't want to. You know this."

She suddenly felt foolish. "Yeah, no, I know. It's fine."

"Okay then. Tell me what happened at school."

Tara stared at her hands and said nothing. A dog was barking outside and its owner was either not around or too lazy and inconsiderate to make it shut up. People should get off their selfish asses and train their dogs to keep quiet, she reckoned. Or give them more attention so they didn't feel so frantic and lonely and bored all the time. Treat them with respect, give them some peace.

"It's alright, Tarabell. Take your time. I don't want to pressure you, but I do at some point need to know what happened and what's going on, how you're feeling. I'm your mom."

"No, I'm okay. I'll tell you; I just need a minute."

"Are you?"

"Yeah. I am now, I mean."

"Okay. Good." Aileen waited, eyes down. She could be patient these days, at least, so that made stuff easier. Easier than things had been in the past. Tara genuinely did have an urge to tell her mother about her day—about some of it, at least—but she had no idea how. She didn't even know where to start. This felt too hard. Everything did, though, to be fair.

"So…" she began, drawing a squiggle on her left thigh with her index finger.

"It's okay. Take your time," her mother said again.

"Yeah I know. I *am*." She rubbed her eyes. Part of what Tara felt was dread, but she was surprised to discover a bit of relief mixed in, too: Relief to have something to talk about that had nothing to do with the bridge, or with the "new school" Nick had mentioned, and so on. Still, the indignation, the anger, was difficult to keep down. "Sorry. Anyway. Whatever. I'm guessing you probably heard about what Mr. Taylor said."

"Nick told me, yes. And Mr. Taylor also called and left a message on my phone. I was driving so I couldn't answer, but I called back when I got home and he was still in his office, so he explained what had happened. Nick was—"

Tara looked up, a sudden burning fury in her throat. "What exactly did *he* say happened?"

Aileen looked taken aback. "I mean, he told me you were very upset when he saw you in the office, and that you got even more upset when he drove you home, and that you jumped out of the truck and—"

"No, I mean Mr. Taylor. What did Mr. Taylor say."

Her mother closed her mouth and straightened a little, as if pausing to rethink her tactics. Tara knew she had probably suppressed a sigh; she'd gotten good at that.

"Well he said the same thing Nick said. He said you attacked and hurt a girl in the bathroom."

"Figures." Tara smoldered, picking at her fingers. She remembered how Nora's face had looked while she was on the floor, screaming and clawing up at her. It had been fear in her eyes; an intensely satisfying look of fear. Tara knew she could have saved herself a whole heap of trouble if she'd simply kept her cool and walked out of the girls' room, but still. The bitch had deserved it. And there was never anything simple about keeping one's cool, in Tara's experience.

This time, Aileen's sigh came unbridled. "Tara, I get it. Trust me, I do. I'm sure you didn't start the conflict, whatever it was. In fact I *know* you didn't; that's just not the sort of thing you *do* anymore. You've come a really really long way, so don't think I haven't noticed all the progress you've made. You're able to *talk* about stuff now, and that's *tremendous*. It is absolutely *huge*. But remember what Cynthia said? It's all about how you *choose to react* to situations that come up. It's about—"

"I know."

"It's about using the techniques she's taught you and making them into habit, a more *ingrained* habit, so they become automatic responses. That way, you don't lose control. And yes, I know you know all this. You know I know you do."

Tara sat stiff-shouldered, eyes on the window, feeling herself break inside one bit at a time. *Go on, break some more, you broken little psycho. Broken little freak of a cliché. That's what I am.* It had gotten dark outside and was still raining; droplets spattered against the glass, glowing golden in the light from the streetlights. Despite the growing knot of anxiety, her stomach was beginning to wake up, annoyingly.

She could sense her mother's nerves. She had to say something. "It's just not fair, Mom. I wasn't the one who started it. And she had it coming."

"Alright then. Tell me what happened. From the beginning."

Tara did, starting with how Nora and her posse had been making snide comments for months, constantly talking shit behind her back and making up lies about her, spreading them, playing petty little games. How it had been building. She mentioned the encounter in the seniors' quad before school, and told what she could remember about the

38

incident in the bathroom later that morning, placing particular emphasis on the fact that the insults against her brother and Dad had been the straw that broke the camel's back. Much of her memory was foggy; she even had a few baffling gaps. She honestly could not recall getting out of Nick's truck, for example.

Her mother only interrupted to express sadness that she and Nora had become so estranged after having once been such close friends. Tara shook her head and rolled her eyes, but said nothing more on the subject; she knew there was no way to explain to Aileen the way things were. As well-intentioned as her mother was, she simply wasn't inside it. She was in a completely different world.

Suddenly, the whole day and all that had happened just felt so silly and stupid, not to mention cruel. Nick clearly had not told her mother about what he'd let slip while they were in the truck together, and Tara didn't think she had the energy to bring it up. An abyss of despair yawned open in her mind, refilling her vision with darkness. She wished there were a way to go back to how life had been before. She wished she knew why she was this way. She just couldn't see a way out, a way through, except perhaps via pain—but even pain was just a temporary distraction. At least pain was something crystal-clear, though; something real. Something she could *feel*.

Wiping a tear from her cheek, Tara flicked a glance at her mother's hands. It was as close as she could bring herself to meeting her gaze. "I'm sorry Mom. I don't know what's wrong with me."

Her mother reached her arms around her and pulled her in close. "There's nothing wrong with you, baby. It's hard, I know. But we'll get through this together. Like we've done before. I promise," she soothed, and the dam smashed open, tears gushing from Tara's eyes like a cataract ripping through a wind-wrecked forest.

They sat there for a long time like that, until her sniffles finally stopped and her breathing returned to more or less normal. She could hear Nick banging some pots and pans around, though the banging was admittedly more subdued than normal. Trying to lie low and keep out of the way, no doubt. Cook dinner, be the good guy. Same old bullshit.

Her mom was tenderly rubbing her hand up and down Tara's back, like she always used to when Tara was little. "Okay, so, Mr. Taylor said you're off school for the rest of the week at least. No surprise there. And they're going to have a meeting to decide if you need to stay away longer than that, so you have a chance to cool off and... so things can settle. But the good news is he's keeping the suspension off your record so it won't affect your college applications."

Tara nodded and let go of her mother, wiping a sleeve across her face. Despite the talk of another "long-term suspension", Tara figured she might actually get expelled this time. The school had plenty of other stuff to worry about besides someone like her, after all. They'd tried to fix her and it hadn't worked, so now they would likely decide to wash their hands of her once and for all.

"So basically, as for when you'll be allowed to go back, the school needs to make some adjustments and will get back to us on that."

"'Adjustments'."

"Right. Put a better management plan in place, that sort of thing. In the meantime, he said, your teachers have all been informed, and are going to be sending you work to do at home. So okay," her mother said, her voice suddenly more upbeat, as if this were just the next item on an exciting agenda. "Now. Tell me, where did you go after school?"

"I walked up to the hospital."

"Oh, you saw Grandma again?"

"No," Tara answered quickly. "I got to the main entrance and there were a bunch of methheads smoking cigarettes and acting like assholes so I left and went to the library for a while." Tara knew her mother knew she hated being around people like that, and wanted her to spend more time around books, so this was a good lie. It was believable. She had no intention of talking to Aileen or anyone else about her time with Grandma; that was *their* time. It was personal, untouchable.

Her mother pursed her lips. "I know how upsetting this all is for you, baby."

The parental lies, the hypocrisy, the big fucking secret elephant in the room, her grandmother's frail neck and shoulders—it was all suddenly too much for Tara. She exploded. "*Upsetting?!* For *me?* Or what, you mean upsetting for you and Nick? Your psycho daughter in trouble at school again, throwing another big curveball right in the middle of all your *important plans*, am I right?!"

Aileen's eyes went wide. "Where is all this coming from, Tara? I was talking about how upsetting it is that Grandma's in the hospital, in... in palliative care. For all of us, yes of course, but that includes you, too, darling. And you know what, it's okay to feel—"

"She *needs* us, Mom," Tara blurted, a fresh wave of tears flooding her eyes.

41

"Yes, of course she does. But other than visiting her and making her as comfortable as possible, there's just not—"

"But Mom! She needs us *here!*"

Her mother hesitated. "Baby, we *are* here...."

Tara folded her arms and crunched forward, breathing hard, staring at the shape of her legs under the covers, her mind a roaring vortex. She did not trust herself to remain calm, keep from exploding again, but she would try with everything she had in her. She needed to be clear.

As coolly as she could—like ice on stone—she stared directly into Aileen's eyes and said, "Yeah well according to your *husband*, we won't be here for much longer. Where exactly are we moving to, Mom?"

There were two distracting spots on the ceiling. Tara felt grateful for them both.

One was a tiny spider that seemed to have lost its web or gone walkabout for some reason. *Maybe it's hunting,* she mused. The sudden recollection of a scene from a show about an infestation of giant brown recluses sent a shiver down her spine. This was just a house spider, though. She watched for a long while as it made its upside-down journey in fits and starts past the dormant ceiling light.

The other was a brown lump only a few inches from the wall, directly above her head and pillows: a little chunk of congealed, dried-up chocolate icing from a piece of Tara's eleventh birthday cake, still right where her friend Nancy had flicked it on a silly late-night truth or dare all those years ago. Now it looked almost black in the dim light from her bedside lamp.

Crash.

Tara didn't jump at the sound of something shattering against the living room wall.

"...yeah well I don't give a flying *fuck!*"

She didn't jump at Nick's angry outburst, either. This particular shitfight between him and her mother had been going on for the better part of an hour, and things finally seemed to have come to a head.

Heavy boots thudded down the carpeted hallway past her bedroom. She heard him wing the front door open, banging it against the stopper, and then slam it shut so hard she was sure the glazing must have cracked. Her mother was still back in the living room, hollering out some choice words. The pickup buzzed to life in the driveway and whined in fast reverse, tires screeching on pavement as Nick sped off. *Good fucking riddance.* After a minute, her mother's tirade trailed to a resentful mumble. The television came back on, and the volume on some silly reality show went up several notches louder than was necessary.

Despite all the racket, the spider did not seem fazed. It was past the light now, heading into the darker shadow of the far corner of the ceiling. Perhaps by morning it would find its way back to its web, or at least stake out a good place for a new one. Tara hoped so.

In her dream, the wall to the right of her wardrobe was shaking so hard the paint started to crack. Suddenly, a crater of sorts formed, about a yard and a half in vertical diameter, buckling the gypsum inward and falling away in goops like chocolate icing with the cake taken out from under it. As though consumed by acid, the plasterboard dissolved outward to the rough edges of the crater, leaving a large hole in the wall. Through it she could see stars, and a lake, and weird swaths of greenish light dancing above a forested horizon. Tara's dream self had somehow left her bed and begun to crawl through the hole, legless until she got to the other side; a moment later, she found herself sitting in the stern of a canoe on still water, stars reflected all around. She gazed in wonder at curtain after curtain of shimmering green light overhead. She thought she could hear a flute or recorder being played in the distance.

Then a wolf howled, and she was so startled she dropped the only paddle. She then watched in horror as a current carried it over the edge of a tremendous waterfall that spanned the entire lake, and felt abruptly nauseous as she realized her canoe was drifting in the same direction the paddle had gone. Searching around in vain for a second paddle, she plunged forward and tried to dig for shore with her hands, but they were tied fast to the gunwales. She screamed. More wolves chimed in, and trees bent forward— hundreds of them—snapping and splintering loudly, and the howling and snapping and splintering all swirled together in a growing tornado of alternating dissonance and harmony. As Tara and her canoe were swept over the waterfall, a spider watched from the ceiling in silence.

She opened her eyes to a vale full of fiery light. All around her were tree shapes with coal-black trunks and flames for leaves. She was squatting down barefoot, staring at tiny finger-width rivulets of lava that braided and coiled across the ground, when a white-hot radiance exploded in front of her and startled her to her feet. An oval of searing energy hung in the air just a couple of arms' lengths away, silent apart from the curling, crackling flames that licked up and down its edges. Dream-Tara stared at it, mesmerized, until something began to change. A blue spot appeared in the center of the oval, and suddenly it was a foot, stepping through toward her. She backed up, breathless, as the tall figure of a man stepped through—except that he appeared to be more god than man, and was smoldering blue all over. He wore mighty armor, and flames of a deeper blue tone shrouded his face. As if ignited by his presence, orange and yellow flames burst from her skin, from every orifice of her face, her body become a fiery garland.

The figure was completely through the oval now and standing directly before her, the gate framing him in a blazing halo. His blueness was intensely luminescent. Somehow, despite the cooler hue, it shone more brightly even than Tara's own orange and yellow fire. As he reached out a hand, she saw his lips part—and very softly, underneath the crackling and roaring of flames both blue and orange, she thought she heard him say her name.

And then it hit her. She knew him. She had always known him, since before the beginning of anything and everything. Her flaming body suddenly roared to life, a tornado conflagration of incandescent energy. Before, she had been but a smoldering coal; now she was a dazzling storm. She burned for him. For *him*, and not for anyone else; not ever, nor would she ever. No longer afraid, Tara stepped regally forward to meet her spectacular mate.

Lugh, she breathed.

The bright god smiled an indigo smile, and their flames crossed the gap between them quickly, as if eager, hungry, swirling around and dancing up both their faces to form fiery crowns atop their heads, weaving together, blending in a howling embrace. His intense eyes stabbed into hers, and

Tara met his gaze straight on. Through his flaming icy pupils, a path was opening up: an azure road. It pulled at every strand of her, tugging insistently. *Go,* the bright blue god whispered, and his blueness and the blueness of the road engulfed her, imbued her, drowned her. Suddenly she was falling, tumbling along it, drawn as by a magnet toward an unseeable destination, completely out of control....

Chapter Three

Morning sounds. Those half-dream noises so familiar they've blended into the background and become part of the mind's furniture, even its very architecture: the low, slow glide of the heavy bathroom door along its runners, the subsequent soft thump as it hits the doorframe; the steady crescendo grumbling of the electric kettle from the kitchen; birds outside, muffled by windows shut tight against the cold; the gas heater building up its bloom of warmth; the flush of a toilet and the running of a faucet; the metal spoon tinkling in a coffee cup, quietly so as not to wake the rest of the house.

Tara drew the blankets over her head, scrunching them close around her shoulders and neck. *Ugh, school.* It took her another second to remember she had been suspended.

As she stared at the ceiling, chasing fleeting traces of the dream she'd had—something involving a waterfall and burning blue eyes—the events of the past twenty-four hours gradually invaded her conscious mind. *This reality is way too real to face so early in the morning*, she decided, and buried her face under her pillow, hoping to avoid another conversation with her mother before she left for work. After several minutes of trying to fall back to sleep, she realized nature was not going to stop its persistent call, so she threw off the blankets in resignation and put on her dressing gown.

Just outside her bedroom, she very nearly tripped over Nick, who was sprawled across the hallway floor, snoring softly. Wrinkling her nose, she stepped around him. The drunktard must have come home so plastered he hadn't even been able to make it to bed. He had apparently just slept right there on the floor where he was still passed out cold, drooling, one boot half off and a hand partway down the front of his jeans.

While she was on the toilet, she heard her mother curse in a low voice and snap at him several times to get up. There were some mumbled protestations and a few thumps of boots or arms against the wall, and then a short bout of more intense arguing. Nick's hung-over slurs were an oily counterpoint to her mother's harsh whispered obscenities and proddings, but after a final strained "I'm goin woman I'm goin", Tara heard him trudge to their bedroom at the end of the hall. A door clicked closed, and a few seconds later, Aileen was speaking at her from just outside the bathroom door.

"Good morning, honey. I'm gonna be late for work, so I have to go, but are you okay? Did you manage to get any sleep?"

"Yeah… I'm fine. Good morning. Mom." *But I'd be a lot better if you'd come to your senses and dump that asshole.*

"Okay. Well, I'm… uh, sorry about that. And I'm also sorry we didn't…."

Tara stared at the floor in silence, waiting for her mother to find her words.

"Hey, I…. Look, I know we should have told you, Tarabell. And asked you first. But like I said yesterday afternoon, this is a great opportunity. And it really is going to make a huge difference, for all of us, so that's how we need to learn to look at it."

Tara ground her teeth, biting back on the acid retort that was ripping through her mind, causing her body to shake. There was so much she wanted to say to her mother, but she knew it would just make things worse. It would be easier just to keep her mouth shut.

"But anyway," Aileen said. "We can talk about it some more, and we will, I promise. I know the idea will take some getting used to. But let's talk later though, okay? I have to go. I'm sorry, baby. I'll have my phone off silent today, so call if you need me. Whenever you want. And then let's have a chat when I get home maybe, or maybe on my lunch break even, yeah?"

"Yeah okay. Maybe."

Another pause, and then, "Alright. Well, just take it easy today. Relax. There's plenty of leftovers in the fridge. Okay, bye now, see you soon…."

When Tara woke up a second time, it felt like mid-morning. The house was quiet, and the sun's rays were slanting in through the window at a steep angle. She cautiously tiptoed her way to the kitchen, but still heard nothing. A brief investigation revealed that she had the house all to herself;

Nick's truck was gone. He had apparently decided she wasn't in crisis any longer and could be left home alone. Or at least that whatever it was he needed to go out and do was more important.

She brewed a cup of tea and sat at the kitchen table for a while, watching a cluster of sparrows outside as they pecked at the winter-browned grass. After forcing down a piece of toast, she spent the rest of the morning in front of the television, feeling too lazy to bother with the Xbox. She flitted from one show to another, unable to decide what she was in the mood for.

At around one in the afternoon, she made herself a lunch of instant soupy migoreng noodles with some sriracha mixed in and logged in to her game, but got bored with it quickly. She turned everything off, then went back to her room to get dressed. It might be good to go for a walk, get some fresh air, she figured. No one had specifically stated that she wasn't allowed to leave the house, after all. She changed out of her pyjamas, put on her favorite jacket—another garment of her dad's, a tattered old army jacket—and headed outside, squinting into the sunshine as she closed the front door behind her. It was colder outside than the blue sky had made it look. Still, the big redbud across the street had already erupted in a flourish of magenta; spring was definitely just around the corner. The thought made Tara sad.

As she wandered around, she noticed a quiet in the neighborhood that wasn't there in the times she normally saw it. This was the middle of a weekday, so most people were either at school or at work. A couple of blocks from home, she encountered a work crew standing around an open manhole in the street. Farther along, an old man looked up from whatever he was doing in his front yard to stare suspiciously as she walked past. Apart from a handful of passing cars, she saw no one else.

Before long, she found herself near the cemetery. It would be nice to say a quick hello to Dad, she decided, so she made her way over to the nearest entrance and went in.

The grass was still damp from the rain, especially the thick patches growing at the shady bases of the larger stones and crypts. Tara wended her way to her father's grave along a path that she reckoned by now she could probably navigate with her eyes shut.

She addressed the name engraved in the center of the tombstone: *Babatunde Yewa*. "Hi, Dad. I miss you." It was how she always greeted her father; it was like a ritual. She sat cross-legged on a sunny patch of grass, not minding if her jeans got a little wet, and plucked a blade of it. She felt unsure of what to say to him; her mind was ajumble. A cold breeze played through her hair as she absent-mindedly twisted the grass between thumb and index finger, the hodgepodge of emotions knocking her this way and that like a petite person in a mosh pit. She hung her head.

"I got in trouble again yesterday," she said. "It was Nora. Remember her? Well, she's changed, Dad. She and her new friends have been hideous to me."

Tara felt sad and a little guilty at the mental image of her father learning of how she had reacted, were he still alive. She pushed her coils from her eyes. "But yeah, I guess I let her get under my skin. I know I should've just ignored her. Water off a duck's back and all that, like you always taught me. Tried to teach me. I'm sorry, Dad."

The nearby cedar branches sighed. The sun was still high in the sky, but it wasn't making the day much warmer.

"Also, *great news*." She rolled her eyes. "I found out we're moving. Nick got some big new job, all the way over in fricking Ohio somewhere. And Mom's completely on board. She says it's gonna be this 'amazing new opportunity', and she'll be able to get a bunch more clients there, better-paying ones, and then all this other shit about how the local high school is a big feeder school for places like Ohio State and how I should just keep an open mind and give it a chance, blah blah blah. But Dad," she said, shaking her head, throat tight. "I don't think I'm going. I don't know how, but I think I need to find a way to stay here in Forestview, you know? Because ... well for starters, the place they want to move to is really far away; it's like more than six hours from here. I mean, how would I visit Grandma? How would I visit *you?*"

Her forearms were on her knees, fingers hanging down, and the blade of grass was now in mangled pieces and tight little knots on the ground beneath them. She sat in silence for a long time, chest tight, head bowed, eyes picking over bits of damp dirt between the clumps of grass, not moving until her nose began to run. She dug out a tissue from her pocket and blew it before bending forward to clear some debris the rain had splattered onto the bottom lip of the gravestone.

When she was done, she got to her feet, and as she did so, something out of the corner of her eye made her turn her head. Next to the big old oak tree and half covered by dead leaves lay a maroon glove. Some kid's mother would be interrogating him or her as to its whereabouts, no doubt. Tara went over to pick it up.

"Fancy meeting you here, friend," a voice said, startling her so badly she yelped out loud and spun around. Standing only a few yards away was the strange young man from the day before. Fran or something.

"Ohmygod you scared me," she said. "What are you doing here? Following me?"

He spread his hands in an apologetic gesture. "Sorry, I didn't mean to scare you, promise! And no, I just happened to be taking a walk through this pretty park here. Total chance, running into you again. What are the odds, hey? And it's Tara, am I right?"

She frowned at him, suspicious. "Yes. And this is a graveyard, not a park. I imagine you knew that. Are you here to visit someone?" Bumping into the same person two days in a row seemed way too much of a coincidence. It was looking more and more to her like the guy might actually be a stalker.

Still, how could he have known she would be here? Had he followed her home and then staked out her house or something? She glanced around, heart pounding, realizing just how alone she was—again—and even more alone, potentially, here in the middle of the cemetery than she had been over in Dee's Park. This was a quieter part of town. On a weekday like this, it was a lot less likely there would even be anyone in earshot out here. She took a step backward and scanned the ground for rocks or sticks to wield, while trying her best to appear composed and calm.

"Oh, yes, I *am* here to visit someone. You could say that, yes."

It was a peculiar way of putting it. Tara's suspicion doubled. She would have to sprint to another exit or climb the fence; the guy was standing in the middle of the path, directly between her and the nearest way out. "Who? You have family here? You don't sound like you'd have family here."

"Well I'll forgive you the generalization, girl, because as it happens, there's a stone with me same last name on it just over yonder, and I am in fact a blood relation, like. As blood-related as a person can be, truly. Would you care to come and see? It's a right lovely grave marker, so it is. A very old one."

Tara took another small step backward, trying to gauge whether she'd be able to outrun him. She wasn't very fast, but she was sure-footed. She could weave around between the crypts and stones enough times to lose him, hopefully.

He put up his hands and raised both eyebrows. "Jaysis, I've given you the fright. Sorry, Tara. I mean no harm, honestly. I can just leave you alone if you prefer." As if to demonstrate that he was not a threat to her, he took a few large strides backward, smiling cheerfully.

Tara hesitated. He certainly looked harmless enough, and there was that apparently sincere friendliness from their first encounter. He was looking at her with kind and patient eyes, letting her make the next move. Perhaps she was overreacting. She'd been known to do that from time to time, she had to admit. Still, some serial killers might put on kind and patient eyes, right? "Well," she quavered, "I just came here to say hello to my dad. I was just about to head back home."

"Ah, grand. I see. Funny you should mention… say," he said, interrupting himself. "What's that you got there? Were you missing a mitten?"

Tara glanced self-consciously at the maroon glove in her hand. "No, just something I found on the ground just now. Not mine. And sorry but I can't remember your name." She was normally better at remembering names, but a lot had happened in the last twenty-four hours. Some of the details from the previous day's events were still quite vivid in her mind, while others were fuzzy at best.

"It's Fin." He smiled again. It was a gorgeous smile.

"Oh, right. Sorry. Well, nice to meet you again, Fin. Anyway, um, I'm sorry but I gotta go." She offered a polite smile, but had made up her mind that it was better to err on the side of caution, so she turned to leave. She could feel his eyes on her back, though, and had taken only a few steps when she heard his voice pipe up again.

"Wait, Tara. I need to tell you something."

"Sorry, I'm going to be late. Have a great day," she called over her shoulder, trying and failing to keep the nerves out of her voice.

"Tara, hold on just one minute. See, the thing is, I know your father."

She whirled around, eyes wide. "You knew my dad?"

"A very good man," he nodded. "I've learned a lot from him, so I have."

"How?" she demanded. It didn't make any sense. This guy would have been a kid when her dad had died, only a few years older than she had been, if she was judging his age correctly. "How old are you?"

"Here, it'll be easier if you just let me show you something. This is actually part of the reason I'm here. But you'll have to read it for yourself for it to all make sense, like. Come, follow me."

She wavered. Threatening or not, the mysterious Irishman was being even weirder than he had been the day before, both at the bridge and afterward when they were saying goodbye to each other in the rain. Nevertheless, he had said he'd known her dad, and was walking off without waiting for her, already halfway around a cluster of graves on the far side of the stand of cedars. Too far away to grab her; she could run the other way if she wanted. But she could feel curiosity getting the better of her, pulling at her. Making a split-second decision that felt more like jumping blind than deciding, Tara stopped looking for rocks and sticks, and instead trotted to catch up.

Fin turned left at the next path and strolled slowly but purposefully along it a few paces before glancing over his shoulder. Without breaking trajectory, he turned around and hurled another of those disarming smiles at her while walking backward. "It's just up here a ways, girl. Almost there. You are really gonna want to see this!" He beckoned to her.

The wind kicked up, more than a breeze now, and thick clouds were closing in from the west. A crow called out from atop one of the cedars. Tara lifted her chin and glimpsed it perching precariously among the highest branches, buffeted and feather-ruffled by the gusts. Another responded from not far away, and a raucous call and response ensued. Fin stopped in front of a small gravestone. Recognizing it, Tara stopped, too.

Finlay MacCarthy.

"Your ancestor," she said, in more of a revelatory "aha" statement than a question. "Wow. You're not going to believe this, but I swear, I was here just yesterday morning. I came here before school and sat right next to that exact same gravestone. This is seriously what you wanted to show me? Who was that? Are you his namesake?" The coincidence had her shaking her head, wide-eyed.

Fin shrugged and smiled that smile again. "Sure look it. But you really should come a little closer; what I want to show you is truly remarkable," he said, kneeling down on one knee and pointing a finger at a faint line of moss-filled text that was engraved at the very base of the stone.

Tara could not recall having noticed it the day before. Intrigued, she kneeled beside him. More crows had joined the noisy pair in the tree and were flapping against the wind, hopping from branch to branch, very agitated and making an absolute racket. Tara shoved her hands into her jacket pockets and bent forward, squinting to read the ancient text.

"Yes, that's it, right there. Perfect," Fin mumbled, and drew his hand away from the tombstone.

Tara felt a solid thud right between her shoulder blades. She tried to scoot backward, but he was too fast. He'd knocked her off balance and was forcing her down with both hands, mashing her face into the grass in front of the grave. She jerked her left elbow up at him with all her might, connecting solidly with his chest. He grunted in pain, but the pressure from his wiry arms only increased. Her cheeks scraped against cold mud and grass and gravel. The crows were screaming. He pressed down harder and harder on her neck and back until she couldn't breathe. Abruptly, a piece of soil beneath her face gave way, and she felt him put a hand on the back of her head and shove hard. She gargled out a yelp at the pain. She tried to kick but could not unbend her legs. The ground softened further... now her shoulders were somehow *in* it... and then her torso, and the rest of her, sinking, falling, blending down into the dirt.

The last thing Tara heard was Fin's impatient voice, barely audible against the din of crows shrieking overhead; he was growling something like, "Stop fighting, girl; just *go*, why don't you...."

And then the world went black as the earth swallowed her whole.

Chapter Four

Wooden floorboards, cold against her cheek. Mouth open; a puddle of sticky, half-dried drool. Dark.

Tara sat up and felt immediately woozy. Glancing around, she saw she was alone in a small room with mahogany walls and low ceiling beams. The whole place swayed in a steep rocking rhythm as though she were on a boat at sea.

Bile rose in her throat. *Where am I? What the hell happened?* She could remember being held face-down in the grass and mud. She touched her cheek; the skin was still tender. But it all felt so distant, like a dream, and made no sense whatsoever. How long had she been out?

Her hair and clothing were wet, and her entire body was stiff, as though she had been lying in the same position for many hours. Perhaps he had drugged her somehow. She carefully moved her sore jaw back and forth, then tried to stand. Dizziness put an end to that idea. Groaning, she leaned back against the wall. A cool weight touching both sides of her collarbone startled her. There was something around her neck, hanging down beneath the front of her shirt.

She pulled it out and looked at it. It was a plain necklace; a simple chain made of silver ball bearings, exactly like the one she had seen Fin wearing. *Twisted gift from a twisted mind*, she thought. Disgusted, she lifted it up past her chin to take it off, but it snagged on her hair at the back of her head. Using both hands, she reached back to lift the necklace from that side, but this time it snagged on her ear. She readjusted and tried again, carefully running her hands around the inside of the circle to make sure no part of her head or hair was in the way. It somehow got hung up on her chin again. She sighed and tried again. And again. No matter how she squirmed and pulled, she couldn't get it off. The stupid thing kept getting caught, which was strange because the necklace was clearly more than long enough to fit around her head.

Muttering obscenities, Tara yanked forward on the silver chain, ignoring the resulting sting against the back of her neck. It didn't break. She grabbed a handful of necklace in each fist, elbows extended out to either side of her, and jerked her arms apart forcefully, putting all her muscle into it. It would not budge or give or stretch, not even a millimeter. Her palms were screaming. She let go and cursed out loud.

Seconds later, she had her chin on her chest and was studying every little metal bead of the chain as she cycled it around, inch by inch, searching for the latch.

There was none.

She cycled it around her neck again, to double-check.

No latch. She tried three more times to lift the necklace over her head, to no avail.

What in the actual fuck?!

She bonked her head against the wall in exasperation. Shivering, she hunched forward, arms crossed and hands on shoulders. She was lightheaded and ached all over. Even her toes hurt. What had the bastard done to her? She closed her eyes and tried to piece together the sequence of events.

She recalled the aggravated crows in the tree and kneeling to read the mossy text on the gravestone, as well as Fin's frustrated voice as he held her down. She remembered how the ground had given way, not unlike the wall in her dream—but he *must* have drugged her, because that part of her memory felt so unreal, so unreliable, as though it had been patched or painted in. And it was impossible anyway. So, psychedelics, maybe. Were date rape drugs psychedelics? She hugged her knees together, relieved to find that everything down there was normal, but felt horribly violated nonetheless. As she parted her hair from her face, a little piece of grass fell from it onto her shirt.

Okay, so being shoved into the grass and dirt—that part had been real, at least. But she still felt like a giant chunk of her memory had been ripped away from her. This still made no logical sense. And the ground in front of the grave... had that been real? *No. Impossible.*

Tara's anxiety was rising fast, on the verge of overwhelming her senses. Beating it back with a mental stick, she forced herself to take in her surroundings. The room was windowless, and the only things in it were a dilapidated cot against the opposite wall, a narrow iron-studded chest at its foot, and an unlit candle lamp swinging languidly from the middle of the ceiling.

She tried again to get to her feet, one hand against the wall for balance. This time she managed to stand, but felt suddenly queasy as the floor pitched, so she had to continue bracing herself. *Definitely at sea*, she thought, to her increasing horror. *But how the...?*

There was a door in one corner of the room. Bending her head to keep from getting hit by the swinging lamp, she stumbled over to it and tried the brass handle. Locked. She tried again, cranking down on it hard while shoving her shoulder against the solid wood paneling, but it wouldn't give. *Prisoner.* She thought of those news stories about human trafficking. Was that what this was? Was she going to be sold to some filthy rich sicko businessman in a faraway country?

The boat swayed more violently, as though rolling through an exceptionally large wave, and Tara very nearly lost her footing. She balled her fists and was about to bang them against the door, but thought better of it. Perhaps she should not draw too much attention to herself. It might be more strategic, she decided, to wait until someone came to check on her; then she could ambush him and make her escape. If they weren't too far from shore, she could even dive and make a swim for it. It had been a while, but she had once been a decent swimmer, back when her mom used to take Tara with her to do laps at the pool while on one of her exercise kicks.

She scanned around for a weapon. The ceiling lamp was anchored solidly, and the chest at the foot of the cot was locked. She got down on her hands and knees to look underneath, then got back up and started stumbling from corner to corner of her prison. She searched everywhere, even in the crevices between the thick boards. Still nothing. Carefully, she made her way to the edge of the cot and sat down.

Everything was rocking back and forth, back and forth, incessantly, the countless boards creaking and complaining in every direction. As she listened, it dawned on her that some of those sounds were muffled voices, like distant shouting. She could clearly make out the voices of more than one man out there, and this was definitely a *ship*, she realized, not just a small yacht or sailboat. *We could be way out, on the open ocean. Too far to swim to shore.* Terror gripped her, and she felt her anxiety ready to peak again. Like a rottweiler straining to jump into the fray and tear its toy to shreds. "Keep calm," she hissed at herself, reaching into her pocket for her rubber band. It wasn't there; she had left it on her bedside table at home. She put her head between her knees and closed her eyes.

Back and forth, back and forth, back and forth…. The world just would not stop moving. Tara's heart continued to race, and in her imagination, the muffled hollers outside the locked door had begun to mingle with various reverberations from memory: Nick's angry shouts, or the hysterical cawing of crows in the cedars. Everything piled into a jumble. Her stomach was churning. She was going to puke; she knew it. Frantically, and despite already knowing there was nothing to find, she searched around for a sink or a toilet or a bucket, *something*. As she did so, she had a mental image of getting motion sickness on the train in the sixth grade while on a school fieldtrip to Washington DC and not being able to make it to the restroom in time. In that moment of impaired reasoning, she had somehow decided it would be good to hurl on the steps right against the exit door so as to get the smell as far as possible from her classmates. Never mind that upon reaching their destination, everyone had of course then needed to walk right through it in order to get off the train....

The memory intensified Tara's nausea. She bent over and spewed violently onto the wooden floor, barely missing the mattress and her feet. The heaves came over and over, and just when she thought she was finished, the boat would sway again and a new wave of vomiting would hit her.

Stomach finally empty and throat burning, she wiped her mouth and chin on a bottom corner of the quilt, curled up into a ball, and hugged the single mildewy pillow tightly to her.

Someone was rattling at her bedroom door handle like a maniac. Tara told whoever it was to go away, and then turned over to go back to sleep. The rattling persisted.

The sour smell of vomit and mildew brought everything back to her in an adrenaline rush. She opened her eyes. The swaying of the cabin, the stained pillow and moldy quilt, the not knowing where she was or where she was being taken or why... it all made her nearly puke again.

A crack of violet light opened around the edges of the door. She sat bolt upright. *Idiot*, she cursed herself, realizing she'd missed her chance at an ambush-and-escape. She glared daggers at the familiar face as he came into the room.

"Awake then, are you?" Fin said cheerfully, as though nothing were amiss.

"Fuck you," Tara snarled.

"Now now, girl, none of that. I mean you no harm, that I promise you. This is all just temporary."

"Oh yeah? Then take me the fuck home, you psycho."

Fin's eyes never left hers as he locked the door behind him with a large metal key. He then leaned against the doorframe, arms folded and ankles crossed, calmly teasing a toothpick into the corner of his mouth.

"Where the hell have you taken me, anyway? And how long was I out?"

Not deigning to answer, her abductor looked her slowly up and down, making her feel for all the world like an object being meticulously appraised at auction. The thought made her skin crawl.

"Hey listen, buddy, my mother's in law enforcement," she lied, hoping to sound more confident than she felt. "Kidnapping's a serious felony, and you're gonna go to prison for a really long time, just so you know. Unless you let me go right this minute."

Fin nodded distractedly, still twirling the toothpick and frowning in her general direction, apparently lost in thought. Tara flared her nostrils. She couldn't get a read on the guy, but reckoned he was plotting something. She had to get out of there.

She squinted at him and tried to soften her voice. "Please. Where are you taking me? I just wanna go home. I promise I won't say anything to the police or *anybody*. Just let me go, okay? *Please?*"

For the briefest of moments, Fin looked pained. Guilty, maybe? But then he raised his hands and shrugged. "Look, don't you worry. Honestly, the less you know, the better. Just try to go with the flow, yeah? And then this'll all be over before you know it. I give you my word, Tara Yewa: Once we're done, I'll take you right back home where you belong. Alive and whole."

"Done with what?" she asked, despite not believing a word out of his mouth. He had lied to get her there; he would lie again.

Fin pursed his lips, looking as though he wanted to say more. But then he shook his head, gave an odd little bow, and turned to unlock the door.

She hesitated for only two seconds. *Now or never.* Launching up from the cot, Tara was across the tiny cabin in two big steps, fingernails clawing at his face. Just as they were about to make contact, however, he calmly held out one very long arm, palm against her chest, stiff and unyielding. Unable to reach his eyes, she shrieked and tore at his elbow and shoulder instead, but he was surprisingly strong. Her brother had used a similar move in their scuffles growing up. She feinted upward with one hand while kicking as hard as she could at Fin's groin.

The move caused him to grunt and bend forward a little, but he straightened just as quickly and caught her ankle with his other hand. Her foot had missed, landing instead against his inner thigh. In one fluid motion he lifted straight up, and Tara went down like a sack of potatoes, hard on her back.

Enraged, she clambered to her feet to attack him again, but by then the Irishman had the door closed behind him and was locking it from the outside. She yelled again and again, beating and kicking at the door.

As she sat back down on the cot, gasping for air and pulse thumping, Fin spoke to her, voice muffled through the door. "A bit later I'll come fetch you. But please, Tara, no more shenanigans. You'll only end up hurting yourself."

She glared at the closed door, panting, refusing to answer. She was a knot, a spring, a bullet. A bomb.

"Listen, just bear with me, girl, and I'll see you safely home. You have my word, as I said" And then he was gone.

She balled her fists. The next time the man entered, she would be ready.

Seconds later, she had gathered the quilt into a bunch and was crouching with it next to the door, keeping as still as she could, prepared to pounce. As soon as the door was open wide enough for her to get out, she would shove her shoulder into her kidnapper's crotch and hopefully foil him with the quilt so he couldn't grab her. Once she was through the door, she had no idea other than to run like hell and perhaps try to reason with the ship's captain, if there even was one.

After several minutes of waiting, the strain on her bent knees had become unbearable. Tara stood, fidgeted, and finally sat down on the floor with her right side against the wall near the doorframe. At least she could still be facing him this way, and she figured it was better to keep low so he would be less able to see her while his eyes adjusted to the dim room.

She wondered if it was nighttime back home. She had no idea how long she had been out or how far they had traveled, but unless they were sailing across one of the Great Lakes, they could very well be in a different time zone by now. Aileen would be beside herself. Nick would... not. No;

that asshole would be quite happy if she never came back, she guessed. Or perhaps not. The bastard did have his moments, she had to admit, even if the vast majority of his parental "efforts" were either consciously or unconsciously designed to win points with Aileen. Furthermore, he had never actually harmed Tara, other than psychologically... but he was still a self-absorbed headcase and an alcoholic, and his behavior afflicted everyone around him. The idiot couldn't seem to hold down a job, either, so money was always a thing. And he never failed to remind Tara of how expensive it was to keep a roof over your head these days and that she and her "whole generation" needed to learn the value of hard work. Never mind that she had been babysitting since she was thirteen and working part time at the diner for almost a year.

Her mother, by contrast, was stable, loving, warm, and more or less reasonable. Even while Tara's father had been alive, her mother had always been the rock of the family. Tara doubted she herself could be even half that patient. If some overgrown manbaby were constantly controlling and emotionally abusing her like Nick did her mother, she'd be out of there without a moment's hesitation, and would not look back.

The whole dysfunctional family unit was certainly a mindfuck, but it was altogether peaceful and wholesome compared to her current predicament. She'd been kidnapped, pure and simple. From what she had gathered from movies and shows on the subject, kidnapped people sometimes got to return home safe and sound after a successful ransom, but way more often than not, they were killed and dumped in some corn field somewhere. Or in the bottomless ocean. She had never experienced such mortal danger; this was fundamentally different from standing on a precipice or watching a train hurtle past, in that what happened next was out of her hands. When it came to finding a way to safety, she had no clue where to start. She would gladly trade this terrifying uncertainty for having to go back and deal with Nick and her mom, and school, and even the prospect of having to move to a different state. She could learn to cope. Or not, but her fate would at least be somewhat on her own terms. But she had to get home first.

Mom, she called out mentally, eyes brimming. Suddenly, she felt very small and lost. But just as quickly, she was angrily wiping the tears away before they could run; she had no idea how, or why, even, but she was determined to survive this.

First things first: She had to escape her prison. She braced herself, waiting for sounds of approaching footsteps.

She awoke with a start, silently admonishing herself for dozing off again. The first thing she noticed was that the shouting and hollering outside had grown louder, more animated; excited, even. The next thing she noticed was that the ship was not swaying nearly as much as before. She could still feel the swells, but they were long, gentle rolls compared to the steeper pitches from earlier. She glanced up at the hanging lamp, and sure enough, it was barely moving. Smaller waves? Smaller waves could mean they were in a harbor, close to shore….

Boots on the deck, getting louder. Tara got back into her crouching position, quilt ready and nerves taut, hoping like hell her captor couldn't hear her heartbeat.

The boot-wearer stopping just outside her cabin. The sound of a key clattered in the lock.

That strange violet light streamed in as a hand pushed open the door. *Not yet*, she told herself.

The door opened wider; almost wide enough to get through it sideways. The hand and arm were Fin's. His head poked in after it, squinting into the darkness.

Now! she thought, exploding into action, quilt held over her head as she slammed her shoulder between his legs.

She hit home. Grunting, Fin reached for her, clutched a fistful of quilt, and yanked it out of her hands, but before he could grab at her again, she had hooked her left fist straight up into his nuts and was halfway out the door, scrambling like mad to get to her feet.

A sharp sting at the front of her throat cut her forward motion short. She lost balance, smashing her hip against the wooden floor as she fell. Fin had a handful of her hair and necklace and was dragging her backward. Savage in her desperation to escape, Tara wrenched free and bolted forward on hands and knees. All around her were guffaws and amused chuckles. As she stood and swept her coils from her face to see where she was going, the sight of the sky stopped her in her tracks.

Her mind wanted what she was seeing up there to be dark clouds roiling, because that would make sense. But no matter how many times she blinked, those things in the "sky" were not clouds. They were more like flowing lumps of violet-brown mud, or a swarm of pink baby rabbits drowning in chocolate, endlessly rolling and climbing over one another. Abruptly nauseated, Tara looked down at her feet and closed her eyes to steady herself.

A high-pitched male voice shrieked with laughter. "I swear that right there was the funniest thing I seen in 'least a century, maybe two!"

Tara opened her eyes. She was surrounded by bizarre-looking figures. Some were impossibly large, some impossibly lanky. Stretched arms, sharply contoured faces, unnatural shapes. Wearing apparel and... costumes? ...of all the colors of the rainbow, but just as many in drab grays and blacks. Hats. Most young, a few middle-aged or older.

And their faces—too many eyes, or not enough. Some with long hair and flowing beards, some with bare skin and bald heads. Tattoos. Ornaments protruding from skin, of unlikely pigments in a few cases. Stained? One man with *horns* on his shoulders and arms....

She blinked. *Gotta go!* she screamed at herself and lurched into motion, forcing her eyes on the deck as she sprinted toward a gap in the gathering crowd.

More guffaws. A barrel voice shouted, "See? Just goes to show, one way or another, these freelancers always bite off more'n they can chew."

Something collided against her back, but before she could react, Fin's arms had wrapped her in a bear hug, immobilizing her. She tried to strike at him with her elbows, but he was too wiry to give her any leeway. Agile, too; he kept dodging his legs out of the way of her backward kicks. She yelped when he vise-gripped her wrists and wrenched them behind her back. A moment later, she felt the rough burn of rope as he tied them together.

"I said no more shenanigans, didn't I?" he murmured, right next to her left ear.

Tara slammed the side of her head against his mouth with a painful but satisfying crunch and felt him yank his head back to avoid further blows. She hoped she'd given him a bloody lip. Riding her fury, she twisted and struggled some more, but to no avail. His grip on her forearms was iron.

As Fin gently pushed her forward, she had no choice but to take a step to keep from falling. "Walk now. This way," he whispered.

Tara's hip and tailbone ached. And her ear stung. Exhaustion was beginning to creep over her, sapping her muscle strength and dulling the knife edge of adrenaline. She bit her lip. She was going to be furious with herself if she cried. Fin prodded her again, and they were walking.

A man-shaped thing with meat hook arms and a mangled chin stepped out in front of them. Tara shrank back against Fin's torso, lowering her head from the sight of the beast. It was too huge and horrible to look at.

"Heh," the monstrosity chortled. It was the barrel voice from earlier. "Looks to me like Finny freelancer can't keep track of his wares."

There was snickering all around, and a few hummed in agreement. When Tara peeked sidelong at the deep-voiced thing, she saw it had planted its feet and was bunching its muscular arms forward, hideous golden cat-like eyes wide open, hands forming into sledgehammer fists. "Perhaps he should be relieved of his *burden*."

"Step aside, sailor." Fin's reply was low and steady. "I'm on a job for The Mother. I'll not warn you twice."

Sailor...? Tara thought incredulously.

"Yeah right, sure you are, pipsqueak," the so-called sailor snorted.

Everything happened so fast. One second the shirtless brute was grinning and shaking its head at the leering audience, and the next it had stepped forward and was taking a swing at Tara and Fin.

As she ducked, she felt a quick tug at her middle, and an instant later they were several feet to the right of where they had been standing. Fin let go of her and was suddenly behind the sailor-thing, touching one hand to its neck and the other into the small of its back, his fingers and thumbs spread in a bird shape: Index finger forward, thumb out, and the other three fingers together, each hand in the same configuration, pressed tight against the sailor's skin.

There was a long, thin cry, like a sick cat. To her horror, Tara realized the noise was coming from the giant man-thing. As Fin continued to press his hands into it, the sailor's body seemed to be *deflating*, like a balloon. Several frightful seconds later, it had completely disintegrated, and all that was left was a vaguely humanoid-shaped smear of blue-black smoke. This rose straight upward, distorting as it accelerated toward the chocolate sky, taking the dying scream with it.

The crowd of onlooking bizarro figures had fallen silent, and several were taking a step or two back, away from Fin. Tara bent over double and retched what little remained of her stomach's contents onto the wooden deck boards.

Fin glared around, turning a full circle, as if to dare anyone else to challenge them. No one did. He seemed utterly spent. Breathing hard, he stumbled back to Tara and reached a hand toward her. She flinched away.

"Come on, we need to go," he panted, hand held out, an urgency in his voice.

She stared stupidly into his fierce blue eyes, unable to think or move. Her hands were still bound behind her back, so she couldn't use them to wipe the strand of drool and puke from her chin. The perpetual violet sunset/sunrise glow had her disoriented, and the rabbit-lumps continued to reel overhead, bringing a fresh round of nausea. She clenched her eyes shut. *Why can't I just sober up?!* Perhaps she was having a panic attack. If so, it was by far the worst panic attack of her life, worse than any she had ever heard of. *Hallucinogens,* she reminded herself. *I'm just having a really really bad trip.* She'd heard stories about acid. Also, that it could do permanent damage to the brain; make a person crazy. *What if I'm already crazy?* But she couldn't think about that right now. It was all just too much. Overwhelmed and in shock, she wiped her mouth on her shoulder and looked back down at her feet. Down was safer; shoes and floorboards did not roil about or disappear or scream.

"Look, I know this is all very confronting for you, Tara, but we need to move, like," Fin murmured. When she just stood there, mind blank, he moved behind her and pressed firmly between her shoulder blades. "Come on, girl. One foot in front of the other."

They were walking again. Numbly, she concentrated on her feet and let him guide her forward along the slippery deck. Her legs were weak. She felt sure she would have fallen at least three times were it not for Fin's support. He seemed to need hers, too; as they made their way forward, he was half holding her up, half leaning on her, still winded. She could hear low muttering and sensed all the wary eyes around them... too, too many eyes... but she didn't dare look up.

They passed a large cabin in the middle of the deck, perhaps the main cabin, and outside it stood a rather normal-looking human woman in a stylish broad-brimmed hat, long olive drab cloak, formal russet vest, and knee-high black leather boots. She was staring at them, watching them approach. Tara's heart leaped.

"Ma'am, please," she started, but Fin clamped his hand over her mouth.

"Mouth shut. *Not a word*. We are *not among friends*."

The captain—or at least Tara assumed that was what she was, going by her attire and the way she carried herself—simply frowned suspiciously at Tara a few seconds longer before nodding tightly at Fin. She then returned to hurling a barrage of curses at a sailor who was perched high up in the mainmast, apparently having a very hard time disentangling a rope. Either this woman was in on the kidnapping, Tara thought, or she at least was tolerating it. Either way, it was clear that this person had no intention of being Tara's savior.

Fin shoved, not so gently this time, causing her to stumble forward. He seemed to have regained his energy; he was no longer leaning against her and had caught his breath. Tara returned her attention to her feet and kept walking.

The ship was very long. Several deckhands stopped what they were doing to gape at them as they made their way past, but a barked order from a tall, thin, stern-faced man with melancholy eyes sent them scurrying back to work. Most of the sailors looked more or less ordinary, like this man or like the captain had, but a few were of outlandish appearance—like demons or ogres from a fantasy novel or zombies risen from the dead. Tara did her best not to look at them. Once again, she bit her lip, this time hoping the pain might wake her up—just in case this wasn't the effect of drugs in her system but was instead some extremely lucid nightmare. She'd never had a dream so real, though. *Dreams aren't like this. You wake up from dreams*, she thought.

They arrived at an area toward the bow of the ship where crates and sacks were being loaded and offloaded over the port gunwale by way of a pulley system, with the more manageable containers being slung over sailors' or porters' backs and carried up and down a rope ladder. Fin took Tara straight over to it and passed something to the elderly, ashen-faced figure overseeing the operation. Some words were exchanged, but Tara could not make them out. The man's face had a violet-brown tinge to it, a reflection from the squirming "sky". *Hallucinating*, she told herself. *I'm just hallucinating. None of this is real.*

Fin lifted her chin with his thumb and forefinger and looked her in the eye. "Alright now. Can I untie you so you can use your hands to climb down the ladder? Or do I have to use the pulley to lower you down like a bag of bricks? Fair warning, things that go down that way tend to get wet, like."

"Ladder," she mumbled.

"Good girl, that's the way. Okay, careful now; watch your footing. If you fall in, I can't promise I'll be able to fish you out again."

Again..? She recalled how drenched and cold she'd been when she had woken up. Had she fallen overboard? Why couldn't she remember?

After untying her, Fin helped Tara up a wide, squat stepladder and over the railing. The sight of the water below disoriented her, and she had to pause to keep from losing her balance. She thought she could see stars in it, but when she squinted at it more closely, they did not appear to be *reflections* of stars; rather, they seemed to actually be *in the water*... or perhaps *through* it somehow. As though the sea were but a layer across the sky, and she was looking up instead of down....

"*Climb*," Fin urged, with a note of what Tara thought might be fear in his voice. Somehow, that thought made everything all the scarier to her. Unclenching her trembling hands from the railing, she placed them one at a time on the top rung of the rope ladder, spotted another rung for her foot, and swung her leg down, heart in her throat, taking on the tiniest shred of faith that the very worn-looking ladder would hold. At Fin's encouraging prompts, she began to lower herself down, hand over hand, maintaining three points of contact at all times like her dad and mom had taught her on backpack trips in the mountains when she was younger.

Halfway down, she made the mistake of glancing over her shoulder in the direction of shore, again nearly losing her balance. The ship was apparently anchored in a wide harbor with a wharf in the middle and a beach stretching to the left and right of it as far as she could see. Despite the churning muddy violet-brown chocolate rabbit-shapes overhead, its sand was bright yellow, almost white—as though lit by the sun—and she thought she could see a faint line of blue on the horizon beyond it. A long pier thronged with people and cargo jutted into the harbor, and several dinghies, weighed down with goods and passengers, were being rowed between it and the ship. One such dinghy floated directly below her feet. The little boat was in the process of being stacked high with crates and sacks from the ship bound for shore. There did not seem to be enough room for all that cargo, let alone for her and Fin, but he was making more impatient noises above her, so she resumed her downward climb.

When she reached the bottom, a man standing in the stern of the dinghy reached out a hand to help her aboard. She hesitated. There was something *wrong* with his face; it was... *blurry*. So was the hand he was extending toward her. She blinked. His clothing appeared in focus, but his head and hands.... She blinked twice.

"Hurry now," Fin said. "Out of time! The Mother is waiting."

Tara nearly giggled, suddenly wanting to make some smart-ass crack about him being a momma's boy or ask in lurid tones whose mother it was he wanted so desperately to please, exactly, but the idea fell flat in her mouth. *I must be getting hysterical*, she thought.

After taking another second to steel herself, she reached out and took the man's proffered hand. Insubstantial-looking or not, his grip felt solid enough, and a moment later she was on board the cramped vessel and seated atop a netted crate against the left gunwale. Only then did she notice that three deckhands—though not any of the ones who had crowded around and jeered outside of her cabin-prison, thankfully—had followed them down the rope ladder and were climbing into the boat after Fin. It rocked from their weight, but Fin and the blurry man leaned this way and that to counterbalance, and soon they were all seated and had somehow managed not to tip the boat over. Fin plonked himself down on the edge of the crate beside Tara, and a minute later, the blurry man had a pair of oars in his hands and was rowing them toward the pier.

The heavy dinghy moved sluggishly through the waves, low enough in the water that it sloshed nearly up to the gunwale. Tara resisted the urge to trail her fingers in it; the stars were still there, and they made no sense. Still, if she closed her eyes and ignored the mental images of everything she had seen since waking up—all those horrible hallucinations, the ferryman's blurry body parts, the sky— and focused on *logic*, then this all sounded and felt as though she really were at sea: She could feel the rocking of the boat; she could hear the shouts of sailors on deck above and behind them as they worked ropes and sails, the squeak of pulleys, the dull flaps of heavy canvas being folded and bound. All the sounds around her were quite vivid, right down to the dip and splash of the oars. She could even smell the salt. Tara therefore figured she must actually be on a boat somewhere, in the ocean; at least that part was real. It had to be.

Two of the sailors moved to sit in the middle with the blurry man, also facing the rear of the boat, and picked up a set of spare ores each. They joked and bantered at the ferryman's expense for a while, but soon were putting their backs into helping him row while chanting something with rhyming lines and plenty of bawdy expletives.

As the dinghy picked up speed, salt spray hit Tara's face. The air felt warm and humid. She gazed back at the ship. They were now far enough away that she could see the full length of it. It had the shape of a giant galleon out of one of those movies about eighteenth-century exploration or naval battles, with heaps of furled sails on multiple masts towering skyward. The roiling "clouds" above still upset her stomach and hurt her head, so she turned her attention to the water and its seemingly superimposed galaxy of stars.

There was a face, right there underwater, peering up at her. Tara yelped and jumped back from the gunwale, falling off the crate and nearly taking Fin down with her. Something surfaced. Kneeling with one hand on the edge of the gunwale, Tara looked again and realized the face belonged to a dolphin. Its head was halfway out of the water, its fins deftly keeping its body in place as it rode the gentle swell of the waves, clicking and snickering playfully. She'd never seen a dolphin up close before.

Everyone had fallen silent, but no one stopped paddling; if anything, they were now digging harder toward shore. All in a matter of seconds, and without breaking rhythm, the sailor nearest to Tara eyed her nervously, shot a suspicious glance at Fin, and then put his head down to concentrate on rowing.

The blurry-headed man muttered something that sounded like a prayer, and they gradually left the dolphin in their wake. Tara stared back at it, marveling that the sea creature seemed to be returning her gaze, looking her right in the eye. An instant later it dove, and as she watched it disappear into the starry depths, she could have sworn the thing had been smiling at her.

Chapter Five

From the dinghy, Tara could see dozens of figures bustling about the pier, stacking crates or carrying various containers to and from shore. A small cluster of gray-robed men and women were on their knees, facing seaward and occasionally kowtowing in perfect unison, their nearly monotone chants rising and falling with the breeze amid the surrounding din of shouts and laughter and general chatter. Several people appeared to be setting up makeshift stalls along the opposite edge, while others were busy loading and unloading boats.

With a shock, Tara realized that a few of the figures on the pier had faces and limbs exactly like those of the man rowing their dinghy: out of focus. *Blurry.* Even after rubbing her eyes, the parts of their bodies not covered by clothing remained completely out of focus. She got up the courage to scrutinize their ferryman's face as he guided them in toward the pier. It seemed incorporeal, or smudged, as if not quite solid.

She leaned over to Fin and whispered, "Hey, would you please tell me what you gave me?"

He knitted his brows. "Gave you?"

"What drug. Some sort of hallucinogen, I'm guessing. Is it acid?"

He frowned and shook his head.

"I just mean… I just want to know what this is, that's all. I'm still tripping super hard here, you know." Hoping honesty might arouse some sympathy in him, perhaps get him to level with her, she added, "I'm really scared, Fin."

Fin shook his head again, tightly this time, and mumbled through gritted teeth, just loud enough for only her to hear. "I *will* explain, Tara, but *not right now*. Later, when it's safe, like. For now, I think it's best if you don't talk." He then turned his attention to their fast-approaching destination and would not look at her again.

"Blessed you are."

Tara looked up with a start and realized that the blurry man was addressing her. Not knowing what to say, she simply stared at where eyes should have been in his impossible face, doing her best not to flinch away.

"Blessed, to be greeted personally by an Engineer," the ferryman continued.

One of the sailors from the ship scoffed out loud, and another echoed the sentiment. The ferryman straightened and glared back and forth at them for a moment, seeming about to say something, but then sighed, shook his head slowly, and returned to his steering duties.

"What did he mean, 'engineer'?" Tara asked her kidnapper, remembering to lower her voice.

At first, she thought Fin might get angry at her for speaking, but after a brief pause, he simply shrugged and whispered next to her ear, almost inaudibly. "Pay him no mind. It's only a myth. A religious obsession, really. Some of the more superstitious in these realms believe the world was built by dolphins and whales."

"Seriously?"

"Yeah. *Quiet* now," he said, finger to his lips.

The blurry man expertly brought the dinghy to a rocking stop alongside the pier between a pair of broad wooden ladders. While they awaited their turn to unload, the sailors stowed the oars and began to gather up their belongings. Before long, the boat ahead of them was fully loaded and had begun to pull away in the direction of the anchored ship, at which point the blurry man guided them up to the front-most ladder. Everyone but Tara stood at once and immediately began to hand the cargo up to the outstretched hands of the people—as well as one who was not exactly a person in physical appearance, at least to Tara's drugged-out mind—who had come partway down the ladder to receive it. When it was her turn, Tara was handed up just as roughly as one of the bags of whatever it was—rice or vegetables or, for all she knew, narcotics.

"Let go, I can climb it myself," she complained, but Fin and the others ignored her and continued to lift. There was a holdup at the top of the ladder while a large container was maneuvered onto its side, and she managed to put a toe on one of the rungs to steady herself while they waited. One of the sailors had a hand under her armpit and was holding her too far out from the ladder for her to reach her hand to it, so she had no choice but to hang there, suspended, feeling awkward and useless.

She tried not to stare too long at the water below her dangling foot. It wasn't easy; the stars were right there, making the ocean depths seem infinite, never mind the fact that she could also see the shapes of fish and seaweed and the pier's thick wood piles rising from a sandy floor. These objects she saw right *through* the stars; above them, in spite of them. The vertigo hurt her head, so she focused instead on Fin's hands around her middle. They were strong hands, with hard lines framing taut tendons and muscle. Despite his youth, they were a grown man's hands. Tara hated being in their grip, despised their owner, yet she somehow knew they would not let her fall.

A long-limbed woman hanging from further up the ladder reached down to receive Tara, and with what seemed a practiced movement, pulled her up with unbelievable strength and passed her on to another waiting porter, who in turn hauled her up the rest of the way and deposited her on her feet atop the pier. For several seconds, Tara just stood there stiff as a board, utterly stunned by the surrounding maelstrom of strange sights and sounds. Her entire body felt rigid and sore, her mind numb from tension and fright. Vaguely, it occurred to her that she should be taking this opportunity to make a run for it and find a phone or a police station, but for the moment, she didn't quite trust her legs' ability to keep her upright, let alone burst into rapid motion.

Fin came up immediately after. No sooner was he standing on the pier than he had Tara by the hand and was tugging her along toward shore, shouldering his way through the press of traders and porters and whatever else they were. Here and there among the "normal" (but still weirdly dressed, for the most part) people were creatures from nightmare: hollow faces, blurred and smudged hands—or even entire torsos, in the case of several who wore no shirts; gaudy outfits, dazzling ornaments and various tools that seemed to actually be extensions of body parts; all manner of weapons hanging from belts or attached to flesh; jewelry, hats, sunglasses, tusks, sleek or clunky footwear, bare feet with either too many toes or not enough. The entire scene felt like a circus of the absurd. Some were maimed, contorted, or deeply scarred, and a few looked as though they should stop what they were doing and get themselves to an ER straight away: a girl with a knife protruding from her belly, complete with a horrific stain of blood that had spread through the bottom half of her blouse to the front of her denim skirt, just going about her business; a square-shouldered man with a large hole in his forehead that Tara could see right through when he looked in her direction; a short person—a little boy? a dwarf?—with a slit throat, darting past while hollering a cheerful rhyme over and over.

She looked away, swallowing down bile. It made no sense; none of them had seemed in any pain or discomfort whatsoever. For the umpteenth time, she shook her head and blinked, wishing she would sober up or, better yet, *wake* up and find herself home, safe and sound in her bed. She tightened her grip on Fin's hand, hating herself for it, but the encounter aboard the ship had left her anxious that another brute might challenge them or try to take her from him, and that something even *worse* might happen next. As he led her forward, however, everyone on the pier seemed too focused on his or her—or its—own business to take any notice of them. *Logic....* Logic dictated that this was all in her head; logic told her she couldn't trust any of what she was seeing, because she'd been drugged and these were all just ordinary people doing ordinary things. Nevertheless, the mental image of that child with the slit throat would not go away, and it made her set her eyes on the back of Fin's jacket and keep them there as they walked. The brown leather was smooth, worn, tarnished. It looked very old, and that was somehow comforting.

Three quarters of the way to shore, the crowd began to thin. Sunlight exploded down, bathing the wharf in golden warmth, as though the clouds had parted suddenly—but when she looked up, she was amazed to see a blue, blue sky stretching as far as the eye could see to their left and right and in front of them. Craning her neck to gaze straight overhead, she caught a glimpse of a distinct line where the dark churning rabbit sky ended and the perfectly blue sky began. It spanned from horizon to horizon, running parallel to the shore, and was more solid and well-defined than any weather front she had ever seen. It also did not appear to be moving. She stumbled a little when Fin yanked her arm and hissed at her to keep up.

She was just letting him pull her along without struggling at all. She didn't know what else to do; her simmering anxiety and the insane freak show all around them had her too emotionally paralyzed to give much thought to what she *should* be doing. Escape? But to where? The entire concept felt abstract and slightly nauseating. She decided she should first figure out where she was, hopefully get her head clear by then, and then see about finding an opportunity to get away. Perhaps ask directions to the local consulate or embassy, assuming there even was one. She might have to travel to a bigger town first. Surely they wouldn't care that she had no passport with her. Or that she was tripping balls from whatever narcotic her asshole kidnapper had slipped her. She reckoned she'd be okay if she could just get free of him and borrow someone's phone. Feeling vaguely hopeful simply from having formed a plan, she began searching for friendly faces, but had to look away again.

The wash of surf against the beach grew more audible as they neared the wide boardwalk that ran the length of the wharf. When she looked down to her left, into the water, Tara was surprised to see the stars had gone. Dark strands of seaweed floated lazily in the shallows like hair in a bathtub, ebbing and flowing, ebbing and flowing with the gentle waves. Little fish darted here and there among them, and sunlight sparkled on the surface. The air was dry and warm and salty.

At the end of the pier, they turned right and had to navigate several large piles of hemp sacks that looked to have been dumped and abandoned there a long time ago; all of them were covered in a layer of drifted sand and gave off a rotten stench, amplified by the hot sun and the close press of bodies. Tara wrinkled her nose. The smell was putrid, though none of the other passersby seemed to mind. As she eyed one of the sacks, something moved inside it, causing her to jump. She looked more closely. Whatever it was wriggled and emitted a desperate screech, punching at the sides violently like a trapped rat or some ghastly fetus trying to exit its mother's womb in a hurry. A chill rippled up and down

Tara's spine, and she hastened her steps until she was walking right alongside Fin, dodging the oncoming foot traffic, focusing on anything and everything that looked even the least bit recognizable and normal. There wasn't much.

They hurried along the boardwalk to a section lined on both sides with storage sheds and shopfronts. The thoroughfare was thronged with people and... *other* things... that were haggling, bartering, or simply having a chat in the sun. Some browsed unhurriedly, others strode past on quick feet. Quite a few sipped steaming hot liquid from mugs or hunkered over smoking grills full of fragrant sizzling meat. All around were vendors hawking their wares, most in very colorful, traditional-looking garb, and among the goods being offered for sale were fruits and meats and flatbreads, including a few things Tara recognized, like bananas and dates. It occurred to her that she hadn't eaten since she left her house... yesterday morning? But she was far too nervy and afraid to feel hungry.

A thick stand of palm trees grew in a gap between buildings. As they walked past, she spotted a magnificently feathered parrot high in the wind-buffeted canopy, hanging almost upside down from the base of a frond. It made soft, melodic chittering sounds while working its beak around a nut or seed of some sort. The subtropical feel to this place added to Tara's growing suspicion that she'd been taken right across the Atlantic and was now in a port town somewhere in Africa. The climate felt too dry for this to be South America or the Caribbean, she thought. Whatever country this was, beyond the wharf it looked very desert-like: Just past the line of buildings rose the most enormous sand dunes Tara had ever seen, including on television. They were so immense they might as well have been mountains. She thought of *Star Wars*. Namibia perhaps? Or was she farther north, in the Mediterranean? Egypt maybe? Or Morocco? All she knew about Morocco was what was shown—and much of it had been a vastly unfair portrayal, no doubt—in that old black-and-white movie, *Casablanca*, set during World War II. Aileen and Nick had made her watch it with them one night during Christmas break.

However, if this was indeed Africa, there was definitely something odd going on, even taking her drug-induced delusions into account: Tara could neither spot nor hear any evidence of cars, or trucks, or forklifts, nor any other vehicle or machinery, for that matter. And not a single person had a phone in hand. Hardly any modern clothing, either, come to think of it, apart from the garments on a handful of people such as that girl on the pier with the blood-stained denim skirt. It didn't add up; Tara had seen plenty of photos from Africa. Admittedly, many of them had been from when her paternal grandfather was growing up in Nigeria, but some had been taken more recently by her father when he had gone there to lecture at a botanical symposium at the University of Ibadan, just a couple of years before his death. He'd been quite snap-happy during his visit, and while Tara's memory from the last time she'd looked at those photos and videos was rather vague, she did recall being struck with the realization that urban culture and technology in Africa were not actually all that different from what she had grown up with in small-town Pennsylvania. But this... by contrast, this port town was... downright *primitive*. Un-technological in the extreme. And most people here were ultra traditional-looking, as though they had stepped right back in time. Or deliberately putting on a show, though that idea seemed even more far-fetched to her.

She planted her feet and glared at Fin when he turned to look at her. "Tell me where we are, this minute."

He pulled at her hand. "Later. We have to go; we're on a schedule."

But Tara leaned back, putting her weight into resisting him. "No. I'm not moving until you tell me where you've taken me."

He was forced to face her again. "Yes, girl, you are," he muttered, then grabbed her by the elbow and yanked her forward. He was too strong; she had no choice but to lurch after him, tripping over her feet and very nearly falling on her face.

"I'll scream!" she challenged, scrambling to find her footing.

"And I'll laugh," he threw calmly over his shoulder.

She shut up then and let him lead her onward, her head down, face burning. He'd called her bluff. She had no intention of screaming, given that she had no desire to attract the attention of any of the monsters and creeps around them.

As they wended their way through the crowd, Tara did her best to ignore the eccentric outfits, the blurry or ashen faces, the mutilated and dismembered, the outright garish and weird. Now and then, heavy thumps resounded in the distance, a bit like muffled explosions. She couldn't imagine it was thunder, as there was not a cloud in sight in that direction, yet the thumps persisted. With each detonation, her panic rose another notch. She fought to keep her head, knowing that if she was in the middle of a panic attack, she could freeze up and potentially miss her only opportunity for escape.

Halfway along the strip of shops, they came to a two-story building with a pair of what looked like guards standing sentry to either side of a service window. Both wore strange armor-like apparel. Despite the heat, the uniforms were thick and bulbous, ballooning out from their bodies as though stuffed with padding or inflated with air. On second glance, though, it looked sturdy and quite protective—a tough, cushioning layer all around their bodies, with not an inch of skin showing. Even their eyes were covered. Tara thought the rectangular plates of semi-transparent, shaded material they had on were easily the most ridiculous-looking sunglasses she had ever seen.

Fin walked her straight up to the window and spoke through the barred opening to a very bored-looking attendant with bloodshot eyes and a scraggly goatee.

"I'd like to register my arrival and wares."

The attendant flicked a glance up from whatever he had been reading, then returned his attention to it as though he couldn't be bothered to even respond. Tara thought the man very rude, but Fin just stood patiently, completely still.

At length, the man sighed, took his time rolling up the piece of parchment, and set it aside before finally regarding Fin. "I am the customs agent on duty. This is not your first time in the Cradle?"

"No, sir," Fin replied before producing a small stack of papers from inside his jacket, which he handed through the window bars. The attendant took them with a tired exhalation through his flat nose.

A moment later, the man sat up straight, eyes wide. "*Official* business, I see," he said, suddenly sounding much more professional, and even a tad obsequious. "Right. Welcome back, sir. You have goods to declare, you say?"

"Only the one, actually," Fin said, nodding in Tara's direction.

She was mortified. *A good to declare?!* She opened her mouth, about to deliver some choice words, but stopped when Fin kicked her foot.

"Farmer?" the agent asked.

"Yes."

"Hey, I am n—" Tara began to protest again but was cut short by a hand compressing tightly around her wrist.

The agent looked her slowly up and down. "She looks quite hale for a farmer."

"Yes, she's new," Fin said casually.

The tension emanating through Fin's fingers made Tara change her mind about trying to slip in a plea for help. Her gut agreed. In addition to this man's overt sleaziness, there was an air about him that made him seem more liable to want to keep a girl prisoner in a secret basement than help her get free.

The customs agent eyed her suspiciously for a lingering moment, but then looked over Fin's papers once more. "Far be it from me to hinder The Mother's affairs. Right," he said, stamped them, and handed them back through the window to Fin. "Registration granted. May The Mother and the Heart thrive forever."

The two guards, silent up to that point, both stomped to attention and repeated his words in unison: "May The Mother and the Heart thrive forever."

Fin took the papers, nodded his thanks, and then took Tara by the upper arm and was herding her in front of him as they continued along the boardwalk.

"What was that all about?" she asked, but he ignored her.

When they were almost at the end of the row of shops, he steered her left into a very narrow, winding alleyway. It was darkly shadowed, cluttered with barrels, and as they made their way deeper into it, Tara realized they were completely out of view of the crowded sunlit boardwalk. Her pulse skyrocketed. Throwing a look back over her shoulder, she wondered if she should make a break for it, and began to scan the ground for something to use as a weapon.

"Relax. This is a shortcut," Fin said.

A minute later, they rounded a bend and sunlight burst into view. They exited the alleyway and a sudden gust of wind hurled sand at Tara's legs, causing her to wince as the grains stung her skin even through her jeans. Squinting left and right, she saw that they had come out behind the line of shops to an area of arid plots separated by dilapidated wooden fences. On the other side of a low wall of boulders, the massive sand dunes towered into the blue like a mountain range.

"Where are we going? It's not.... There's nothing out here," she said with a tremor.

Fin merely tightened his grip on her arm and propelled her forward, pausing only long enough to help her over the boulders. From there they continued upward, leaving the town behind, apparently heading straight into the desert wilderness. Tara discovered that most of the sand underfoot was not loose like beach sand; it was hard-packed and therefore much easier to walk on, especially in the scattered patches where sprigs of some kind of hardy little plant grew. Even so, steep as the incline was, she soon found her leg muscles burning.

It was a long slog. Fin was ruthless in his desire to get wherever they were going; he would not let her rest until they'd crested the top of the giant dune. When they finally got there, Tara bent over, hands on her thighs, panting for breath. The view was stunning. What they were standing on was but the first of an endless expanse of sand dune ridges rolling all the way to the horizon, unbroken beneath what in the direction they were facing was a cloudless sky. Down the slope in front of them was a shallow saddle connecting the ridge they had just climbed to the next, and in it nestled a trio of tent-like structures. Fin only gave her a brief respite before prodding her forward, and a moment later they were trudging down the slope, leaving the ocean and the wharf and the awful pink chocolate rabbit sky behind.

Tara was very conscious of the fact that the farther they went, the more distance was being put between her and home. She was hitting herself for not trying to get away and find a police station or a phone while they were in town, and could feel the panic spiraling through her, pulsing up from the hot sand and into her feet with every step she took, snaking through her legs, into her belly. From there it pierced her, expanding into every part of her body, stretching her insides like crystalline lattices of sharp-edged ice; pushing distending twisting wrenching until she could barely breathe.

She closed her eyes and tried to focus on the warm wind, on the sensation of her hair whipping against the side of her face. It helped; it was a distraction. Anything physical was. But so far, ever since she had woken up in that dark ship's cabin with the swaying lamp, the primary force that had carried her forward had been the knife edge of fear. Fear of her abductor and whatever fate he had in mind for her; fear of all the terrifying hallucinations; fear of losing her mind and never getting it back. Fear was what had kept the panic at bay and stopped it from consuming her; fear was what had prevented her from collapsing into a heap of depression and hopelessness. Each time she wanted to give up, that knife edge would saw and chop mercilessly at her spine, flaying her senses into hyperawareness.

At the same time, she could feel exhaustion creeping up to take fear's place, slowly but surely wilting her, mitigating the effects of adrenaline, sapping her strength of will. Soon exhaustion would reign supreme, and fear would no longer be enough to stop her from seizing up, from breaking, from letting go; from sinking into that sweet familiar abyss that was despair. It was already so tempting; she could simply shut down, curl up, and disappear, lost forever in the loose strands of her mind. Running her tongue right along the bumpy roof of her mouth and into the crevices behind her teeth, she could actually taste the despondency that was beginning to envelop her. It tasted sour.

But she still had enough fear and sense of self-preservation to want to survive this. To escape; to get home. To *make* it. All around her was sand and more sand. Nowhere to run, and certainly nowhere to hide. But she would bide her time and hope for another chance. She would find a way.

The dusty tent-like structures at the bottom of the hill had resolved into a small, semi-permanent-looking garrison or checkpoint of some kind. It appeared to be manned by a dozen or so guards, and as they drew closer, Tara could see that they wore the same sort of armor as the ones outside the customs office had. These guards, however, looked much less bored and a lot more mistrustful: They were sporting weapons—spears or pikes—and as Fin and Tara approached, they arranged themselves into a defensive formation.

"Papers," one of them barked, stepping forward. The voice was female and extremely unfriendly.

Fin retrieved his papers and handed them over. The guard took only a second to examine them, then whistled a sharp, rising note through her teeth. A bird—it was huge; an eagle, Tara thought, eyes wide—appeared out of nowhere, swooping around from behind one of the large tents and landing on the guard's outstretched arm. As it pinned its sharp gaze on them, cocking its head, the guard rolled Fin's papers up tightly, stuffed them into a leather tube tied to the eagle's talon, and flung the bird skyward. With a shrill cry, it beat its powerful wings until it had caught a thermal, circled up and up and up, and then made a beeline for the next ridge. Tara followed the majestic creature with her eyes, in complete awe, as it vanished over the top of the giant sand mountain.

The guards had already gone back to whatever they had been doing before she and Fin arrived. It was suddenly as if she and her captor were not even there.

"Now we wait," Fin said, and walked over to a shady spot at the corner of one of the large tents. There he sat down with his back to a wooden pillar, legs crossed, eyes half closed.

The sight of the eagle had been like a salve to Tara's worn-out mind; though she had never seen anything like it before, it was nevertheless recognizable on some level, being a mundane animal, and therefore a very welcome break from the bizarre. Perhaps it was simply that it had looked so vivid and so *real*; so like an eagle *should* look. No slit throat; no protruding knife; no extra wings or horrible limb extensions; no blurry face or torso; just two eyes, a beak, a body, a tail, talons, and a pair of wings. Now it was gone, she looked around at the guards and their bulbous armor, the exotic sand dunes rolling from horizon to horizon, her abductor incongruously taking a snooze—though he was clearly keeping an eye on her, even now—and the feeling that she was losing her mind weighed her down even further, dragging at her like rocks around her ankles, threatening to take her under. She searched for a mental image to cling to, something to keep the niggling sourness in her mouth from overwhelming her. If she had a blade, or a rubber band, she would use it.

She closed her eyes and pictured home. Her bedroom. The clothes scattered across the floor. The messy desk. The photo there of her smiling father with a backpack on, red sweaty bandana across his forehead, making him look more like a hippy than an academic. She recalled watching the backs of his boots as they'd hiked up a trail, one foot in front of the other.... *Always plan your steps... avoid rocks and roots; find the flat spots... much easier on your feet, over time....*

A rush of apprehension. The world tipping. Tara's mind suddenly unsteady, clinging desperately to reality, fighting hard to ignore that troubling what-if thought. Abruptly, she whirled to face Fin. "Wait. What did you mean when you said you knew my father?!"

Startled by her sudden outburst, he lifted his head and stared at her for a moment, apparently not comprehending.

"In the cemetery. Before you drugged me and kidnapped me. The way you said it, it sounded like you really knew my dad. How did you know him? Or was that just another lie?" she demanded.

Several emotions seemed to play over Fin's face at once, but then he smirked and shook his head. "Oh, that. Yeah, sorry about that. You're right; I was lying. I don't know your dad. I never knew your dad."

She nodded, returning her eyes to the ground. She had suspected as much, but the sudden recollection of the conversation in the graveyard had made her feel compelled to ask anyway; he had seemed so earnest at the time. But sure enough, this guy was just a liar, through and through; he'd have said whatever it took to get her to follow him, and that had done the trick quite easily. She had even provided him with the ammo herself, by telling him she was there visiting her dad; and then, sure as a hollow-point bullet, he'd used it, and she'd fallen right for it, as blind and stupid as a deer in headlights. Rather than infuriate her, however, this admission of his only made her feel sad. Like just another nail in that foolish, childish hope of a second chance at goodbye.

"I mean, I'm sure he was a great fellow and all, and it'd have been my honor to know him, like. But no, I just said that to get you to follow me."

"You're a bastard," she said simply.

"Yes, I can be."

Tara thought she heard a chuckle from the direction of where the guards were sitting together in the shade of one of the tents.

"Look, girl, for what it's worth, I really am sorry."

She glared at Fin, riding the faint spark of anger, cultivating it, using it to take her away from the sadness, to keep from losing her grip. It was a different sort of edge, but every bit as useful as fear. "Sorry for what? For lying to me? For kidnapping me? Or for drugging me?"

"All of the above."

"Well then why did you do it?"

He stood and brushed the sand off his trousers. Somehow, through all of this, his white T-shirt looked just as clean and unwrinkled as it had when she'd first met him on the bridge. It seemed so long ago to her, that rainy day.

"Well? Why did you drug me? And when is this trip going to wear off?"

"Trip?" he asked, looking genuinely confused.

"These hallucinations. It's acid, right? Or what is it?"

He looked toward the horizon and nodded. "Ah. Right. Yeah, that's the one."

He was being evasive, and she wanted to slap him, but at least he had confirmed it. It was both reassuring and frightening to think that so much of what she had seen since she'd woken up aboard the ship had been caused by chemicals—chemicals that were still circulating through her body. Chemicals that might do lasting damage to her brain, or so she had read. Deep down, a piece of her still had trouble believing it, though. Everything looked and felt and sounded so *real*. There was that tipping sensation again. She could feel the panic attack rising, puffing out its ugly chest. It was going to win. She wasn't going to be able to stop it. She clenched her fists and tried to concentrate on one thing at a time.

"How long will they last, do you think? These hallucinations," she quavered.

Fin was shading his eyes, gazing in the direction of the top of the next sand ridge, where the eagle had flown.

"Well?"

"Huh? Oh," he said absently. "They should wear off by... oh, tonight sometime, I'd think. Tomorrow morning at the latest."

"Tomorrow morning?!"

"At the latest. Come on, we need to move. Our escort has arrived."

Something was glinting brightly in the sun at the top of the ridge, and above it she could see the eagle circling lazily, a tiny dot against the vast blue.

The whole thought of walking even one step further into the unknown was suddenly just too much for her. Her mind could not cope. Right then and there, her mind stopped working, like a blown spark plug. Despair cracked open its toothy maw directly beneath her, and the sourness in her mouth bloomed.

Time to disappear.

The sounds of Fin's exhortations faded to background noise, a distant static against the clamoring abyss. Empty, exhausted, and utterly alone, Tara plonked herself down on the ground, focused on her feet, and let herself sink.

Chapter Six

You know it's rude to ignore your elders like this, Tarabell."

"Nick," her mother warned, voice pitching upward.

Tara glared fiercely at her stepfather from where she was sitting on the couch, then returned her attention to picking at the skin around her fingernails. Only her mother got to call her Tarabell.

"No, see? She hears me. She hears me. She's just being stubborn." He sneered. "It's not anxiety or depression or any of that crap. It's just normal teenage bullshit, pure and simple. Am I right, Tara?"

"Nick!" Her mother was shouting now, tugging at his arm, but he was in steamroller mode now.

"Well? I'm right, aren't I?" He tipped his beer bottle up to his lips, having apparently forgotten it was empty, then slammed it down on the coffee table in frustration. "Answer me!"

Tara had one thumbnail under the other and was pressing it into the sensitive nerves there as hard as she could, trying to feel something. Clinging to the sensation for dear life; following it like a light in a storm.

Nick pulled at his hair with both hands. "Jesus fucking Christ I swear, if people in this family would just toughen the FUCK UP. You think life is hard, little girl? Shit. You don't even know what hard is. You kids… every single one of you, your whole goddamn generation, just sitting on your asses, whining away in the dark."

Her mother was pleading with him, face flushed. "Nick! Please! Stop this, now!!!" She sounded pathetic, Tara thought.

"Well guess what, kid? There's a whole world of light out there, just waiting for you. And all you have to do to see it is walk out that front door! All it takes is some guts!"

"Stop it Nick! Now!" Aileen was screaming, trying to shove him by the shoulder out of the room, but even without the extra strength the booze had given him, he was way too massive for her to budge.

"You know your mom here just wants to protect you from the world. But I think it's pretty fucking clear that strategy isn't working. It's time to toughen the fuck up and face life, Tara. And stop hiding from it. I'm only saying this shit because it's something you need to hear. And you can hear me, can't you. You're hearing what I'm saying, right? Right, Tarabell?"

Tara stared at the carpet between her shoes, as still and silent as stone.

"Well?" Nick bellowed.

"Leave her alone!" Aileen was begging.

"Well?! Do you hear me?! Yeah, she fucking hears me. Goddamn fucking teenagers I swear. Answer me when I talk to you! FUCKING ANSWER ME YOU LITTLE SHIT!!!"

102

Tara opened her eyes. The sand was still there between her sneakers, and Fin had raised his voice a few notches.

"Look, just say something, won't you? *Anything.*"

The nerves under her left thumbnail were on fire.

"Please, *please* snap out of it, alright? We need to go. We need to *move.* We'll be safer where we're going, and then we can rest, but we aren't there yet. *Please,* girl. Get up, okay? I'll carry you if I have to, but I *really* don't want to have to...."

She thought he was going to come over and kick her, or cuff her ear, or grab her by the hair and drag her against her will. She was so sure of imminent violence that when he sat down peacefully beside her, she flinched and hugged her knees to her chest.

Fin's eyes were on the back of her neck. She could feel them touching her skin, like fingertips. She kept hers glued to the sand. A million silent grains stared back at her. She was waiting for him to do something, or say something, but for the longest time, he just sat there quietly next to her, knees drawn up in a similar position.

The roar in her head gradually receded, her vision clearing. She rubbed her eyes. She hated that she was like this. She felt like a cripple. A weakling. Inept. If this was a test of character, she knew she was failing. But she also knew she couldn't just sit in the sand forever. It led nowhere, and she knew where that led.

She looked up at Fin. "Okay."

The relief on his face was palpable. "Okay?"

"Okay," she repeated, nodding.

"Alright then, up you get." He stood. "There are people waiting for us—"

"But I'm not moving another inch until you tell me *why*," she blurted.

"Why? Why what?"

"Why the fuck did you *kidnap* me? And why *me*, of all people? What exactly do you want with me?"

He paused. "Okay," he said, and then paused again, eyes darting left and right, as though considering. "Look, some of it I won't be able to explain until we get to where we're going, because... that's when it'll all start to make sense, like. That's later today, assuming all goes well. And I *will*. But... well, as for the 'why you' part, honestly, it was just a case of being at the exact right place at the exact right time. The wrong place and time from your perspective, I suppose. But as for what my reason was for bringing you here? All I can tell you right now is that I needed to do it; I had no other choice. I need you to help rescue someone, see. And that's the honest truth."

Tara mulled this over. "Who?"

"My mother."

"Rescue your mother? I thought you worked for her."

He shook his head. "That's not my mother; that's *The* Mother. She's the ruler of this realm; that's just what people call her. Ancient as the hills, Mother to all. No one knows her real name, 'least as far as I can figure."

He was clearly spinning a whole heap of bullshit, but Tara could not for the life of her fathom why. *They say the best lies contain elements of truth.* But which elements were BS and which were true? Or was everything he'd said so far a lie, designed to distract her for some reason? Keep her guessing, stop her from freaking out until he could get her—his "wares"—to wherever it was he was taking her? Sell her into

104

slavery, or whatever the scheme was? Was this Mother person some sort of madam? A human trafficker? But he already had her out here in the middle of the desert in some faraway country; even if she could escape, she probably wouldn't get far, or might get lost and die of thirst in the attempt. So why keep up the illusion? Why act all sympathetic, like he was sorry for kidnapping her? She didn't buy it.

"Okay, so your mom needs saving. From what? And how is it, exactly, that a *seventeen-year-old girl* can help…?"

He sighed, glancing again toward the glinting object at the top of the next sand dune. "Now that right there is a long story. Look, I promised I would answer all your questions eventually, and I aim to keep that promise. But please, Tara, we really are out of time; I can't protect you here, not truly. There are unfriendly eyes about. And I mean *unfriendly*. If we happen to attract the attention of the wrong sorts—and we may already have—then your, um, nothing is going to keep you safe. And no *one*, either, including me. Not *anything*, see? And then you'll never get home. So just bear with me for the moment, yeah? Help me out, like, and I'll get you back home safe and sound, promise. Okay, girl?" He winked.

"Okay," she said, forcing a wan smile. Feigning trust. Biding.

Atop the rise, they were greeted by a company of three leather-armored soldiers, six camels, and by far the strangest figure Tara's drugged-out mind had conjured yet. He was man-shaped, towered above everyone else, and appeared to be made of glass: a thousand broken pieces from head to toe, all joined together and shimmering in the intense sunlight. In his hand was a rope, the other end of which was attached to a very colorfully knitted muzzle and bridle worn by the largest of the mounts, and on his shoulder perched the eagle. Wings folded and intently observing, it was a dark brown slash of razor eyes and jerky head movements.

"Freelancer." The glass figure's voice resounded from his chest like marbles dropping into a deep porcelain vase.

"General," Fin said reverently, bowing low and holding that position for several seconds. As he straightened, the glass man handed him a tight roll of papers, no doubt the same ones the eagle had carried.

Fin nodded his thanks. As he pocketed the papers, the general turned a pair of dreadful, empty eyes toward Tara, and she inadvertently took a step backward. His body—her hallucination of it, anyway—was extremely upsetting to behold, in large part because it was so difficult to focus on. The "head" was a cascade of mirrored triangles, iridescent in the perpetually shifting reflections of sunlight as he moved. His fingers were sharp shards of glass, yet the rope he held looked neither cut nor frayed. When he turned to signal the soldiers to mount, Tara was startled to see her splintered image reflected in his broad shoulders and back. One of her eyes seemed to sag, and her left leg extended in an improbable direction.

"Ever ride a camel before?" Fin asked her.

Tara narrowed her eyes at the animal he was leading over to her. It made a loud, throaty grunt and raised its head, appearing both wise and aloof at the same time. When she touched its neck, it blinked and swiveled slightly, making further guttural sounds.

"Put your right foot here, and I'll help you up."

She did as she was told, and after an awkward moment of straining arms and legs and elbows and very nearly falling on her butt, she was mounted in the saddle and had the reins in a death grip, terrified of letting go. The animal grunted again and shifted forward a couple of steps, but then stood still and chewed its cud.

No sooner was Fin on his camel than the tall shining general raised an arm and motioned the company forward. Without a word, the soldiers fell into formation, one riding abreast of the general and the other two taking up the rear behind Fin's and Tara's mounts. As the pace quickened, the eagle flapped its wings in place a few times and whistled out a series of high-pitched notes as it readjusted its balance on the general's glass shoulder. There it remained, apparently comfortable, until a minute or so later when he leaned his gleaming head close as if to whisper something into its ear. With a shriek, the bird launched into the air, wheeled a tight turn, and swooped back down the sand mountain in the direction of the garrison.

The company traversed ridge after ridge, dropping into shallow valleys between but always gaining to a higher altitude than that of the dune before. Occasionally, they came across another small checkpoint or garrison, but were never stopped; the guards on duty would merely stand at attention as they passed, saluting but not uttering a word unless the glass general had spoken to them first. By the time the sun had sunk behind the distant wall of violet-brown "clouds" at their backs, the little caravan had ascended the tallest of the ridges, and at the top they turned right to travel along its spine, sloping gradually upward. Here and there the way was marked by rock cairns that stood a good six or seven feet above the shifting sand, tall stacks of stones that were black and porous like lava.

Tara's thighs were aching. She had never ridden a horse before, let alone a camel, and would never have guessed that sitting still for hours on end could be such hard work. Her tendons were fire, her shoulders and back a compound of knots, and she had a throbbing headache that radiated from the base of her very taut neck into the back of her skull and right around to her left eyeball. Exhaustion battled with adrenaline. She felt like she could sleep for a week straight, but didn't dare close her eyes for longer than a blink.

At length they reached the summit. A fierce wind stung her eyes, whipping at her coils and the hem of her army jacket, forcing her to squint into the tremendous view that spread before them. Below, the rock cairns continued along the steeply downward-slanting spine of the sand ridge, dwindling all the way to a point where the dunes stopped and a broad green valley began. A river meandered through lush fields dotted with herds of animals, and in the distance she could see the forest-shaded slopes of a snow-capped volcano. A thin wisp of smoke rose from its peak, drifting sideways and blending with the sunset-rouged clouds above it. It was breathtaking.

Tara spotted a settlement—a large town, really—along the banks of the river. It rose in marked steps around a low hill, culminating in a big tree-wreathed structure that likely commanded a view of the whole valley. Lights were winking on here and there in the gathering dusk... fires, she guessed, by the way they flickered... all over the town and for quite a ways upstream and downstream from it.

The general leaned forward, causing his camel to break into a gallop. Abruptly, Tara's mount was speeding down the slope with the rest of the entourage, sand flying. She hunkered down with her arms wrapped tightly around the camel's neck as it grunted in rhythm, absolutely sure she was going to slide off and get trampled.

Somehow, she held on. The dune ridge gradually gave way to flatter ground, and soon the sand gave way to hard-packed dirt studded with tufts of grass. The vegetation grew denser as they approached the river. By the time they were at its edge, thick brambles and occasional swaths of shoulder-high reeds were crowding in on all sides. The soldier who had been riding alongside the general most of the journey took the lead then, expertly picking out a path that kept the camels' legs free from entanglement. Strange insects or frogs trilled in the shadows as they passed, and the unfamiliar sounds made Tara feel farther from home than ever.

The river took a wide bend. Halfway around it, the brambles began to thin out and disappear, and a short while later they came to the first of many tree-lined fields. Even though the light was fading fast, there were still farmers about, busy harvesting or planting or whatever it was they were doing. A few stopped to watch them as they rode by, but most kept their attention on their work. There were no tractors or irrigation machines; everything seemed to be done by hand. Tara was reminded of how the customs agent had referred to her as "farmer" back in the port town, and again thought about asking Fin why. The stern looks on the soldiers' faces made her decide against it.

The path broadened until it was a well-traveled, hard-packed mud road, still paralleling the river. By the time they reached the town walls, twilight had sapped all color from the land and the first stars were shining overhead. The air was warm and humid, but Tara shivered anyway.

A pair of solid wood gates blocked their way, with torch-lit sentry posts to either side atop a twenty-foot wall that extended to the left and right, presumably encircling the entire community. As they drew near, Tara heard a shout, and the gates parted in the middle, heavy and slow on whining hinges, swinging wide to let the travelers inside. A number of people—soldiers as well as civilians, by the look of them—stood inside, having stopped what they were doing to see who the visitors were. As they spotted the glass general, further shouts went up.

"General!" called the soldiers, saluting at attention; "Angle Man!" cheered some of the townspeople, including quite a few children.

The general rode past stiff-backed, responding to the greetings with only a slight nod and wave. Tara looked over at Fin to mouth the question, "Angle Man?" at him, but the young Irishman didn't see her; his eyes were forward and his jaw rigid with something akin to worry.

After crossing an open space—a common area, surrounded by thatched houses on wooden stilts—they turned right and followed a narrow street that took them to a long stone bridge. It spanned the river in a trio of arches, and at the far end was an even taller wall with another manned gate. This one was torch-lit, too, and one of the sentries there barked out a challenge as they drew near.

The leading soldier brought his mount to a halt while the Angle Man continued slowly forward a few more paces.

He then lifted his chin and declared in a formal voice, "General Aguilar, to see The Mother."

"General," the challenger acknowledged just as formally. "May The Mother and the Heart thrive forever." A shout was relayed, and seconds later, the thick doors swung open.

On the other side was paradise. Trees overhanging crystal clear ponds, balconies sticking out over the water with long, flowering vines trailing down, candle lamps and brilliant blossoms everywhere, some even floating on the surface. Lanterned boats drifted lazily about, their passengers either fishing or simply relaxing, chatting and sipping from cups. Many of the buildings were connected by narrow, rope-railed suspension bridges. The place felt alive in the twilight, with torches lit in sconces in the trees along the paths and larger fires burning on small islands. The brightest source of light was a bonfire, a huge inferno of steepled logs built on a crescent beach at one end of the main pond—a lake, really—and Tara could hear laughter coming from the crowd gathered around it. Someone was plucking a lively tune on a stringed instrument, and a pair of voices rose and fell in jaunty call-and-response accompaniment. More people were making their way toward the bonfire along the many paths, wearing all manner of clothing, some dressed casually, some more elegantly, all carrying wicker chairs and plates and jugs of food and drink with them. Among these was the occasional bizarre or ghoulish figure with blurry features or unnatural appendages and strange adornments, or even with a mortal wound of some kind. One man looked to Tara as though he had half a spear piercing his shoulder. Suspended from both ends of it, like loads on a carrying pole, were a completely ordinary picnic basket and thermos. Unnerving as such hallucinations were, however, the whole scene and atmosphere reminded her of a family festival day at the park.

Without warning, the general and his deputy—for that was what she guessed him to be after having observed their interaction over the past several hours—dismounted. After Fin helped Tara down, the deputy and the two other soldiers gave their commander a salute, took the camels' reins, and led the animals along a path to the right. It vanished into a natural tunnel formed by the overarching boughs of a wall of very old trees that were so thick their trunks had fused right into one another. As the general headed in the opposite direction, Fin motioned for Tara to follow.

The glass man took them around the lake, keeping left to avoid the oncoming groups of scattered foot traffic, skirting the beach until they had arrived at a steep wooden staircase. It followed the contour of the hill, bending left and right in a series of switchbacks that made the climb easier than it otherwise might have been. Even so, Tara found it difficult to make her legs do what she wanted them to do. She felt stiff from the ride and mentally exhausted to boot.

At every turn, a guard stood in full regalia next to a pole with a hanging lantern. These lights were not electric, Tara noticed, nor did they look like gas or kerosene. The light appeared to emanate from neither bulbs nor flames, though she was unable to pause long enough to get a decent look. The guards all eyed Fin and Tara critically as they passed, as though weighing them up.

She just wanted this day to end. Dog-tired and beginning to wonder if she might actually fall asleep on her feet, she only made it up the last flight of steps thanks to a string of quiet but insistent pushes and prods from Fin.

At the top was an ornate archway, on the other side of which was a giant hall that was open on all sides. A dozen or so gnarled baobab columns that looked as though they might still be growing held up a magnificent thatched ceiling, woven and shaded in a thousand intricate patterns. Opposite the landing, right in the center of the expansive area, stood a dais made up of six cushioned ebony terraces, and on the highest of these was a stunning thirty-something-year-old woman. She was sitting upright, her posture regal but not arrogant, and was looking intently into Tara's eyes, her lips curled in an amused smile.

The general took position to the left of the entrance, arms at his sides and staring forward, completely motionless. The people—courtiers?—who had been conversing in small groups around the hall fell silent as they turned to look at the newcomers, and even the servants stopped bustling to stand with their chins on their chests. The queen—for that was what she looked like to Tara—flicked her wrist without breaking eye contact, and everyone immediately bowed toward her and left, servants and all, shuffling through the wide archway and down the steps behind Tara and Fin and the general without so much as a muted whisper. Within minutes, they were alone with the queen-like figure.

Tara faltered, flinching under the woman's continuing gaze. Despite the youthful smoothness of her chestnut skin, her gray eyes appeared as ancient as granite, like tunnels into a distant past, a time of primordial legend. She wore a formal-looking maroon headband, her cheekbones were tattooed in a delicate array of thin black dashes, and she had gorgeous green and black feathered eyelids and perfect lips. However, there was nothing doll-like about her; this woman looked like a predator. And there was something utterly unyielding and... relentless... about the set of her jaw. The regal garb she wore was a riot of stylish earthy colors and patterns, flowing down her body like a waterfall, spilling into the cushions all around her. It was only when she shifted her legs that Tara realized the clothing was actually separate from the upholstery.

Fin took Tara gently by the hand. "Come, I'll introduce you," he whispered as he led her forward. Upon reaching the middle of the floor below the dais, he kneeled, gesturing for her to do the same. Tara had never knelt in obeisance before. It felt strange.

"Mother, may You and the Heart thrive forever," Fin said as he kowtowed, deference in his voice.

"Freelancer." The woman atop the dais chuckled, a lovely clear sound like a bell ringing. "So, you have really gone and done it, eh?"

Fin nodded, his head practically touching the floor. "Indeed, Mother. I've followed your instructions, and here she is. Everything worked out as we'd hoped. In fact, it all went a lot easier than I thought it would, so it did. Thank you, Mother, for going out on a limb for me."

The Mother laughed again. "A limb? Only a limb that I, too, plan to ride until it bears fruit. Make no mistake, young Finlay: We are in this together. Attached at the hip, as all you modern *citta* like to say."

Finlay, Tara thought to herself, her head suddenly abuzz with the cawing of crows.

"Yes, Mother," Fin said, eyes still on the floor.

114

"Rise."

Fin stood. "Up you get, girl," he whispered at her.

Tara glanced back over her shoulder in the direction of the steps, wistfully wondering whether she might be able to make a dash for it. The general had moved to the center of the archway, where he stood guard like a statue, blocking all passage in or out. He seemed to be staring hard at her. Before she could turn back around, Fin had grabbed her by the armpit and was yanking her roughly to her feet. She shrugged his hand off angrily and glared back up at the woman, who was still studying her from the throne of cushions. Tara tried her best to maintain a look of defiance, but all she could manage under those granite eyes was timid and sheepish.

The Mother had her chin propped in one hand, head tilted, and was tapping a finger against her temple. "You look familiar, girl. Where are your people?"

Tara glanced at Fin, but he simply stood there next to her, eyes down.

"Answer for yourself, child. Where are they?"

"Pennsylvania."

"Pennsylvania," The Mother repeated slowly, drawing the word out as if mulling it over. She raised an eyebrow briefly at Fin, then returned her attention to Tara. "Well, Pennsylvania, I rarely forget a face. I will know the truth of you eventually. Now, come, I'll pour you both some warm *oshikundu*, and Finlay here can regale us with a tale of how he managed to bring you to the Afterrealms from the land of the living *without* rising into the Antim."

The land of the living. The world, tipping again. Blood rushing to her head. In that instant, all Tara could think about were gravestones, and being forced into the ground, and singing children with slit throats and girls in denim skirts with knives protruding from their bellies. Behind her was a grinding sound, like glass on glass. Tara turned to see the general's hollow eyes, still staring hard in her direction. She clenched her own eyes shut and shook her head, struggling to keep from sinking.

"Ma'am," she began, voice wavering, then stopped, feeling faint.

"Speak, child."

Tara opened her eyes but kept them focused on her feet and the cuffs of her jeans. "I... I don't know what sort of deal you have with this man, but... well you should know, ma'am, that whatever he might've told you, the truth is he's kidnapped me and drugged me and brought me here against my will. And that's *illegal*. So... so I'm asking you, please, ma'am, please take me to the nearest American embassy, and... and I'm sure my government will reward you, and... and it will be the right thing to do." Even as she stammered the words out, Tara knew she sounded foolish. She wished her parents were rich; she wished she could promise an easy ransom. She wished the crow call and the word "Finlay" would stop teasing through her mind.

The Mother stood and crossed her arms, that amused smile twisting at her lips again. "A valiant effort, Pennsylvania. I admire your courage, I really do. But this *man* works for me."

"So... okay, then please, just call the embassy. They'll pay, I know they will."

Glass ground against glass again. The Mother seemed to be having trouble keeping herself from laughing. "And if I do not, child?"

Tara stammered. "I mean, why wouldn't you? You're just after the ransom money, right?"

The Mother's barely suppressed giggles bubbled up then, spilling out around her tongue, between her teeth, through a widening break in the seam of her lips as she shook her head.

Tara felt weary. Her body ached all over. She also felt stupid, like she wasn't getting some joke that everyone else got. Like she had been brought to some insane amusement park where all the patrons were actually employees who were in on the whole charade. That terrifying "general" was still boring holes in the back of her neck; she could feel it. She also felt the weight of the necklace, pulling down against her skin toward the level floor, a floor which nevertheless felt so slanted she thought she was going to fall over.

Exasperated, she turned to anger. "Well if you don't want money, then what exactly *do* you want?! What are you gonna do to me? Pimp me out? *Kill* me?!"

At this, The Mother's face went abruptly serious. Her mouth still had the shape of a smile, teeth half visible between parted lips, but all the mirth had drained from her tattooed face to be replaced by a fleeting but intense look of envy. "*Kill* you? Why, child, you are the only one here who isn't dead!"

Chapter Seven

Tara could hear them talking; they were both just chatting away as if she weren't even there... but their voices sounded distant, and none of what they were saying made any sense whatsoever. It all had her mind doing somersaults. She felt ill. Spinning; off balance. Once again, the panic was rising to fever pitch, and she thought she might throw up.

"...did not think you would succeed, it's true. You have surprised me, young Finlay. And I must thank you, for it has been so long since this old woman felt truly surprised."

Fin had walked over to stand on a balcony to the left of the dais, his hands clasped loosely behind his back as he gazed out over the dark valley and the twinkling lights below. He turned toward the dais and gave a dramatic bow, smirking as he did so. "It's forever my aim to please, Mother. Forever my aim to please."

The Mother ignored the sarcasm. "So, alright, now we have a live girl. But as I said to you months ago, obtaining one of the living is only the *first* step. The stakes are high, boy. We have much planning to do. Much, much planning, and we cannot afford to make a single mistake."

Fin cleared his throat. "Yes, Mother. If you'll pardon the assertion, I do recall your words, every last one of them. And I hope you recall mine: I'm in this to the end, and will do whatever it takes to get us there; don't you worry about that. We are gonna have to…" he trailed off, glancing sidelong at Tara.

The Mother nodded. "Perhaps we should continue this conversation in private. Aguilar, take this girl to one of the larger *!haru-oms*; choose one with a nice view of the valley. She is our guest, and here in the Cradle, we treat our guests well. Our *guest*, child," she repeated, smiling that toothy shape of a smile at Tara before addressing the general again. "See that she is brought a light refreshment, and have the helpers bathe her and provide her with something more… comfortable to wear."

"Mother," the general said, bowing his head.

"When she has been bathed and changed, take her down to the fires personally, and let her partake in our bountiful food and drink. The freelancer and I will be along shortly."

"As you wish, Mother," he said, bowing again.

"And General," the Mother said.

"Yes, Mother?"

"When it comes to guarding my most prized possessions, I put only my most trusted men in charge. This particular duty is not to be delegated. Understood?"

"Understood, Mother." The glass general bowed deeply. He then straightened and began to walk toward Tara.

In a sudden panic, Tara took a step backward and looked over at Fin, but he had returned his attention to the view from the balcony. She pivoted, searching for another way out.

"If you know what's good for you, Pennsylvania," The Mother said, having paused halfway down the left side of the dais, "you will do your level best not to irritate the Angle Man. He has sent more *citta* to the Antim than just about anyone in the realm—and trust me, that is not a fate you wish to befall you. Now be a good girl and go get cleaned up. We will talk more, and soon."

The general stood in place, patiently waiting for Tara to relent. She threw a furtive glance past him in the direction of the steps, then toward each of the four corners of the hall, and then over toward the balcony, where The Mother had joined Fin. There was no way out.

The last Tara saw before being ushered through the ornate archway, the two of them were chatting in low tones with their backs turned, Fin's figure towering over that of the diminutive ruler, silhouetted against the starry sky.

As the glass man herded her down the steps, Tara was frantically erecting walls in her head, desperate to block from her conscious mind everything that had just been said. Failing that, she rationalized.

It couldn't be real.

She wouldn't let it be; it was impossible, so she would not accept it.

She *was* a "live girl", but then everyone else here was alive, too. This was all just one big stupid farce.

Blurry faces and bloody denim skirts and disintegrating screaming sailors were horrible hallucinations, nothing more. She still had drugs in her system, potent ones, and they were affecting everything she saw, everything she heard and felt, even her very thoughts. She was simply experiencing a very, very bad trip. She'd heard of this sort of thing before. *Logic.*

The man walking behind her was not made of glass at all. It was in her head.

He was probably not even as tall or menacing as her delusions made him seem. He was definitely scary, but the way he acted, he did not come across as creepy or mean.

Perhaps deep down he was actually a reasonable man. Perhaps he never thought working for that woman would get him involved in something as ugly as human trafficking. Perhaps it didn't sit right with him, the fact that his boss and her hireling had kidnapped a teenager like this. Perhaps he was conflicted. Perhaps she could convince him to take pity on her, help her get away. Perhaps....

"Excuse me, sir," she said. "Mr. Aguilar, right? Could you please tell me where we are? Like, what country we're in?"

All she heard in response was the repeated crunch of heavy footsteps, like hiking boots through morning ice.

Tara stopped and turned to look up at his many-angled face. "We're in Africa, right?"

The tall general touched a hard glass palm to her shoulder and pressed lightly, but his strength was such that she nearly lost her balance anyway. "No talking. Move," the deep, marbly voice resonated.

Halfway down the series of switchbacks, he gestured for her to turn right onto a tree-lined side path. This led around to a string of structures that were significantly larger than most of the buildings she had seen so far, not just in the town outside the gates, but here as well, in what she was coming to think of as the palace compound. The general spoke to a guard standing sentry at a lantern-lit intersection. A moment later, the guard hurried off.

"We wait here," Aguilar said.

A breeze rustled through the leaves overhead, carrying with it the fragrance of something that reminded Tara of wisteria or jasmine. She looked up, and shining down through gaps in the canopy were by far the most brilliant stars she had ever seen. Forestview did not have bad air pollution, relatively speaking, but even so, she could not remember ever having seen such a clear sky, not even during family trips to the mountains out west. The dizzying shawl of galaxy spread from horizon to horizon, an infinite sea of countless pinpoints of light—and these included not just the whites and yellows she was used to, but reds and blues and purples, too.

When the guard returned, he was accompanied by two rather short women dressed in simple brown smocks and strange-looking headdresses, their hair intricately plaited. As they approached, one of them smiled and reached up to touch Tara's shoulder, gently urging her to walk with them. Not knowing what else to do, Tara nodded and followed them up the path. The guard returned to his post by the lantern, and she felt relieved when the general stayed to have words with him. A moment later, however, she was disappointed to hear the heavy crunching footsteps resume their steady rhythm several paces behind her.

The women led the way to one of the largest of the nearby buildings. Halfway along its windowless frontage, directly opposite a steep, densely vegetated knoll with overhanging rocks at its crest, a shallow stoop led up from the path to an entrance draped with patterned bead curtains. The two smiling female "helpers" stood to either side, holding the beads open for her, and as Tara ducked her head through, she noticed out of the corner of her eye that the general had not followed them up the steps. His fractured glass outline loomed in the dead center of the bottom step, barring all passage the same way he had obstructed the arched exit in The Mother's hall, only with his back turned this time.

The !haru-om was even more spacious on the inside than it had appeared from the outside. It was a large single-room dwelling with a sweeping hardwood floor broken only by a small cluster of modern-looking settees and a carved wooden coffee table in the middle; to the left was a luxurious copper bathtub with attending benches and shelving; and sprawling against the right wall was the biggest bed Tara had ever seen, piled high with comforters and decorative throw pillows. Taking up two-thirds of the wall opposite to the beaded doorway were a pair of enormous mahogany bifold doors, which the two women immediately walked over and slid aside to let in the night air.

On the other side of the doors was a magnificent deck that overlooked the valley. When Tara went to the railing and peered down, she saw the tops of trees several yards below her feet, and even farther down were a tumble of house-sized boulders, ominous in the gloom. From there, the landscape sloped steeply down to the river. Her eyes followed its bends all the way up to the head of the valley where the volcano's dark massif shouldered skyward, its high snowy peak glowing a soft blue under the light of the stars.

"Please," one of the women said behind her, her voice soft and heavily accented.

Tara turned. The servant was gesturing toward the bath. Tara shook her head. "I'm fine. Where are we? What country are we in?"

The woman grinned in apparent embarrassment and repeated her gesture toward the bathtub.

She must not speak English, Tara decided. "Here… is… *where?*" she tried again, pointing an index finger at the floor between her sneakers and then shrugging with both arms spread wide.

Still smiling, the servant nodded demurely, then patiently motioned toward the bathtub once more. The other woman, who was standing next to the bifold doors, joined in the effort then, gesticulating in the same manner. "Please," she entreated.

Sighing, Tara took one last peek at the volcano, then followed them back inside. She could probably use a bath, she knew. A shower would be way better, but a dip in a tub of warm water—*Please, please let the water be warm!* —might do wonders for her weary mind and aching muscles. She walked over to the deep metal basin and stared into it. It was full of steaming water, and to one side was a small wicker stand with neatly folded washcloths, a towel, a few small bottles, and a leaf-shaped brass plate that held an etched oval of what she guessed was soap. She nodded thanks at the women and waited for them to leave.

When they just stood there, Tara awkwardly nodded again and placed one hand over her heart—her way of trying to convey thanks—and pointed at the beaded doorway. "Thank you, I can take it from here," she mumbled.

The two servants looked utterly confused and were smiling in embarrassment or amusement or both. One walked over and reached up to take Tara's army jacket from her shoulders. Out of reflex, Tara dodged backward and shook her head. "No, I'll do it myself."

"Please." It seemed to be the only word of English they knew.

Tara shook her head firmly. The two women looked at each other, then back at Tara, and made a concerted effort to undress her; while the one went for her jacket again, the other squatted down to undo Tara's shoes.

"No!" Tara shouted and dashed around to the other side of the tub.

The helpers weren't smiling anymore. One appeared on the verge of nervous laughter, and the other had her brow knitted in worry or exasperation or both. They exchanged a few words in a soft, fast-paced chatter. It was a language Tara had never heard before, full of rapid tongue clicks and strange consonants. After a minute, the one with the knitted brow shrugged, tilted her head, and gestured toward Tara's side of the bathtub. "Please," she said flatly before turning around. The other woman joined her, and now they stood side by side with their backs to Tara, whispering softly.

"Okay," Tara mumbled, half to herself. "So I guess this is their idea of privacy. Alright then."

With an eye to the door to make sure no one was looking in, she undressed quickly. She tried again to get the necklace off, to no avail. Dumping her clothes in a pile on the floor, she stepped over the high copper edge into the steaming water. It was almost too hot, and she had to suppress a yelp; she didn't want to startle them into turning around and seeing her naked. Cautiously, one elbow braced on each side, she lowered herself into the bath.

The strange women continued to stand with their backs turned, whispering to each other almost inaudibly. Tara put her arms in the water and stretched her legs out; her body was beginning to adjust to the temperature. Closing her eyes, she leaned back and let herself slide all the way under.

The seconds went by, and her heartbeat began to slow. The panic was still there, just beneath the surface. If she were to follow those anxious trains of thought that had been teasing at her thoughts, tapping on the doors of consciousness for hours—that she was no closer to finding a policeman or consulate now than she had been back in the port town; and worse, that she may well have undergone a complete psychic break and would never be normal again—then the anxiety would surge right back to the front of her mind with a vengeance. Mentally exhausted as she was, though, it did not take too much effort to sidestep her anxiety for a moment and focus instead on the warm sensation of bathwater embracing her skin, her scalp; the buoyancy of her limbs and hair; the little bubble that rose from one of her nostrils, tickling as it went up. She wished she could stay underwater forever.

Reluctantly, she sat back up to take a breath, glancing around to see if the helpers were still there. They hadn't moved an inch. She slumped against the warm copper and closed her eyes again.

"Please…."

Tara opened her lids to see that one of the serving women was kneeling at her left shoulder, pointing at Tara's hair, while the other was squirting something that looked like shampoo into her palm. Water splashed as Tara raced to cover her chest with her forearms, scar-sides down. The woman with the goop in her hand kneeled behind her right shoulder and, smiling patiently, tenderly ran her fingers through Tara's wet coils. Face hot, she drew her knees up and kept her arms as tightly folded as she could.

It was not a comfortable experience, having her hair washed for her while being almost completely exposed. The women worked very professionally and efficiently, however, and when it was all finished and the shampoo and scented oils had been rinsed out, one of the helpers gently worked through her coils with a wide-toothed bone comb, simultaneously massaging her scalp with strong fingers. It felt nice, and Tara felt some of the tension ease from her forehead and neck. When her hair was to the helper's liking, she stood and gestured at the soap. "Please," the women said, almost in unison, before turning their backs to give her privacy once more.

After she'd finished bathing, Tara dried off with the folded towel, and was alarmed to find that her clothing was missing. She wrapped the towel around her and confronted the servants. "Um, excuse me, where are my clothes?"

The women turned around, both smiling and nodding, then bustled off in different directions—one toward the shelving, the other toward the bed. The latter retrieved an outfit from a closet-like enclosure and brought it over. It was gorgeous: a long, patterned dress, ankle-length, with round neck and half sleeves, of similar earthy tones to what The Mother had been wearing—marigold, rust, deep navy, and ivy green, the irregular patches of color outlined strikingly in thin borders of white. It was not as formal or fine as the ruler's garb, but still very fancy-looking to Tara. She balked at first, but when the serving woman politely averted her eyes, Tara took off the towel and allowed her to help her into the dress.

"Please." The other helper—the one who had struggled to suppress her laughter earlier—was indicating a platter of snacks and drink she had placed on the small carved table.

Tara walked over to it, realizing with a start just how long it had been since she had eaten anything. She thanked the woman, sat down on one of the settees, and leaned forward to study the refreshments. The women left her alone to eat then, leaving through the bead curtains, but not before they drew the bifold doors closed and locked them. *Still a prisoner*, Tara thought to herself.

On the table in front of her was a tall ceramic mug of water, clear and cool; a little basket of flat round biscuit-looking things; a shallow bowl half filled with a rich brown dipping sauce that lingered spicy and oily on the tongue; and another small bowl of something akin to sweet, pitted dates. She hadn't felt hungry until the moment she tasted the food. Abruptly famished, she devoured three of the biscuits with sauce and half the dates.

The food energized her. As she felt her brain beginning to work again, self-doubt and fear gradually gave way to matter-of-fact determination. When the women returned to check on her, she sat up and addressed them in a clear, steady voice. "Excuse me."

The women widened their eyebrows at the refreshments, smiling, and asked her a question in their language. One made as if to go fetch more.

Tara shook her head. "No, thank you. That was delicious. Thank you." She then lowered her voice and spoke to them very slowly, enunciating each word carefully. "Look, I know you don't speak English, but I need you to understand me."

The brow-knitter knitted her brow, and the other raised hers doubtfully.

Tara pointed at her own chest. "Tara."

"Ta-ra," the doubtful one repeated, her face melting back into a friendly smile.

"Yes!" Tara exclaimed, feeling suddenly hopeful. "Tara. That's my name! Tara."

"Ta-ra," they both repeated.

"Yes!" Tara said. "Tara Yewa."

"Ta-ra Yew-wa," the brow-knitter said.

"And you? And you?" Tara gesticulated at them each in turn.

The doubtful one grinned and touched her index finger against the other woman's head playfully. "Au-p 'khari." She then pointed at herself and covered her mouth with one hand in a gesture of modesty. "Gamiro-b."

Both names were framed in palatal clicks and contained complex rising and falling tones. Tara tried her best to repeat what she had heard, but failed miserably. "Gammyba."

The doubtful one snorted with laughter. "Gamiro-b."

"Okay. Sorry. Gammy roba." More laughter, from them both this time.

"Au-p 'khari."

"Oop...."

"Au-p 'khari."

"Oopgari."

The woman whose brow had previously been knitted in worry or apprehension was now giggling so hard she had trouble catching her breath.

Patiently, the other woman repeated both names a few more times, and Tara did her best to mimic the sounds. She did get closer, but eventually shrugged at the helpers and apologized.

"Sorry, ladies. I'm afraid that's the best I can do. Your language is really really hard!" She held up a finger to get their attention, then pointed it at her chest and said, again very slowly, "Tara Yewa. I, Tara Yewa, have been kidnapped. Kid – napped. Do you understand?"

The knitted brow returned. The other one giggled, clearly having no idea what she was talking about. She seemed to think this was a game of some sort. Tara tried again, using all the hand gestures she could muster. She cast about, searching for pen and paper, but saw none.

"Um... Home," she said, forming a roof shape with her fingers. "My home, *not here*. My home... *there*," she said, waving in the direction of the bifold doors, hoping they would get that she meant a place far beyond them. "Here, *not* home. Understand?"

The giggles had tightened into uneasy titters. Two sets of shoulders were shrugging. The doubtful look had returned, and both grins looked forced.

Tara raised her voice a notch, desperate. "Me, *kid – napped*. Not home! *There* my home! Not here my home. *There!* I miss my mom. My *mom*. You know? Mom? *Parents?*"

The serving women both stared at her blankly... and listening to herself, even Tara thought she was starting to sound like an idiot. She gave up.

A little while later, the helpers convinced Tara to follow them out through the beaded entrance. As she exited, she saw that the hulking glass man was still standing sentry on the steps. He appeared not to have budged. *Well, he speaks English at least.*

She tried asking the other question that had been on her mind. "Excuse me, Mr. Aguilar, I was wondering if you might ask these women for me where they've put my shoes."

"You don't need them," he replied gruffly. "This way. Follow me."

Without a word, the two helpers bowed a formal goodbye and scurried up the path. As the general started off in the other direction, Tara turned around to go back inside and hunt for her clothes. It wasn't just her shoes she wanted; she felt very anxious at the thought of being separated from her father's old jacket.

"You can get them later," the porcelain voice rumbled. "Now come."

Tara hesitated in the doorway, remembering The Mother's words about the glass man. He looked quite menacing where he stood on the shadowy path, a tower of cracks and sharp edges. An eruption waiting to happen. She backed down.

When they reached the intersection with the lantern, the guard they had spoken to before saluted. The general nodded curtly, and they continued down the steps toward the lake. Tara could hear music and the sounds of many voices laughing and singing and conversing, and the air was fragrant with the tantalizing scents of food cooked with otherworldly spices.

The bonfire was still going strong, but by now, the high flames had given way to a red-orange mountain of coals. Dozens of figures were dancing to the music, but not very perfectly. It was obvious alcohol was involved, because there was quite a bit of stumbling and laughing and colliding into one another going on. A large gathering of musicians were jamming hard on the far side of the fire, playing all manner of instruments to keep the dancers energized, and seeming to have a joyous time doing it. The drums were the most prominent; there must have been at least twenty drummers, all working together in perfect counterpoint, like an engine.

The general took Tara to a slightly elevated wooden platform off to the side with a view of the party. It supported a few elegant, cushioned chairs with a long narrow table in front of them, on which was arrayed a sumptuous feast of food and drink. As they sat down, a pair of helpers brought even more dishes to put on the table.

"Will Fin be coming?"

The general stared impassively at the bonfire, apparently either too rude or deep in thought to answer.

One of the helpers—a man with blurry head and blurry hands like the ferryman—offered to pour a dark liquid from a tall glass bottle into the ceramic cup at Tara's place. Assuming it was alcohol of some kind, she covered her cup with her hand and shook her head politely. The last thing she wanted was to get tipsy on top of already being drugged out of her mind.

Dancers came and went. Some would stay at it for several dances in a row and then collapse on the sidelines in heaps of jolly laughter; others would just do a short set before returning to where they had been feasting with friends or family or… coworkers? Tara had no idea. She didn't care. It was all so foreign; so *different*. She just wanted to go home. Every couple of minutes, she would turn her head to scan around for Fin. As much as she hated her abductor, he was the closest thing there was to a familiar face in this entire bizarro country.

Eventually, she spotted him. He had changed into more formal attire, of a style Tara had never seen before. It almost looked like a pant suit, only he actually looked good in it. He had The Mother on his arm, and they were making their way down the path from the palace, still engaged in what appeared to be rather intense conversation.

"Pennsylvania!" The Mother called, letting go of Fin and waving both hands in greeting. "Marvelous. A good look on you, as I thought it would be, that dress."

Tara refused to return the smile, but was too frightened to be rude. "Thank you… for the clean clothes and food and bath. I appreciate your hospitality, ma'am."

"You are very welcome, girl."

Tara decided to take a gamble. "This is a wonderful place you have here. But may I go home now, please?"

The Mother chortled. "Ha! Such spirit. You remind me of myself, Pennsylvania. Relax now; have something to eat," she said, taking the seat between Tara and the general. "These are the fruits of my people's labor, and the finest you will find in all the Realms. You can be sure of that. If you taste one of those, for example"—she pointed at a dish that looked like plums stewed with onions and some sort of meat or legume—"I promise, you will forget your homesickness for a while. Quite possibly a long while! Now go on, enjoy yourself. There is much to be grateful for, this night."

Tara stared at the squishy plum-looking things. Perhaps if she refrained from saying or doing anything that might antagonize this woman, she could get on her good side. Make her change her mind about whatever fate she'd had in mind for her. She picked out one of the questionable morsels with her fork and sniffed it. It smelled delicious. She bit into it and had to jump to avoid the juices that squirted onto her chin and threatened to dribble down onto her dress.

"I believe she likes it." Fin chuckled. "Or it likes her, anyway."

She shot him a dark look, even though the flavor was amazing. She'd never had anything like it. Before she knew it, she'd eaten three more.

The helper offered alcohol again, and again Tara refused it. Thankfully, The Mother did not push her to drink it; she was whispering something to the general. Tara glanced sidelong at Fin. He sat with his legs stretched out and crossed at the ankles and was staring up at the sky. His chair was very close to hers; she could almost feel the heat from his broad shoulders. Or perhaps it was the fire. She shifted in her chair to put some distance between them, being as subtle as she could.

"Are the stars in Ireland like that?" she fished.

Fin shook his head. "You know, it's been so long, I honestly don't remember. I honestly don't. But I wish I did."

"Well, maybe you could go there. You know, go to the nearest city, wherever that is, and buy a plane ticket."

Fin smirked, still gazing upward. "Ya, I know what you're trying to do, Tara, but it isn't going to work. You're trying to get me to divulge info: what continent we're on, what country we're in, what city we're near, whatever else you think you need to know. And you're hoping you might be able to convince me to take you home. Well, as I told you, I *will*, but first I need your help."

"You mean you and your employer need my help."

Fin looked over Tara's head at The Mother, who was still deeply engaged in discussion with the glass man, then nodded and lowered his voice. "Yes, we both do, in that our goals happen to have aligned." He leaned in so close to Tara's ear she felt his breath on it. "But just you remember, *I* am the one promising to take you home afterward. She has made no such promise, nor is she likely to. Understand?"

Tara mulled this over. "But when will it be?"

"Hard to say."

Tara clenched her jaw. "Alright, but ballpark?"

"Again, hard to say. I'm sorry, Tara, I really am."

"Sorry my ass. This is fucking bullshit." She had raised her voice without meaning to.

"Now now, there is no need for such language, Pennsylvania!" The short African-looking woman had turned away from the general and was regarding Tara with an amused expression on her face.

I don't give a shit who you are or what the fuck place this is. Just take me home. Please. Now. But rather than voice the thought, Tara made herself say, "Yes, ma'am. I'm sorry ma'am."

"No need for sorry, either, child. You are free to express yourself in my presence, just as all my people are. Always better to voice one's thoughts than to hide them, I say. Far too many *citta* are not living their dreams because they are living their fears. Remember that, child."

"Citta?" Tara asked.

Something deeper than thunder boomed in the distance. A second later, two more booms resounded, getting louder as they went, until they stopped just as suddenly. They sounded like what she had heard shortly after coming ashore.

"Go!" The Mother snapped at the general, who stood immediately and strode off into the night.

The Mother returned her attention to Tara. Briefly, her eyes raked over the scars on the insides of Tara's forearms. Tara self-consciously pulled at the sleeves of her dress, but they were too short to cover past her elbows, so she crossed her arms in her lap.

"Our word for what you would call 'people'," The Mother continued. "*Citta* is the essence of a being. It continues on after the crossing—what you think of as death—until it vanishes into the Antim, the forevernothing. Once it goes there, that is *true* death. It comes sooner for most, but some of us hold on, here in the Afterrealms, delaying the inevitable for as long as we can."

"So what you're saying is that you're... dead."

"Yes, child, that I am, in a manner of speaking... although at my age, that means very little. You see, once one is rid of one's physical body and only *citta* remains, one becomes an elaborate recording mechanism. *Citta* observes and records everything that happens to us, and in the process, creates sensations, emotions, impressions, thoughts, desires, attachments. We are in a constant state of flux—and for a time, that flux is wonderful, unpredictable, delicious. Most never grow out of that, you see. Most."

"I still don't really get what *citta* means."

"Ever the philosopher. You're confusing the poor girl," Fin drawled, still staring at the sky.

The Mother smiled patiently. "Think of it as a person's rainbow spectrum of consciousness and perception, all balled up into one unified essence of existence. For all intents and purposes, here, in the Afterrealms, a person's *citta* is who a person *is*."

"But you're alive. You're sitting right here next to me, talking to me, just as alive as I am. How can you be dead if we're both sitting here eating the same food? Besides, I'm not stupid. I know there's no such thing as ghosts. And you can't convince me this is some afterlife or whatever, because on the way down here just now, I felt every single bit of gravel and sand under my bare feet. It *hurt*. It was real. So I'm not dead and this isn't heaven or hell; there's no such thing. The truth is that your employee here has drugged me and now you're both keeping me here against my will, lying to me for whatever reason. Trying to distract me or make me go crazy or something." She took a breath. "Ma'am," she added. She hadn't meant to vent like that.

Movement caused Tara to look up. The general was returning, striding swiftly back toward the platform, his face expressionless as always.

The Mother touched her forearm and leveled one of those condescending grown-up gazes at her. "Yes, yes; I can see how it all must seem, from your perspective. Well, the *truth* is that you will understand more in time, dear. How about this," she said, folding her hands, eyes darting in the direction of the other side of the fire where the general had come from. "Tomorrow, after breakfast, we will walk together; I will show you my private gardens, and there will be plenty of time to answer all of your questions. Alright? For now, however, I'm afraid young Finlay and I have further business to attend to. My apologies. I am normally a much better host. The Angle Man here will take you back to your *!haru-om*."

The general inclined his head.

"Good night, Pennsylvania. I advise you to do your best to stop worrying about everything and get some rest. It will all work out for the best. It always does." She turned to the general. "Bring a pair of extra guards with you to keep watch."

At that, she stood, spoke to the blurry-faced servant in the same clicking language the two female helpers had used, and left with Fin. Tara stared after them, vaguely annoyed that Fin had not even bothered to say goodbye.

The glass general led the way back up the switchbacks to her *!haru-om*, where the same two women helped her undress and get ready for bed. When she asked them to open the bifold doors for her, they shook their heads and smiled apologetically, either not understanding or pretending not to understand. They then bowed, put out the light, and left.

Tara lay back on the pillows in the dark and closed her eyes, struggling desperately to keep the events of the day from replaying through her mind. She just wanted to go to sleep; to be rid forever of this charade, this bullshit world of hallucinations and monsters and nightmares and lies. Again she tried to erect the walls, but the tumult of images assaulting her over and over and over were as relentless as a set jaw, as a pair of wings against the blue, as a smelly wriggling hemp sack, as a shriek fading into an impossible sky, as a pair of milky brown eyes in a hospital ward.

She knew the general was standing guard right outside her door, but it did the opposite of make her feel safe.

Chapter Eight

The torrent thundered into a bottomless abyss. Down was not down; the river flowed sideways. Nevertheless, she felt herself being pulled along with it, all that volume of water rushing, taking her piece by piece like loose strands of seaweed or a clump of twigs and leaves slowly being drawn back into the current from a swirling eddy. There were big boulders under the surface, and the force of the cataract hitting up against them boomed erratically, violently, like a dozen sledgehammers dropping onto windshields from two floors up, or guffaws of cruel smiling laughter erupting from a barrel chest.

In the back of her dream-mind, she suspected that she was not fiery orange enough in color to slow it; she had to be bluer. She had to merge with the torrent somehow, without being torn apart by it. She had to learn to *flow*. Tentatively, she dipped a finger into the river, and watched as it was abruptly severed from her hand and carried sideways, downstream. The wormy piece of meat bobbed in time with the waves, with the erratic booming against the boulders, with the surges and ebbs of whitecaps. Deep down, she understood that there was something ultimately tragic about the loss. It wasn't simply that she was now missing a finger; it was more to do with the realization that she had forgotten something. It was something important, something vital. She further recognized that something had gone wrong as a result—a terrible thing—and it was all her fault. And so she wept, right there on the bank of the sideways river, utterly devastated, for she knew deep in her bones she would never, ever get it back, and that regret would own her, always, for the rest of her life....

Opening her eyes to a near pitch black room, Tara was immediately disoriented.

The loud booms brought her back to where she was. They sounded closer now, more pronounced, and for the first time, she wondered if there was a war going on. Shuffling off the comforters, she walked over to the bifold doors, but they wouldn't budge. She tiptoed to the bead curtains and cautiously poked her head through, keeping as quiet as she could.

The stoop was empty; the general was not there.

She looked left and right and spotted four guards; one pair were under the lantern, the other twenty or so yards up the path. She quickly ducked back behind the beads and sat on the floor with her back against the wall, thinking.

There was no way she would be able to get past either pair of guards without being noticed, and the overhanging rocks and thick shrubs on the opposite side of the path from her *!haru-om* prevented any possibility of cutting through that way. *Think*, she told herself, but could not come up with an alternate escape route. Regardless, she would need her shoes, and preferably her own clothes. She stood.

It was almost too dark to see inside, but her eyes were slowly beginning to adjust. She went over to the part of the room with the bathtub and felt each shelf with her hands, but came up empty. Along the wall were a few cabinets; she opened these, and again was disappointed. Determined, Tara strode back to the side of the room with the bed, pulling at the bifold doors on her way past. Still locked. A sudden idea made her hopeful. She got down on her hands and knees to look under the bed, but then sighed and stood back up. She searched behind the pillows, then sprinted around to the closet-like corner enclosure on the other side of the bed, searching it up and down three times thoroughly before finally giving up. *They must have taken my stuff with them.*

She was on her way back to look near the bathtub again, just on the off chance that she had missed something, when the beads to her left exploded as the general burst into the room. Tara yelped and cowered down on the floor next to the tub.

"Come. We must go, *now*." The tall glass man beckoned, one hand held out toward her.

"W-Why?" she managed to stammer.

"No time. Come with me." He sounded tense, if marbles dropping into cavernous porcelain could sound tense.

Tara hesitated for a few more seconds. Seeing no alternative, she stood, took one last look around the room, and followed Aguilar outside.

As she exited the *!haru-om*, a heavy object clamped down on her left shoulder. She tried to push it away, but she might as well have been shoving at a parked truck.

"Relax. Please. This is for your protection," the general rumbled. The heavy object on her shoulder was his glass hand. With the other one, he was pulling her necklace out of her dress from behind her neck. Before she could do anything other than squeak in surprise, he had let go of her shoulder and was feeding the necklace rapidly through thumb and forefinger, all the way around its length.

"There. Safe now." His deep voice reverberated as he let go.

Tara flinched back against the wall, eyes darting from where the necklace hung against her chest up to the general's horribly shattered face and back. The silver necklace shimmered in the starlight; it seemed to be coated with something shiny and see-through, like hard plastic shrink-wrapped around each bead.

"What did you do…?"

"You cannot be tracked now. Come, we need to go."

Tara held the necklace out in front of her, pulling her chin in to get a closer look. The coating appeared to consist of tiny pieces of glass, all molded together, though it was smooth and somehow flexible; she had no problem bending the necklace and sliding it freely between her fingers.

"But what…."

"This way," he said, cutting her off, his voice low and menacing as he grabbed her upper arm and pulled her down the stoop. The pressure from his glass fingers stung.

"Let go, you're hurting me!" she hissed.

He let go. Where he had gripped her, a bit of blood was welling up. "Sorry," he said and retrieved a cloth from a pouch at his belt. Bending down, he dabbed gently at the cut with it.

As he did so, several loud booms went off, sounding even closer this time; they couldn't be more than a half mile or so away, Tara thought. Adrenaline pumping, she glanced furtively down the path, and then up it, and could see that the guards had still not returned to their posts. Something was happening—something big—and she had no idea what to do. She suddenly wondered where Fin was.

"Excuse me, sir, but where is Fin? Is he coming?"

Returning the cloth to his belt pouch, the general left the stoop in one big stride and crouched down in the branch-shaped shadows. He scanned up and down the path, then turned his huge head to regard her. Bizarrely, he seemed scared, or at least apprehensive. Tara did not know whether actual fear was an emotion the general was capable of, but something clearly had him rattled. The slate-dark shadows waved slowly back and forth in the night breeze, starshine glinting periodically from his myriad facets. She stood completely still, her back to the doorframe, mesmerized by the sight of him.

"Tara is your name, yes? Tara. Listen to me now. I will not compel you, but I strongly advise you to come with me. I do not know what exactly The Mother has planned for you, but I know her well enough to know that she does not intend for you to survive whatever it is; you are far too tenacious— far too powerful—to be set free. I cannot speak for Finlay MacCarthy, but that man is contracted to her and therefore cannot be trusted. Once The Mother is done with you, she will undoubtedly send you to the forevernothing. You must believe me. I can get you out of here, Tara, but there will not be another chance. Now, decide."

Ever since she had met the general atop that sand ridge, he had been nothing but stern and terrifying; based on her limited experience, this behavior seemed very much out of character for him. He was normally a tough, unapologetic leader of very few words; this was by far the most she had heard him say. He also seemed to be genuinely sorry he had hurt her. Baffled, she squinted in the direction of the lantern. "Is this about those noises? Are they bombs?"

The general put a finger to where his lips should have been. "I will explain later, if you come with me," he whispered, sounding like breath through a pipe. He then strode several paces up the path, turned, and stared at her. "Decide. Last chance. I am going, with or without you."

Tara shuddered. Those hollow eyes always gave her the heebie-jeebies. She looked at her feet, wavering, not knowing why she felt so reluctant to leave without the very man who had lied to her repeatedly and drugged her and abducted her. For all she knew, however, this General Aguilar would turn out to be a liar, too. In fact, she should probably assume he was lying, she figured. Peering back over her shoulder, she saw the lantern glowing softly a little ways past the *!haru-om*. In that moment, she had absolutely no idea which way was home.

If she tried to go back and hide under the bed, the glass man would just find her and drag her back out and… she was loathe to think what else. It was easier when all she had to doubt were her drugged-out senses. Now she did not have much confidence in her judgment, either. She felt very small and very helpless.

She hated that feeling. She was getting sick of it.

Blinking, she took a wary step toward the glass man.

It was unclear whether he was smiling or not when he nodded at her, but within seconds he had turned, dashed up the path, and reached the top of the rise. There his hulking figure squatted in the shadows at the side of the path, waiting for her, beckoning impatiently. Tara trotted to catch up, careful to avoid stepping on rocks or roots with her bare feet.

"Follow close," he whispered as she joined him.

They kept to the shadows, skirting behind the *!haru-oms* and other buildings whenever possible. Periodically, the path took them to another lanterned junction, but the sentries were always busy craning their necks to get glimpses of whatever commotion was happening down the hill in the direction of town, so it wasn't difficult to escape their notice. Tara could hear orders being barked from near where the bonfire had been, as well as frantic shouts and even the occasional scream-like noise out beyond the gate. She hurried to keep up with the general.

When they arrived at the bottom of the hill, he made a sharp left, following the forested side of the lake around and darting from tree trunk to tree trunk until they came to a long, thatched structure positioned at the intersection of two main roads. Several torches were burning at its front, and Tara could hear a raspy female voice speaking in low tones. Now and then, a couple of male voices would respond with grunts or assenting murmurs.

She followed the general as he slinked around the back. When they reached the far end, they had to flatten their backs against the wall as a detachment of guards or soldiers trotted past along the road.

The general bent down to deliver an airy whisper into Tara's ear. "Wait here. Do not move."

With his back still to the wall, he inched his way to the end of it and cautiously peeked around the corner. Tara started to follow, but as if reading her mind, the glass man shot her a severe look, rooting her feet in place.

The trotting soldiers had apparently stopped to exchange words with the murmuring people at the front of the building. Tara could not make out much of what was said, but an order was barked and she heard the scuff of feet standing to attention, and then the barking voice snapping something like "put those away, now's not the time for a game of stones", and three voices "yes sir"ing in unison. Someone asked a question and the commander responded, but Tara didn't catch it. A moment later, the soldiers shuffled off and the low murmuring of the woman and two men resumed.

Aguilar waited another minute, still as ice, then sprang into action, vanishing around the corner with surprising agility. Tara heard a scuffle and a muffled cry, and then another, and then two heavy thumps. When the general poked his head back around to tell her the coast was clear, he was standing fully upright, apparently no longer worried about being seen. She followed him around to the front.

The building was a long, open-faced stable, with a dozen or so camels kept in hay-bedded stalls. The woman and two men whose voices Tara had heard were nowhere to be seen.

The largest of the camels grunted out its complaints as the general quickly saddled and bridled it, then led it out of its stall to the torch-lit dirt road.

"Quickly," he urged, as Tara struggled to get her foot into the stirrup. Losing patience, he grabbed her with both hands by the middle and lifted her into the saddle. He then vaulted up behind her and leaned forward to whisper into the camel's ear, and seconds later the humming beast was loping down the road at a fast clip.

They rounded a corner, and Tara saw that they were already catching up with the column of trotting soldiers. Beyond them she could see the main gate to the palace compound, and dozens of people, mostly soldiers, were standing at attention just this side of it, as if preparing to exit. The gate parted in the middle and began to swing open.

Aguilar pulled the reins hard to the right, and they bolted between two ponds and into a manicured thicket of ornamental trees. Small, pebbled trails braided in every direction, but he seemed to know exactly where he was going. He pressed the camel forward, occasionally barreling straight through the underbrush to connect to a new path, and the peel of shouts that rose behind them only made him egg the animal on faster.

They reached the compound wall at a spot a hundred or so yards up from the gate. Looking left, Tara saw several armed soldiers sprinting along it in their direction. The general dismounted, strode up to the thick wood pillars that made up the wall, and placed both palms against them. A spiderwork of glass shot out from his hands, penetrating the wood like roots or frost, and a deafening CRRRAACK ripped through the air. A split-second later, a six-foot-wide section of the wall exploded outward, evaporating into a cloud of dust and splinters.

The soldiers were almost upon them now, but they were on foot. The general sprang back into the saddle, kicked the protesting camel with both feet, and they flew through the cloud of still falling dust and splinters, riding like mad for the segment of river upstream from the main bridge.

A trio of sentries guarding the small stone bridge stood no chance. The general squeezed the camel, leaning forward, and the animal grudgingly accelerated. The pressure of his hard chest against Tara's back was excruciating. They hurtled past, and the three guards had nowhere to go but over the stone railing and into the drink.

They traversed the field that lay before them in a matter of seconds, and while speeding between two huts on the other side they very nearly knocked over a man carrying a basket on his head. He hurled insults after them as they careened past. When they reached the outer town wall, the general dismounted again and performed the same trick as before, though the explosion was smaller this time; this wall was neither as thick nor as tall as the wall surrounding the palace compound. As he got back up on the camel, Tara turned and saw several mounted soldiers on the other side of the river, heading their way in hot pursuit.

Back in the saddle, the general clicked encouragingly, whispering again into the beast's ear, and it sprang forward with renewed vigor. The burst of speed was so sudden Tara felt herself slipping out of the saddle, but a steady hand caught her and righted her as they bulleted through the gap in the wall and across the fields.

It was soon apparent that they had the faster mount. Now and then she would crane her neck to look back, and she could see the pursuing cavalry were gradually falling behind. She wasn't surprised, given how long this camel's legs were. The animal was huge. She wondered if it was the same mount the general had ridden the day she'd seen him for the first time, and realized with a start that that had only been the day before.

They hurtled across field after field, keeping as far from the river road as possible. The brush was thick, and in places they had to backtrack, but never far enough that their pursuers caught up. Ahead and to their right she saw the outlines of the giant dunes, sloping steeply up toward the starry sky.

At one point they had to leave the vegetation and cut through an area with hard-packed sand to avoid being cliffed at a spot where the river made a tight bend. They had to go up and over. As they emerged from the bushes and stands of reeds, a shout went up to their left; they had been spotted by a second contingent of soldiers, this one galloping hard down the road from town, looking increasingly likely to intercept. Not hesitating for a second, the general urged the camel up the rest of the incline, and soon they were trotting precariously along the top of the bluff.

"They're going to cut us off!" Tara shouted into the wind.

The general ignored her and pointed their mount down the other side, its wonky feet skidding in scree. When the way had leveled out enough for Tara to dare to look up again, she could see that they were now beyond the farmland; before them stretched the broad expanse of brambles they had passed through when they'd first reached the river the day before. Rather than continue around to the right, however, the general angled left—*toward* the intercepting contingent of soldiers.

"What are you doing?" Tara shrieked.

No sooner had they burst out of the bushes and onto the road than the general leaped from the camel's back, landing directly in front of the soldiers. The leading mounts were so frightened by his sudden appearance they reared backward, necks straining skyward, grunting gutturally as the camels behind them collided into their rumps. Angry shouts ensued; one of the soldiers, clearly confused in the presence of their general, dismounted and attempted a salute.

"General, we were told—"

The Angle Man reached him in one long stride and slashed a glass hand downward, slicing right through the soldier's bulbous armor and inner clothing. In the blink of an eye he had both hands against the man's bare flesh, and with a wailing cry, the victim of the general's onslaught deflated into a puff of blue-black smoke, just as the brute onboard the ship had, and shot skyward.

Within seconds the general had annihilated two more soldiers in a similar fashion before they could even get off their mounts. The remaining soldiers dodged out of his way and regrouped several yards up the road.

"General Aguilar, I am sure there is some misunderstanding here, but I have orders to apprehend you!" one of them shouted, apparently the one in charge. "Please, let us do our duty peacefully. No more *citta* need be detached tonight."

In response, the general jumped straight at them, his arms arcing through the torchlight in a shining blur. Glass tore through armor, camels screamed, and before Tara could close her gaping mouth, the rest of the soldiers were gone. Simply gone, as though they had never existed. The general murmured something to their mounts, and the beasts turned in unison and trotted back toward town. Aguilar then took a moment to scan the brambles on the side of the road the soldiers had gathered on, as if making sure he hadn't missed any, before returning to Tara and their big camel.

As he approached, she heard a pipe-like *thump* from the shadows off to the left, and the camel spooked and loped several paces down the road toward the dark dunes. She fought with the reins, but the animal would have none of it. It grumbled, yanking its long neck left and right, and then started bucking. Tara managed to hold on for a half a minute, but then was thrown, landing in a heap in the middle of a thick bramble, arm twisted and face mashed against the sandy ground. The camel grunted indignantly as it trotted away.

Tara held one hand to her hurt shoulder while awkwardly trying to find her feet. From back up the road, she heard many voices shouting, and then three more deep *thumps*. The thorny branches kept catching at her dress, but at length she was able to disentangle herself enough to get both knees on the ground. Sticking her head up between the clusters of leaves, she cautiously peered toward the ruckus.

The general was on his knees, too, but in the middle of the road, surrounded by soldiers. They all had pike-like weapons, which they were pointing directly at him. Some sort of netting had him immobilized. The thick strands were dark and metallic-looking, and the corners looked like they were bolted into the ground. Further up the road, Tara saw more soldiers approaching on foot, racing down from the compound.

Tara sat back on her heels and rubbed her shoulder for an anxious moment. She really only had one choice. Before anyone could think to look for her, she gauged which direction she figured the port town was most likely in, then gingerly picked her way out of that side of the bramble and ran as fast as she could into the night.

Chapter Nine

For the hundredth time, she shot a glance over her shoulder, back down the sandy slope toward the river. The vegetation here had thinned out, and the bushes and clumps of grass were much shorter; she could no longer keep her head low enough to stay completely hidden as she dashed from one thicket to the next. Worse than that, she could see that up ahead, in another couple hundred yards, the plants stopped, giving way to sand and more sand. She would be completely exposed.

It did not appear that she was being followed, at least not yet. When she'd bolted, she had not looked back, not until she'd stopped for a brief rest behind a small outcropping of boulders; and for quite a while the soldier's voices had carried clearly enough through the dry air that she didn't think any of them had sent up an alarm to go hunt for her. The general hadn't said anything, either, nor had he given away her whereabouts after he was subdued, at least not that she could hear. She hoped this meant she still had a good head start, perhaps good enough to lose them, though the thought of running camels niggled at her confidence. Taking one last look at the distant patch of torchlight where the soldiers were clustered on the road behind her, she exhaled and sprinted past the dwindling bits of brush and grass toward the sand dunes.

The incline was gradual at first, and the ground was still hard enough to make good headway, but as it got steeper, the sand grew looser. Soon, she found herself expending a lot of extra energy just to walk through it, let alone run. Her bare feet would sink in to the ankles, the sand would slide down on top of them, and she would have to fight all that extra weight when pulling them forward to take the next step. Before long she was winded, and in order to make any progress she was having to use her hands almost as much as her feet. Her breaks became longer and more frequent. The adrenaline was there, as always, but her body could only go as fast as it could go. Knowing how easy she would be to spot out here under the stars with nothing around for cover made her feel very vulnerable indeed, but the physical exhaustion was replacing that fear with a mix of optimism that she might get lucky and fatalistic resignation.

The dune was enormous. More like a mountain, she reckoned. Periodically she would glance back at the valley below, but there was no sign of pursuit yet. Pushing herself to her very limits, Tara strained up the steep sandy slope, wishing she had her shoes and jeans instead of this silly dress. The arms and shoulders were fine, but the skirt part kept getting in the way of her feet. She wished she had a knife or scissors so she could cut it; the fabric was too thick to rip by hand.

When she finally reached the top, she collapsed and lay on her back for several minutes, breathing hard, staring up at the stars. She wondered what time it was. Surely it was getting close to morning. When she looked over at the volcano, however, she saw no sign of any dawn glow in the sky beyond it. Remembering the sentry post with the eagle and its sharp eyes, she forced herself to get up and keep going.

She jogged along the narrow winding ridge, scanning for rock cairns. She saw none, but then couldn't recall whether there'd been any on this ridge or not. A little while later, the ridge crested and sloped downward. She paused and took one last look at the volcano and valley behind her to reorient. Then, feeling certain—certain enough, anyway—that she was still headed in the right direction to reach the port town—or at least the coast, she hoped—she ran down the slope and started up the next one.

She kept hearing her dad's voice in her head, telling her to pace herself. And she knew he was right. But she also knew time was running out. By now, The Mother would have heard of her disappearance, and as soon as the sun came up— or sooner more likely—she would send more forces out searching for her. They probably already were, with their camels and their net guns or whatever. So Tara continued, moving slowly but surely up the uphill parts and then letting her feet fly down the downhill parts.

Besides, the physical exertion felt wonderful; her heart was pumping, which was another clear sign that she was alive and awake and not imagining all this. Her muscles burned and her lungs heaved, and the sand under and around her feet was genuine, honest-to-god sand-grainy sand. It reminded her that this was an actual place, a place on Earth; this was a real desert with real sand dunes. It could not be anything else. That terrible, troubling dread—that The Mother hadn't been lying; that this really was some sort of afterworld land of the dead rather than simply being a very strange and foreign country; that the things she'd been seeing all this time had been... actual monsters and horrors, instead of hallucinations from some toxic substance still loitering in her blood—that sickening, dreadful feeling was beginning to lift from Tara's mind like a cast-off morning blanket. And that sudden lightness was exhilarating. She could almost taste freedom, sweet on her tongue and in the excess saliva she had to spit now and then from her panting mouth. *I can do this. I'll find a ship back to America and I'll get home. They'll get me detoxed and fix my head, and this will all stop.*

Sand dune after sand dune, she trudged onward, only stopping just long enough to catch her breath when she needed to; then she would plunge down to the next saddle, sprint across, and scramble up to the top of another rise. She had no sense of time, but at one point she noticed that the sky was starting to get lighter; there were not as many stars out as before, and it was growing ever so slightly paler on the horizon at her back. The night had felt unending, so this was a bit of a relief, but logic reminded her that in daylight she would be even more exposed.

At the top of a dune, she stopped in her tracks, suddenly feeling that something was off. After a moment, it dawned on her that she hadn't seen any rock cairns or sentry posts.

She turned a full circle, but all she saw was ridge after ridge of dunes, rising and falling in every direction. She couldn't even see the top of the volcano anymore, only the growing luminosity on that side of the sky. She was in the middle of a sea of sand.

Tara had never been truly lost before. Turned around, sure; she did not have the best sense of direction in the world, certainly nowhere near the level of that of her father, or her brother Ronnie, for that matter. Still, it couldn't be called terrible; she at least knew how to find the north star, and most of the time had a vague sense of which direction she had come, especially if she had been paying even a little bit of attention.

But the remaining stars above her right now made zero sense. She had learned a handful of constellations, but nothing up there looked the least bit familiar. All she had to go by was that imperfect awareness in the back of her mind— an elusive feeling which, however accurate most of the time, had not been sharp enough to keep her from getting lost in the park that one time, much to her chagrin.

Anxiety, that ugly beast that refused to let her be, clawed its old way up from her stomach and into her chest, spreading its spindly disjointed fingers throughout her shoulders, along her arms, and up and down her spine, then settling in a spot at the base of her skull where it festered like a parasite. *Fuck you*, she told it, struggling to keep calm. Right now was the absolute worst possible time to be having a panic attack. *Fuck you fuck you fuck you fuck you.* Shaking her head vigorously, as though she could shake the panic right out of her, she lined herself up with the glowing horizon directly behind her and willed her feet forward.

As she put one foot in front of the other, Tara occupied her mind with ideas of what she would do once she got to the port town. The sleazy customs agent did not seem like a good bet, but perhaps there would be other offices around with people who might listen to her tell of her plight with sympathetic ears. She could ask around. Or, rather than announce her presence and then hang around naïvely where she might get caught, she could pretend to be a young merchant looking to ship her cargo across the ocean, and find out what ship would be headed that way. She would have to be careful when it came to what people she approached, but perhaps with the right story, she could convince someone to take her—the problem being, of course, that she had no cargo. She frowned. Perhaps the best course of action would be to find a ship going to America and then somehow sneak aboard, she thought. If she hid well enough, then by the time she was discovered, it would be too late for them to take her back; they would be far from shore by then, halfway across the Atlantic maybe, and would have no choice but to deliver her to the port authorities wherever they landed. She might get in a lot of trouble, but at least someone somewhere would eventually allow her to phone her mother. The plan wasn't perfect, but it was something to work with.

She slogged up a particularly steep dune, again having to resort to using all four limbs to scramble up the sandy incline. When she reached the top, she was greeted by a sight she never thought would make her feel glad: Before her, spreading from left to right as far as she could see, was a wall of roiling pinkish brown clouds. Below it lay the ocean, lead-gray in the dawn gloom. Tara whooped and sprinted toward it with a sudden burst of energy.

There were still a few more ridges to traverse, but none as high as the one she was currently on. It didn't take long for her to cross over the final big dune, and when she did, her heart sank. The bustling port town with its docks and markets and ships at anchor was nowhere to be seen. She had misjudged. She had made it to the ocean but was either too far up the coast from the town or too far down it. She studied the landscape, but could not see any sign of civilization. There was nothing in either direction but miles of waves crashing against the beach. *Well shit*, she thought, and sat down.

The sky was getting brighter. The glow behind her had transitioned from a pale peach to a vanilla bordering on light blue. Once the sun was up, which she figured would not be that long, she would not only be much more easily spotted, but would have to contend with heat and thirst as well.

There was only one thing for it, she decided. She could pick the right direction and reach her destination, or she could pick the wrong one and die, lost and alone. Making up her mind, Tara turned northward and cut diagonally down toward the beach.

As she got closer to it, she saw that there was, in fact, a small road meandering along the coast, disappearing in the distance to who knew where. In the dim light, it had been lost in the sand from her vantage point atop the dune, but now she could make it out clearly. The discovery made her simultaneously happy and nervous; a road meant harder packed sand and thus easier walking, but it could also bring unwelcome eyes in the form of travelers or The Mother's sentries. She trotted the rest of the way down the slope, paused to make sure no one was coming, and set foot upon the road. Soon she was jogging briskly up it with the ocean to her left, feeling mildly silly for running in such a fancy dress. *Not a good look*, she thought to herself, and smirked ruefully. But then she didn't care if the dress got ruined, and there was no one around to see her anyway. The important thing was that she was still free, for the moment, and therefore had a chance to get home.

She ran, her legs settling into a rhythm. Occasionally she would flick her eyes seaward to scan the waves for boats or dolphins the way she had done when she was little on a trip to California with her family. They had camped just inland from a little beach near Point Reyes, and one night before dinner, her brother had escorted her down to the water. There they had hunted for seashells, spotting all sorts of peculiar shapes and colors and bits of flotsam among the sand, and then had gotten into a fiercely competitive water fight, knee-deep in the surf. She remembered looking up and being thrilled at the sight of what she at first took for a dog, floating in the waves just beyond the break, staring straight at them with curious brown eyes and long, dainty whiskers. "Seal!" Ronnie had pointed, having seen the face at the same time. Later, when their parents had joined them and they had all taken a walk together up the shore, the seal had followed, bobbing up and down, always keeping just beyond the wave break, staring from not very far away in terms of physical distance, but from across the infinitely vast gulf separating land mammals from sea mammals, and humans from other animals in general. Sometimes the thought of that gulf depressed Tara.

To her left, she saw no inquisitive mammalian faces, no fishing boats or whale spouts; only rolling leaden waves, with the wall of unnerving squirming clouds above. She returned her focus to the road; while daydreaming, she had stepped on a couple of painful rocks with her already very sore feet and did not want to repeat the experience.

By the time the sky was azure and the sun had poked its fiery crown up above the dunes, Tara was beginning to feel satisfied that she had chosen the correct direction. Up ahead was a smoky haze, and here and there she passed a small roadside hut. At first, these were dilapidated and abandoned-looking, but as she went farther, she began to come across more and more that looked inhabited. It occurred to her to get off the road so she wouldn't be seen by anyone she might encounter, but there really was nowhere else to go other than walk around to the right through the dunes, and she was too tired to do that. She decided to take her chances. Slowing to a walk so as not to attract any extra attention, she put her head down and hoped against hope that no one would question her.

A short distance on, houses and buildings abruptly increased in frequency; she was definitely approaching a town. There were people about now, busy with morning chores, and some not-people, too. She did her best to keep her eyes averted from the disfigured, the maimed, the blurry. At one point she looked up and saw the unmistakable shapes of mainmasts sticking high into the sky, and she knew she had arrived at the port town. She quickened her pace.

A morning market bracketed the street, jammed on both sides with vendors and shoppers and children darting about. There were animals, too; in addition to the occasional camel or mule, she spotted a long-tailed monkey sitting on a chair next to two old men playing a board game that looked a bit like chess. One of the men handed a deep bamboo cylinder to a sandy-haired adolescent in flip-flops who had been absorbed in their game; the girl put her mouth over the wide end, inhaled, and bent over in a fit of coughing as the old men guffawed and slapped their knees. A little farther on, a woman with half her face missing had a cooing dove perched on her shoulder as she calmly folded laundry. Tara hurried past.

At last, the sand road turned to dirt, and this gave way to the broad wood planks of the main thoroughfare which, at its far end, widened into the boardwalk Fin had taken her along when they had first arrived. The street was getting more crowded as she approached, and several yards ahead, she spotted a pair of armored guards standing with their backs against a wall. She shrank back, then darted into the mouth of an alleyway she had just passed. Fire and laughter crackled off to her right; through a half-open doorway, she caught a glimpse of a group of men hunkered around a breakfast hearth in a hazy room. She hesitated, unsure of what to do. A gust whipped sand down the alleyway, stinging the side of her face and her exposed ankles. She pulled the hem of the dress down as far as it would go, then skipped through to the other end of the alley.

As she peered out, she could see she was closer to the wharf now. The alley fed onto a dockside area that wasn't nearly as busy as the main street. Up ahead she saw the trio of piers with their dinghies being loaded and unloaded, and anchored a short distance out in the harbor were not one but three large ships. Judging by the string of heavy-laden dinghies bobbing out toward the nearest of the vessels, that one would be leaving sometime today, perhaps even this morning, she reckoned. Tara threw a furtive glance toward the boardwalk and the windows to her right, then made a dash across the short open space between the alley and a bunch of barrels that were stacked at the shore end of the nearest of the piers, just down from a structure that looked like it might be the harbormaster's office. There she waited, studying the activity just past her hiding spot, racking her brain for an idea of how she was going to get aboard one of those dinghies.

The sound of a barked order a dozen or so yards off to her right made Tara turn her head. Coming down the boardwalk toward the wharf were a column of soldiers, all armed with pikes and other weapon-like objects. A pair of camels led the entourage. On the back of one of them was someone who looked like a commander, and—she gasped—riding the other one was none other than Fin. Just as she spotted him, he turned his head in her direction.

Tara ducked behind a barrel, heart pounding. Fin! Here! He had guessed her plans! *Of course he did*, she thought. *Where else would I go?* Tara fretted. How would she get aboard the ship without being seen? Had he seen her already? Cautiously, she peeked around to see what else she could see.

Fin and the commander had dismounted and were leading the camels up toward the second pier. Tara exhaled. He had apparently not spotted her after all. She crouched down close to the ground so she could stick her head out from behind the barrels and study what was happening on her pier without as much risk of being seen by Fin and the soldiers, should they turn back her way.

There did not appear to be many more crates or sacks to be loaded from the end of the pier; most of the cargo had already been handed down and ferried across the harbor. She could see Fin shielding his eyes with one hand, scouring the wharf from the middle of the second pier. She ducked back down, careful not to move a muscle, hugging close to the barrel. She could see that he was talking to others he came across, and it suddenly occurred to her that he might know some of the dockworkers. Something exchanged hands, and a few of them seemed to join him. She watched in horror as the expanded group methodically worked their way to the end of the pier and then back to the wharf, checking every nook and cranny. Upon reaching the wharf, Fin and the commander and a few of the soldiers turned left to search the farthest pier, while the rest turned right and began making their way back toward the main street market.

Tara's knees were starting to hurt from crouching for so long. From her perspective, the wharf bent to the left ever so slightly, and after a long while she saw Fin's figure disappear around it. The relief was only momentary, however, because she still had no idea what she was going to do.

She returned her attention to the activity at the end of her pier. The last crates and sacks were being loaded. There wouldn't be another boat after this one, she reckoned, and then her only way of getting aboard that ship would be to swim. She grimaced at the choppy water, not liking her chances.

A gust of wind carried the voices of the men and women handing cargo down the ladders from the end of the pier. They sounded jovial, but she wasn't fool enough to assume that meant these people would be friendly. At least they did not look menacing, she thought. Besides, what choice did she have? Squinting once more toward the farthest pier, she stood and darted around to the other side of the stack of barrels, nearly tripping on a coil of rope as she legged it toward the near end of the pier.

She slowed suddenly, trying to look normal, and was just about to set foot upon it when sharp edges closed around her waist from both sides, like huge scissors or metal boxes. The world spun, and everything was a blur of movement as she was jolted off her feet. Something jagged and unyielding had her pinned against what she at first thought was a wall. It took Tara a couple of seconds to realize that the wall was General Aguilar's glass torso; he had her under one arm and was trying to get her balanced as he catapulted forward. Fractals of shattered glass blinded her in the sun, and the docks and buildings blurred past. She glimpsed the alleyway she had just come through. Seconds later, it was gone.

"Let me go," she rasped, trying to squirm free. His vise-like grip around her waist stung. When she looked down to where she was pinned between his huge arm and his body, she saw spots of blood staining through the dress.

"Don't move," Aguilar's deep voice rumbled. Then the world spun again as he switched her over to the other arm and continued to sprint in long strides away from the harbor, carrying her like a doll in the opposite direction to where Fin had disappeared.

"Fucking let me go! I want to go *home!*"

Aguilar ignored her, glass feet crunching repeatedly as they flew along. They were almost past the dockside area already, speeding away from the harbor and behind the buildings and houses that lined the main street.

"Say, what happened to not compelling me to go with you?" she managed to croak out.

He kept running in silence, ignoring her.

"I said let me go!"

"Quiet," he said simply as he vaulted over a low wall of rocks.

Intimately aware of the sharp edges of his arm and side, Tara dared not struggle too hard. She even stopped trying to crane around to get a glimpse back toward the harbor. The bare skin of her neck was precariously close to his rising and falling thigh; her hanging necklace was clinking against it over and over, bouncing violently with every stride. She let her body go limp. That seemed to make the general relax a bit; he stopped crushing her so tightly against him. When she felt the slight loosening of pressure, it crossed her mind to take advantage and try to break free, but she was more worried about cutting herself in half in the process. She decided to wait for a better opportunity.

The morning breeze had picked up, and sand from the dunes gusted sideways across the ground. Aguilar's gait was machine-like. With his long-legged lope he kept a fast pace, speeding behind the houses, and soon they were on the outskirts of town. He cut left between two structures, glancing behind them only briefly as he bolted across the sand road. From there he barreled on up the slope, his glass feet thrashing through the looser sand as he headed into the dunes.

He had shifted Tara to a more secure position, and she was now able to glance backward around his arm without risk of slicing her throat on it, but the view continued to be shaky. She saw the smudge of town and the ship masts against the blue, bouncing up and down with the glass man's movements, already small in the distance.

For a brief moment she hoped Fin would spot the general's glass body from afar as it sparkled in the sun and come rescue her. Duplicitous though he had been, he had so far never been cruel to her. He had promised more than once, after all, to take her home "once we're done", whatever that meant. But she knew it was a flimsy hope. As the general had pointed out, Fin was The Mother's employee, so no matter how hard Tara might try to convince him to let her go or take her home, he had other motives. She knew she had to consider everything he had ever said to her to be a lie. Still, she wanted so badly to get back to the port town and board that ship! She had been so close!

Aguilar was unbelievably strong. Despite her frustration, she found herself amazed at how quickly he had reached the top of the first dune. Behind them, the ship masts disappeared from view as he dropped down to the other side of it. From there he kept to the valleys between dunes whenever possible, only risking the exposure of crossing a ridge when a valley ended or curved in the wrong direction. They were angling inland, but were still heading more or less southward, Tara judged, and would soon pass the spot where she had made it out of the dunes and reached the coast.

"Where are you taking me?" she shouted.

She was surprised when he answered her this time. "A safer place."

At length, they crested the highest ridge. Far to their left, rising above the sands, was the volcano, its snowy peak bright white against the blue. The ocean spread behind them and to their right. It looked choppier now, and a golden haze hugged the coast where the waves pummeled the shore. Forward was the most difficult direction to look, Tara found, but when she strained to arch her back and lift her chin, she could see the sea of dunes stretching on and on and on until, far, far ahead, the land folded upward to form a range of gentle reddish mountains. Moments later, the view was obstructed again as they continued down the other side of the ridge.

A wind hit them as they traversed the next one, and Tara could hear a tinkling sound as sand grains hit the general's glass body. She had learned to keep from looking at any part of him whenever they were in the direct sunlight, and do most of her glancing past him to the right when they were in a trough between dunes. The reflections were so bright they were painful, and she preferred to keep her vision clear so she could see where they were going. It was not easy, however; the refracting glass was always right there, blocking much of her frame of view. She wondered again how a hallucination could be so unwaveringly consistent, and immediately buried the thought.

Instead, she gazed at the sand blurring past a few feet below her face. She might have been a drone, humming over the dunes, her eyes twin cameras scanning the surface. Except that this drone was a prisoner and dripping blood. She shut her eyes and found it easier to calm her anxiety. The steady lope, the rhythmic *crunch crunch crunch* of footsteps, the sun warm on her face… these sensations lulled her, and her mind wandered.

When Tara next opened her eyes, the sun was much lower in the sky. With a surge of anxiety, she realized she must have been out for hours. The general did not appear to have slowed; he was still racing forward at the same steady pace, eating up the miles. She wondered how many miles they were from the port town. Far more than she could make by herself in a day, she reckoned. The thought threatened to pull her deeper into despair.

She strained to peer forward through her flopping coils. This elicited a head rush, swirls and blotches of color momentarily clouding her vision. When it cleared, she saw that the land had changed; all around was still sand, but they were no longer in the sea of dunes. Scattered here and there were clumps of palm trees, or something like them. As the general sprinted past, she heard a lonely bird call from the fronds atop one of the trees, though it was unlike any birdsong she had ever heard before. Again Tara wondered what fate this strange man had in mind for her, but again tried not to think about it. She was getting weary of that train of thought, for it only intensified her apprehension. She closed her eyes and tried to go back to sleep.

His long legs crunched across the distance, glistening in the last rays of the sun. Tufts of grass and shrubs were all around now, and the clumps of trees were becoming more frequent. When Tara looked up again, she saw that they were fast approaching a thick stand of them, rising from the desert like a bright green island. All that lushness was a welcome break from the eye-stinging sand.

As they reached the oasis, the general finally slowed his gait. Without a word, he set Tara down gently at the base of a large palm. Then he turned, walked back to the edge of the copse, and stood as still as a statue, glass arms hanging at his sides, staring back northwestward.

The sun had drifted below the horizon, and swaths of unbelievable hues were spreading up through the vast blue, transforming it into an otherworldly conflagration. Tara slumped against the tree, feeling numb inside. She knew that even if she waited until dark to make her move, she could never hope to survive all that arid distance on her own. For the first time in her life, she wished she had been more serious about getting physically fit. Her family had done a lot of hiking when she was younger, but she had avoided organized sports like the plague and had generally ignored her mother's and Nick's advice to get some exercise.

"I'm cold," she said, but the Angle Man just stood there, either not hearing or not caring.

"I'm thirsty, too," she said, a little louder this time. There was movement in one of the trees a short distance behind her. A bird perhaps, or something else. She was too exhausted to even turn to see what it was.

Wordlessly, the general walked over to a bush with large leaves, bent down, and gripped it at its base. He then stood, uprooting the whole thing in one fluid movement, and then strode over to toss it onto the ground in front of Tara.

She stared at it for a full minute. "What the hell am I supposed to do with that?"

Aguilar stood over her for a moment, his shattered glass eyes seeming to study her. Tara glared right back. Sighing one of those airy sighs, he picked the plant back up, pinched the fat sandy root cluster with both hands, and effortlessly pulled the outer layer right off.

"Drink," his hollow voice said as he pointed at the moist white flesh inside the tuber. "And eat."

He took a step closer. Tara flinched, but all he did was bend down to hand her the plant. When she accepted it with both hands, he nodded once, straightened, and returned to his post.

Tara sniffed suspiciously at the root, but nothing was setting off any alarm bells. She wiped the tip of her pinky finger on her dress, dipped it into the moist mass of white fibers, and then carefully touched it to her tongue. It tasted slightly sweet. Throwing caution to the wind, she let her thirst and hunger take over, ripping stringy flesh out with her fingers and teeth and sucking down every bit of moisture she could get like a ravenous beast slurping marrow from bone. It was nasty and exquisite all at once.

Refreshed, she stood, wincing as she did so. Through the night and into the morning, adrenaline had helped her ignore the pain of running all that distance barefoot, but now that she hadn't stood on them for hours, contact with the ground made her very aware of just how raw and sore her soles were. She found a patch of soft sand to stand in and leaned against the tree. A few yards away, the general still stood in silence, apparently watching for pursuers. The first stars had begun to appear, and a stillness was settling over the desert.

"So why do they call you 'Angle Man'?" she asked, hugging her shoulders. It was a lot colder than it had been the night before.

The general turned to regard her for a few seconds, then walked off into the underbrush.

"Okay then," she muttered, and sat back down with her back against the tree.

She heard a crash, then the snapping of branches, and a minute later he returned, dragging a small tree behind him in one hand and holding a bundle of sticks in the other. He dropped the wood in a heap not far away from her feet, then squatted down and made a shallow pit in the sand. He then proceeded to build a fire. Once the kindling structure was complete, he did something that made Tara's eyes go wide with awe. As he reached his hand toward the little teepee he had fashioned, the glass shards that comprised his fingers began to emit an incandescent white glow, causing the wood beneath them to smoke and then erupt into flame. After that, he pulled a couple of green fronds from the small tree he had dragged and then sat down cross-legged in the sand across the fire from Tara.

She scooted forward, reaching both hands toward the flames. The warmth felt nice against her skin. The wood popped and crackled and smoked, clearly still green inside, but it seemed to be burning well enough. After a moment, she noticed Aguilar was staring at the scars on her arms. She withdrew them quickly, hugging her shoulders.

"This glass," he said in his porcelain voice, "for me, is a memory of pain. Not unlike those scars of yours."

You know nothing about me, mister, was her initial reaction, but she immediately recognized how childish the thought was. "What pain?" she said instead. At least he was talking now. It had been a long, terrifying day, and words were a distraction from the fear, even if they were coming from this intimidating figure.

He was ripping the fronds into long ribbons, braiding them together. A nervous pastime, she assumed. Or maybe he was just bored. He looked over at her with those hollow eyes, again causing her to flinch away. "The pain of losing my heart. My child, my wife."

"Oh. They died?"

"I killed them."

"Oh." Tara mulled this over for a moment. "You… murdered them? Why?" she stammered.

Aguilar shook his head slowly and stared into the fire, his fingers still working at the fronds. "Well, no. Not on purpose. See, I was not paying attention. I was drunk. And emotional. And I can list a thousand more excuses, a million more, but in the end, I was the one behind the wheel; I was the one who lost control and smashed into that tree. Smashed them to their deaths."

Tara didn't know what to say. Other people she'd met had told them about people they'd known who had died, mostly older people, and she hadn't known how to respond then, either. She scratched the side of her nostril, trying to think of something sympathetic and appropriate, but it was hard enough just trying to wrap her head around the idea that this hulk of glass was actually a person.

"That must have been hard," was all she could come up with.

He nodded. "Harder still was living without them. I tried, I really did. I tried to work through grief. I tried to move on. I tried to do what I knew she would have wanted. I tried to let go, but I just couldn't."

The fire crackled, and coals formed. Aguilar carefully placed a few more sticks in, leaning them at an angle so they would catch more easily.

"So what did you do?"

"I ended myself."

"Ended yourself? But you're still alive."

He turned his empty eye sockets toward her. "No, not alive. But I still exist, yes. You see, when I first arrived here and realized death was not the end, it hit me that I had tried to take the easy way out, like a coward. All my life, I was always looking for an easy way out, always trying to find some sort of angle, some trick, something that would make money from nothing and get me up that ladder far above the rest of the rabble. I was too good for everyone else; I was too smart to be associated with them. And even after the tragedy of losing my family, I still refused to see. I continued in my habit of searching for yet another angle, yet another way out. Another route to escape shame and pain. And it wasn't until after I'd killed myself that I realized just how despicable I truly had always been.

"So, I wear this glass as a reminder to myself—not just of the windshield I put the beautiful faces of my wife and child through, but of the truth, which is that I do not *deserve* an easy way out, nor have I ever. I do not *deserve* to go to the Antim. The only justice for me is to remain here in existence forever, with the agony of memory and regret my eternal companion."

Tara stared into the coals, jaw clenched, as a chill went up and down her spine. Despite the proximity of the fire, she shivered, hugging herself tighter and rocking forward slightly. Snot was puddling in one nostril, threatening to drip. She wiped at it with the back of her hand and sniffed.

"This is all real, isn't it," she said finally.

"Yes."

"And you're… you're really dead. And this is… this is not… I can't just take a ship back across the ocean and be home, can I."

"No. I'm sorry. You cannot."

"Am I dead too?"

He shook his head. "No. I'm sorry. You are not."

Everything Fin had said was true. Everything The Mother had said was true. This was the land of the dead, and she was trapped here.

She curled into a fetal position, sobbing uncontrollably. The Angle Man returned to braiding the fronds, reflections of flames dancing eerily across his glass facets.

She must have cried herself to sleep. When Tara opened her eyes and sat up, more stars had come out, the sunglow almost gone from the sky, and the birds had quieted. In the sand in front of her were a pair of shoes made from braided palm fronds. She looked around, but the general was nowhere to be seen. She tried putting her sore foot in one of the shoes. It fit. She put on the other and stood.

He wasn't in the spot where he'd stood guard, so she wandered around the fire past the clump of trees in the direction of where he had gone to collect firewood. The forest was even denser here, with underbrush and vines climbing in-between. Everything around her was lush green, and the trees towered overhead. Dusk made everything feel darker, stranger.

She came to the top of a hill. It was studded with boulders, and a short distance beyond them, the ground sloped downward. After a while, she caught a glimpse of glass through the trees, and continued down to the bottom of the hill.

Aguilar stood on the bank of a big river that flowed from left to right, straight out of the side of a mountain. It churned out of the darkness from an enormous cavern, arcing in a series of green-blue tongues over a broad precipice before pounding down in a short but massive waterfall. From there, the roiling rapids gradually flattened as they bent around to their right. To the left of the giant opening, Tara spotted a much smaller cave, several yards up a steep, rocky slope.

She stood next to him, staring at the massive body of water, twirling her fingers distractedly through her hair. A small shape darted overhead, then another, arcing around in erratic patterns over the river.

"Come. I want to show you something."

She followed the glass man up the bank toward the smaller cave, scrambling with hands and feet through the rocks and from ledge to ledge. The palm frond shoes were surprisingly sturdy.

"Here," Aguilar said, pointing at the ground just to the right of him. "Stand here, with your arms and legs spread wide, like this." He formed an X shape with his body, blocking the left two-thirds of the cave entrance.

She did as she was told, and just as she was reaching her arms into the air to mimic his stance, something winged out of the cave straight at her, darting around her head in a near miss. Too late, she ducked.

"It's okay. The bats will not hit you. They have sonar, remember?" the general said. Tara thought she heard a chuckle in his voice. "This is the time of night they come out en masse. Brace yourself; there will be more than just a few. Way more. But they will not hit you, I promise. Just stand with your arms and legs out, exactly like this."

For the first few minutes, the tiny bats darted out one at a time or in twos or threes. Then larger groups began to come, and soon it was a flood. If she had wanted to chicken out and leave the cave entrance, she should have done it sooner; now there were so many bats careening out of the cave, zooming past them, around them, under their arms and between their legs, that she did not dare move an inch.

The rush of bats continued to grow in intensity over the next several minutes, a never-ending torrent of webbed wings and furry bodies. Once Tara realized that they really weren't going to hit her or get tangled in her hair, she relaxed, allowing herself to feel the excitement. It was exhilarating. Aguilar looked over at her, then tipped his head back to stare up at the endless flow around them. Tara stretched both hands up as high as she could, tipped her head back as he had, and shouted at the top of her lungs.

It was the first time she had laughed in days.

Chapter Ten

The cavern mouth yawned before them, its pocked ceiling slanting parallel to a scree slope that dropped steeply for several yards before ending at a black hole not quite large enough to fit a VW Bug through. Tara squinted down into it, but it was like trying to make out shapes in her closet in the middle of the night. The stream of thousands upon thousands of bats had finally finished exiting the cave, for the most part; only the occasional straggler flitted past, with increasingly long gaps in-between.

"Are you kidding me?!" Tara looked at Aguilar ludicrously. "In there?!"

He nodded. "I told you we were going to a safer place. This is it."

"But it's a cave," Tara said, pointing out the obvious.

"Yes."

With that, he set off down the slope, enormous glass feet sliding through the scree a little as he found his footing.

As he reached the hole, he held one hand up, and radiant white light burst forth just as before, illuminating the walls around him but penetrating only a short distance into the abyss below.

He turned and beckoned. "Come. Follow me," his voice boomed, seemingly at home among all that rock. He then proceeded to lower himself over the precipice until all but his head had disappeared behind it. "Quickly! I'll help you down."

Tara hesitated. Behind her, the river flowed swiftly around the bend; she assumed toward the ocean. She could follow it....

The first few yards after the scree slope were nearly vertical, but the rocks were dry, not slippery, and she was able to find enough shelves and handholds that it was not too terribly difficult. At one point, there was a drop that was too far for her legs, but when Aguilar offered to lift her down, she refused. Hunkering down on her hands and knees, she got sideways to the ledge and eased one leg over it. She then maneuvered until she was on her stomach, bracing with both arms, and stretched her toe all the way down until she could touch the next outcropping.

When they got to the bottom of the initial descent, the rocks gave way to a damp, level floor that felt soft and springy under her makeshift shoes. All around them was the sound of water dripping. Tara took a last look back up toward the opening. Although it was dusk outside, the ragged patch of sky appeared as bright as day compared to the darkness that now enveloped them. A crack led down along the center of the slanting ceiling to just past their heads. In it she noticed two small furry shapes, their bodies flattened to fit into the crevice: a couple of bats still sleeping, apparently too lazy to join their fellows in the early evening bug hunt.

Sleep as late as you want, little guys, she thought, and wondered if they were dead.

The general had stopped to wait for her, his glowing hand creating erratic shadows on the walls and ceiling around him. Beyond him was a dark passage about twelve feet tall and six or seven wide. Tara said a mental goodbye to the bats and to the sky—but not to the hope of finding her way home—and followed the twinkling glass figure into the depths.

The cave had a moldy, dusty smell. It wasn't exactly unpleasant, but she found herself crinkling her nose more than once. It made her wonder how there could be mold in the afterworld. Did mold have souls? Or, what was the world they had used—*citta?* It all seemed a bit ridiculous to her. She vowed to ask the general more about it, but later, when she didn't have to concentrate so hard on not spraining an ankle or donging her head on an overhanging wall.

The passage got narrower, but above them the ceiling lifted even higher until she couldn't see it in the gloom. "How big is this cave?"

"Big," Aguilar said.

After a time, she began to see stalactites jutting down from the upper reaches of the walls. A few times the walls curved inward to the point that they very nearly met in the middle, a thin crevice of black the only indication that there was more to the passage above, but then they always widened back apart. The air was cool. Tara remembered hearing something about it always being a constant temperature if you got deep enough underground—but then what was "ground" in the land of the dead? What was "air", for that matter? The concept did her head in. Still, her brain would not stop, so she let herself keep on wondering, and made more mental notes.

She guessed the passage was following the river upstream through the mountain, because now and then she heard the faint roar of rapids or waterfalls through the wall to their right. After a couple of hours, however, she stopped hearing it, and the passage seemed to be gradually slanting downward.

The passage got narrower and narrower until the general had to walk sideways to fit his broad shoulders through. When Tara looked straight up, she noticed the ceiling was low enough to be visible again. It was bristling with delicate, straw-like stalactites, so thin the light from the general's hand shone right through them. She was so engrossed in their pastel beauty that she bumped into the general, who had stopped abruptly to squat down and peer at something.

In front of them was what looked at first like a dead-end to her, but Aguilar calmly rocked forward onto his hands and knees and proceeded to crawl into a low, narrow tunnel.

"Um…." Tara paused.

Aguilar's voice came back muffled. "Don't worry, we don't have to crawl very far. It opens back up after a while."

Reluctantly, she got on her hands and knees and crawled in after him.

Tara had never been claustrophobic, but after a while, the ceiling came down so low she couldn't crawl normally. She had to scrunch her head and shoulders and butt down, lest they scrape against the rock. She could feel the fabric of her dress stretching and fraying under her knees, and wondered how the much bigger glass man was able to fit through. However he was doing it, it was loud.

Her hands and knees were starting to hurt when she noticed to her left and right it was pitch black; the walls had suddenly fallen away. The ceiling at this point was one massive slab of grayish rock, extending into the darkness as far as she could see to the left, right, and in front of them.

"Are you sure about this?" She hesitated, trying unsuccessfully to keep from thinking about all that rock collapsing on them, burying them alive. The blackness to either side of her seemed to stretch into infinity. One by one, childhood nightmares and campfire ghost stories began to creep into her conscious mind. She kept thinking she could see a whitish form lurking in the dark far to her right, almost owl-like in shape, but whenever she looked straight at it, it was gone. She would look again with her peripheral vision, and there it was. A chill crept up her spine.

"Keep up," Aguilar hollered back at her. He was now crawling on his stomach, and the cacophony of glass grinding over gravel was making Tara wish she had earplugs.

"I want my own lantern," she grumbled, but then hastened onward, ignoring the tender scrapes on her knees and elbows as she grunted to catch up with the glass man's refracting silhouette.

The gravel crawl seemed to last forever. When they finally reached the end and could stand, Tara felt both profoundly relieved and rather proud of herself for having kept it together. Rubbing her elbows, she surveyed their surroundings.

They had entered a small room with enormous fin-shaped stalactites hanging down, almost but not quite touching the tips of similarly shaped stalagmites that protruded from the floor. The near perfect mirror images were disorienting.

"Rest," Aguilar said, pointing to a stalagmite. It had a flat spot on its side that was just big enough to sit on.

Tara sat. The general pulled something from one of his belt pouches and handed it to her. In the glow from his other hand, which he thoughtfully kept raised to provide more light, she saw that it was a clump of the stringy white tuber flesh she had eaten back at the oasis. She accepted it and raised it to her mouth, chewing and sucking down the sweet juices, feeling suddenly parched.

"What about you?" she asked between mouthfuls.

"Hunger and thirst, like all attachments, are illusions."

She mulled this over as she ate. Considering her suddenly growling stomach and how good the moist root fibers were tasting, she had to disagree. "Illusion my ass. I'm *hungry*, and this tastes *good*." She slurped down the last of the snack and licked her fingers, not caring that they tasted like dirt.

"No, you are not actually hungry; your body is not here. You think it is, because physical sensation is what your mind expects. It is what your consciousness and perception are accustomed to. But you are not here, not in the way that I am."

"But I *am* here. See? Look at me. I'm here." She smiled sweetly, holding out her sticky fingers for him to see.

Aguilar nodded. "You are here, yes. But your body is not."

"So I'm a spirit," she said doubtfully.

He shook his head. "You are *citta*; you are consciousness and perception. But unlike other *citta* here in the Afterrealms, *you* are still attached to the realm of the living. You have not yet left it; you have not yet died."

"You mean my body is still... there? Alive? Only my mind is here?"

He thought for a moment before replying. "Not in any normal sense. Your body is... suspended in-between, connected to both realms; you cannot leave it, nor it you. As far as I know, this cannot be undone unless you die. And once you return, the balance between your... parts, your states... this will be restored, and then you will be whole again. Once that happens, you—your *citta*, which is more than just your mind, you understand—it will be back with your body, in the physical realm."

Tara couldn't get past the idea that this wasn't her body, sitting right here, elbows and knees stinging. This *was* her body; she even had bloody scratches to prove it. "But I saw other people eating and drinking at the feast, next to the bonfire. It wasn't just me. I remember clearly."

He nodded. "Most *citta* are willing to go to great lengths to maintain the illusions that make them feel comfortable, in less turmoil. Such illusions are formed easily by those with sufficient tenacity."

"I've heard that word a few times."

"Probably. Tenacity is, for lack of a better word, power. It is the capacity to hold on—not just to attachments, but to these very realms. Another word for it is 'grip'. The more tenacity one possesses, the greater the illusions one can maintain and the more secure one's grip on the world is.

Without any tenacity at all, or when completely drained of it, that 'grip' ceases to exist, and one is pulled inexorably up into the Antim."

"Which is the end."

"Yes. The forevernothing."

"Like, death? Death death, I mean? Final death?"

"As far as anyone knows, yes."

She nodded and looked around. "So, what about this rock?" She slapped the palm of her hand against the stalagmite she was sitting against, causing it to resonate around the chamber like a drum. Amused, she slapped it again, harder this time. It made a satisfying *thump*, sending even louder echoes. "Wow, that's really cool."

"That rock was... formed. Much of what you can see in the Afterrealms was formed by those with great tenacity—The Mother, for example. She possesses enough tenacity to fashion and maintain the Cradle—her realm; the realm we have just left—as she sees fit. But some of it..." he trailed off, hollow eyes wandering up toward the ceiling. "No one quite knows."

She followed his gaze. The cave looked pretty natural to her. "You know a lot of stuff. What were you before you... came here? A teacher? Professor? My dad was a professor."

The general hung his chin against his chest, arms folded, and shuffled his toe from side to side in the dust. Tara thought he looked uncomfortable.

She shrugged and stared at her feet for a while, then glanced back up at his cracked glass face. "You said 'once I return.' How do I do that? How do I get back home? Do you know the way?"

"I do not, I'm afraid. But this is a question you can ask the Elder."

"The Elder?"

"He is the *citta* I am bringing you to meet."

"So, what, he's really old or something?"

"He has been here for a very long time. Not nearly as long as The Mother, but a very long time nonetheless."

"And he'll know the way home?"

Aguilar paused, as if choosing his words carefully. "If anyone does, he will."

'If, he said. The world was tipping again. Tara rubbed her eyes. She needed a distraction.

Looking around, she got to her feet, walked over to another stalagmite, and thumped it with her palm. It produced an even deeper tone than the one she'd been sitting on. She thumped it a few more times in a brief rhythm, marveling at the way the sounds reverberated. Making her way in a circle around the chamber, she struck all the stalagmites and stalactites she could reach, each one producing a different musical tone.

"Hey, you hit that little one way up there. I want to see if it makes a higher pitch," she said, pointing at the stalactite hanging near Aguilar's shoulder. He stared at her blankly.

"Come on! Just do it. Please?" she said, sounding suddenly very girly to herself. She did not quite understand where this lighter mood was coming from; she was lost in a cave, with a monster, in the land of the dead, apparently. But at least there was now hope that she had not, in fact, lost her mind. Moreover, she now had a reason to follow the general that was other than simply not knowing what else to do or where else to go.

If a hulking glass man with hollow sockets could roll his eyes, Aguilar did. But then he reached up and smashed his palm solidly against the stalactite. A higher tone rang out, accompanied by the sharp *clink* of glass hitting rock. Tara thought she also heard a cracking sound, but wasn't sure whether it was from his hand or the stalactite.

"Enough. We must go," he said, turning to continue down the passage that led from the chamber.

The next mile or so involved quite a bit of up and down, with an emphasis on the latter. It grew steep in places, and more than once the general had to carry Tara over a precipice that was too tall for her to navigate by herself. She felt awkward in her dress, clinging to his massive back with her arms around his neck, and each time resulted in a fresh cut or two.

At length they came to a low chamber roughly the width of her school auditorium, with a giant pile of rubble in the middle. At the top were several long, flat boulders that must have weighed many tons each. The glass man stopped in front of the pile, shining his light left and right. Tara waited patiently for him to pick which way to go, but he just stood there, apparently at a loss.

"Where to, General Aguilar?" she asked, her voice deadened by the relatively low ceiling. There didn't seem to be any way around.

"No need to call me 'General'."

"Okay then. Mr. Aguilar. Which way?"

"This was not here, the last time I came through," he muttered, surveying the array of dusty boulders and rocks. "The ceiling has collapsed. And you can call me Luto."

Tara looked up at him. "Luto. Funny, why didn't I guess. You look *exactly like* a Luto," she said smirking, but the sarcasm seemed to go right over his head. Humor wasn't something that translated very easily across worlds, she decided.

Going by the light from the glass man's hand, she rock-hopped around to the right, but came up against a dead end. She circled left, but again found no way around or through. She looked up. There was at least five feet of space between the top of the pile and the ceiling, she figured. After taking a moment to plan out a route, she began to climb.

"Careful," Aguilar said, following close behind. "Perhaps I should lead...."

She ignored him and kept going all the way to the top of the pile. Between two of the largest boulders, there was enough space for them both to squeeze through. On the other side, it was less steep going down, and she spotted a horizontal shadow at the very bottom of the opposite wall.

"Down there," she pointed, waiting for him to catch up. "I don't know if that's an opening or just an overhang. Here, I need your light."

She scrabbled down to where the rocks had slumped against the wall and crouched to inspect the dark spot more closely. It was indeed an overhang, it turned out, but as she ducked her head underneath it, she could see a low tunnel continuing downward at about a forty-five-degree angle. The floor appeared to be hard-packed dirt, though there was no sign of footsteps. In fact, Aguilar could have told her that no one had ever set foot in this cave, and she would have believed him; it felt utterly wild, untouched by humans. Thoughts of what other denizens of this realm might have been there, or might perhaps still be there, teased through her mind, and she did her best to shut them out.

"Hey Luto, shine your light. Think you can fit through here?"

"I think so. But I should go first—"

Tara did not wait for him to finish. Sitting on her butt with her legs forward, she lay back, braced her hands against the musty rock walls, and started easing herself down the steep dirt slope. Aguilar was hollering at her to stop, but she felt happy to be taking the lead for a change. She'd been the one to find this passage, after all.

For the first couple of minutes, everything went fine. The shadows cast by the light behind her sometimes made it difficult to see very far past her feet, but now and then she caught a glimpse of the dirt slope and could see that it continued unbroken for quite a ways. But then her left hand slipped from a less than ideal grip she'd found on the ceiling, and she was suddenly sliding down the incline, out of control and accelerating, already too fast to stop herself. She yelped.

"Tara!"

Aguilar's voice already sounded a long way behind her.

This was quickly beginning to feel like the stupidest thing she had ever done. She couldn't see anymore; she was flying straight down into a pitch-black abyss. She turned onto her stomach and frantically tried to dig her fingers in to slow her descent, but the ground was too hard and she was skimming over it too fast. Just as she was starting to whimper in panic, the slope abruptly leveled out, and she stopped.

Unable to see a thing, Tara carefully reached a hand above her head and felt for the ceiling, but there was nothing there. She sat up and stared wide-eyed into the black.

Moments later, a faint light lit the walls and ceiling around her as Aguilar came sliding down after her, revealing the passage to have broadened considerably. If they'd had camels, they could have ridden them through it with ease. Tara stood and brushed herself off as the glass man came to a stop.

He stood and hunched over, his shadowy sockets seeming to glare at her. "Don't do that again."

"Why not? My body's not here, remember? So I can't exactly get hurt," she countered, but felt a lot less cocky and a lot more shaken than the words made her sound.

"Listen to me, Tara." His deep voice filled the cavern. "There are *many* things in this place that can indeed hurt you, and worse. Much worse. You would be wise to keep close and not let yourself get separated again. Understand?"

"Yes sir," she found herself saying.

"This will become imperative as we get closer to where we are going. I cannot protect you unless you let me. Understand?"

"Okay! I said yes. Got it," she exclaimed, shrugging her shoulders upward with her hands outstretched in exasperation. Still, despite his menacing appearance, Aguilar had sounded more worried than cross. She'd begun to notice a softness behind his voice when he spoke to her during their trek into the caves; something like concern. It almost sounded fatherly.

The passage meandered a hundred yards or so before bending sharply to the left. As they rounded the corner, Tara stopped in her tracks. Just in front of them, the walls and floor and ceiling stopped; beyond that was an enormous hole, gaping into blackness.

Aguilar trudged onward, slowing as he reached the opening. When she joined him, a wave of vertigo made her take a step backward. She did not trust herself not to totter over the precipice, so she crouched down and touched the floor with both hands, in part to find her balance and in part just to reassure herself that it was still there.

They were standing at the mouth of a hole in the side of a sheer cliff. It was immense. Looking up, Tara saw only darkness; the ceiling was too far away for the glass man's hand to illuminate. Craning left, she saw that the wall gradually curved around for a hundred yards at least before disappearing in the distance; and to the right, it went completely straight until it vanished. She couldn't see across the chamber, though to the right, very faintly in the distance, she thought she could make out what looked like colossal slanting columns, perhaps giant stalactite-stalagmite formations of some sort. Bracing herself, she inched up to the edge and looked straight down. Far below them, just barely visible in the dim light from Aguilar's hand, was the cavern floor. The dusty-brown terrain down there was covered in a thin veil of haze. Going just by what little she could see, this chamber was easily the size of a few indoor stadiums, only much greater in height.

But it wasn't what she could see that boggled her mind. It was dawning on her that the cavern was much, much larger than that, for drifting to her ears from way off to the right, from what sounded like miles past the columns, was the distant roar of a mighty river. Tara's conception of just how vast this cave was exploded, expanding the bounds of her imagination radically outward. It made her feel suddenly very tiny and insignificant, their little patch of light but a delicate mote, all but lost to darkness at the brink of infinity.

Chapter Eleven

To their left, from where it was bolted to the rocky cavern floor, a tattered rope ladder led straight down the cliff face, disappearing into the misty gloom. Tara studied it, full of misgivings. In the light from the Angle Man's hand, the maroon-colored fibers appeared far too ancient and eroded for any sane person to trust.

"No, I don't think so." She shook her head. "There's gotta be another way down."

"This is it."

"It'll break."

"It hasn't yet."

"And when was the last time you used it?"

Aguilar bent down and tugged one of the ropes against its bolt, testing it.

"Well?"

He stood back up, still studying the ladder. "Years."

"Years. How many years?"

"A few." He touched his fingertips to his chin, as if stroking a goatee that wasn't there. "Several."

Tara raised an eyebrow.

"Okay, more than several," he conceded. "But not a lot more."

Tara returned her attention to the rope ladder. "Well, I hope your feet don't cut through that."

His chest emitted something akin to a chuckle, like stones rattling around in a barrel.

Tara shook her head again, following the ladder with her eyes all the way to where it disappeared into the misty depths. "If I die here, do I die there, too? My body, I mean."

"There is no death here. Only the transitioning of *citta* to the forevernothing."

"You know what I mean."

Aguilar leaned over the cliff to peer down into the gloom. He shrugged his massive shoulders, glass fracturing here and there. "I cannot say for sure."

Tara swallowed. "Alright," she said and, pulse racing, began to gather up the skirt of her dress.

"However, I will go first. That way you don—"

"No, I will," she interrupted, tying the dirty fabric in a knot just above her knees. After double-checking her palm-frond shoes, she got down on her hands and knees, with her backside toward the precipice, and reached her hand up. "Here, give me a hand. Please."

Aguilar bent at the knees to grasp her hand as she awkwardly slid her leg over the edge of the cliff, stretching a toe down to find a rung. Very carefully, she slid her foot forward so that it was centered on the rope and tested her weight on it.

"Here goes nothing," she breathed, and let go of Aguilar's hand, wincing as the edge of a facet sliced her skin. It stung when she gripped the right side of the top rung with it, but it was bearable. *Three points of contact at all times*, she quoted in her mind as she squeezed her left hand around the other side and proceeded to lower a foot down to the next rung.

She did her best to not look down, focusing instead on the mechanics of climbing. This grew easier as the light from Aguilar's hand faded above her and the ladder rungs grew harder to see. Before long, she had to go by feel. Thankfully, the ropes were stiff and thick enough that the ladder did not twist much. As she descended, however, she soon encountered another problem: Her movements were causing it to sway slowly from side to side, which presented the danger of smashing her fingers between the rungs and the cliff face. The arcs were subtle at first, but as they grew more pronounced, she had to pause occasionally to let the ladder settle back into place. Hanging there in the dark, Tara felt very thankful that there was no wind to make things worse.

Her arms and shoulders were burning, and the balls of her feet were sore. She felt as though she'd been at it for hours. She was inside the layer of mist now, she reckoned, because the air felt cool and damp on her face and the distant light above had shrunk to a faint, fuzzy glow. She hoped that meant she was close to the bottom. Just as she was beginning to wonder whether the mist had risen higher, her foot squished ankle-deep into a thick layer of dust and came up against something solid underneath. Cringing a little, she withdrew with a start, her imagination squirming with thoughts of bugs or worms tunneling through the dust. A moment later, her practical side took over, and she dipped her toe back down to feel around with it, making sure it was ground underneath and not merely an outcropping. Satisfied, she let go of the ladder and squinted up toward the tiny, diffuse spot of light.

Cupping her hands to her mouth, she leaned back and shouted. "Okay, I made it!" She had expected echoes, but her voice fell flat against the vastness of the cavern. She may as well have been yelling in the outside air.

Slowly but surely, the glow grew brighter as it descended. At one point, it occurred to her that the general's glass hands really might cut through the ropes. Using the cliff face as a guide, she shuffled very carefully to the side to be out of the way in case he fell. Then she felt stupid; if that did happen, his body would likely shatter into a thousand flying shards, piercing right through her like so much shrapnel. Even if it didn't, she would never survive this place on her own without the light his hand provided. Annoyed at her overactive imagination, Tara waited, alone in the dark, the only sounds the soft back-and-forth shifting of rope against rock and the faint but constant roar in the distance.

To her relief, Aguilar made it down without mishap. The light emanating from his hand created a warm bubble against the void, small but intensely welcome. Without a word, he plodded off through the dust in the direction of the giant columns. Tara closed her eyes briefly and drew in a deep breath, wishing she could wake up from this nightmare and find herself in her bed back home, all clean and warm and safe. Then she opened them to the murk and trotted to catch up.

The ubiquitous dust looked as though it hadn't been disturbed in millennia. Their passage left a shifting trail through it. In the light and shadow, she watched the powdery substance swirl in the still air behind them where they had stirred it from its age-old resting place, and wondered how many hours or days it would take for it to settle again completely. Over the next several minutes, she took to scanning around for other tracks through the dust. She was mildly reassured when she did not spot any.

Their progress was slow, and the columns were farther away than they had appeared in the dim light from the clifftop. Time had very little meaning in the dark, and Tara had no watch or phone clock to gauge by. She figured it had taken them at least twenty minutes to wend their way to the base of the first one. She gazed upward. The mist had cleared, and she could see the enormous pillar of rock rising at a steep angle from the floor to disappear skyward—for without any visual evidence of a ceiling, that was how it felt. There were no stars up there, of course, but she had no problem pretending it was overcast. It was easier than trying to fathom just how immense the cavern must be.

As they plodded through the thick dust, Tara thought the slanting columns appeared almost man-made. Their bases looked natural enough, and were quite similar in shape to the fin-like stalagmites in the room with the funny tones and echoes, though on a much larger scale. As she followed their shafts upward into the darkness, however, she could not help but wonder at their uniformity, their evenness. Had they once stood straight? What had caused them to topple? Or was this just another of nature's bizarre coincidences, like a skull-shaped rock she had once seen on the Maine coast or an old oak tree with a face in its bark—only resembling such things to humans due to their inherent need to find familiar patterns in the unknown? She wasn't sure which thought unnerved her more: that the slanting columns of rock had been formed over eons through natural processes which should not be possible in this land of the dead, or that they were walking through some ancient ruin, perhaps the remnants of a towering stone hall built before the dawn of time by titanic godlike beings. At this point, she was almost ready to believe anything.

The general marched on through the dust, picking a careful route around steep boulders and precipitous pits that yawned open without warning in the cave floor, a glass man on a mission. Tara struggled to keep up with his long legs. After a few hours, he stopped, seeming to have suddenly remembered that continuing on and on without breaks was impossible for some.

They rested on a large flat boulder that was almost table-like in shape. It was so uncanny that when Tara cleared the dust from a spot so she could sit, she leaned close to inspect the surface, but it revealed itself to be nothing but ordinary rock. Aguilar handed her the last of the tuber, and she slurped it down thirstily. Afterward, they sat in silence for a few minutes, staring in different directions into the gloom, and then continued on their way.

At one point, she looked up and noticed that there was indeed a wall off to their left. It was close enough to be visible now, and it angled inward as they progressed. Several minutes on, they found themselves walking in the middle of an impossibly tall corridor, the walls only twenty yards apart and getting closer. They could have been walking through a cathedral, only there were no stained-glass windows. That, and the scale was off; if this was a cathedral, then she and the Angle Man were miniscule dolls.

The walls continued to close in. Soon she could almost touch them, and a ceiling had come into view, slanting steeply downward. The cathedral-like hall shrank quickly until it was a normal-looking passage, not far different from the ones they had passed through in the earliest sections of the cave. That already seemed a fantastically long time ago. She wondered how long it had been since they had stood spreadeagle in the stream of bats. It felt like days.

The passage became even more difficult, slowing their progress. It twisted this way and that, climbing up or dropping down, and there were many more boulders and pits to navigate. The air here was moist, and the river-like roar had grown much louder. At times they had to inch their way along a slippery ledge, taking care not to fall into a crevice below. Some cavities were so deep she couldn't see the bottom; the rock cliffs dropped and dropped until they vanished into the black. More than once, Tara had to swallow her pride and allow Aguilar to carry her, hopping with his long legs from shelf to precarious shelf.

After one such stint, they came to a step-like formation that led down to a small chamber with a low ceiling. Aguilar put Tara down, and as she followed him in, even she had to bend forward to keep from hitting her head. Before them lay a wide, shallow puddle of water about ten or twelve feet across. In the bright light from his hand, she could see ripples spreading out from the vibrations they had caused when stepping to the pool's edge. The water was perfectly clear and looked to be only about an inch or two deep. Tara was about to step into it when Aguilar put a hand out to stop her.

"Slowly," he said. After studying the shallow water for a moment, he picked a direction, took a careful step...

...and plunged straight in up to his hip.

"Shit! It didn't look that deep!" Tara gawked. What had appeared to be the "bottom", beneath the thin layer of water, was actually the surface of a few feet of light brown mud.

Aguilar held his glowing hand up near the ceiling to light the way. As he turned toward her, his body made a sucking sound in the mud. "You will need to hold on to me. I cannot recall how deep this gets. It may have worsened over time."

Tara hesitated, bracing herself, then stepped in after him and sank all the way up to her chest. She yelped at the sudden cold. The general reached a hand under her armpit and dragged her unceremoniously through the mud to him. Once she had her arms around his middle, he began to squelch forward.

The mud was watery and loose, but it still clung enough that movement took a great deal of effort. Tara held on as Aguilar trudged forward, ignoring the sharp pain, terrified that they might sink even deeper. One wrong step, and she could slip under, never to be seen again. Scenes from a dozen old Saturday morning technicolor movies were flashing through her mind all at once. There was always a remote jungle dotted with quicksand, and there was always some poor unsuspecting fool who disappeared into it.

When they dragged themselves out the other side, she thought they both must look like they'd been dunked in a vat of milk chocolate. She paused to wipe gobs of the stuff from her torso and arms and legs, but gave up after a while, knowing she would never get it all. As they pressed onward, the mud-caked dress clung to her in thick, wet folds. She was too tired and cold to care.

A short climb up a rocky slope and around a bend brought them face to face with the river. It ran from right to left past a rock ledge not ten feet in front of them, dark waters churning. The cavern through which it flowed was not nearly as big as the cathedral-like chamber had been, but still large enough that Tara would not have been able to throw a stone from one side to the other. As Aguilar held his hand over the side of the ledge, she pulled her coils from her face and peered with him into the swift current. It was mesmerizing. The rapids flowed on and on, curling twisting leaping, as powerful and unstoppable as time or the end of consciousness, disappearing into the darkness beyond their little island of light.

"This part will be challenging," Aguilar said, his voice almost inaudible against the roar. "You will have to jump."

Tara searched in vain for a bridge or rope ladder to cross, then looked back down at the rushing water. "There's no way."

"I cannot carry you. If the current were to push us into a wall, you could get pinned between it and my heavy body, and you…. It would not be good."

Tara looked upstream and downstream. "Is there no other way across? Maybe another tunnel somewhere?"

Aguilar shook his head. "We are not going across. We are going down. That way." He pointed left, downstream.

"You're insane."

"I may be. I have not decided yet. Regardless, that is where we must go."

"But won't that take us back to the entrance?"

"No, this is not the same River. There are many Rivers, many Conduits; this is the one we must take to reach our destination."

Tara shuddered, remembering how the waterfall in Dee's Park had pummeled down to rocks and raged through that wind-whipped ravine. This felt even more dangerous to her, though she couldn't quite put a finger on why. It was the same, in a way. All she knew was that this time, she was one hundred percent sure she had no desire to jump whatsoever.

"I will go first. That way I will reach the Cavedwellers' sanctuary before you. I'll be able to catch you as you float past."

Tara stared at him in horror.

"I am sorry, Tara. There is no other way. We must do this."

She peered into the water. It was too dark to see the bottom, and the current looked frigid, unforgiving. Everything in her told her this was a terrible idea. She squinted downstream to where the waves disappeared beyond their circle of light, but found nothing reassuring in that direction, either. Her heart was beating very fast, and she realized she was shivering.

"How far down do we have to swim?"

"Not very far, as I recall."

She felt as though her feet were glued to the ground. Logic, her gut, and all the wilderness survival lessons her parents had ever taught her were screaming at her, telling her to rebel against this foolhardy proposition.

"Come," Aguilar rumbled in what Tara was beginning to recognize as a sympathetic tone. "It will be over before you know it."

He stepped to the edge and turned his head to regard her. "Because I will go first, you will be without light. After I jump, count to ten and follow. Shield your head with your arms if you can, and just let the current take you. I will be waiting at the end; I will catch you. Understand?"

Tara nodded mutely, eyes wide.

He jumped, falling several feet before splashing into the river. Despite his significant weight, the current took him immediately, and the light with him. For a few seconds, Tara saw the bright glow from where he held his hand above the waves, but then the circle of light curved quickly around a bend and was gone, swallowed by the dark. Far more abruptly than she had been prepared for, Tara could not see an inch in front of her face. She closed her eyes, then opened them. No change; the dark was absolute.

Panic rose suddenly as she realized she had forgotten to count to ten. *One, two, three....* She inched forward, not knowing exactly where the ledge ended. She would have to jump out as far as she could to avoid striking it on her way down.

She closed her eyes, held her breath, and leaped.

As her body smacked the surface, cold stabbed inward from all sides, penetrating bone deep. The unexpected rush was deafening as the current grabbed at her feet, wrenching them straight downward, and she was tumbling underwater, completely submerged. Tara dug upward with both arms, kicking for her life, only to discover that what she had thought was up was down. Opening her eyes, she saw nothing but black. She wanted to scream, but managed to keep her lips shut.

Seconds later, a large object appeared directly in front of her. It was too dim to make out, but had a vague fish shape to it and was looming rapidly. The thing cycled in and out of her field of view as she tumbled along with the current. *No light; imagining it*, she thought. *Way too big to be a fish anyway.* Then it was gone, and her face broke through the surface, sucking at the sweet air.

The water took her and took her, but she fought to keep her head up. She had only the sensation of movement; in every direction was oppressive, unbroken black. Belatedly, she remembered to shield her head with her arms, and then tucked her knees up, too, frightened of breaking a leg on a passing rock. That didn't work very well, however; it caused her head to roll back underwater. She adjusted so that she was floating on her back, going down feet first, hands behind her head with her elbows tucked upward. This felt like a better position; now and then her body would dip and roll through what felt like an extra-large set of rapids and she would have to readjust, but for the most part she was able to breathe freely.

There was a roar up ahead, and it was getting louder. She had her eyes shut against the black, but the sound made her open them wide. She thought she could see a dark rock ceiling rushing past. She blinked, but it was there, getting more visible. She was careening down at an unbelievable speed. When she lifted her head, she could just make out the shapes of the toes of her palm-frond shoes sticking up from the water, as well as the choppy waves beyond. They were silhouetted; the light was getting brighter. It was clear now that she was in the dead center of the river as it shot around a wide bend.

Up ahead she could see a straight line, smooth and unbroken, running from left to right across the river passage. Her heart sank as it dawned on her that she was headed straight for a waterfall and there was not a thing she could do about it. She thrashed about in desperate panic for a few seconds, but the smooth line just got closer and closer. She braced herself, hugging the sides of her head, wanting to shut her eyes but not daring to at the same time.

As the river swept her over the edge, a whimper of utterly helpless fear rose from deep within her. Eyes wide, she caught an adrenaline glimpse of a large pool below with a light on the shore shining steady and bright. In a semicircle around it were several dark shapes, closing in on it.

Then she was weightless, and the world became thunder.

Chapter Twelve

It was worse, much worse, than when she had jumped into the river in the first place. Her body was yanked this way and that, legs and arms wrenched in opposite directions, turning, twisting, out of control. She screamed, then immediately shut her mouth against the cold. For a heartbeat, she could not tell whether it was open or closed. All around her were bubbles, bubbles in the dark, rising in every direction. Her back struck something hard, and more bubbles exploded out of her. Her vision began to dim.

A light was approaching. Then everything went black.

Tara dreamed of glass hands grabbing at her ankles, dragging her bloody from a seething lake onto a hard pebbly beach. Something heavy bore down on her stomach, but she could not lift her arms to shoo it away. The annoying thing kept pressing and pressing, and a distant voice was yelling her name over and over. She hoped it wasn't Nick.

Then her eyes shot open, and she was sputtering up icy water. Someone was shining a flashlight in her face. She averted her eyes and continued to cough, water and drool dribbling from her chin onto the ground next to her upturned hand. Her fingers were curled. They looked very small to her.

There were voices around her, speaking in another language. She tried to sit up, but the dull pain in her back suddenly became excruciating. She lay back halfway and propped herself up on her elbows. Behind her, the cataract roared endlessly. It seemed smaller, somehow, now that she had survived it.

Tara looked up and saw Aguilar's back. He was in a defensive stance, glowing hand raised high, and he was saying something in what she thought sounded like Spanish. The light blinded her. She couldn't see very much beyond his figure, but there was movement. She shielded her eyes, and her sight adjusted in increments.

The dark shapes she had seen from the top of the waterfall were humanoid, with arms and legs, but their heads were all wrong. She breathed in sharply, then broke into another fit of coughing. When it stopped, she saw that they had enormous bat-like ears and their eyes were various shades of lime green, with black vertical slits in the middle like a cat's. Their fingers, longer than a grown man's fingers by half, were bony and slender and ended in razor-sharp talons. The creatures had them surrounded; they were trapped against the shore, and the only escape was back into the maelstrom.

One of them—their leader apparently—took a step closer with talons at the ready and growled out something in

Spanish in a commanding voice. Linking the monster's arm and side was a sheet of leathery fabric. Like a bat wing, Tara realized in horror.

Aguilar crouched protectively between her and the beast. He bellowed out a reply, his porcelain voice calm and steady. "Te lo advierto, no te acerques más. Estas manos son las mismas manos que derrotaron a Xie hace treinta años, y salvaron la vida de su líder. Sé que no lo has olvidado."

The giant bat-thing raised the talons of both hands, causing its terrible wings to spread wide, and one by one the others did the same. Even so, whatever Aguilar had said seemed to give them pause; neither the leader nor its cohorts advanced any closer. As she gaped at them, something moved in her peripheral vision, and she looked up to see more of the things hanging from the ceiling or perched on ledges around the walls, glaring down at them, cat eyes gleaming in the light from the general's hand. There must have been dozens. *We need to get out of here!* Trembling, Tara tried to get to her feet, but pain ripped through her again, forcing her back down.

The leader let his arms drop to his sides, wings folding as he did so. "Recuerdo que fuimos desterrados a estas cuevas. También recuerdo que no te quedaste mucho tiempo."

As soon as he said these words, a resentful muttering of agreement echoed around the chamber. The leader's fierce lime-green eyes raked over Tara, lingering briefly on her dress. "And you," he accused in English. "You are obviously from the Cradle. You wear The Mother's colors."

"This girl did come from the Cradle, yes," Aguilar said, also in English, "but she is not of that realm, nor does she work for The Mother. I have brought her here deliberately."

"Why?" The bat-thing seemed taken aback. "You know full well what the penalty is for bringing an outsider to the Caves."

Aguilar straightened slowly and lowered his hand. "Respectfully, Ion, this is a matter that is between me and Kavi."

Another round of low murmurs from the other bat-things simmered around the chamber. The one called Ion regarded Aguilar and Tara for a full minute, eyes narrowed in an outright murderous look. Any moment, he would slash them in two with his dreadful talons, she thought.

At last, the creature's hideous mouth twisted into a sneer. "The Elder does not waste time with *traitors*."

"Be that as it may, I humbly request that you at least inform him of my presence. If he chooses not to grant an audience, then you and your friends here can do with me what you will. I only ask that you spare this innocent, in honor of the bond you and I once shared."

An acrid look spasmed across the leader's face. He turned to the bat-thing nearest him and muttered something in Spanish. It nodded its head, spread its giant wings, and launched into the air, wheeling over the pool before flapping downstream to disappear around a tall rock outcropping.

"I used to think there was such thing as an unbreakable bond," he said to Aquilar. "You taught me otherwise. So, *respectfully*, Luto, no. As far as I am concerned, you and your companion are both intruders, so you will both suffer the consequences."

They waited in tense silence, the winged creature staring the glass man down, the latter calmly returning his gaze. After a couple of minutes, Ion shook his head in apparent disgust and walked over to the other bat-things that were gathered where the pebbly bank met the rock wall. Most of the ones that had been positioned about the chamber glided down to join them, but one bat-thing remained where it was, hanging upside-down directly above Tara's and Aguilar's heads, its smoldering eyes never leaving them.

"What are these things?" Tara whispered as quietly as she could.

Aguilar sat down next to her. "They are *citta*. We are in the realm of the Cavedwellers now, and these are members of the Elder's elite guard. They have used their excess tenacity to form bodily apparatuses that are more conducive to hunting and doing battle in the pitch dark."

Tara winced as she tried to face him; her back was killing her. She experimented with rolling over on her side and found the pain to be a lot more bearable in that posture. "Seems like you and this Ion fellow have history."

Aguilar leaned close, lowering his voice. "There are things that he does not know which, were he to know, he would likely not be so hostile toward us."

"Then why not tell him?"

He considered. "It's not that simple."

Tara stared at the huddle of winged shapes, feeling again like she was trapped in an endless nightmare, unable to wake up. "So what were you two talking about?"

The general drew a slow circle in the pebbles with one of his glass fingers, going round and round absently, as if lost in thought. "A long time ago, we fought side by side in a battle against a powerful *citta* named Xie Yuanzhan. It was grisly. And devastating. We lost in the end, and a great many of our brothers and sisters were sent to the forevernothing. I got lucky, and managed to defeat Xie in one-on-one combat, but I failed to vanquish him completely. I was too slow, and he escaped to regroup with his forces. But I'd bought enough time to save myself and a handful of others from the assault, including Ion. And my friend Kavi. Their leader," he added, nodding toward the bat-things.

Tara made a face. "So shouldn't they be grateful?"

"That was thirty years ago. A lot has happened since then," Aguilar said without explaining further.

When the messenger returned, she—Tara was beginning to be able to discern gender—came sailing around the bend in the company of three more of the winged elite guards. Each carried a torch, which they lit as soon as they landed next to a narrow crevice in the wall, just to the left of where the other elite guard members were gathered. The torchbearers stood at attention to either side of it, and the light from their flames cast flickering shadows that exaggerated their features, making them look even bigger and more frightening than they already were.

The one named Ion turned to call out to the general, gesturing in the direction of the torch-lit passage. "Luto, aquí. Vamos."

Aguilar stood. Despite Tara's lack of Spanish, it was clear enough that the bat creatures meant for them to follow. She struggled to get into a sitting position. "I... I don't think I can walk."

"You're hurt," Aguilar rumbled, that softness returning to his voice. "What hurts?"

"My back."

Reaching one arm under her knees and the other gently around her back, he lifted her from the ground. With her cradled in his arms, her dress and hair dripping, he strode off toward the flickering torchlight.

Half a dozen bat-things escorted them up the passage, with Ion and two others in front and three behind. In the torchlight, Tara could see they were armed not just with their razor-sharp wing tips and talons, but with short swords that hung in scabbards from their belts. Their bodies were covered in thin but sturdy-looking leather armor, greaves, and gauntlets, each overlapping rectangle intricately fringed and burned in decorative spirals. Only their heads were left bare, perhaps so that their oversized ears would be free of any hindrance. She wondered if they were able to use echolocation like real bats.

The way became steep. Unlike all the passages Tara and Aguilar had traveled through to get there, this one had clearly been fashioned; at the end of a short incline, a set of stairs spiraled upward between perfectly vertical walls, each stone step smooth and even. When they got to the top, Tara was surprised to find a door in front of them. One of the lead guards turned a key and pushed. The thick panels creaked open on rusty hinges.

Beyond was a dizzying view across yet another enormous cavern. This one, however, was even bigger than the cathedral, at least in terms of how long and wide it was—she could not even see the ends in the distance—and the entire cavity was filled with blue-green light. At first, Tara could not make out the source of the luminescence, but as her eyes adjusted and she squinted up at the vaulted ceiling, she saw something that looked like faintly glowing moss or fungus. Whatever it was, the substance sprawled across the entire ceiling and more than halfway down the walls, producing so much light she could see color, albeit not quite in the normal spectrum. Had she been told she was outside, in a moonlit pasture, she would have believed it. Her gaze drifted to the ground passing underneath her, and the sight of her foot hanging down with its unraveling palm-frond shoe sent a burst of homesickness and despair though her, mixed with a strange sense of claustrophobia.

After going through the doorway, the six escorts turned left and took them along a broad, straight road that paralleled the base of the vaguely concave wall. Tara found herself staring upward, past Aguilar's bobbing head; it was the easiest position for her neck. In addition to the glowing moss, other plants and fungus grew in the wall from cracks and holes and anywhere else they'd been able to gain a foothold. The fungus-looking growths were not like anything Tara had ever seen before; they didn't have a traditional mushroom or shelf fungus shape, though they were predominantly gray or white or, in the case of one species, covered in charcoal splotches. Silvery tendrils or roots hung down in clumps from the distant ceiling, some easily several yards in length.

Lining the road were row upon row of tall, hedge-like plants with white stems thicker than Tara's arm. These climbed and spiraled around each other, as if vying for top spot, and ended in a canopy of brown petal-like surfaces bigger than an elephant's ear. From her vantage point in Aguilar's arms, Tara could just see over them. Field upon field of the plants spread across the subterranean valley, making her wonder if they were a crop of some kind. She spotted scores of squat round structures nestled among the fields, many of them with lit windows and curls of blue smoke drifting up from hidden chimneys. As they passed, she heard voices, too; there were people working along the lanes between the fields or carrying bundles from place to place. These were not bat-shaped like their escorts, but human-looking. On closer inspection, however, she could see that some of them did have grotesque appearances; none with blurry faces, but several with irregular protrusions: tool-like appendages, extra arms, even one monstrosity with a back that extended below its muscular shoulders into a flat, rectangular surface on which the thing carried a basket that was piled high with black artichoke-looking objects.

Tara felt the anxiety building again, spidering up between her shoulder blades, invading her chest, penetrating the flanks of her mind like worms through meat. Her back was killing her, and she felt sure she'd injured her spine. The terror of permanent disability was only slightly mitigated by the vague idea that whatever happened to her "body" here might not have happened to her actual body, back in the land of the living. But the uncertainty and fear were generating a pressure in the back of her mind that threatened to overwhelm her. She had that sickening, tipping feeling; her sense of control was beginning to slip away. She wanted to ask the general to stop, maybe see if he would put her down so that she could shut her eyes for a moment and get grounded, get centered. Then, hopefully, the wave of anxiety would pass. That sort of thing sometimes worked.

But she knew he wouldn't, because these creatures were clearly not going to put up with any dawdling. Besides, they only seemed concerned with Aguilar's presence, and not in a good way, which meant they would probably consider her to be quite disposable. Absently, she groped at the spot below her hip where a pocket would be if she were wearing pants. She needed something to hold, preferably something elastic that she could squeeze. Or something smooth she could rub. Her eyes darted to the sides of the path, but the rocks there were too big, and she would have to ask him to stop to pick one up anyway. She took a deep breath and closed her eyes, biting down hard on her lip until she tasted blood, doing her level best to ignore the rising panic.

The road took them to a T-intersection. Without waiting for their escorts, Aguilar was already turning right, apparently aware of exactly where to go. His long legs picked up the pace, and the elite guards shuffled to keep in front of him. The dirt path was narrow, and broken here and there by little meandering brooks; each of these they crossed by hopping over a series of raised flat stones. Powerless to do much else, Tara stared up at the "sky". In the distance overhead, the blue-green moss and hanging white tendrils had grown across the cavern ceiling in a dazzling, almost starlike display, their very randomness creating the impression of pattern and order when taken in as a whole.

At the fourth brook crossing, one of the elite guards motioned for Aguilar to wait while their commander, Ion, leaped into the air and flapped a short distance upstream. He landed in front of one of the round abodes, this one significantly larger than the others they had passed. As his feet touched the ground, a door opened. Ion ducked inside, shutting it behind him. Moments later he re-emerged to shout an order to the other bat-things, and they ushered Aguilar and Tara onto an overgrown trail that meandered along the stream and through a thicket of light-green, waist-high fungal bushes. The house stood on the other side of a clearing that was covered in thick, spongy moss, and was nestled between a pair of landscaped gardens full of otherworldly subterranean plants or fungal growths—Tara wasn't sure which.

A man who looked to be in his early sixties was watching them approach from the doorway. He was slim, and not much taller than Tara, with salt and pepper hair graying at the temples. The smooth teak skin of his high cheekbones reflected mosslight, and he had deep-set eyes that returned a look of intelligent curiosity. She looked away in embarrassment.

"The prodigal son? Or the bearer of bad news?" the man called out as they approached.

"Both. And neither," Aguilar said, coming to a stop a few yards in front of the house. "And perhaps both."

"And this is?"

"Tara. She stays with me."

The man nodded slowly, still studying her. His gaze seemed to take everything in: her attempts to hide behind her hanging coils, her ragged damp dress, her makeshift shoes, the scars on her arms. She was too exhausted and in pain to bother trying to cover them. Ion and the other bat-things had placed themselves at casual attention about the mossy yard, but the atmosphere felt anything but relaxed.

"Tara. Welcome. I am Kavi. You will hear my people call me 'Elder', but that appellation always makes me feel old and feeble." The man's smile was disarming. Off to the side, Ion seemed to bristle.

Kavi returned his attention to Aguilar. "And are you still hell-bent on executing your one-man crusade against the pleasures of the palate?"

The glass man shifted, seeming to sigh. "I have never been against eating, Kavi. I simply choose not to waste time with such fanciful sentimentalities myself. You know this."

The Elder chuckled and shook his head. "Luto, Luto, Luto. Still just as touchy as ever. And thus, the dance begins anew, of me stirring and you reacting. Come, old friend; we have much to discuss, and Aarov has cooked up one of his delicious stews. I imagine Tara here might like to partake, even if you will not."

"Elder," Ion said and took a step forward, his bat face red and his tone incredulous. "No puede.... Surely you cannot ignore the crimes of this *traidor*."

The Elder raised an eyebrow at the commander. "I was not aware that it was within your purview to question what I can or cannot do, soldier."

Ion bowed his head, quickly backtracking. "No, Señor, I simply mean...."

"You simply mean to say, 'My sincerest apologies, Señor, for being so presumptuous right here at the doorstep of your own home.'" Any trace of humor was long gone; the Elder's tone had turned to steel.

"My sincerest apologies, Señor. That was not my intention," Ion said, his voice subdued but still with an indignant edge to it.

"Relax, commander. You are not in possession of all the facts. You will join us inside so that I can explain everything to you."

Ion's face looked like it was about to explode. "¿Y la chica? She is an intruder, with no prior permission to enter our realm. The law is the law, Señor."

218

The Elder bowed his head and spread his hands. "You are not wrong, Ion. The law *is* the law. We will get to the bottom of why they have come, and we absolutely will prosecute to the law's fullest extent if we collectively deem it appropriate. That I promise you."

Ion finally seemed satisfied. Though he continued to scowl suspiciously at Tara and Aguilar, he did not offer any further protests.

"Come," the Elder said. "Let us go inside and warm ourselves by the fire." Addressing the other guards, he spoke a few words in another language—not Spanish this time, Tara was pretty sure—and they gave a strange salute with their wings, leaped into the air, and flew back in the direction of the stairway.

Smiling, the Elder gestured toward the open door. Aguilar and Ion both had to stoop to fit through, the glass man turning sideways to keep from bumping Tara's head against the doorframe. The smaller man followed them in, pulling the door closed behind him.

Inside, it was indeed warm, despite the spaciousness of the large round room. In the center was a cozy stone hearth, with a large steaming copper pot hanging over it. A tall, slender man with white hair tended to the fire, squatting on his haunches while creating a spot for a new log over the coals. The smoke rose through a hole in the ceiling directly above the hearth, and whatever was cooking smelled divine. Tara felt suddenly famished.

"Your companion, she is injured?" the Elder asked, pointing to a cushioned hardwood sofa whose six short legs were inlaid with a latticework of what appeared to be ivory or bone.

Aguilar walked over to it and carefully laid Tara down, propping one of the pillows under her head. "Her back. From the falls, most likely."

The sofa was close enough to the fire that Tara could feel the heat on her skin. She shivered. She hadn't been aware of just how wet and cold she was feeling until that moment. The general sat at the other end of the sofa, just past where he'd stretched her feet out, and leaned forward with his elbows on his knees, rubbing his hands together like an old man come in from the cold. She could not imagine that the glass man actually felt cold, so she wondered if he was doing it out of habit.

The Elder approached and reached down to touch her shoulder, pausing just before he made contact. "May I?"

"What are you going to do?" Tara recoiled.

"I'll heal you, if you let me, daughter," he said. He had kind eyes, and his face was an intricate landscape of smile lines.

"I'm not your daughter." That liar Fin had had kind eyes, too.

The Elder laughed out loud, as though she had just said the funniest thing he'd heard in a very long time.

"It's just an expression," Aguilar rumbled at her. Tara glanced over to see him nodding at her encouragingly.

"Alright then," she said hesitantly. "I guess."

The Elder placed his hand down between her shoulder blades and gently touched her bony spine with his fingertips. He then pressed them against her temples, closed his eyes, and rubbed them in a tight circular pattern. The pressure released as he let go, and instantly, the debilitating pain in her back was gone.

She sat bolt upright. "How did you…?"

The Elder winked at her as he took a seat on an ordinary-looking stool across from Aguilar, his back to the hearth. "Aarov, dear, we have guests," he called out over his shoulder.

Tara experimented with lifting her arms and stretching her back. She stood, then sat back down, then stood and sat back down again, gob smacked. Everything seemed to be in working order. In her peripheral vision, she saw Ion eyeing her skeptically. She stopped and hunched forward with her elbows on her knees and her feet together, avoiding eye contact.

The white-haired man calmly finished placing a last log on the fire. He then straightened, dusted off his hands, and walked over to join them, carrying a pair of stools with him. After blowing one nostril unceremoniously, he placed a stool in front of Ion and plonked himself down on the other. Ion waited until the man was settled, then took a seat, the points of his folded wings towering over his head.

"Luto. Long time." Aarov nodded from his stool before throwing Tara a cheerful wave.

"This is Tara," the Elder said.

"Yepo. Nice to meet you, Tara." Aarov grinned, tossing his bangs aside. "Welcome to our humble abode."

The man had a goofy, down-to-earth way about him. His voice was loud and straightforward, and he gave the impression of a person who would never lose his shit over the little things. Tara felt instantly comfortable with him.

She waved meekly. "Hi."

He copied her meek wave and mouthed a sassy 'hi' in return, teasing her. She smiled and looked down. The white hair belied his age; up close, he looked quite fit and energetic, and could have easily passed for someone closer to her mother's generation.

"So, my friend. Let us not beat around the bush, as they say. You would not have come all this way, after all this time, unless you had good reason. Now out with it," the Elder said, his dark brown eyes glinting in the firelight. "What has happened?"

Aguilar glanced at Ion. The elite guard commander's erect posture hinted at heightened alertness, his batlike features smoldering with scarcely concealed contempt.

The Elder followed Aguilar's gaze. "Oh, him? You can say anything in front of Ion. He has become my second-most trusted advisor in all matters, military and otherwise. He has proven himself loyal."

"Has he," the glass man said, sounding surprised. "Well then. In that case, Commander Ion, you have my full congratulations." He turned back to the Elder. "Should we go ahead and tell him then? Perhaps he would take it better coming from you, Kavi."

The Elder nodded slowly, scrutinizing Aguilar's refracting face for several seconds. Presently, he turned and addressed his lieutenant, sounding suddenly cheerful and upbeat. "You see, ever since he left, our old friend Luto here has been deep under cover."

Ion's narrowed eyes flitted from face to face, blinking rapidly. "What do you mean?"

"Our own little man inside," Aarov drawled as though impersonating a character from a movie.

"A spy, Ion," the Elder said. "Luto went to the Cradle to spy for us."

"To spy… on The Mother?"

"Indeed."

"More to keep an eye out than anything else," Aguilar put in.

The Elder nodded. "Exactly. And his instructions were to report back if—and only if—something happened, or he learned of something, that might pose a threat to our existence. We had already lost our home once; that was very fresh on our minds, and not something anyone wanted to go through again, as I know you understand very well."

Ion's eyes searched the ground, as if trying to find sense in what he was hearing. "But… Señor… this cannot be true. Everyone knows this man abandoned us, right when we needed all hands; right when we were at our weakest. One of our most tenacious assets, and he up and *left*."

The Elder spread his hands. "Yes, things were falling apart, and he left. Pretended to be done with us; departed for greener pastures. And now it is my turn to offer my sincerest apologies, commander. You see, at the time, The Mother had nearly as many spies in her employ as Xie, so we could not be sure whom to trust. We decided it would be prudent to restrict all knowledge of the plan to the three of us." His finger drew a triangle in the air, pointing to Aarov, Aguilar, and himself.

Ion stood, clearly agitated. "You kept this from the small Council?"

"Sit down, commander" the Elder said calmly. "This happened before the small Council had even been established."

"Bygones," Aarov piped.

Ion's face was red with indignation and humiliation. He scowled at Aguilar. "And how do we know he's not a double agent?"

"We have no evidence either way." The Elder sighed. "However, in my heart, I know."

The elite commander glanced toward the door, and for a brief moment, Tara thought he was going to storm out. He glared suspiciously from face to face for half a minute. Then, visibly forcing himself to calm down, he made a formal bow toward the Elder, performed the wing salute the others had done outside, and sat down heavily on his stool. From there he glowered at the ground between his legs in silence, eyes jittering left and right as though a thousand thoughts were racing through his mind.

It's not over, Tara thought to herself. She did not trust him.

"Good." The Elder turned to Aguilar. "Now then, what has happened, or what have you learned?"

Without further ado, the general pointed at Tara. "You see the necklace she wears. That is a tracker, placed 'round her neck by a freelancer."

The Elder shrugged. "By the laws of the Cradle, it is not a crime in that realm to wish to keep track of one's property."

Tara bristled at the word "property", but kept her mouth shut.

"And as I understand it," the Elder continued, "freelancers in the farmer trade need to protect themselves against loss more than most, as they have neither guild nor government to fall back on."

"It does more than track," Aguilar said.

"And what does it do?"

"It hides what she is."

Suddenly curious, the white-haired man, Aarov, stood and walked across to squat down and squint at the necklace. "May I?"

Tara nodded, lifting it for him. He slowly ran the glass-coated silver beads between his fingers, smirking. "Nice handiwork, Luto."

A stunned look came into Aarov's eyes. He straightened and walked back to his seat, locking eyes with the Elder and blinking slowly. The Elder's brows knitted briefly, then he opened his own eyes wide in amazement. "We can see that someone has gone to great lengths... someone with *enormous* tenacity... superior even to my own...." Realization seemed to hit him. "This... this is The Mother's doing?"

Aguilar nodded. "The freelancer I mentioned is in her employ."

The Elder frowned. "She must have doubled her tenacity."

"More than doubled," Aguilar said.

Tara was staring at her feet. The ground under them was solid, and so was the sofa beneath her weight; she could feel her body pressing down on the felt-like cushion covers, and the wood edge was hard beneath her fingertips. She took a deep breath and closed her eyes, swearing to herself that the air filling her lungs was air. It could not be anything else. When she opened her eyes again, she made herself focus on the steam rising from the copper pot.

The Elder's brow furrowed. "But why? Why expend such a colossal amount of tenacity on a—pardon, my dear— a mere farmer girl? I mean you no offense, young Tara. We all do what we can to remain attached to this world, and many have no choice but to work for others for a time."

Aguilar folded his arms and leaned back against the pillows, his long legs crossed at the ankles. "Do you remember the early years, Kavi? When we first began to realize that we had underestimated our enemy. He and his forces had gathered so much more tenacity than we'd ever dreamed possible, and we were feeling absolutely stumped, remember? And even then, in retrospect, the extent of his onslaught was only just becoming apparent. We brainstormed and brainstormed, searching for a plan that stood half a chance of defeating him."

The Elder nodded. "Yes, I remember well. And in the end, we came up with the best strategy we could have. I've replayed this history in my mind many a time since, and I have no regrets."

"None," Aarov said.

Ion grunted in agreement.

"Nor I." Aguilar nodded gravely. "But there was a moment, when we were at our wits' end, and you joked about a 'what-if'."

"Remind me."

"It was after we'd decided to accept The Mother's offer of temporary alliance. We were in the Heart, standing around her big sand table, and you said something like, 'If only we could bring one of the living across. Then we would have more than enough tenacity to defeat Xie.'"

The Elder's lips parted. "Surely not...." He turned to gape at Tara with something akin to horror. "I was only... I was only being whimsical. Wishful thinking, nothing more. The stress had gotten to me."

Aguilar stared meaningfully at him.

The Elder seemed flustered. "But even if that were possible, *no one* would risk the consequences of doing such a thing. Least of all The Mother. She is wiser than all of us combined."

Aguilar's hollow sockets went around the room, gazing at them each in turn. "She has done it."

"The Mother has brought a...?" Ion sputtered, eyeing Tara nervously, wings unfolding slightly.

"Yes, she has," Aguilar said. "Rather, the freelancer has done it, with the help of The Mother's tenacity. Apparently a very clever and resourceful fellow, that one. Finlay MacCarthy is his name. In fact, from what I heard shortly before we left the Cradle, this whole thing was his idea in the first place. Although, my guess is The Mother must have given it some serious thought over the years, perhaps even tried it herself."

The Elder regarded Tara, eyes wide with astonishment, causing her to squirm under his gaze and look back down at her feet. "So... just to be clear... you mean to say that this girl is... *of the living.*"

"I do."

Kavi and Aarov exchanged a long look. Then the Elder straightened and turned back to Aguilar, suddenly tense. "You of course know what this means."

"I do."

The Elder's eyes flicked around the round room absently, as if he had misplaced something. "We will need to bring this matter to the Council."

"I thought you would be of that opinion, but hear me out first, please, old friend," Aguilar said, stressing the last two words. "I have promised this girl sanctuary. My main purpose in rescuing her was to keep such a powerful weapon out of The Mother's hands. But just as importantly, I believe we also owe it to Tara to honor the oath I made to her. *I* owe it to her."

Weapon? Tara frowned. When she glanced over at Ion, he looked away immediately, but she thought she'd seen hunger in his eyes. She scooted a couple of inches closer to Aguilar.

"You know even better than I do how dangerous it would be if The Mother were to acquire such a wellspring of tenacity," the glass man continued in his porcelain baritone. "I think we can all agree that the very world is at risk, with every moment that this living being remains here. The potential...."

"...The potential is so destructive, it could send us *all* to the Antim," Aarov finished for him. "Everything—gone."

"Yes. And that is why it's my strong belief that we should find a way to send her back across. Whatever it takes."

The fire crackled as everyone sat in taut silence. Tara concentrated on suppressing the hope that was beginning to bloom in her chest. She needed to push it back into the dark where it couldn't lie to her, break her mind, take her down by the ankles, make her sink.

"And you think I have the power to do this," the Elder mumbled. The kindness in his deep-set eyes seemed to have drained away. In its place was a troubled look.

"He knows you do, dear," Aarov said.

Aguilar spread his hands. "We could pool our tenacity, but you would be the key, of course—"

Ion stood suddenly, wings trembling behind him. "Elder, may I speak." It was more of a statement than a question.

The Elder sat up straight and nodded at the commander.

Ion's cat eyes went from face to face, though not to Tara's, she noticed. He cleared his throat, a coarse, guttural sound. "If this is indeed such a weapon, Señor, then should we not... use it? This could be our chance, our only real window, to take back our realm. To take back that which was annexed from us. And...." He frowned and shook his head.

"Go on," the Elder prompted.

"Thank you, Señor. I mean no disrespect. But is it really our fate to be banished to these caverns forever?"

"These caverns are our home now," the Elder said.

Seeming to have lost interest, Aarov got up and went back to tending the fire.

"Our home, si, but it wasn't by choice. What was ours was *taken* from us. And now we can get it back! Señor."

For a long time, the Elder just stared at the fire, lost in thought. Everyone else seemed to be waiting for him to speak. Finally, he stood and turned to Aguilar. "I hear your concern, my friend; please do not think otherwise. You are suggesting that we send this *citta* back to the living in order to rid the Afterrealms of the threat she poses, as well as to remove all possibility of her falling into The Mother's hands or—worse—into Xie Yuanzhan's. I see your point, I truly do. And I happen to agree with it."

Ion shook his head again, tightly, but held his tongue.

The Elder eyed him sidelong and continued. "But I cannot make such a decision unilaterally. That is not our way."

"Nope, not our way," Aarov echoed from the fire.

"So, yes, Luto, while I do respect your opinion and see the logic in it, it is only one opinion, and this matter is out of my hands. I'm afraid we must bring it to the Council for discussion—the small Council, of course; we'll only inform the general session once we have decided what to do. And until then, none of us," he said, leveling his eyes first at the elite guard commander and then at Tara, "*not one of us* will breathe a word of this matter, or of your true nature, to anyone outside this room."

"Yes sir," Tara mumbled.

Aguilar stood and bowed deeply. "Elder." As he sat back down on the cushioned sofa, he angled his glass face slightly to look at Tara, seeming about to say something. Then he leaned forward to stare mutely into the flames, and the reflections dancing across his facets made it even harder for her to guess what he was thinking.

Chapter Thirteen

A little fish, perhaps two inches long, was hiding behind a boot-sized rock in the brook, facing upstream, its tiny pectoral fins waving in the current. Now and then it would dart out to nab something floating downstream before hurrying back to cover. Bright turquoise lines ran along its sides, fanning out to the blunt ends of a forked, see-through tail, and when the fish turned, Tara could see it had a shiny white belly, though its back was as black as the rock. Delicate sprouts of faintly luminescent seaweed grew here and there between the smaller stones of the streambed, bending with the flow of the water to flatten just below the surface, their foot-long streamers undulating back and forth, back and forth, back and forth, forever pointing downstream.

She remembered staring into the maelstrom from the bridge, watching those massive green tongues of water race over the edge. She remembered sensing the nothingness, the calmness the nothingness had presented, as well as how tempting it had been to just let it take her. The idea had been clear, simple. She'd have released herself, and all the pain and confusion would've gone away. Her life would have ended, of course, but that would've been okay.

The end would have made sense, in a way. Like a neatly folded napkin, or how shiny and reflective a slate surface always appeared after being swept free of debris.

She recalled other encounters with that feeling of nothingness as well, though she hadn't had a name for it yet. She remembered wanting it desperately; craving it. She remembered *needing* it. Needing its simplicity, its tranquility, its peace. It had been right there in front of her, plain to see. In a curving stretch of train tracks, a gleaming razor blade, a midnight balcony. Ostensibly easy to follow, but fear had always stopped her from committing.

And now here she was, either lost forever to madness or genuinely on the far side of death itself.

In truth, she had stopped wondering whether she had lost her mind; everything she'd experienced had just been too real, too constant, without even the slightest reprieve. There had been zero moments of clarity or sanity, nor of lucid wakefulness for that matter. She wasn't asleep, and she wasn't crazy. She was something else. Not dead, but with the dead.

She was with the dead, and they saw her as either a weapon or a curse. She was with the dead, who right then were gathered in a big fortress on the far side of the dimly glowing cavern, deciding her fate. Deciding whether she would be allowed to go home or be forced to remain a prisoner.

If she had jumped from the bridge, she wouldn't have been able to go home anyway. Would she have ended up here? Or in some other place?

She felt a bit numb. It was a feeling she was getting tired of. She wished in her bones that she were just a little fish, simple-minded, existing in a simple little world of breathing cool water and finding morsels and darting between light and shadow.

"I like your dress. Did you form it yourself?"

Squatting on an outcropping not five feet to her right was a little girl, staring at her intently. Tara was so startled she lost her balance, very nearly falling face-first into the brook. When she had caught herself and found her footing, she stood and frowned. The girl appeared to be around eight or nine years old, with hazel eyes and straight, shoulder-length blonde hair that looked almost platinum in the mosslight.

"Hi. Who are you?" Tara asked, keeping her tone guarded.

"I'm Jenny. You're Tara."

"Yes," Tara nodded, looking around. Behind them, splinters of light from the single window on the near side of the round house shone through gaps in the fungal shrubs of the landscaped garden, and the spongy moss lawn stretched unbroken to the bank of the brook. There was no one else around. "Where are your parents, little girl?"

Jenny shrugged. "At a meeting. They needed someone to look after you. I volunteered."

"You volunteered, did you?" The girl seemed quite mature and confident for her age. Tara scanned the fields on the far side of the stream, then searched again in the direction of the house, but they were alone.

The child nodded, smiling cheerfully. "So?"

"So what?"

"Did you?"

"Did I what?"

"Form it yourself."

"Form it? This dress?" Tara ran her fingers over the stiff, dirty fabric. The once bright white borders had gone brown, the hem was torn and frayed, and the skin of her knees was visible through various rips and holes. Much of the middle was stained with old blood. "I don't know what you mean."

The girl did not appear convinced. Tilting her head, she smiled that conspiratorial sort of smile a child might use when she's on to the fact that a grownup is kidding with her, and she is waiting for the grownup to stop playing around and tell the truth.

"I was given this dress. It was… a gift." Remembering the Elder's words, Tara realized she should be careful not to reveal too many details about where she'd come from, even to a child.

"So you traded for it?"

"Sure. I traded for it. Where do you live, Jenny?"

"Well I think it's pretty. And your eyes are pretty, too. See? We're alike," Jenny said, touching the tips of her index fingers to the freckles she had on her pale, dimpled cheeks.

Tara found herself smiling. "Well, I suppose we are," she said, mimicking the girl's gesture by touching her fingers to her own freckles at the corners of her eyes. "Freckle sisters."

"Freckle sisters!" The child's gleeful laugh rang out over the clearing, and for a second, it almost seemed to make the seaweed in the brook glow a fraction more brightly; but when Tara glanced directly at it, the bluish light it emitted was just as dim as it had been before. Feeling silly, she looked back at Jenny's face. The little girl was still grinning at her.

"So where did you say you live?"

"Over there, most of the time." Jenny shrugged and bobbed her head toward the round house.

"Most of the time?"

"I've been with them a long time, so I sometimes take breaks and go visiting. What about you? Where are you from?"

Tara didn't know what to say. The girl's curious eyes were relentless. She decided to go with honesty. "I live in a place called Forestview."

"I've never heard of it. Is that in another cavern?"

"No, it's... up on the surface."

Jenny tilted one side of her face away and narrowed her eyes in another playful, disbelieving look.

Tara thought it might be safest to change the subject. "Hey, I have a question. People keep calling me 'farmer'. Do you know what that means?"

Jenny looked down and picked at a patch of dirt on the bank. Tara was not used to seeing a frown on the girl's face. "Yes, I do. Intimately. I used to be one, too. I'm so sorry that happened to you. It's not an enviable position to be in, to say the least."

Intimately. Enviable position. Tara marveled at the child's vocabulary. "Why not?"

The girl scrunched her face at her. "Why *not?!* Because, it's just not. Who in their right mind would *choose* to be a farmer?"

Tara frowned. "Okay. But what do you mean you used to be one? You mean your parents used to be farmers?"

Jenny straightened and gave her another strange look. "No, my dads have never been farmers. Before I met them, I was one for twenty-two very long years, over at the main palace in Prosperity. It felt more like a couple hundred. During the war, Aarov rescued me and brought me here."

It took a moment for Tara to realize her mouth was gaping open. She closed it and continued to stare, examining the girl head to toe. "You're older than you look."

"However did you guess," Jenny smirked, but with a playful glint in her eyes.

Tara mulled this over. "Sorry, I'm not used to..." she began, then reconsidered. She shifted her eyes over to the stream. The fish was no longer hiding near its rock; it seemed to have moved on, perhaps frightened by the sounds of their voices. "I just mean, I'm still feeling pretty tired from the journey down here. So I guess I'm not thinking straight."

The girl smiled and nodded, but her curiosity only seemed to intensify, and she was now scrutinizing her as one might a previously undiscovered species. Tara wondered if she had said too much.

She flicked her eyes down to Jenny's little hands. "So why... why do you look so young?"

Jenny shrugged. "I go back and forth. Sometimes I save up a bunch of grip and use it to make myself look like an adult, most often in the prime of womanhood, all beautiful and strong and elegant and commanding and what have you.

But then I get to feeling like a hypocrite, because there's always a few things missing; like, I'll never truly know what it's like to have children, be a mother. Just for example. It doesn't matter most of the time, but I do sometimes dwell on stuff like that, I must admit."

"Oh," Tara said. "How old were you when you…."

"Died?" Jenny finished for her. "I was nine."

The thought of never experiencing anything past childhood both horrified and depressed Tara. At the same time, she felt a vague sense of envy. "I'm sorry."

"Sorry? Don't be sorry. I mean sure, it's sad I never got to experience certain things. But then, you grow up wherever you are, no matter what you're doing. You have to. You know?"

Tara nodded, pretending she knew what the girl was talking about.

Jenny continued to study her. "But no, I usually default back to this appearance, or something similar. Not because it was my death form, but because I find it makes a lot of *citta* underestimate me. And I mean a *lot*. And that can be fun." She smiled mischievously.

Death form. Tara thought of the monstrosities she had seen at the docks, at the bonfire, among the fields while being carried through the cavern. She wanted to ask about them but did not want to make the girl suspicious.

She thought subterfuge might be best. "I still don't get why anyone in their right mind would want to look the way they looked when they died. Especially if they had a violent death."

Jenny giggled. "The age-old argument. Yeah well, I guess some *citta* do it for personal reasons. Me? I can't imagine wanting to have a hammer sticking out of my head all the time."

They both laughed. Tara was beginning to like her. She seemed funny, easy to be around, if a little strange. And the fact that she was a woman in a girl's body somehow made her seem more vulnerable. Tara found herself feeling a bit sorry for her.

"So what about…. Is this how you looked when you were a farmer?"

Jenny went abruptly sullen, lips pursed in irritation.

Tara realized she was in way over her head. "I'm sorry. Did I say something wrong? I meant no offense. I'm just tired, like I said—"

"It's okay," Jenny said cheerfully. "The important thing is I'm not one anymore, and neither are you. Right? Otherwise, you wouldn't be here."

"…Right."

Now the girl was frowning at Tara, a doubtful look spreading across her features.

"Right," Tara repeated. "Because I left that job. Because, well like you said, being a farmer is not something anyone would choose to be," she fished, feeling curiosity getting the better of her. There was so much she did not understand about this place.

"Of course not!" Jenny exclaimed in a burst of exasperation. "Who would *choose* such a miserable existence? Always teetering on the brink of oblivion, just barely scraping by in that in-between state, farming tenacity for some selfish arrogant bastard for months on end until your body goes all fuzzy and insubstantial? And never having enough extra grip to fully form it back to normal, no matter how long and hard you might work to try to scrape together that tiny bit extra, except of course once in a blue moon when your master deigns to give you a day or two off? And then afterward you feel stupid for falling for it, for ever having *been* so vain, because that little bit of extra grip you gathered from soaking your arms in the River water during your time off never lasts long anyway, 'cause your master inevitably gets tired of seeing your face look anything but dismal, and of course he then has to drive home the point that as his *farmer* you don't *deserve* to have the form you want, not even your death form, and so he ends up siphoning it right off anyway, and then drains you even further just out of spite, laughing as he does it, taking you right to the edge, leaving you starving and half mad and ugly as sin, until even you yourself become convinced from looking at yourself through your own pathetic eyes that this is the only fate a disgusting grub like you is worthy of? Always feeding the master, feeding the master, feeding the master, wearing thin over and over and over until you start wishing someone would just fix you right, put two hands against your skin and be done with it, send you straight to the Antim in a puff of smoke just so you can escape all the self-loathing? Now who in the hell would deliberately submit to such an existence? *No thanks.*"

When she was done, the girl was breathing hard and had a wild look in her eyes. After a moment, she hung her head and picked absently at a cluster of tiny toadstools. "Sorry. I didn't mean to get so carried away there."

"It's okay. I get it." She didn't, but she recognized overwhelming anxiety when she saw it.

"I… I try not to think about it; it was a lifetime ago. But the memories still upset me." Jenny looked back at the ground, yellow-white bangs obscuring most of her face like half-drawn curtains.

"I'm sorry you went through that, Jenny. It sounds horrible. I guess I've been lucky; I haven't been… I mean, I wasn't one for anywhere near that long." Tara studied the girl in front of her, wondering how old she was, how long she had been… *dead.*

Jenny looked up to meet her gaze. "Yeah? How long were you one? In the Cradle, right? Did Luto save you?"

Tara nodded and looked at the ground, feeling herself sinking deeper and deeper into the lie. "Yeah, he, ah… he bought me."

"What do you mean he bought you? He traded for you? Why would he do that?"

"I mean… he…."

Several huge shapes obscured the light from the "sky". Startled, Tara looked up to see four elite guards sailing overhead in formation, their enormous bat wings fully extended. One of them peeled off and spiraled down to the yard, glancing over his shoulder at her and Jenny as he landed, his momentum carrying him forward a few steps toward the door of the house. "Jenny. A word." It was Ion.

Jenny stood hastily and smoothed her pants with her hands, a very adult-like frown pulling at her young features. "To be continued. It was nice to meet you, Tara." She then hurried across the yard toward the house, skirting around the edge of the garden.

When Tara got up to follow, Ion shook his head and pointed a taloned finger at where they had been seated. "Not you. You wait there."

"Did they decide...?" Tara ventured.

Ignoring her, Ion stalked to the door, yanked it open, and ducked inside.

Without stopping, Jenny did a half turn to give Tara a bewildered look and a shrug, then disappeared after him.

Tara hugged her knees to her chest, feeling suddenly chilly, which in turn made her wonder whether she was *really* feeling chilly or if it was just habit, imagination. She couldn't wrap her head around why, if this wasn't her body, it felt exactly *like* her body. *Pain, cold, hunger. Emotions.* It made no sense. But none of it would matter if the Elder and his Council had decided to send her home. She peered at the closed door again, then over her shoulder at the path that led back through the bushes and along the brook. She was trying not to let herself get too excited at the prospect, but was failing utterly.

The door opened and Jenny walked out, closing it behind her. As she swept her blonde bangs from her eyes, she glanced sidelong at Tara, then straightened and waved, apparently having seen that Tara was looking at her. Then the frown returned, and she shoved her hands in her pants pockets and walked purposefully down the path in the direction of the road.

The wave had seemed rather reserved when compared to the cheerful enthusiasm Jenny had shown earlier. Tara wondered if the girl had gotten in trouble for talking to her. She stared at the door for a while, expecting Ion to emerge soon after, but it remained closed.

She didn't know what to do; she was desperate to learn what the small Council had decided, but could not make herself go inside. The thought of being alone in a room with the fierce commander unnerved her.

On pins and needles, she stood and looked around for a minute, then wandered over to the landscaped garden. There she sat on a stone bench beside one of the weird fungal bushes. It had twisting, knobby stem-branches that were studded with large, gilled blossom-like structures that might have been orange in normal light.

On the ground below it she noticed a scattering of olive-shaped objects, each about the size of a small chicken egg. She bent down to pick one of them up. It was spongy to the touch, with a porous surface. She squeezed. The strange spore pod—or whatever it was—was firm enough to give a satisfying resistance, and collapsed almost like a rubber ball before slowly recovering its shape. Tara squeezed it three more times. The thing was apparently quite durable; it expanded back to shape each time without crumbling or splitting. She held on to it.

Even though the ubiquitous moss light and the vast height of the ceiling above went a long way toward making the cavern feel less cave-like, Tara still felt very aware of the lack of real sky above her. She had never been in a giant indoor sports arena, and knew that those were nowhere near this size, but it was mildly reassuring to pretend she was under a human-built dome, perhaps some giant international greenhouse constructed as an agricultural experiment for exploring new strains of mushrooms to help solve the world hunger crisis.

The world. Whatever that word meant, it was so much bigger, and so much smaller, than she could ever have imagined.

When they finally returned, Aguilar and the Elder had their heads bent in intense discussion, the shorter man taking swift steps to keep up with the general's long glass legs. Behind them, white-haired Aarov loped along the path, looking a lot more relaxed than his companions. He had his hands in his pockets and was gazing up at the distant ceiling, whistling softly. As they approached the round house, he threw a casual glance at Tara and beckoned her over with a toss of his head.

Hesitantly, heart suddenly pounding, she stood and walked over to join them. The others continued inside, but Aarov waited for her, holding the door open and smiling patiently. Tara dipped her head politely as she went in, mouth set in an anxious line.

Ion stood near one end of the sofa, his muscular body rigid. The expression on his bat-like face was hard to fathom, but he did not look happy. Over by the hearth, the Elder was stoking the coals, sending wafts of sparks and smoke upward. Aguilar sat on one of the taller stools, elbows on his knees and fingers steepled, head turned toward the door. As Tara entered and took a seat to the right of the door, she returned his gaze nervously for a second, then stared at her feet.

"I'm making tea," the Elder called over his shoulder. "Would you like some, young Tara?"

"No thank you, sir."

The Elder regarded her as he dropped a fat pinch of a dried substance into a pot and placed it on the flat surface atop the hearth. "You are no doubt eager to hear what has been decided, so I'll spare you any further suspense. After much discussion, the small Council has concluded that in light of the potential instability and danger your presence poses—not just to this realm, but to *all* the Afterrealms—the wisest course of action would be to send you back across."

Tara could hardly believe her ears. "Across?"

The Elder nodded. "Yes. Back, to the realm from which you came."

"Home," Aarov added, squinting his kind eyes at her.

"However," the Elder said. He paused to glance at Ion, who was staring stony-faced into the fire from the sofa. "The unfortunate truth is that there are at least two major obstacles to accomplishing such a feat. The first problem is, of course, the need to focus sufficient tenacity on such an endeavor. That we feel confident we can do, though it will take some coordination. The second problem, I'm afraid, may prove to be the larger of the two, for it involves our inherent lack of knowledge. You see, the fact remains that we do not know exactly *how* The Mother and her freelancer managed to bring you across. We do have a few theories, and we have discussed various possibilities to try, but the process will take time, you understand. And in the end, Tara, we cannot promise that we will succeed."

Tara nodded mutely, heart sinking.

"If she could do it, we can," Aguilar said.

The Elder dipped his head. "Indeed, Luto is right. The Mother figured it out, so in all probability, we will, too. Eventually. However, I thought you should know there are no guarantees. There is no precedent to go by, and since we cannot allow her to learn of your location, we cannot exactly go and ask her. One thing we do know is that her freelancer was able to travel to your world and back again. For all we know, however, for a still-living *citta* such as yourself, the major Conduits may prove to be one-way."

Tara felt herself sinking. She needed to understand more. If she had more knowledge, she might be able to help think of something. "Conduits, sir?"

"Call me Kavi, I told you! No need to be so formal in our home, eh Aarov."

"Aye-aye cap'n," the white-haired man said.

The Elder pretended he hadn't heard him. "The Conduits are what brought us all to the Afterrealms. Yourself included, if I understand correctly. You see, when a *citta*'s physical body dies, that *citta*'s consciousness is drawn through Conduits... streams, in a way, which is why we often refer to them as the 'Rivers'... and these flow straight toward the Antim. The journey begins slowly, but then the current, so to speak, accelerates as one crosses over and draws nearer the Antim. Do you follow?"

"I think so. And the Antim is like the ultimate death, after you die. The forevernothing. Right?"

"Well, to call it death would not be the most accurate—"

"Now, now, professor. Watch those academic tangents," Aarov cut him off.

The Elder grinned and spread his hands. "Just so. I will attempt to be more straightforward. My apologies, Tara. For all intents and purposes, yes, what you say is true. Or true enough."

Tara frowned. "You said people... *citta*... flowing along the conduits get pulled into the Antim. Okay, fine. But then how did you all get here?"

"By way of smaller Conduits. You see, shortly before the final, quickening approach to the Antim, there are channels that branch off and flow here to what we call the Afterrealms. These smaller Rivers route—"

"Have been routed," Aarov interrupted.

"*Route*," the Elder continued, arching a stern brow at his partner, "around and through the Realms. A bit like circling eddies, if you will. Eventually, these braids meet back up and resume their flow toward the forevernothing."

"They're more like detours," Aarov said.

Tara looked back and forth between him and the Elder.

"Some believe the realms were created deliberately—" the glass man explained.

"Many of us do," Aarov said.

"Many," Aguilar conceded. "Many believe the Rivers that lead here were… fashioned. Formed. But they are so ancient, no one really knows."

Steam was billowing from the pot. The Elder pulled it from the hot surface and poured three cups; one for Ion, one for Aarov, and one for himself, and then resumed his lecture. "So you see, young Tara, the vast majority of *citta* have no choice but to float obliviously along the main current straight into the Antim. Only a handful are either lucky or unlucky enough, depending on one's perspective, to get caught by the eddies, or these *detours*, if my esteemed colleague's theory is correct," he teased, making a face at his partner, "and end up on the shores of these our realms. Most *citta* arrive in our world with no memory of the journey, but enough have recalled snatches over the eons that we have been able to piece the process together. By now, we have quite a decent understanding of it. Mind you, when I came across sixty thousand years ago, the journey was much more arduous; there were no guilds or freelancers to fish me out of the drink and haul me aboard their ships. I had to wake up all by myself, realize what was happening, and swim as hard as I could to make it to a branching River lest I be sucked back into the flow of the major Conduits and taken to the forevernothing. Getting to the Afterrealms is *much* much easier now than it was back then."

Tara gaped. *Sixty thousand....*

"Yes, yes, old man. Things were always harder back in the good old days," Aarov chuckled, turning a playful look toward Tara. "And you got here by pure skill, my dear Kavi; no luck involved whatsoever. No helpful nudges from anyone or any*thing* else, either."

"Sixty *thousand...?*" Tara blurted.

"Oh, that's nothing," the Elder laughed. "I am but a tyke compared to some. The Mother is... well, no one knows for sure, but at least double my age."

Tara tried to let that sink in, but simply could not fathom existing for even a fraction of that many years. "Really?"

"She came to the Afterrealms a very long time ago," the glass man said.

"Too long," Ion grunted. It was the first sound he had uttered since Tara had entered the house.

"Many of us believe she was the first," the Elder said.

Aarov arched an eyebrow at him. "The first *citta* of homo sapiens origin, that is."

The Elder snorted.

"Wow." Tara hesitated. "So...."

"Speak your mind. You are among friends here."

Tara wasn't so sure. She deliberately avoided meeting the elite guard commander's severe, humorless eyes. "Um, so, how long will it be before you know?"

"Whether we can send you back home, you mean? That is hard to say, but in the meantime, you are safe with us here in the Caves." The Elder put his cup down and walked over to offer his hand. Tara took it hesitantly, and the old man grasped it in a firm, warm grip, staring steadily into her eyes. "Aarov and I will let you know personally, Tara, just as soon as we know ourselves. That I promise."

"Yes sir," Tara nodded glumly.

"Good. Now then, I can see that this is all quite distressing for you, so let us talk of other matters. We would like to offer you the bungalow attached to our home as a place to rest and recuperate while you wait." He pointed to a door on the far side of the hearth.

Tara looked over at Aguilar. He nodded at her reassuringly.

"You met our daughter Jenny earlier," the Elder continued. "She will be staying there with you, so if there is anything you need, just ask. She is happy to help, and quite capable."

"Understatement," Aarov drawled.

"However, I must insist on one thing, Tara," the Elder said, squeezing her hand, "and that is discretion. As we discussed before, you must be exceedingly careful not to divulge your true nature—where you are from, I mean—to anyone. Even to our daughter. This is a matter that *must* be kept between those of us in this room and the four other members of the small Council. Can I trust you to be discreet?"

Tara nodded, feeling anxious as she recalled her inquisitive conversation with the blonde-haired girl. "Yes sir," she resolved. She would have to get better at lying.

"Excellent. Alright, then. There is just one final item on the agenda." The Elder winked, squatting down to examine her feet. "That right there is some truly artful craftsmanship, Luto, but I believe we need to do something about Tara's shoes. Wouldn't you agree, Aarov?"

Aguilar kept his attention on the fire, but a long glass finger rose slowly upward from the middle of his right hand. Aarov chuckled, and Tara allowed herself a shy grin.

The elite guard commander continued to smolder in silence where he sat, his mouth twisted in a dark frown. Out of the corner of her eye, Tara watched as the toe of his leather boot twitched ever so slightly back and forth, erratically, like a nervous tic.

Chapter Fourteen

It almost felt normal. Like she was simply out for a walk after dinner, the sun just set and the neighborhood dimming in twilight. She could imagine the streets around her house with their eroded sidewalks, the parents beginning to call their kids inside; Mrs. Jeffers raking old snow-flattened leaves into a pile by the driveway, the patches of new grass poking up through the yellow. A squirrel darting up a tree, silhouetted with the still mostly bare branches against the sky; a cat disappearing under a wooden fence. If Tara closed her eyes, she could see and hear everything so vividly.

It was the shoes, she decided. And perhaps even more so, the jeans. She knew it was silly, but just wearing them made her feel like everything was going to be alright. Once she'd finally recovered from being gob smacked by how easily the Elder had formed the articles, from mid-air right in front of her as if by magic, and then handed the jeans to her all neat and folded like one might find a pair of pants on a shelf at a department store; and the shoes a lovely white pair of sneakers that fit her feet perfectly, with unblemished laces—once Tara had regained her composure and found her words, she'd thanked the old man profusely, eyes brimming. And truly, she felt grateful. It had been a wonderful kindness.

Aguilar had watched in silence, and Tara knew he must have been shaking his head inwardly; like food or drink, he would have called such things sentimental attachments. But she didn't care. It had been a genuinely lovely, thoughtful gift, designed to make her feel better, more at home.

In her view, everyone needed something to hold on to, something to make them feel safe and secure. She was starting to see how things worked here. As she understood it, *citta* formed objects by way of their tenacity, just as the Elder had formed her shoes and pants; and then those objects were traded for things others had formed elsewhere. She thought of the crates at the pier, being loaded into the dinghies, and could imagine now why so many *citta* were keen to barter with each other for such mundane-seeming items—clothing, delicacies, materials, baubles of one sort or another. They were reminders of life; they were familiar. Powerful *citta* with heaps of tenacity had formed entire realms just so that everything around them would feel more familiar. The Elder and other Cavedwellers had formed these caverns, and The Mother had fashioned the Cradle to her liking.

Tara got it; it made sense. Because right now, walking in these shoes, these pants, along quiet lanes through fields of bizarre fungi and even stranger crops, she felt just that little bit closer to normal, like not everything was going to swallow her whole or put irrevocable cracks in her sanity.

Like she might actually be able to get home. It was a huge source of comfort, so she could only imagine how much stronger an attachment the dead must feel toward familiar things.

Plus, she was a ton more comfortable in jeans; she had been incredibly relieved to get rid of that awful dress. She didn't think she would ever wear one again.

A man with long dreads and a red bandana waved from where he was harvesting objects that were blue and round, perhaps seedpods or a fruit of some sort. Tara waved back and smiled. She had seen him several times over the past few days, always working hard, always offering a friendly wave. Life in the Caves was good; everyone she had met seemed happy. Almost everyone.

A little farther on, she turned left at the junction she recognized by the tall spindly "tree" growing on the corner, and glanced up at the hundreds of purple bell-shaped spore bags hanging from its branches as she passed underneath. The path led up an incline and through some dense bushes before opening to a vale on the other side. To her right, a little creek flowed over a sandy rock shelf before dropping several feet into a deep, clear pool. Their own secret swimming hole.

Jenny was already there, wearing cut-off jeans shorts and a cute pink top. The pigtail braids Tara had put in for her that morning were still there.

Tara smiled. "So you changed your mind about jeans, huh?"

Jenny looked up in surprise. "Here so early! I thought you'd be another half hour yet."

"I got bored. Decided I might wander down and see if you were here early."

"Well, I am!" The girl-woman beamed, patting the flat patch of sandstone next to her. "Take a load off. And no, I haven't changed my mind; I just thought I should entertain your suggestion and give them a try. You know, for *science*," she said, imitating the Elder.

Tara sat down, replying with her own best imitation of him. "Yes, of course; for science." They both giggled.

Spreading above their heads like an enormous sun parasol was by far the largest mushroom formation Tara had seen anywhere. It spanned a good eight feet in diameter, and the underside rippled with thousands of musty-smelling gray-green gills. The first day they'd come to the swimming hole, it had taken her a while to grow used to the fragrance, but now she quite liked it.

"Wanna take a dip?" Jenny squeaked, jumping to her feet and already bounding to the edge. "Race ya!"

"Hey, not fair. You gave yourself a head start!" Tara complained, leaping up and sprinting over to the low cliff, her longer legs putting her even with Jenny just as the smaller girl was jumping.

Both of them landed at the same time, sending up plumes of water that splashed against the overhang. They surfaced laughing. Jenny kicked water at Tara's face, grinning mischievously.

"Hey!" Tara turned aside to avoid the onslaught, then cupped both hands and sent back a barrage of splashes.

The water fight continued intermittently, broken by the occasional teasing banter. At length they hauled themselves onto the opposite bank, Tara breathing hard as they walked sopping wet back around to their spot at the top of the rocks. When they sat down, Jenny did her heat-and-light trick, as Tara thought of it. The girl closed her eyes and drew in a deep breath, holding it until all the nearby fungus began to glow. After a minute, the giant mushroom cap above their heads was vibrating with a brilliant turquoise radiance, sending light and heat down to warm their skin.

Tara lay back with her eyes closed, basking in the warmth. It was almost like sunbathing. Not quite, but almost.

The past few days had been peaceful. She felt rested for the first time in as long as she could remember, and found herself in a state of constant wonder at the sights, the sounds, the sheer eye-popping variety of "nature" as she explored the subterranean farmland. Much of what she'd discovered puzzled her. What made the wild fungi grow? Where had the little fish come from? Were such creatures *citta*, too? Had life in the Afterrealms evolved? Could you even call it "life" if everything was dead? *Was* it dead? It would take years to understand it all.

Despite her curiosity, however, she earnestly hoped she never would, because she didn't want to be here that long.

"Hey, I've been wanting to ask you something, big sister."

It had become their little joke. Jenny was decades older than Tara, at least—she was always evasive whenever Tara asked just how old—yet she appeared several years younger. On their first night of hanging out together, Tara had said it felt like they were having a slumber party. After cautiously explaining what that was, Tara had at one point called her new friend "little sister". Jenny had responded in kind, calling Tara "big sister". They'd laughed and laughed, and the names had stuck.

Tara cracked an eye open. "Yeah? What's that, little sister?"

"One thing I've always been curious about."

"Go on." Tara knew Jenny would go on anyway. The girl could be quite forthright when there was something she wanted to talk about.

"What's it like going on a date?"

Tara's smile faded. She chose her words carefully. "You've never been on one?"

"Of course not, silly. I died when I was nine. The only boys I ever got to spend time with were my brothers."

"Oh, right." Tara felt very nervous. This wasn't the first time it had felt as though Jenny were fishing for something. But she knew she might be being paranoid; it had likely just been an innocent question. Tara suddenly felt a tinge of guilt for not being able to talk freely. She was no good at this stuff.

"Well?"

"Um," Tara stammered. "Well, I wish I had more to share in that department. But I'm not exactly, um, experienced, when it comes to boys."

"You've never been on a date, then?" Jenny was lying on her side, chin propped in one hand, staring at her intently.

"Well, I don't know if you could call it a 'date'. But I went to get ice cream with a guy after school one time."

"Ice cream," Jenny repeated slowly. "What's that?"

"It's… frozen milk and flavors and stuff. It's yummy."

Jenny sat up and crossed her legs, leaning over her to peer down into Tara's eyes, clearly intrigued. "And what happened?"

"I mean, what do you mean?"

"Did he kiss you?"

Tara felt herself blushing. "No, of course not."

"Why not? You're really pretty."

The further the conversation went, the more uncomfortable Tara felt. She did not trust herself not to let something slip. Sitting up abruptly, she hugged her knees to her chest and stared at the pool.

"You don't think so? You are," Jenny said, her voice softer now.

"I don't know."

"Well you are."

"Thanks."

The glow from the mushroom was beginning to fade. Normally at this point Jenny would close her eyes and put some tenacity into "recharging" it, but instead she lay back and gazed at the gills above, apparently lost in thought.

Tara picked at her fingernails. "Well, I'm feeling tired. I think I'll head back."

"You want to be alone." It was more statement than question.

"Yeah. Is that okay?"

"Of course it is, Tara," Jenny said, her tone suddenly very adultlike, and reached over to touch the back of Tara's hand.

The sudden bright glare was so intense Tara had to shield her eyes. The mushroom cap above them was shimmering with incandescence, and the temperature had skyrocketed. She watched in awe as the edges of the gills began to singe and curl while nearby fungal bushes radiated accelerating pulses of dazzling turquoise light.

"What's happening?!" Tara yelled. As she gaped at the flaming gills, she saw that beyond the mushroom cap, way up above them on the faraway ceiling, a broad swath of moss was rapidly pulsing, too, already ten times brighter than normal.

Jenny wrapped both hands around Tara's wrist and squeezed hard. Tara's necklace bounced upward as if jolted by electricity. She yelped. Jenny was staring straight at her, eyes wide, mouth half open. Tara stood, and Jenny stood up with her, leaning in, holding on even more tightly. The brightness all around them increased. Out of terror and reflex, Tara yanked free and dodged out from under the burning mushroom.

The ceiling and surrounding fungus stopped glowing immediately, and within seconds everything had returned to its normal luminosity. Tara looked at her wrist. Jenny's little hands had gripped it so tightly her fingers had left marks.

"What did you do?" Tara said, backing a couple of steps away.

Jenny was gaping up at the smoking underside of the mushroom, as if in a daze.

"Well?!" Tara demanded.

"Um... I don't quite know...." There was a tremor in the girl's voice, but her face was alive with excitement. When she turned her bright hazel eyes on Tara, she opened her mouth as if about to say something, but then just stood there and eyed her slowly up and down.

"Did you like malfunction or something?" Tara said.

Jenny pushed a strand of still damp hair from her forehead, blinking rapidly, eyes drifting to Tara's wrist.

"Um… I'm sorry. I guess… yeah, I must have gotten carried away. I… I didn't mean for that to happen…."

"Why wouldn't you let go?"

Jenny just shook her head. She was shivering, but Tara didn't think she was cold. She seemed exhilarated.

Tara took another step backward. "Well that was pretty intense, Jenny."

"I know," Jenny finally said. "I'm sorry, I'll be more careful."

Tara held her wrist up to look at the marks more closely. They were fading.

Jenny cocked her head for a moment, then walked over to stand in front of her, one hand held out. "Still friends?"

Tara hesitated. Whatever had just happened had felt *dangerous*. But here Jenny was, looking enthusiastically cheerful and friendly and apologetic all at once, offering a handshake. Tara took her hand tentatively. Nothing happened. They shook.

"Sure. Friends. Of course," Tara said.

"Yay!" Jenny exclaimed and threw her arms around Tara's middle. "I'll be more careful next time, I really will, I promise."

Not knowing what else to do, she patted the girl's back, feeling all the more awkward knowing Jenny was at least old enough to be her mother. Tara frowned at the tree-sized mushroom behind her. It looked charred and slightly wilted, and smoke was drifting out over the pool.

"Okay, well, I guess I'll go now." She tried to pull away.

"Alright," Jenny pouted, giving her one last squeeze before letting go.

As Tara reached the start of the path where the bushes grew, Jenny called out to her and waved cheerfully. "See you later big sister!"

Tara returned the gesture, putting as much enthusiasm into it as she could muster. "After a while, little sister."

On her way back to the house, she replayed the incident in her mind, as well as the conversation they'd had beforehand. She could not shake the feeling that something terribly wrong had just happened. Over and over, a series of images flashed through her thoughts: That intent look in Jenny's eyes, the fingermarks she had left, the fierce thrill that had seemed to pass through her.

The side of her neck itched suddenly, feeling as though something had gotten caught between her skin and the necklace. When she held it out from her neck to inspect it, she saw that the glass around one of the silver beads was touched with blood. On closer examination, she realized it had fractured. *I'll have to tell Aguilar about that*, she thought, and readjusted it so that the jagged section was no longer rubbing against her skin as she walked.

Day 4. Yesterday Jenny nearly cooked us alive by accident. Then she seemed weirdly happy about the whole thing. And then all last night she was acting super strange, always wanting to do things like sit right next to me or hold hands or get me to give her a hug. It was a bit creepy. Then this morning I went for a walk and came across her and Ion whispering in the garden. I said hi because I knew they'd seen me, and she smiled and waved like everything was normal. Ion looked pissed though, so I said sorry for interrupting and went inside. Later I heard him fly off but then

Jenny didn't come in and I haven't seen her since. I guess she's avoiding me.

Tara put the pen down and stared out the window. Every afternoon since Aarov had been kind enough to form the booklet and writing implements for her, she had sat at the little desk for an hour or so to jot down her thoughts and details of her experiences among the Cavedwellers. But today she just wasn't feeling it.

She was trying not to let it stress her out that the Elder and his Councilmembers still hadn't come up with a solution. Aguilar would be over in an hour or so to tell her of the day's progress; he always showed up at about the same time. She told herself she shouldn't get her hopes up. It would take time. They'd said that.

She stared at the words she'd scrawled in her chicken scratch across the page. It suddenly felt like a pointless pastime. She certainly hoped it was pointless, anyway. Because if they figured out a way to send her home, then the diary would cease to exist, at least for her. Every day she wrote an entry was another day they'd failed. The only reason to keep writing would be so that she'd have something to occupy her anxious mind while in the Afterrealms. Therefore, the very act of keeping a diary was essentially an act of giving up.

Feeling ill, she slapped the booklet closed and hurled it into the corner, then stalked to the kitchen.

It was not a kitchen as she ever would have thought of one, but it did have a small fungus-burning hearth in the wall, some pots and pans, and a table with three chairs. She fanned the coals and put the strange kettle-like vessel on; it felt like it had enough water in it for a cup of tea. She was sick of the flavor, but there wasn't anything else to drink except plain water.

Thirst was a strange thing. She'd noticed a pattern since arriving in the Caves; she only felt thirsty if she thought about it first, and never otherwise. Same thing with hunger: She only ever got hungry if someone mentioned food or if it had occurred to her that she *should* be hungry because it had been a while since she'd eaten. Then she would be suddenly ravenous.

Sleep was different. Tara seemed to get tired all the time; even through the relative calm of the past few days, she would get so mentally exhausted she couldn't think straight. It happened quite often. Then she would have to take a nap, or lie down for a longer sleep at night—Jenny had to tell her when it was nighttime, because she otherwise would never have known. To Tara, the moss always seemed to glow at the same level of brightness, freakish-burst-of-energy incidents notwithstanding. But then she never slept very long, even during the longer "nighttime" sleeps.

With the exception of the night before, the two girls had gotten into the habit of staying up late and getting up early together, spending practically every waking moment in each other's company. Last night, however, Tara had stayed up by herself, listening, waiting, occasionally opening the front door to gaze across the brook. At one point she'd heard voices through the door to Aarov's and the Elder's abode, but hadn't been in the mood to talk to them, so had made herself go to bed. As soon as her head had hit the pillow, she'd been out like a light.

There was a knock at the door.

"Come in," Tara called. It would be Aguilar. He was a bit early, she thought, which in turn got her hopes up. Nearly knocking her mug off the table, she sprinted over to the door. It opened just as she was reaching for it.

Ion's hulking torso filled the doorframe, his chin just becoming visible as he ducked his head down to peer inside. Tara took a step back, alarmed.

"Tara." He hardly ever spoke to her directly, let alone addressed her by her name.

"Yes…. Is everything okay?" She stood in the doorway, unwilling to invite the commander in. It still made her uncomfortable being around him even when others were present.

"Si. Yes. I need you to come with me."

Tara hesitated. "Why?"

Ion appeared flummoxed, apparently not used to being questioned. "Because, you have been summoned."

"By the Council?" Her hopes flared.

"Yes. I am to take you there."

The Council had never summoned her before. It must mean something, she thought. And it had to be good news, because why summon her if it had just been another fruitless day of failed attempts and Councilmembers arguing back and forth over theories, the way Aguilar had described the other sessions so far?

"Okay, coming. Let me just get my shoes."

"Hurry."

"Yes sir," she muttered. Not bothering to untie the laces, she slipped her sneakers on as quickly as possible and raced out the door.

Ion had gone over to stand next to one of Aarov's fishponds. When he turned, his face was scrunched up in a rather menacing expression. "If you… allow me to carry you, we'll get there faster." Even when not angry, the commander's voice was like a low growl.

"Um… carry me?"

"Si." He nodded. "Don't worry, I will not drop you."

Tara frowned at him doubtfully.

With an impatient sigh, he spread his wings all the way out, flexing his powerful arms and shoulders and stretching the membranes taut. "See? Plenty strong enough to support us both."

Tara eyed the wings, then looked past his muscular torso at the far wall of the cavern. Somewhere over there, the small Council met. She had never ventured in that direction, having been forbidden to attend, but judged it to be at least a twenty-minute walk. That wasn't far, but she was dying to know what they had discovered. There was logic in what Ion was suggesting.

Feeling very nervous and excited at the same time, she relented. "Alright. But don't you dare drop me."

It was hard to tell whether the sneer on his face as he walked over to pick her up was one of amusement or contempt or both. Tara flinched a little when he reached for her shoulders with his sharp talons, but while he was turning her around, she didn't even feel them. Before she could change her mind, he had hugged his arms around her, and with a loud billowing *fwhoop*, the ground dropped away.

The huge wings beat mightily, taking them up and up. Tara's body had gone still with fright, and it took her a few seconds to realize she was emitting an unconscious whine.

She bit her lip and stared as the house and gardens shrank below, looking for all the world like miniature models. As Ion flew them toward the far wall, the brook became a thin, curving line, and she had a view of the fields spanning across the subterranean valley in every direction, cut by the straighter lines of dirt tracks. Here and there she saw little puffs of dust or smoke.

The commander's grip was firm and steady. It did not seem as though he had to put any effort at all into carrying her weight. When they reached altitude and leveled out, he fell into a pattern, his wings beating confidently a few strokes before gliding for a stretch. During the gliding stretches, Tara heard nothing but the soft brush of air against their bodies. The quiet was almost serene. Gradually, her panic subsided, and she let herself feel awe. It amazed her that he and the other elite guards could do this anytime they wanted. His form was streamlined, athletic, and graceful in flight; by comparison, her dangling legs looked spindly and awkward. *It's good my shoes are tied*, she thought randomly.

The trip was a lot shorter than she'd expected. Already they were getting close to the far wall, and by the mosslight shining down from the ceiling above, she saw that they were rapidly approaching a narrow balcony carved right into the side of the cliff. Ion's landing was flawless, skimming just over the railing to alight halfway between it and a door in the cliff face. As his strong arms deposited her gently on her feet, she turned to gaze some more at the view of the cavern. The fields spanned left and right, far into the misty distance, appearing a mellow blue-green under the glow of the ceiling moss and hanging tendrils, and a breeze whistled through the nearby rocks.

"This way," Ion growled.

Tara followed him through the door. It led onto a narrow landing in a spiral staircase cut from the rock, similar to the one they had traversed the day they'd arrived in the cavern but much broader. Ion ascended two steps at a time, making her have to struggle to keep up.

At the second landing, he knocked before pushing open a heavy door. The room was roughly oval-shaped, with a high ceiling and tall windows that overlooked the cavern and its fields far below. At first glance, the long table in the middle of the room appeared to be carved of wood, but as Ion walked her around it to where the Councilmembers were gathered, she realized it was fashioned from some kind of dense fungus. Her father would have been fascinated, she thought.

The Councilmembers were standing in a circle around a shallow stone bowl that was at least ten feet in diameter and half filled with clear liquid. On the other side of them gaped an enormous fireplace. Despite the height of the ceiling and the open windows, the chamber was warm from its embers.

Aguilar stood between Aarov and a woman with auburn hair dressed in a flowing black outfit. Opposite them, next to the Elder, was a man wrapped in barbed wire. Cringing inwardly, Tara looked again and saw that the wire was fused to him; it studded his face, his neck, and wound right down his arms. She could even see the shapes of barbs poking out from under his tunic and trousers, and wherever metal entered or exited his flesh, the skin appeared pale and clammy and splotched with purple and yellow bruises. An elderly lady with cloudy eyes and deep wrinkles leaned on his arm, and next to them stood a handsome woman with short hair who wore a cutaway tailcoat, wool twill trousers, and a top hat, looking as though she had stepped right out of the nineteenth century. Perhaps she had, Tara thought.

"And here she is," the Elder said, spreading his hands as she and Ion approached. "Tara, welcome."

Tara could feel them all eying her in silence. She wanted to go stand next to the general, but there was no room there, so she reluctantly followed Ion to a spot next to the man with the barbed wire.

As she took her place between him and Ion, he wrinkled his nose, eyeing her up and down. "Well, she doesn't look like much."

"Looks can be deceiving," the auburn-haired woman snapped while contemplating Tara with suspicious, penetrating eyes. "And intentions are often hidden."

"She's just a girl," Aarov said from across the circle. "Remember? The innocence of childhood and all that? Oh, never mind, m'lady; that was literally eons ago for you."

The woman rolled her eyes.

"Time is of essence," the Elder interrupted. "Tara, we have brought you here to help us try something. So far, despite the considerable tenacity we collectively possess, all our efforts to open a crossing to your realm have failed. It has been posited that your nature, being still… alive, as it were, may just give us the nudge we need."

"Okay," Tara muttered shyly, fighting the urge to look at the floor. "What do you need me to do?"

"Stand right here, child," the elderly woman said, pointing at a spot by the edge of the stone bowl without looking at it, making Tara wonder if she was blind.

After Tara had done as she was told, the barbed wire man reached for her hand. She recoiled. The woman in the top hat chuckled.

"It's okay, Tara. He won't bite." Aarov winked. "Much."

She glanced at the general. When he nodded reassuringly, she let the man take her hand, cringing a little when one of the rusty steel barbs touched her finger.

The elderly woman on his arm took her neighbor's hand, and so on, right round the circle, until all seven of them were linked to Tara by a chain of hands.

"Now just relax, and look into the bowl," the Elder said. "I want you to visualize something from your home; something very familiar. It needs to be so familiar to you that you could draw it with your eyes closed."

"I'm no good at drawing," she stammered.

"That's okay. Just pick something or someone you wish with all your heart you could return to. We will call that object or person your anchor. Keep your anchor in mind, and whatever you do, do not let your eyes stray from the essence in the bowl. Are you ready?"

Tara closed her eyes and pictured her mom's face. She could see her standing there, right in front of her, clear as day. A lump was growing in her throat when she opened her eyes again. "Yes sir."

She stared into the bowl, and the Councilmembers bowed their heads in unison. A moment later, the room shuddered as though from an earthquake tremor, and the water began to ripple. As she watched, it became apparent that the surface was moving in patterns. At first, the ripples started in the center and radiated concentrically outward, but then they switched to straight lines running from one side to the other. Then to spirals. Before long, she found herself mesmerized.

"Remain mindful of your anchor."

Tara stared into the patterns, imagining her mother's eyes. She wanted to reach out to her, put her arms around her, feel her comforting embrace. She remembered the last time she'd seen her mother, in her bedroom. Tara had been angry and hurt and had said hurtful things. She swallowed against the lump. It ached. *Please let this work. Please let me go home. Please please let me go home.*

The vibrations intensified, and she thought she heard a low hum emanating from somewhere. Then the liquid went completely flat.

The man with the barbed wire cursed and let go of her hand. "Well that did nothing."

Everyone was talking at once, except for the Elder, who continued to stare into the bowl, deep in thought.

"Perhaps using her as an amplifier is not enough," the auburn-haired woman said. "Maybe it's more than just the strength of our tenacity that matters. We might need to do this at a specific location, perhaps even at a specific time."

"Are you suggesting that we take her to the Conduits?"

She nodded. "All the way upstream to one of the major ones, would be my guess."

The woman in the top hat dipped her head politely. "With all respect, we have no evidence that location or time or anything other than tenacity matters. Theoretically, a crossing should be able to be opened from anywhere. The right amount of tenacity and focus should do it."

"Those theories could be wrong," the elderly woman countered.

"We have no evidence either way," Aarov said.

"Enough. We will try again," the Elder said simply.

They tried again. This time Tara focused on the sound of her mother's voice, and tried to remember what she smelled like. Amid the ripples moving over the surface, she saw sunlight shafting through the kitchen window and her mother sitting at the table, smiling up at her. Tara called out to her. Afterward she wasn't sure whether she'd cried out loud or just in her mind.

The patterns intensified as before, but moments later, the surface of the liquid went flat again. Tara's excitement and hope were quickly changing to despair.

"Again," the barbed wire man grumbled.

The room shook as they tried again. And again. By the fifth time, Tara was feeling quite useless and small.

Between attempts, the Councilmembers floated various ideas, and most had begun to ask her questions about all kinds of seemingly unrelated things. She answered as patiently as she could, but deep down all she wanted to do was close her eyes and go to sleep. She was exhausted, and felt like a fool. She'd gotten herself into this mess, after all; had she never gone to the cemetery that fateful morning, she wouldn't have come across Fin's grave. And then perhaps she would still be in Forestview, miserable but home at least, and none of this would ever have happened.

"I wish I'd never even seen that stupid stone," she mumbled to herself.

The elderly woman reached across the barbed wire man and touched her arm, clouded eyes staring blankly past her. "Stone, dear?"

Tara looked up, embarrassed. "Sorry, ma'am. I was just talking to myself."

"What stone, Tara?" Aguilar said from across the bowl, his hollow glass sockets aimed straight at her.

"Nothing. Sorry. I just meant I wish I'd never seen Fin's grave, because then none of this would've happened."

"Whose?" the woman with the auburn hair asked.

"Finlay MacCarthy's. She is referring to the freelancer who brought her across with The Mother's help," Aguilar explained.

"Ah. And you believe it was somehow your fault," the woman said.

Tara nodded emphatically. "This all started because I went near his gravestone, I'm sure of it. And it might've also had something to do with crows, I don't know."

"Crows? As in, birds?" the Elder asked.

"Yes sir."

He frowned, contemplating, as several conversations broke out at once. He waved for everyone to be quiet. "Alright, yes, this is indeed an extraordinary coincidence, but regardless, it should not matter."

"Unless," the auburn-haired woman said, holding a finger up. "Unless you *did* something to that man's grave?"

"No, ma'am."

"Or to his remains?"

"Ew, no." Tara scrunched up her face.

"Did you know this man before he died?"

"No, ma'am. He died... a couple hundred years ago, I think." As far as Tara could recall, the dates etched on his headstone had been from the late 1700s and early 1800s. She shot a glance at the woman in the top hat. *Earlier than when she was alive, probably.*

"We should keep trying," the Elder insisted. "Perhaps we simply need to focus harder. Tara, what did you think about before?"

"My mother."

"Good, but this time, try thinking of something else. An inanimate object, perhaps."

They tried again and again. Each attempt, Tara thought about some familiar aspect of her home—her bedroom, a poster on the wall, the backyard, her stereo, a stain in the hallway carpet that had been there for as long as she could remember, the old throw pillows on the living room couch. Inevitably, her thoughts wandered back to her mother's eyes, and then to her grandmother's sleeping face in the hospital. With each attempt, Tara felt more and more like a failure.

"Well that was fun," the woman in the top hat mumbled as she broke away and strolled over to gaze from one of the tall windows.

"It may well be that Finlay MacCarthy is the key to getting her back across," said Aguilar, shaking his head. "I'm sorry, Tara," he rumbled.

"Or it may well be that the key is for us to keep at it, take the time through a process of elimination to figure out what exactly it was that he and The Mother did, and then replicate it. Don't give up so easily, Luto," the wire-studded man said.

Tara felt sick at the thought that she might not be able to get home without Fin's help. Her anxiety was rising, she was running on fumes, and it was getting harder and harder to focus. She could feel despair beginning to reach up through the rock of the floor and pull at her like a hungry toddler. Carefully, so that no one would notice, she slid a hand into her jeans pocket and gripped the spongy spore pod she kept there. Very slowly, she squeezed and released it repeatedly, in regular rhythm, just as Cynthia had taught her.

"Señor, if I may," Ion said suddenly, voice tense.

When Tara looked up at him, she saw his face was contorted with something like disgust. The Elder raised his eyebrows, seeming taken aback. Everyone else stopped talking.

"Of course, commander," the Elder said. "You are part of the small Council now and may speak your mind at any time. All ideas are welcome here. Please, proceed."

Ion scowled around, fidgeting. "Gracias. Okay, well, since this obviously isn't working, and might not *ever* work, isn't it time to start discussing alternative courses of action? This opportunity we have, this weapon we now possess," he said, pointing his chin at Tara, "it changes everything. We could take back our realm. We could take back what's rightfully ours."

It. Tara glared at him.

"Yes, Ion, you have voiced these thoughts already," the elderly woman said calmly. "And once again, I point out to you that Xie's forces are not to be underestimated. Just look at what happened to us last time. You were there."

Ion bared his fangs at her. "Yes, madam, I was. And many of my fellow soldiers were lost. I was there. Make no mistake about that."

"We could strike another truce with the Cradle," the woman in the top hat said with a smirk on her face.

A din of ideas sprang up, with several people talking at once. A couple of voices grew heated; Ion's was getting louder, tighter. Tara tensed.

Aguilar stepped to the edge of the bowl suddenly and bellowed in his deep, loud voice. "Madness! This is madness. Allowing this living *citta* to remain here would be far too big a risk to us all! Have we not already decided this matter? Besides, we've been down the path of alliance with The Mother before, and it was never going to work out, even if her forces hadn't been defeated along with ours. After the years I've spent with her, observing her, I can tell you with full confidence that she would never agree to *any* terms that we would find acceptable, not unless they happened to help her achieve her own goals as well. And even then, she would stab us in the back afterward. Don't forget that from her ancient perspective, it was not all that long ago that *she* was the preeminent ruler in the Realms. I know in my gut that her ambition has not abated; Xie's relatively sudden takeover was but a setback for her. She has been biding her time. Do you really think she would allow us to take such an opportunity from her, or share in the new balance of tenacity it would create? No. Madness. The only way forward is to take The Mother's endgame piece out of play by sending Tara back across. And that is infinitely safer anyway."

The Elder stepped forward, gesturing gently for Aguilar to return to his spot. "I hear you, friend. And I agree, Commander Ion, that it is awful what happened to our people. But that was a long time ago, and we have made a life for ourselves here in the Caves. It is not a bad life, I think you must admit."

Ion huffed. "No, not bad at all for two old men who've given up and stuck their heads in a deep dark hole in the ground."

There was a lot of mumbling and shaking of heads at that.

The auburn-haired woman turned to Ion. "Commander, I would remind you that however strong your convictions may be—and they clearly are quite strong—you are but one member of this Council. We do very much value your contributions thus far, not least of which have stemmed from your vast military perspective. And you are new here, so we do take that into consideration. However, I must insist that you take a step back and learn to compromise. As Luto has pointed out, this matter has already been decided. You had your vote, so now is the time for you to put such thoughts to rest and accept the decision of the majority. Will you abide by it?"

Ion glared around the room, seething in place, but after a long tense moment he relaxed his shoulders, gave a tight bow, and physically took a step backward.

"Good. Good," the Elder said. "Now, on second thought, I think it best that we stop here for today. First thing tomorrow morning, we start fresh. Tara, you will join us."

The Council disbanded. Over the next several minutes, the members approached Tara one by one to give their personal greetings and appraisals, making her feel like an animal at a zoo. She mumbled her replies as politely as she could, but inside her was a raging torrent.

To her relief, Aarov pushed in between her and the man with the barbed wire, who was pontificating away about the subtle differences between varieties of blanket moss. "Walk home with us, Tara? We have more fun on foot, you know." He made a funny face.

She nodded and turned to search the room for Ion, but he had apparently left without her. When she followed Aarov over to join The Elder and Aguilar by the tall windows, she looked out and spotted the commander just as he was launching from the rock balcony below. From it he surged upward on powerful wings, then leveled out and beat back across the valley at breakneck speed.

Chapter Fifteen

She didn't know how long she'd been out. It could have been one hour or seven; the mosslight seeping in through the window was the same dim level as always. As she stared at the ceiling, she knew she'd been dreaming of her mom and brother. She could still feel them. They'd been in a car together, driving down a two-lane highway. Row after row of frozen cornstalks had spread out in every direction, brown and dead beneath a churning graywater sky, the nearest ones blurry from the speed of their passing. There had been an uneasy feeling that the brakes might not be working, yet they'd been accelerating. She'd heard someone calling her name in a harsh whisper that had gotten louder and louder as they hurtled toward the horizon.

"Tara!"

Tara opened her eyes again and rubbed the sleep out of them. The voice was real. She sat up and looked out the window just in time to see the back of Jenny's head as she disappeared into the fungal bushes between the house and the brook.

There was no light coming from under the door to Aarov's and the Elder's abode. They had not yet woken her to attend the small Council session with them, so she judged it must still be too early. It was strange that Jenny had called to her from outside. Why not just come in? The door wasn't locked.

Tara got dressed quickly and went to open it. Ion stood a couple yards back from the entrance, facing her, his wings half unfolded and a grimace on his face.

"Hi, Ion," she muttered unenthusiastically with a yawn from just inside the door. She'd have preferred to walk with Aguilar and the others, but perhaps they'd already left. "Did I oversleep?"

"Jenny needs to talk to you," he snarled, gesturing back over his shoulder.

No sooner had Tara stepped outside than a large figure reached toward her from the left and grabbed her in a bearhug. Tara shrieked. A hand with long, slender fingers clamped over her mouth. She struggled against the constricting embrace and tried to bite her captor's hand, but sharp talons pressed firmly against the soft flesh of her cheek until she yielded. Looking wildly around, she saw that there were two of the bat-things in addition to Ion; they must have been hiding to either side of the door. She let her body go loose in an attempt to drop and squirm out of the creature's grip, but then the other one had her by the middle and was lifting. She kicked air, twisting with all her might, but they had her.

Ion walked slowly toward them and raised a dark brown sack to her head. Tara grunted and flailed, elbows jabbing, but her assailants held firm. For a moment, the edge of the sack got stuck between the back of her head and her captor's chest. She slammed her head backward, thudding solidly, and then again, but nothing she did would loosen the elite guard's grip on her.

As the hand over her mouth was replaced with a cloth gag, she managed to get out a partial scream, but seconds later they had it knotted tight, and her voice came out muffled. The sack's coarse fabric slid the rest of the way over her face. She felt them cinching it off around her neck, so close to choking her that she stopped squirming. Immediately after, she could feel someone tying her legs together at the ankles.

"¡Rápidamente!" a voice hissed.

They bound her wrists. Tara tried to communicate, tried to plea. She tried to say, "Commander Ion, please," but it came out, "kayada Aya, ffwaaff."

"Dame la chica." It was Ion's voice.

She felt strong hands take her from the one who'd been holding her, and thought they might belong to Ion. His arms wrapped securely around her middle, squeezing so tightly she had difficulty breathing. She emitted a series of muffled yells. *Let me go!* "Nwah nga ngoo!"

"Vamos," a gruff voice murmured, and they took off.

Terrified of being dropped, Tara stopped struggling but continued to yell and shriek at her abductor as loud as she could. Nothing was visible through the thick fabric, but she could feel the strength of his wingbeats through his chest and the air rushing past her body, and knew they were gaining altitude at a fast clip.

"Put me down!" she tried to roar, but it came out an incomprehensible garble. If the one carrying her was indeed Ion, she could imagine him ignoring her as he flew, a grim scowl on his face like the one he'd worn the whole time in the Council chamber. Tara shouted a few choice curse words at him, but they were lost to the wind.

He never stopped working his wings long enough to glide. Without any visual reference points, she had no idea where she was being taken, but at the speed they were going they should already have reached the far wall by now, so she reckoned they must be flying lengthwise along the cavern toward one of its ends instead. No one talked, but now and then she heard the swooping wingbeats of others nearby. It sounded as though several more had joined them.

Tara felt the panic building in her as they flew on. With every passing second, she was being taken farther away from the house, from Aguilar, from the Council. From any possibility of getting back home. Tears stung her eyes. She raged against them, biting down hard on the gag in the hope she might sever it with her teeth. It was too tough. Jaw aching, she went abruptly quiet and surrendered to the helplessness of her predicament, doing her best to focus on a mental exercise to keep calm.

The air ripped past, her captor's chest muscles bunching and stretching over and over against her back in rapid rhythm. The sensation drove a cold anger into her belly, a murderous loathing, and she began to plot what she would do once they landed. Most of the guards carried weapons, she'd noticed, and most of those had long, sharp blades. She would get her hands on one when Ion let his guard down and plunge it straight into his chest as hard as she could. Then she would try to reason with the other bat-things, tell them their commander was dead so they might as well just take her back to the Elder and Aarov. That part she didn't feel so sure about. She kept brainstorming.

Someone nearby murmured some words in Spanish, and moments later she felt her captor's body tilt. She could feel them banking to the left, and then to the right. This continued erratically for a few minutes. Before long, the sounds of their wingbeats grew suddenly louder, as though reverberating from nearby walls. Her stomach flipped as they dropped, lifted again, and banked hard to the right. The elite guards spoke softly amongst each other in short sentences as they flew, keeping their voices down, but she couldn't understand what they were saying.

"Aquí," her captor growled. *Definitely Ion.* She felt him lift her body upward, then a soft thud as they landed. All around them were the sounds of other bat-things setting down. There must be dozens of them, she thought.

"Was the bag over her head really necessary?!" It was Jenny's voice.

"In my experience, *citta* who cannot see are much less likely to struggle," Ion said.

"Take it off. Her hands and feet are tied; she's not going anywhere."

Tara felt Ion set her down on a hard floor. The sack was lifted from her head, and she could see again. The sudden light made her squint, though as her eyes adjusted, she could see that it was only a dim glow coming from a woven garland and wristbands Jenny wore. The girl-woman stood regarding her from the other side of a broad shelf, surrounded by bat-things, some of which were still landing and tucking in their wings. Her expression held no trace of the eager friendliness she'd shown her before. Tara turned to look over her shoulder, past Ion's legs, and had to recoil at the sight of a chasm disappearing into darkness directly below them. She'd been deposited very close to the precipice, with only Ion standing between her and the edge. Looking up, she saw rock walls rising straight up into the gloom, forming a roughly cylindrical shaft about fifty feet in diameter.

It was all in Spanish, but an argument seemed to have broken out. Ion was involved, as were Jenny and several others. They sounded tense. After a while, Jenny stopped talking, and it came down to two of the elite guards, apparently with opposing views, each trying to persuade their commander. One of them had a sword that hung scabbarded at his belt. Tara eyed it closely. The words grew heated until Ion barked a command and the two bat-things fell abruptly silent. No one said a word after that.

Some of the guards sat, but most crowded along the edge of the chasm, peering intently down into it as if waiting for something to happen. Before long, there was a whoosh of air as a lone bat-thing appeared out of the darkness, careening up into the light, saluting Ion and cocking an eyebrow at Tara as she landed.

"Commander," she said in English. "No sign of anyone following. The general troops were mobilized," she breathed, "even more quickly than we anticipated. But they seem to have taken the bait. By all appearances, the Elder doesn't know we came this way."

"It's only a matter of time. My fathers are no fools," Jenny said.

"Agreed," Ion said. "Vamos."

Scooping Tara into his arms, he spread his wings and was springing upward before he even had her fully positioned. Jenny's dim light fell below them as they spiraled up the cylindrical shaft, Ion's wings pumping powerfully. The last thing Tara saw before the light faded completely was a faint impression of wingtips just barely missing the walls as they climbed into the pitch black.

The shaft seemed interminable. They went higher, gaining several times more altitude than Tara thought possible when she recalled how deep underground she and Aguilar had traveled. After a while, she wasn't even sure they were still flying upward. Then a tiny circle appeared above them, so faint she thought at first it might be her imagination, but it grew and grew, silhouetting Ion's head, until she recognized it as a distant rock ceiling.

They burst from a hole in the floor of a vast grotto, one half of which was open to a starry night sky. Vegetation crowded in from all sides of the opening, sending roots and vines down like bushy wigs or beards. The stars were breathtaking, and surprising; for some reason Tara had thought it would be daylight outside. *That'll make it easier to escape*, she thought, but then remembered the bat-things could see just fine in the dark.

Ion landed just inside the broad cave entrance, in the shadows a few steps back from where starlight hit the cavern floor. Looking outward, Tara could see rocky gray crags all around. They were on top of a mountain and surrounded by sharp, rugged peaks. Stunted trees and shrubs clung to the cliffs here and there, but many of the surfaces were sheer.

The others flooded out of the hole, a mass of leathery wings and ears and armor. The one carrying Jenny came to a stop just behind Ion. Jenny closed her eyes, and Tara watched as her garland and wristbands faded until they no longer produced any light.

They waited in silence. Tara could hear her heart beating in her ears. A few minutes later, the scout rose almost silently from the hole and landed gracefully next to Ion with a salute.

"Still no sign, commander."

Ion grunted and put Tara down, then got down on hands and knees and crawled up to peer over the rim of the grotto. No one moved or said a word. At length, he beckoned them to his position.

Jenny and the elite guards joined him at the opening, keeping low. Tara was left sitting alone in the shadows, hands and ankles tied. The gag had long since rubbed the corners of her mouth raw. As she narrowed her eyes at Jenny's crouching figure, her mind swam in dark currents.

"There," she heard Jenny say. The girl was pointing at something, and a few of the others murmured assenting sounds in Spanish.

Ion stood, apparently no longer afraid of being seen, and walked back to Tara. When he bent down, he undid her gag. She spat at him.

He hmphed, then bent down again to untie her arms and legs. "Don't try to run, little girl," he said. "You wouldn't get far. And keep quiet, or I will put this back on you."

"Just take me back. Please. I promise I won't tell them where you went. I just want to go h—"

She was reeling, cupping one hand to her cheek, face screaming in pain. She hadn't even seen him raise his taloned hand to smack her.

"I said *quiet.*" There was a threatening edge to his voice.

Tara nodded mutely, too stunned to do anything else.

"Get up," he said. "We walk from here."

As she followed him to the opening, she focused on the line of sharp craggy peaks in front of them. On the other side of those high rocks was the ocean, its distant rolling waves clearly visible beneath the night sky. *Or a River,* she thought, though she could not see to the far shore. The sight was disorienting; she had assumed they'd have come out on the other side of whatever realm they were in, and that the water, if visible at all, would be back behind them somewhere. She realized she had no concept of where and how far the Caves led.

Before them was a cliff that dropped a few hundred feet to a rocky scree slope, but to the right were a series of grassy shoulders slanting steeply downward. Jenny was already heading that way, looking sure-footed and dainty at the same time, her hair almost silver in the starlight. The bat-things followed, and the scene struck Tara as a bit absurd: a bunch of hulking monsters tiptoeing down the mountain, being led by a nine-year-old.

"Go," Ion said gruffly. "I will be behind you."

"Why don't we just fly down?"

"Quiet. And watch your step. If you fall, I'll just let you; I'm not going to catch you. Entiendes?"

Tara glowered at him for a second, but then followed the train of guards down the grassy shoulder, keeping her weight centered and carefully planning her steps.

It took them an hour or more to descend into the pine forest that blanketed the ravine at the foot of the mountain. The trees towered overhead, easily as tall as the Redwoods she and her brother had seen in California when on a "botany excursion" with their father. Really, the trip had just been his excuse to spend part of a summer vacation with them out on the west coast. The bark of these trees looked similar, but the needles underfoot were over a foot long.

No one talked as they marched along. Occasionally she heard animal noises, but even they sounded as though they were trying to keep quiet. There was virtually no undergrowth, and the needles deadened their footsteps. It almost appeared as though they were following a road or path, but if that was the case, no one had traversed it in a very long time.

The ravine opened up, and they came to the edge of the forest. The bat-things and Jenny hunkered down behind roots and rocks, and Ion made Tara do the same. Dawn had arrived; there were still a few lingering stars out, but these were beginning to fade against the pale. Before them was a broad flower-dotted meadow, on the other side of which rose the walls of a fort, hundreds of vertical logs lashed tightly together, all ending in spikes at the top. Several figures were garrisoned in turrets above an iron-banded gate, their curved helmets and long pikes silhouetted against the sky.

One of the bat-things made a signal, and several of them split off to make their way along the edge of the forest to the right. Another group headed left. Jenny, Ion, Tara, and about two dozen others remained where they were, apparently waiting for the flanking groups to get into position.

Jenny pulled a hood over her hair, stood, and trotted over to Tara, keeping low. Tara stared at her coldly as Jenny produced a braided band from her pocket.

"Where is this place?" Tara asked.

Jenny smiled suddenly. "This place? This place was once known as Svargaloka. It is the realm from which the Elder and his people were driven by Xie and his armies. This place is by far the most beautiful of all the Realms."

"Cool. Whatever. If you feel even one ounce of friendship for me, Jenny, then please, take me back to the Elder so I can get home."

Jenny sighed. "I know you're angry, and I know you feel betrayed. And I'm sorry, Tara, I really am. But this is bigger than both of us. Bigger than *all* of us. You must see that. Now hold out your right arm. Please."

Tara kept both arms in her lap.

Jenny rolled her eyes and glanced up at Ion. The commander took Tara's skinny arm roughly and held it out straight so that Jenny could tie the braided band in a tight figure-eight, wrapping one loop around Tara's wrist and the other around her own. The girl-woman then touched her hand to Tara's, closed her eyes, and took a deep breath. Instantly, the band blazed with blue-green light. Tara gasped as she felt it tighten around their wrists, its braided strands seeming to fuse together. Then the light was gone.

"Come. You're with me now, big sister," Jenny said as she straightened and tugged Tara toward the edge of the forest.

"Fuck you," Tara said, but went with her, very aware of Ion's looming presence behind them.

A burning arrow shot out from the forest to the right and stuck into the dead center of the gate. One of the sentries shouted, and more helmets appeared atop the wall, peering in the direction from which the arrow had flown. Two of the bat-things on that side walked calmly out of the trees and stood there, taunting. One of them turned and bent over, mooning the sentries. There was a bit of muffled giggling among the bat-things around Tara and Jenny.

The sentry atop the wall shouted something, but Tara couldn't make out his words. The pair of taunting bat-things continued to jeer. A projectile sailed in an arc from the wall to land just shy of the one doing the mooning. He and his companion laughed and gestured a moment longer before walking backward to the cover of the forest, shouting obscenities the whole way.

Several minutes passed in silence. There was a creaking metal-on-metal sound, and the gate swung partway open to let out a party of ten heavily armed sentries. These trotted in formation over to where the decoys had disappeared behind the tree line.

Jenny leaped to her feet. "Quickly," she hissed at Tara, pulling her into the grassy clearing with astonishing strength.

When they were halfway between the edge of the forest and the gate, Jenny removed her hood from her face and held a hand in front of her, palm outward, squeezing Tara's fingers as she did so. A wave of light rippled outward through the grass, growing in intensity as it approached the partway open gate. To either side of the clearing, Tara thought she saw several of the giant Redwood-like trees bend a little just as the wave hit.

The gate erupted in a column of splinters. She heard screaming, and saw at least two figures through the smoke, burning alive as they ran. Jenny picked up her pace, and Tara had no choice but to run with her. They were sprinting toward the now demolished gate. A roar rose up from behind them to their left as that flank of bat elites took to the air and rushed forward. The right flank came out of the forest just as Tara and Jenny reached the gate, apparently having defeated the ten sentries who had chased them into the trees. Tara could see several curls of blue-black smoke rising above the treetops.

Just past the breached outer wall was mayhem. As they stepped over bodies and singed log splinters, Tara saw bat-things swooping down to rain death from above, slashing the sentries' armor with talons or weapons and jamming their hands in immediately afterward to touch their victims' skin, sending them shrieking skyward just as she'd seen Fin do to the brute on the ship.

An inner gate opened, and soldiers thronged into the fort's courtyard, many of them still putting on helmets or fastening metal armor into place. It was too late. Jenny squeezed Tara's hand and held her palm out. There was a great cracking sound as glowing branches came flying in from the forest, arcing over the walls to strike the soldiers and flatten them like bowling pins, tearing them to pieces. And there were the bat-things, ready to rend their metal armor apart as if it were nothing, exposing flesh, sending them wailing up to the forevernothing.

"Why are you doing this?" Tara mumbled in a daze.

"They deserve it. They could have found refuge in any other realm, but they chose to work for *him*, as occupiers. They *chose* this," Jenny said through gritted teeth as she pressed forward.

Tara stumbled along after her, enthralled and stunned at the same time. Wherever there was resistance, Jenny and the other Cavedwellers took it out with ease. Several times, Tara glimpsed Ion's dark shape sailing overhead, picking off the sentries still up on the walls. Soldiers were screaming everywhere.

The compound was quite large. In the middle were several buildings, and these Jenny systematically obliterated, laughing with apparent glee as she did so. To the left Tara caught a glimpse of the wharf, and a small sailboat coming in to dock, half obscured by the smoke from the fires Jenny was causing.

"Allá, allá!" someone bellowed from overhead as he swooped past. Jenny turned to where the bat-thing had been pointing. Several soldiers were running at them. As they sprinted past a garden growing at the side of one of the buildings, Jenny squeezed Tara's fingers and ignited it. Green tendrils of flame licked out at the passing soldiers, and they fell to the ground screaming.

Tara knew she was in shock. The anxiety from all the carnage around her, the shrieks as the elite guards dispatched the sentries and soldiers and sent them skyward in curling puffs of blue-black smoke, the almost maniacal bursts of giggling from Jenny—it had her stumbling along, stunned, hardly able to process. As the last of the soldiers were cornered in what was left of the stables, Tara felt a glimmer of hope that they might be spared, but then Jenny brought the structure crushing down in a blue-green tornado of fire.

By the end of it all, not a single building was left standing, and not a single prisoner was taken.

"Why are you crying?" Jenny demanded. "Get up."

Tara hadn't realized she was on her knees. She struggled to stand, still sobbing.

A figure was walking along the dock from the direction of the sailboat. Tara saw Ion leap into the air and dive straight at the figure through the curling smoke and cinders, talons at the ready.

The figure stopped and calmly regarded the commander as he swooped down at him. At the very last second, the figure dropped to one knee and raised his hand. There was a loud *thump*, and Ion crumpled as if he'd slammed into an invisible wall, his body slumping off to the side and dropping into the surf with a splash. The figure stood and appeared to take a moment to catch his breath, then resumed his trajectory along the dock.

Tara felt Jenny bristle. The girl-woman stalked forward, practically dragging Tara behind her, muttering under her breath.

Tara squinted through the smoke. It was now clear that the figure walking toward them was a man, in a leather jacket and a white T-shirt. With scruffy jeans and dark ringlet bangs.

"*WAIT!!!!*" she screamed, just as Jenny was raising her hand to unleash fury at the visitor.

An entire tree came sailing over the wall like a giant's plaything, dazzling blue-green flame rippling along its 300-foot length as it arrowed straight down toward Fin. Tara planted her feet and yanked her arm backward, halting Jenny's forward motion like a boulder, causing the girl-woman to spin around and stumble.

The collision was imminent. Tara looked down at her shoes, drew a desperate breath, and closed her eyes.

Chapter Sixteen

Something was wrong with the air. It slumped and shifted, separating, like an overwhipped meringue or curdled milk. Everywhere Tara looked, she caught barely visible glimpses of see-through, hair-like strands slipping through her peripheral vision, winking in and out of existence, fading before she could lock on to them. Above, the cloudless morning sky seemed to be shuddering, distending, shifting apart.

Movement in the water caught her eye. As Tara squinted through the still settling dust and debris, she saw many sets of eyes peering straight at her from just beyond the surf, bobbing up and down with the waves, watching her intently. It took her a moment to realize they were dolphins, and that the larger shapes behind them were whales. Time seemed to stand still. Then the sun crested the gray crags along the coast to the left, beaming down brightly, and a tension released, as though the air had snapped back to its normal shape. As she stared, the whales and dolphins sank beneath the waves and were gone.

What was left of the tree Jenny had sent flying at Fin lay in a million shards, scattered in a loose circle across the dock and beach like a deconstructed wreath, with him at the epicenter. He was bent over double, hands on his knees and coughing. He tried to straighten, but then seemed to lose his balance. He tottered a little before sitting down heavily on the dock, breathing hard.

Other than the breeze playing through her yellow-white hair, Jenny hadn't moved, but Tara could feel the rage and frustration radiating from her like heat from a bull. She turned and stared coldly at Tara for a moment, as if sizing her up, then set her jaw and took a step in the direction of the other side of the dock, where Ion had fallen. Tara tried to plant her feet again, but pain shot through her shoulder when Jenny pulled with inhuman strength, and she had to stumble to keep from falling.

As they continued past the dock, Fin looked up and waved at Tara, a smirk on his dust-smeared face. "Howya, girl. I see you made some friends."

"How'd you find me?" Tara nearly sobbed, so relieved to see him she wanted to run over and embrace him. It was a very confusing emotion; he had done what he had done to her, after all. Still, he was a familiar face. And the way back home, she hoped.

He pulled his necklace from under his T-shirt and shook it between two fingers, then was racked by another fit of coughing.

As Jenny dragged her along, Tara lifted her necklace and searched for fractures in the glass, but the coating appeared intact. Augilar had re-sealed the break as soon as she'd shown it to him, but it must have been too late.

When they got to the beach, several of the elite guards were gathered there in a circle with their heads bowed, and more were arriving in a great flutter of leathery wings. A few of the bat-things stood aside to make room for Jenny and Tara.

Ion lay at their feet in a heap, one wing clearly broken. His subordinates had turned him onto his side. Half his face was crusty with wet sand. To Tara, he looked quite dead.

"Pick him up," Jenny ordered. "Carry him up to the bailey and set him down next to what's left of the orchard. I'll attend to him shortly."

As several of the bat-things moved to follow her instructions, three more glided down to land at the edge of the circle. One of them stepped forward to give a formal salute. "Mistress. We've swept the village, and all survivors have been taken care of. Some attempted to flee, including a few soldiers and their platoon commander. They boarded a craft, but we struck it down over the channel."

"They were headed toward Might?"

"Yes, Mistress."

Pulling Tara along with her, Jenny walked right up to where the waves were breaking on the sand and gazed to the right. Half a mile in that direction, the beach curved around and ended in a low, sandy point that jutted out into the blue. Jenny seemed to be watching the point expectantly. As they stood there, the surf from a wave rushed up the strand to wet their shoes. It smelled salty and hissed with tiny popping bubbles as it receded.

"I am confident that no news of our attack got out. We triple-checked, Mistress," the elite guard called from behind them. "The only other runners died in the forest."

"So Xie is still not aware of our presence here."

"I don't see how he could be, Mistress. We were thorough."

Jenny continued to stare in the direction of the point, taut with alertness, though Tara did not think she seemed apprehensive; her demeanor was more one of impatience or eagerness. Abruptly, the girl-woman turned and stalked back up toward the garrison, dragging Tara along behind her.

Fin hailed them from where he'd managed to get back to his feet. "Oi, lil' boss lady! Where're you off to in such a hurry?"

Jenny paused to regard him. "You're the freelancer I've heard so much about." She did not sound impressed.

"The one and the same. Now if you don't mind, I'll be asking you to hand that girl over to me, as we have some unfinished business to attend to."

Jenny raised her hand, palm outward, and Tara heard tree trunks straining and cracking in the forest to either side of the clearing. "What unfinished business?"

Fin smiled as he ambled forward. "Just never you mind. A simple matter of reclaiming a bit of lost property, this is. Now hand her over."

Jenny giggled. "Hand her over? Or you'll what, pray tell?" More trees and branches cracked in the forest.

"Now now," he said, eying the tree line nervously. "We saw what happened when you tried that last time. Do you really think it's gonna work this time? Something tells me young Tara here is the one with the upper hand, not you. Am I right, Tara?"

Tara knew she had somehow stopped the tree. Or that something had channeled through her to stop the tree; she didn't know which. She had no idea what had happened or what she had done, if anything. She glanced around, noticing that in addition to Fin and Jenny, several of the bat-things were staring at her, awaiting her response.

"I… yes. I'll do it again," she stammered. "I will. And worse." When she saw Jenny's eyes, she knew she hadn't been very convincing.

A tenth of a mile or so behind Fin, just off the craggy coast not far from where they'd emerged from the cave, the air over the ocean buckled, sloughing apart in a fissure of gelatinous wrinkles to reveal the huge outline of a ship under full sail. Tara blinked as it slid through the distorted air rapidly, as though along a steep downhill flume. Its huge prow smashed into the water, sending gigantic waves to either side, the ship rocking as it evened out. A diminutive figure balanced right on the end of the bowsprit, and a multitude of others clung to the shrouds and masts.

A shockwave shot out from the figure on the bowsprit, causing the air to shimmer in a cone that sped toward the fleeing shape of a dolphin. It dove just before the shockwave hit, and in that spot the surface boiled and ruptured, whitewater and steam billowing upward. The ship was approaching fast, and at least half a dozen more vessels had already appeared behind it and were slipping through the impossible fissure in single file.

"To the bailey! NOW!" Jenny shouted at the stunned elite guards as she raced back up the slope with Tara in tow.

As the ships drew nearer, Tara looked over her shoulder to see Fin jogging to catch up. Most of the bat-things flew up to position themselves on the half-destroyed battlements, with eight or so staying near Ion's crumpled form where he had been deposited next to the small orchard. Jenny belted out orders as she and Tara joined them.

"The numbers are on their side, but we have the air, and we have the girl. Keep the orchard clear, and I'll do the rest. If we get overrun, we'll fall back to regroup at the forest's edge." Jenny kneeled at Ion's side and touched his brow with her tiny hand, closing her eyes. The grass around him began to glow. Tara felt a surge flow from her hand into Jenny's, a sensation she hadn't noticed before. Little tendrils shot up from the soil, pulsing with blue-green light, and climbed over his bat-like features, curling around his ears and through his thick brown fur, down along his jaw and into his mouth. Jenny hummed, and the pulsing light from the plants intensified.

A deep groan came out of Ion's chest, and his cat eyes opened, pupils narrowing to slits against the light. He sat up, uprooting the tendrils as the light faded from them.

"Commander. We're out of time. The Mother's forces have taken us by surprise. Can you carry us both?" Jenny said.

Ion took a few seconds to squint in the direction of the charred battlements where his subordinates were readying themselves for battle. Then he nodded and got to his feet. He flexed his wings, causing bits of vine to fall to the ground. The broken one appeared to be as good as new.

"El comandante esta despierto!" someone shouted, and a loud cheer went up.

"I need to be in a position of height. Take us to the top of the wall," Jenny ordered.

Ion reached down to gather them up, one in each arm, and vaulted gracefully into the air, sailing up to the tallest remaining section of the battlements. Tara felt queasy from the sudden motion and the acrid air. They landed atop a narrow platform that ran between two walls of sharpened vertical logs, broad enough for two people—or one and a half bat-things—to stand shoulder to shoulder. The far end of the platform was a mess of still smoking cinders.

Tara looked down toward the water just in time to watch the largest ship as it came straight at the shore, not even bothering to drop anchor. Furrows of sand and water went flying as its prow rammed into the beach with a horrible grinding sound. Before the ship had come to a stop, the small figure balanced on the bowsprit dropped all the way down, landing on her feet, and began to walk calmly up the strand toward the garrison.

"She's here!" Jenny shouted. "Be ready for anything!"

Tara felt the little fingers grip her hand. Heart racing, she shot a glance over both shoulders to scan the courtyard and bailey behind them, but Fin was nowhere to be seen.

As the other vessels came to shore to either side of The Mother's flagship, dozens of figures wearing bulbous armor leaped from the gunwales and charged up the beach behind her. She was level with the dock now, and so close already that Tara could see the tattoos on her face.

The Mother was staring right back at her. Then she stopped abruptly, one arm in the air, and the soldiers came to a ragged halt behind her, some of them bumping into the ones in front of them.

"Why hello, Pennsylvania. How lovely to find you here, amongst all… this."

Fin sauntered out from between the shattered walls, calling out cheerfully. "You tracked me!"

The Mother laughed. "Would you have expected anything less, freelancer?"

Fin shook his head and did a shallow bow. "To the contrary, I'd have been shocked if you hadn't." Without turning, he pointed a thumb over his shoulder at where Jenny stood rigid next to Tara, her light blonde hair flowing in the smoky breeze. "We have a problem."

"Oh, 'we', is it?" The Mother tilted her head. "You still believe we are a 'we'? Well now, that *is* interesting." She said this to Fin, but ever since she'd landed on the beach, her eyes had not strayed from Tara for even a second.

"Well, a deal is a deal, after all," Fin said. His tone was full of bravado, but Tara had never heard him sound so unsure of himself.

"We should strike," Ion whispered to Jenny. "Now, while she is distracted."

"Yes, strike; please, by all means, go ahead," The Mother said, pinning her eyes on the commander, clearly having heard him despite his efforts to lower his voice. "Or—you can make the smarter choice."

"And what would that be?" Jenny shouted in her high, clear voice.

The Mother tilted her head to regard the girl-woman. "Ah, yes. I remember you. You were there, with Aarov and Kavi. They refused to let me have you. One of our minor bones of contention, as I recall. But that is in the past."

"Let you 'have' me? I am no one's possession," Jenny snapped.

The Mother smiled disarmingly and dipped her head. "As you say. Not anymore, correct? You now belong to no one but yourself. And I can see that you would make a formidable ally! In fact, our interests are quite well-aligned, wouldn't you say? These *citta* you lead," she said, spreading her hands to encompass the elite guards who stood tensely atop the walls and to either side of the bailey, "if I am not mistaken, they are hoping to get their realm back. And you… well, you, I am willing to wager, would like your revenge. Who wouldn't?"

There was a lot of murmuring, most of it in Spanish. Jenny said nothing. In the distance, tree trunks were cracking.

"So let's make a deal, shall we?" The Mother continued. "I promise not to stand in the way of what you want, if you promise not to stand in the way of what I want. How does that sound to you?"

"She cannot be trusted," Ion said in a low growl.

Fin crossed his arms. "And what about what I want? What of *our* deal? You are the honorable, benevolent ruler at the heart of the Heart, are you not?"

The Mother dropped her hands to her sides and snorted. "Always the presumptuous one. Tell me, young Finlay. This *deal* of ours—did you have it in mind when you sneaked off to find our ward without informing me? You are going to tell me you merely wanted to spare me the effort of searching for her, yes? No. I think not. You have served your purpose, freelancer."

As if shooing a fly, The Mother flicked her fingers, and Fin went flying backward to hit the wall with a muted thud, his body sliding into a heap on the ground.

"No!" Tara shrieked, leaning over the wall to stare down at Fin's inert form.

Jenny yanked her back. She then squeezed Tara's fingers and casually placed her other hand on the sharpened end of one of the vertical logs, palm outward. "I can see what striking a deal with you entails, Mother. No thank you. I'm happy to agree to disagree, and part ways," Jenny said as she nodded at The Mother's flagship, an arrogant sneer on her young face.

The Mother's granite eyes hardened. "So be it," she said calmly, and flicked the fingers of both hands.

Jenny lifted her palm, and a wall of pine needles came funneling across from the forest on both sides with incredible speed to form a barrier halfway between The Mother and the top of the wall, just in time to stop her assault. The impact caused the green barrier to rock backward, but it held firm, absorbing it easily. Jenny gripped Tara's fingers harder, humming under her breath, and the needles drew together into a vortex. This spiraled faster and faster, then drew into a narrow cone and shot down at The Mother in a barrage.

The Mother staggered backward with her arms held up to shield herself as dozens of her troops were knocked off their feet.

Ion bellowed. All at once, the elite guards drew their weapons and leaped into the air, diving down at the enemy with an ear-splitting battle cry. Tara felt the flow from her hand into Jenny's fingers as the girl-woman brought on another assault, watching in horror as half the forest seemed to be uprooted and sent tumbling at The Mother.

The Mother narrowed her eyes at Jenny and snarled. Crooking her fingers, she pulled her shoulders upward as if lifting a heavy object. The ground erupted around her. Pillars of rock and dirt rose up to meet the barrage of flying trees, and the sudden thunderous cacophony of two titanic forces colliding made Tara squat down and squeeze her eyes shut. Jenny's palm was open toward The Mother again when she forced Tara back to her feet.

A look of surprised amusement rippled across The Mother's terribly beautiful face. Planting her feet shoulder-width apart, her multicolored robe flowing in the torrential wind, the woman closed her eyes and balled her hands into fists.

The tether holding Tara's wrist to Jenny melted like butter, and a gut-twisting blast wave hit them. Then Tara was falling, arms and legs flailing as she tried desperately to grasp onto tilting, slanting logs, chips of burned wood, anything she could reach. It all came crashing down in an avalanche. Something hit her head, and her vision went splotchy.

She was on her back, blinking at the sky, sight gradually returning to normal, ears ringing. Tara watched as an elite guard soared overhead only to be speared by a lance that sent him whirling to the ground. She sat up. A piece of log was on top of her legs. Grunting, she shoved it aside, and the ache that shot through her shin made her cry out. The scuffed jeans were stained with blood.

A deep loud *boom* reverberated from the direction of the sea. It sounded exactly like the ones she'd heard the night she and Aguilar had escaped from The Mother's compound.

Another sounded, and another, getting louder, closer. Bat-things were falling from the sky—either diving or being shot down, Tara didn't know which—and shouts and screams filled the air.

A jet tilted overhead, flying low, engine roaring. *What the...?!* She gaped as the aircraft banked to the right and disappeared toward the coast, obscured by smoke clouds from the still burning fort.

"To me! To me!" The Mother was shouting. Tara was dimly aware of soldiers doing an about-face and sprinting back outside from where they had been scrambling through the rubble.

She looked around for Jenny, but she was nowhere to be seen. Tara bent her knee, testing her leg. The pain was acute, but it didn't seem to be broken. She tried using a piece of wood to pull herself upright, but it slid out of place and she fell back down. Rolling onto her side, she made it onto her hands and knees and then got shakily to her feet. Her ears were ringing.

Boom, boom, boom, BOOM.

It sounded like cannon fire, or bombs exploding.

Fin. I have to find Fin.

She slowly picked her way out of the smoldering rubble, grimacing as she stepped over a shredded bat wing. On the other side of what used to be the wall was utter chaos, or what sounded like it; the air was choked with ash, and the pile of debris was too tall to see over. She walked around it to get a view of what was happening.

Through breaks in the smoke, she glimpsed The Mother's forces double-timing it back to their ships, climbing aboard as their leader stood knee-deep in the surf while pushing the vessels from their moorings with her tenacity. Half a mile to the right, Tara spotted other ships approaching from around the low sandy point. These were sleek and streamlined and had massive engines instead of sails; Tara could hear them, could feel their vibrations in her belly. The plane sped past. She watched as it banked over the beach, bomb bay doors open, and several objects dropped from it. She was too slow to plug her ears. *BOOM! BOOM! BOOM!* Columns of sand and water exploded skyward, somehow not touching The Mother but destroying dozens of her soldiers.

The plane circled back around to rain hell down on the clearing between what was left of the fort and the edge of the forest. Through the flying debris, Tara caught glimpses of Cavedwellers beating a hasty retreat. For a split-second, she thought she saw Ion carrying a small figure with yellow-blonde hair in his arms, but could not have been sure. The elite guard wove back and forth, dark wings banking sharply to avoid another strafe from the plane, then vanished between the enormous trees.

Tara found Fin beneath a pair of splintered logs. One was propped on top of the other, both sagging to just inches from his chest. He was still unconscious and had soot all over his face, but appeared otherwise unharmed.

"Fin!" she hissed. "Fin! Wake up!"

She looked over her shoulder. "Fin! Come *on!*"

Touching his soot-smeared face, she leaned down to whisper right into his ear. *"Fin! Please! I need you to wake the fuck up!"* She slapped him on the cheek.

He groaned.

She slapped him thrice more, each time more forcefully. "Come on, please, please wake up."

He opened his lids halfway. "Tara...."

"You're awake," she breathed, almost crying with relief.

He looked around for a moment, blinking, then held a hand to his head and groaned. He shut his eyes again.

She put a hand on each of his cheeks and forced him to face her. "Look at me. *Look* at me."

When the lids parted to reveal those penetrating blue eyes, Tara shook him hard. "Are you listening? Can you hear me?"

"Mmm," he said. "Yeah. We need to go." He tried to get up.

"No. Wait. Listen. I need you to tell me something first, and I need you to *not fucking lie to me*. Got it?"

He nodded, blinking some more, and seemed to focus. "What is it?"

Tara swallowed, looking over her shoulder again, then stared back into his eyes through her disheveled coils. "How you got me across. To the Afterrealms. Was it because I saw your grave?"

He frowned and shook his head. "No, not exactly. Come on, we should go." He propped himself up on an elbow, grunting.

"I said *listen* to me, goddamnit. This is *important*. What do you mean, 'not exactly'? How the fuck did you do it?" She squeezed the sides of his face.

He winced. "It was a one in a million chance. One in a billion. Trillion, maybe, I dunno."

"What was?!"

Fin sat up, careful not to hit his head against the sagging logs. "We should get out from under these."

"I swear I'll fucking leave you here and make them all come down on top of you if you don't answer my question right this instant."

His eyes went wide, as though suddenly seeing her for the first time. "Yeah, okay. Sorry, Tara. Okay. Um, so, it was rather complicated, but, ah, basically it was when you said my name out loud right next to my remains. I heard you, like."

"From here? From the Afterrealms?"

He nodded.

"And that's what made you able to cross over to my world?"

"Yeah. Well, that and a bit of a push from The Mother, as well as some help getting back."

Tara felt despair slithering up along her spine. "So in order to cross over, you need someone to say your name out loud next to your grave."

"That, and you need to be listening. I, ah... I just happened to be listening right at the right moment. A fluke occurrence, so it was."

She put her face in her hands.

He touched her shoulder. "But for you, Tara, none of that matters. I'm fairly certain."

She looked up at him, hope surging. "Fairly?"

"Yeah, well, see, your body is still there. Sort of. It's like, hanging in-between, as far as I understand it. But it's there, not here. Or more there than here, anyway. Come on now, help me up. We need to get out of here."

"So what? What does that mean?"

"It means you can go back," he said, grunting in pain as he leaned forward. "But I can't, not unless someone calls my name at my grave again and I happen to be listening just at the right time. Like what happened with you and me. But you don't need anyone to call your name to help you find the way back across, because you're not dead, see. You just need someone to give you a shove, like. Someone who knows the exact right direction to send you. Someone who's been to that exact spot before."

Tara's eyes were stinging from the thick smoke all around them. "And are you that person? Can you do that? Give me a shove in the right direction?"

Fin eyed her in silence, considering.

"Well? Can you?!"

He nodded. "I can. But."

"But? But what?"

"But only if you help me."

"Help you? With what?"

"With what I've wanted help with from the get-go. I need your tenacity, so as I can free my mum. I told you this."

Tara sat back on her haunches. "But I just want to go home."

Fin shook his head. "I know you do, girl. And I want to get you there. But I can't free her without you. I just can't. She's in a prison I can't break into by myself; I just don't have enough tenacity. Not anywhere close to enough. I'm sorry to do this to you, but I'm afraid I can't let you go back until she's free. But once she is, then I promise, I'll send you straight back across. Just as I've always promised."

Tara rubbed her eyes and looked around, feeling numb. The bombs continued to drop, and people were screaming in the distance. Something roared in the direction of the ships, like a great machine or a beast a hundred times the size of a lion, though the smoke was too thick for her to see what was happening.

"I hate to do this, I really do," Fin said.

"You're a bastard," she said matter-of-factly.

"Yes, I can be. We've been over this before."

She mulled over what he had said, but already knew she had no other choice. "Okay. But just to be clear, will you *swear* you'll take me home? Just as soon as we've freed your mom?"

"I swear I'll *send* you. I can get you home, but I can't take you there; I can't cross with you. Good enough?"

She nodded. "Good enough."

"Good girl." He groaned in pain. "Now, help me up from this shitpile, and let's find us a way out of here."

Her leg was sore, but she could walk on it. They crept back behind the pile of rubble, occasionally leaning on each other for support, and made their way across the bailey, taking cover wherever they could, sometimes having to limp from one pile of debris to the next. No one was around; the fight seemed to have transitioned to a naval battle a few hundred yards out from shore. As they scurried along, Tara caught glimpses through the smoke and dust of projectiles hurtling from ship to ship, some of them scoring hits and sending up plumes of smoke and flame. Pieces of what appeared to be a fuselage and wings littered the beach.

"Wait. Are you sure?" she hissed. They were crouched behind a boulder, about fifty yards from the dock. At the end of it, Fin's little sailboat rocked in the waves where it was tethered, still intact.

"It's the only way I know to get us where we have to go."

"Can't you just, you know, focus your tenacity or whatever and open one of those portal things?"

Fin screwed his face up, looking at her like she was crazy. "Oh, that. No, no one can do that but The Mother."

"Why not?"

"Doesn't matter."

"What makes her so special?"

"She's been here longer than anyone, so she knows shortcuts, like. Hence how she caught up with me so fast."

"And you can't do that? What about just a little one?"

He shook his head and pointed at the sailboat.

Tara scanned the beach to the left and right. Most of it was obscured by all the smoke, but it seemed clear. She glanced back at the burning remnants of the garrison and up toward the edge of the forest. Everyone was either gone or... gone. *Dead dead. Gone forever.*

The sailboat bobbed up and down in the waves, looking very small and fragile. "Fine. But if we get sunk by one of those bomb things and drown, I'm gonna kill you."

Fin snorted. "You do realize I'm already dead."

"You know what I mean."

"Come on, time's wasting."

He grabbed her by the hand and helped her up. After one last look around, they made a dash for the dock, feet thudding over the boards as they raced toward the little boat.

A section of the dock exploded right in front of them. Tara was thrown onto her back by the blast, shielding her face from the flying splinters and sand out of reflex. Fin was hugging his chest next to her, gasping, eyes shut tight.

"That's far enough, Pennsylvania. Time to come with me."

The Mother strode up through the smoke, a furious look on her face. A pair of soldiers ran up from behind her and bent down to clamp irons onto Tara's wrists, then moved to do the same to Fin.

"No, not the freelancer. Dispatch him."

One of the soldiers tried to tug Fin's jacket and shirt up, but Fin was sitting on the hem, thrashing about, doing everything he could to keep his skin from being exposed. The soldier drew his sword.

"Wait! Please!" Tara shrieked. "I need him! Please, please don't kill him!"

The Mother narrowed her eyes at Tara. "Hold."

The soldier stopped, and The Mother turned to regard the battling ships for a moment. When she looked back at Tara, one of her eyebrows was arched. "On second thought, bring him with us."

"Don't you have more pressing issues to worry about, Mother? Why not just leave us be? We'd only get in your way." Fin grunted as the soldiers clamped him in a second set of irons.

The Mother ignored him. After being hauled unceremoniously to their feet, Tara and Fin were made to march behind her as she led the way back to the beach. A small dinghy was waiting there, tossing to and fro in the surf. The Mother continued right up to the side of the boat without stopping, thigh-deep in the water.

Once they were all aboard, she grabbed Tara by the chain between her wrists and tugged her up to the bow, seeming not to care when the movement caused the dinghy to rock precariously. The two soldiers held Fin face-down in the grimy bottom of the boat, the sharp points of their swords touching the back of his neck.

"Let us go," Tara pleaded. "I'm begging you. Please. I just want to go home!"

"This is your home now, child. *I* am your home."

The Mother grabbed her by the armpit and slid her fingers into Tara's sleeve until they were touching her skin. Bucking suddenly, the boat surged forward with unbelievable speed, smashing through the breakers and skimming across the surface toward The Mother's flagship. The Mother's face twisted in a maniacal grin.

A rope ladder was lowered as they approached, but The Mother ignored it. Reaching down with her other hand, she grabbed Fin by the irons, pressed her fingernails painfully into Tara's armpit, and jumped skyward, hauling them both straight up with her. Tara yelped as the air crackled around them. When they came down onto the deck of the ship, soldiers and sailors scattered to get out of the way, and the boards under their feet bowed and splintered from the force of their landing.

"Move!" The Mother yelled, striding forward on her short legs, dragging Fin and Tara along like rag dolls.

Tara managed to get to her feet and tried to reach over to help Fin, but was yanked stumbling forward. The Mother pulled them across the deck and up the stairs, Fin shielding his head with one arm and Tara only barely able to keep up.

"I said let us go!" Tara screamed into the salt wind.

"Enough from you." The Mother turned and smacked Tara across the face.

They were almost to the bowsprit. Through stinging tears, Tara could see the enemy flagship and its accompanying vessels spread out in formation. Most of them spewed smoke and fire, and a few appeared to be sinking, though not as many as were sinking on The Mother's side. Fin was on his feet now, but The Mother's strength was so great his efforts to haul back on his chains had no effect whatsoever.

Tara gritted her teeth, fuming. It was happening again: She was being dragged, pulled, tugged, made to do someone else's bidding, serve as someone else's tool. She was over it. *Sick* of it. Sick of being kidnapped, sick of being carried off, sick of being compelled to go places she didn't want to go, sick of being forced into horrible situations. Sick of having no choice.

The Mother pulled them up onto the end of the bowsprit. Across a span of water, the enemy flagship was turning, its prow slowly swinging around. On it stood a tall figure in what looked like a suit and a fedora.

"How did he know you'd be here?" Fin shouted.

The Mother took a moment to look him up and down, scowling. "I wonder."

The volleys between the smaller ships continued, the sound deafening. Facing Xie's flagship, The Mother lurched forward along the bowsprit, causing Tara to lose her footing. For a second, she felt herself slipping, about to plummet to the water below, but then The Mother grabbed her by the wrist and steadied her. The diminutive woman laughed then, a horrible rupturing sound, and a demented look broke into her ancient granite eyes, as though her very mind was cracking apart. Then Tara winced as The Mother squeezed her wrist hard, raised her other hand, and crooked her fingers to send out a shockwave.

Just then, the figure in the fedora crossed his arms, and the air around him warped like melted plastic. A shining silver object the size of a canoe formed in front of him and came hurtling straight at their bowsprit.

"*STOP!*" Tara screamed.

The projectile was only meters away. The Mother yelled with rage, her bony fingers crushing down on Tara's wrist, and the immense shockwave ripped forward to meet it.

Tara closed her eyes. *Just stop.*

When she opened them again, time seemed to have slowed. A sphere of air and water was expanding outward from her, snapping the bowsprit in two and collapsing the front third of The Mother's ship like a bowling ball rolling into the side of a cake.

The sphere contracted slightly. Just as Tara grabbed hold of Fin's hand, it detonated.

A crater in the ocean ripped open, and the air seemed to cave away, shuffling apart in a million squiggly translucent threads that surged in every direction. The force of the explosion sent The Mother flying to one side of the ship and Fin and Tara to the other.

They were hurled a hundred feet at least, and she lost her grip on Fin's hand. When they came down, the impact knocked the wind out of her.

She opened her eyes to numbing cold water. Sunlight gleamed from above, shifting and sparkling with the waves. It was getting farther away, she realized. She kicked toward it, but for all her effort, she seemed to be sinking. The iron shackles were incredibly heavy.

A pair of hands closed around her waist, propelling her upward. She kicked harder, fighting to keep her mouth closed, desperate not to inhale water. They broke the surface together, Tara coughing and sputtering, spitting salt.

"Come on," Fin shouted. "We need to swim. Can you swim?"

"These things are heavy," Tara breathed.

"Give me your hand," Fin said. She did.

Interlacing his fingers with hers, Fin concentrated on the shackles. A molten crack formed, and seconds later, they split apart and fell away, sizzling as they sank into the water. He then did the same to his.

Despite being freed from the heavy irons, their progress shoreward was excruciatingly slow. Tara did her best to keep from swallowing water, and Fin kept close to her, using one arm to prop her up whenever she started to lag. She could hear cannon fire and distant shouts behind them, but she made herself keep her eyes forward. At the crest of each wave, she could see that the dock with the little sailboat bobbing at the end of it had inched only a tiny bit closer. They were approaching at a snail's pace. Dread pulled at her, weakening her arms and legs, threatening to sink her; at any moment, she thought, The Mother would find them and capture them again.

By the time they finally reached the sailboat, she was exhausted. Fin hauled himself over the gunwale first, then reached a hand down to pull Tara up. She collapsed into the boat like a fish, gasping for air, and shut her eyes against the bright sunlight. Most of the smoke had cleared, but enough remained in the air to make her cough. Her ears were still ringing from the blast.

"Here, take this," Fin said.

As Tara took the coil of rope he passed to her, she heard a soft sequence of descending notes, coming from one of several cloth-covered crates wedged into the stern.

"What was that?"

"An eagle. Nothing to worry over," Fin said as he untied the mooring line and jumped back in.

"An eagle?" Tara recalled majestic wings flashing over the dunes.

"There's a pair of oars there." Fin pointed as he sat down and slid his own pair into the oarlocks.

After watching how he had done it, she sat in the spot he'd pointed to in the bow and followed his example, locking the oars into place and dipping them into the water as quietly as she could. The noises from the battle and the waves washing up on the beach were loud enough to drown out anything, but she didn't want to take any chances.

Fin steered the sailboat from the dock, turning it away from the wave break. Once they were free of the shallows, he pointed it into the rolling waves, angling toward the sandy point, with the battling ships behind them and to the left. Tara forced herself to ignore the silvery adrenaline taste in her mouth, the tingly sensation between her shoulder blades. If Xie or The Mother were to spot them, they would be toast.

"Dig. We need to *move*," Fin urged.

"Why not use the sail?"

"It's big and white. Don't want to attract attention."

She put her back into it, and they soon found a rhythm together, rowing as hard as they could in tandem.

The distant screaming and explosions continued. At one point she looked over just in time to see a shockwave push out from the prow of one of The Mother's smaller ships toward Xie's big flagship. Several smears of blue-black smoke rose skyward from the flagship's deck all at once. *She survived.* Tara was not surprised. Shuddering, she put her head down and pulled on the oars with renewed vigor.

Even after they were on the far side of the point, long after they were out of sight and out of earshot and Fin had felt it safe enough to unfurl the sail and send them underway, Tara could still hear the explosions and screams reverberating over and over through her mind along with the cracking sounds of splintering tree trunks, burning logs, and The Mother's unhinged laughter.

Chapter Seventeen

Tara knew they were sailing along one of the so-called Rivers, but it looked like the open ocean to her. It had been hours since the rocky, pine forested coast of Svargaloka had disappeared behind them, and in every direction dark blue waves trundled beneath a leaden sky.

"Why does this place look so much like the normal world?" She had learned about the curvature of the Earth in school. "Are the Afterrealms or whatever shaped like a sphere?"

"Sphere?" Fin looked up from his reverie.

They hadn't spoken since he'd let the eagle out to hunt. Watching it dive into the water and come up with a fish half its size had been spectacular, though she could have skipped the part where the bird had ripped the fish's guts out and eaten the poor thing right on the side of the boat. Tara had had to turn away.

"Yeah. You know, like a planet."

"Ah," Fin said, sitting up straight. "No, well yeah. The Realms are similar to the place of our birth and death in a lot of ways. In most Realms—not all, but most—conditions are mimicked. Sun, sky, ground, stuff like that. The air, even. Smells, tastes. Sounds. Hell, pretty much everything. I can see why it's got you confused, now I think on it."

Tara thought about that. "Mimicked, as in copied? Like, formed to look like planet Earth, you mean?"

"Well, so, we aren't exactly *not* on the Earth, you see. But we aren't exactly *on* it either. The Afterrealms aren't anywhere. Or any when, for that matter. This world is more like… like a pause, I guess. A pause between where we all came from and the next place."

"And over the years a bunch of *citta* with humongous tenacity formed all this so it would look and feel familiar, right? Like home."

Fin shook his head. "Maybe. Some say otherwise. I don't know. Don't really care, to be honest. It just is what it is."

"So like a pause, you said, between the real world and the next place."

"Oh, this place is plenty real, believe you me. But well, yeah. A pause, like. Delaying the inevitable, I suppose, though my plan is to hang on for as long as I possibly can. Who wants to go to the forevernothing and just be done with existence? Not me. As it was, I didn't get to live long enough when I was alive, so I'm in no hurry to find oblivion, not on your nelly."

The wind picked up, causing the taut sail to flap loudly. Fin worked some ropes for a while, and the angle of the boat slowly changed. Tara shivered and hugged her arms around her shoulders.

"Oh, that reminds me," Fin said, turning around to rummage through a crate. He pulled out a bag, and from it he produced a folded stack of clothing.

Tara's heart leaped. They were the clothes she'd had on when he had abducted her and taken her to the Cradle. They appeared to have been cleaned. She received them mutely, reeling from a mix of emotions. On top of the pile was her favorite jacket. She held it up to her nose and inhaled deeply.

"Thank you," she murmured, stifling tears.

"Think nothing of it," Fin said, leaning back with his hands behind his head to gaze skyward. He seemed to have relaxed his vigil a bit. During the first part of their journey, he'd stood every few minutes to peer back behind them through his peculiar black spyglass, but now he seemed satisfied they weren't being followed.

The light in the sky changed gradually. It seemed divided in half, with the left side having zero clouds and very little detail in it. It looked strange, almost unformed. The other side, directly above them and to the right as far as she could see, looked like normal sky, with high wispy layers of cloud that morphed and stretched over time. She took to staring into the passing waves, searching for dolphins, but none appeared.

There was a distant smudge on the horizon to their right. Over time, it resolved into a coast, dim and plum-colored in the distance. They seemed to be angling closer to it. After a while, Tara noticed land on their left, too. It looked like a perfectly flat plane and was uniformly gray. As they sailed on, the coasts converged. Fin guided the little sailboat closer to the plum-colored shore on the right, but kept a respectful distance from it. The water was very riverlike here,

Tara thought, with the two shores only a mile or so apart, though there did not seem to be a current.

"Are we going to land?" she asked.

"No. It's just safer to keep to the right through here."

"Why?"

He squinted off to the left. "Oh, that realm over there is called Might. One of Xie's territories. Too many unfriendly eyes over that side. Best to avoid it if at all possible."

The waves had diminished to the gentlest of swells. They were close enough to the shore on the right that Tara could hear the water lapping against the rocks. Here and there were signs of habitation: a thatched roof, a mud trail through the wet yellow grass, some livestock. The river curved around a gradual bend, and they soon came to a small jetty. Fin steered left to give it a wide berth. There was only a slight breeze, but they were still traveling forward at a decent pace.

There were figures on the dock. Fishermen, Tara thought. As they drew abreast, she saw that every one of them was dressed in a hooded gray robe. One of them stopped what he was doing and walked over to stand at the end of the jetty, watching silently as they sailed past. Fin didn't wave, and neither did he.

"I saw people dressed like that back in the Cradle, when we first arrived at the wharf," Tara said.

Fin sighed. "Yeah. More and more of these buggers in recent years, it seems."

"Who are they? I think that guy's staring at me."

"More likely he's just being curious. Maybe wondering if we'll stop and trade with them. Or who knows? They're a strange lot, those ones."

"Yeah?"

"Yeah. And they have a funny name for themselves, but I can't recall what it is." He shrugged. "Just another whack job religious cult if you ask me. Dunno why some *citta* had to bring all that nonsense with them when they crossed over."

After an hour or so of the dreary, sparsely settled coastline, the drab unformed land on the left fell away completely, and the wisps of cloud above them fluctuated to sunset pinks and oranges. Strangely, the sky to the left of the invisible dividing line remained the same. Soon the land on the right fell away, too, as the River broadened into open ocean again.

"Can we navigate in the dark?" Tara asked, pulling the collar of her jacket up around her neck. The light was beginning to fade.

"It won't get completely dark," Fin said. He was staring intently ahead. Tara followed his gaze, but saw nothing.

Sure enough, the light only dimmed to a point. Behind them, the sunset was brilliant, but up ahead was a dull sky—no clouds, no color. It just seemed like a nothingness; a void. The wind picked up, and they had to lean against the starboard gunwale to keep the boat balanced. When some spray from a cresting wave hit Tara's face, she was surprised to find the water didn't taste salty anymore.

Fin saw the land before she did, another flat-looking plane similar to Might. Fin stood and opened the eagle's cage. As before, the bird would not come out until he had inserted his forearm for it to perch on. Grimacing a little as the bird gripped tight, he whispered something into its ear, and it exploded into motion, careening over the waves and then banking to climb up past the mast. As it circled higher, it emitted a series of high-pitched whistles, then shot forward.

Fin smiled at Tara and pointed at the eagle's trajectory. "Almost there. I bet you'll be ready to get out of this boat."

"Where?"

"Prosperity."

"That's where your mom is?"

Fin nodded, eyes never leaving the approaching land.

It was hard to think of it as land. The closer they got to Prosperity, the more it looked like a false array of shapes and angles. Tara kept rubbing her eyes; the view was disorienting. Something wasn't right. It seemed unformed, even more so than Might had. Even the water here had gone weird. It was completely flat, smooth as glass, and pitch black.

They drew nearer and nearer the shore, but still it hadn't resolved. "It doesn't look real," Tara said, rubbing her eyes again.

There were no details in the land, and no color. It was just a flat slab of dark gray with bits of tan here and there, only varying in shade if she looked far enough to the left or right and used her peripheral vision, but even then, she didn't trust her eyes. She glanced up, and noticed to her horror that the sky was just as featureless. The land, the water, the sky, it all looked more like fuzzy graphics from a 1980s video game than anything real.

"What is this? What's happening?"

"You'll get used to it," Fin said as he furled the sail and guided the boat up to a smooth bank that slanted at a perfectly even thirty or so degrees.

Tara stood to let Fin help her ashore, feeling suddenly nauseous.

She waited on the shore as Fin fetched his bag and the eagle's crate. As she stood there, she did her best to focus on him and the boat, the only things that made any visual sense. Everything in her wanted to reject what she was seeing around them. She had a strong desire to get back aboard and leave. Anywhere was better than here.

The eagle gliding back down to land on Fin's outstretched arm was a welcome sight. As he returned it to its cage, it whistled nervously, and he soothed it with soft reassurances.

Tara heard a throaty purr from off to the left. When she turned to look, she was struck dumb by the sight of a pair of headlights, fast approaching along a slant of uniform gray. It was a bright yellow sports car, convertible. She was so disoriented she had to sit down.

Fin held out a hand. "Stand up, girl. Our ride's here."

As she stood, she saw a handsome young man with raven hair in a stylish suit and tie open the door and walk around the front of the car. He was heading straight for them, a broad smile on his face. He had perfect white teeth and unblemished skin, and his black dress shoes appeared to have just been shined.

"I was wondering if I'd ever see you again!" he greeted.

"You knew you would," Fin said, embracing him warmly.

The man clapped him on the back. When he pulled away, he looked Tara up and down. "Bossman's pissed, you know."

"He has good reason to be," Fin chuckled.

"Sho nuff, sho nuff. Well, I've been planting seeds in his ego, getting him all hot and bothered about The Mother's inevitable encroachments. Warning him she's gonna make her move soon, so he'd best be vigilant. I guess it worked, because he relocated to Might two days ago."

"Much appreciated." Fin bowed.

The man's eyes seemed to linger on Tara's necklace for a moment. "This is her then?"

Fin nodded. "She goes by 'Tara'. Tara, meet Tang Ping. We, ah…."

"We ah we ah came up together," Tang Ping said. "Very nice to meet you, Tara. Welcome to Prosperity! Where all your dreams can come true. As long as you realize they don't really belong to you."

Fin was carrying the backpack and bird crate over to the car. Tara stood rooted in place, wondering if she should pinch herself. She glanced over her shoulder at the boat. It sat still as a statue in the flat black water. *This isn't real.*

"Come on, let's get out of here," Tang Ping said. "This part of Prosperity is ugly. Sit up front with me, and I'll give you the grand tour."

Mutely, Tara followed him to the bright yellow sports car where Fin was already climbing into the back seat. Tang Ping held the door open for her, and she sat, pulling the seatbelt into place out of habit. The seats were black leather, and everything looked pristine, with not a speck of dust on it. It had that brand-new-car smell.

Struggling to make sense of it all, she thought about the jet and the ships with engines, then turned suddenly to look at Fin in the back seat. "Say, I thought technology didn't work in the Afterrealms.'

Both men laughed. "You can do whatever you want here, as long as you have enough tenacity." Tang Ping said. "There are no rules. Rules are for suckers."

"Most *citta* aren't very mechanically minded," Fin explained. "And even those who are, most tend to prefer simpler, more nostalgic surroundings. But Xie Yuanzhan—whose realm this is—was once an engineer."

"Chief engineer to the emperor," Tang Ping chimed in as he turned the key in the ignition, firing the engine to life.

"Emperor?" Tara asked.

"When he was alive. Back in the Ming Dynasty. Okay, hold on to your seats, folks. This here is my new toy, and I *like* to go fast!"

Tang Ping gunned the engine twice, then floored the accelerator, lifting up on the handbrake at the same time. The car spun around in a 180.

"Hey, you're gonna make the eagle sick," Fin said.

Laughing like a lunatic, Tang Ping floored the accelerator again. The car lurched forward, tires squealing against the indistinct gray surface of the "ground", pressing Tara's back against her seat so hard she had to gasp for breath.

Chapter Eighteen

S he couldn't shake the feeling that they were zooming through the middle of a video game landscape. There was a clearly defined road in that it was a lane with thin black borders that traversed the featureless gray, but when she stared out the window at the passing "ground", it appeared so uniform she had the impression they weren't even moving. Looking up was no better; the "sky" had a lighter shade of gray but was just as featureless. Even the horrible pink chocolate rabbit sky would have been better than this. As claustrophobia pressed down on her, it occurred to her that she might throw up. Using the old-school crank handle, Tara rolled the window down in case she needed to hang her head out in a hurry.

Tang Ping laughed. "Hey Finny, looks like your girl here is goin' a bit green."

Tara wanted to punch him. And then she wanted to punch Fin, too, for not saying anything on her behalf. She sank back into the seat and closed her eyes, but then the car lurched to the right, causing her to open them wide again in a panic. They were going around a series of sharp bends, climbing up the slope of a mountain with a perfect triangular peak at the top and covered in digital-looking squares of gray and tan. She focused her eyes on Tang Ping's knee, and the very real-looking cloth of his slacks helped her to get a grip and calm her stomach.

"Don't worry darling, you'll get used to it," Tang Ping chuckled.

"I already told her that," Fin grumbled from the back seat. He seemed to have fallen into a dark, apprehensive mood, though Tara was still largely unable to read him.

"Why does it look like this?" she managed.

"Xie is a selfish bastard, that's why," Tang Ping said.

She turned around to look at Fin for an explanation.

"He leaves most of his realms unformed," he said. "Xie only ever puts any tenacity into forming the parts where his many abodes are or where he likes to visit. Most *citta* here have no choice but to exist in the gray. As Tang Ping said, he's selfish. Extremely stingy with his tenacity."

A series of switchbacks took them up to the shoulder of the mountain. As they crested it, the car bumped and slid sideways a little, its undercarriage scraping for half a second as though along a sharply angled crease in the road. If there had been a roof, Tara would have hit her head on it. For the fiftieth time, she mashed her foot against the imaginary brake on the floor, eliciting a cheerful snicker from the driver.

"So, how does it feel, my man?" Tang Ping said, beaming his white teeth at the rearview mirror. "Finally gonna happen, eh? You all good buddy?"

Fin said nothing. When Tara glanced at the mirror, she saw he was staring out at the passing gray, forehead pressed against the window, lost in thought.

They shot forward along the mountain shoulder, and a dazzling view spread before them. The gray video-game-like road zigzagged down the slope in perfectly even turns into a broad valley that was more of the same unformed gray and tan expanse, but the opposite side was something else entirely. It was draped with vineyards, bright green and shining beneath what was probably the bluest sky Tara had ever seen. These extended up to the walls of a picturesque village perched at the top of the hill, the stucco white walls of its houses roofed in red clay tiles and nestled amongst a forest of flowering trees.

Rising above the village were the terraced walls of the most tremendous palace Tara had ever seen. It reminded her of a photo she had once seen of the Dalai Lama's traditional winter palace in Tibet, only this was easily five times as big. The terraces were green with what looked like gardens, though Tara couldn't be sure from this distance. To the left, white puffy clouds drifted on the horizon, and birds with huge wingspans wheeled in the distance. It was the most beautiful thing she had ever seen.

The race car engine hummed louder, and she had to close her eyes to keep from vomiting as Tang Ping wove like a crazy person down the impossible slope of the gray- and tan-patched mountain. When they at last reached the bottom, the road made a sharp bend to the left. They were fast approaching a wide blue line that looked like it was supposed to be a creek, but she thought it was more like a cartoon impression of one. The line cut left and right through the center of the valley, straight as a board, and as they got closer, it appeared to be made up of square blue tiles.

The bridge was out. Tara braced herself as Tang Ping accelerated straight for the gap, ramping off its jagged upturned end to sail airborne over the light blue "creek". They just made it across, tires screeching as they landed on the other side, flinging a shower of sparks that winked out against the featureless gray in the rearview mirror.

This isn't real. This isn't real. This isn't real, she told herself over and over, hand working the spongy spore pod.

As the road slanted upward with the terrain, the digital-looking uniform grayness gradually gave way to reality, or to what seemed like reality to Tara. She saw grass growing alongside the road—which was an actual road now, complete with asphalt and narrow cracked shoulders and even a dashed white line down its center. There were ditches to either side with water flowing in them, and as they flew past, she even spotted dew or leftover raindrops clinging to the delicate branches of red berry bushes. Though Tang Ping hadn't slowed down—they seemed to have sped up, if anything—her stomach slowly began to settle as the world around them returned to relative normal.

There were people, or *citta*, standing or walking along the streets of the town, some of them carrying satchels or briefcases. Many were dressed in business attire, and almost all of them had faces and hands that were blurry to varying degrees. Tara thought of Jenny, of the vengeful rage she had witnessed in the girl-woman's eyes, and the thought made her sad. Even though she clearly had her own agenda, and had tried to use Tara to that end, the brief friendship between them had felt genuine. Parts of it, at least.

Tang Ping raced on, not slowing for anything or anyone, occasionally swerving to miss a pedestrian by mere inches. Tara's right foot was getting sore, and her nerves were stretched taut. A few times she turned to look in alarm at Fin, but he didn't seem to be fazed one bit.

At the top of the village, they turned onto a narrow driveway that rose steeply upward, a damp stone wall to the left and a line of thick old trees to the right, with a steep drop-off just beyond them. The pavement shone wet in the shafts of sunlight that made it through the dense canopy above, and the smell of the upholstery and the reflections flitting across the windshield felt far too familiar for this not to be the land of the living. The feeling of disorientation grew, adding to Tara's anxiety. The car took a hairpin turn to the left, then right, and just as they came even with the tallest treetops, she caught a brief view of the valley and its wine fields on one side and gray and tan blankness on the other, the straight blue line running in-between. Then it was gone as they made a ninety-degree turn into a tunnel in the side of the hill.

Electric lights lit the way, fluorescent semicircles evenly spaced along the tunnel's ceiling. As the road curved ever upward, Tang Ping slammed the heel of his hand against the car horn in a series of short shave-and-a-hair-cut bursts and laughed his lunatic laugh.

"Is that really necessary," Fin mumbled from the back seat.

"Bossman's not here. Nothing to fear!" Tang Ping laughed. "Might as well have some fun for a change, don't you think? You're way too serious, my man. Need to learn to enjoy the little things!"

Fin ignored him, seeming deep in thought.

They exited the long winding tunnel onto a small brick plaza situated in the middle of one of the terraces Tara had seen from the other side of the valley. Cranking the wheel all the way right and pulling hard on the hand brake, Tang Ping brought the sportscar drifting to an abrupt halt between two parked vehicles that were also very fancy-looking. Steam rose from where the hot tires had skidded over wet bricks.

Tara blinked. They were stopped, but it felt like they were still moving.

"Did I pass?" Tang Ping turned and asked her, deadpan.

"Huh?"

He shook his head with a chuckle and got out of the car, leaving the keys swinging in the ignition. As Tara numbly unbuckled her seatbelt, she realized with a shock that the driver's side didn't even have one.

"I'll get those, my man," Tang Ping said to Fin, reaching for his bag and the cage with the eagle.

"Gently," Fin grumbled. "She's been through a lot."

"I'll give her food fit for a queen, don't you worry. Want me to come up with you?" the man said, suddenly serious.

It took Tara a moment to realize they were talking about the eagle.

"Wait, no," Fin said as he got out of the car and closed the door behind him. "On second thought, I'll take her up." He took a deep breath, held it, and let it out very slowly, his eyes fixed on the towering heights of the palace above.

Tara got out of the car on the other side and closed her door too softly at first, failing to get it to latch. Her arms and legs were weak. She opened it and closed it again, harder this time, then followed Fin's gaze. The incline was so steep she had to lean her head back to see the highest terraces.

Tang Ping nodded and handed the cage back to Fin with great tenderness. "Alright then. You take her, buddy. I'll give you guys some privacy. Come find me afterward; I'll be in the grand dining room. The one with the fountain." He reached his arms around Fin and gave him a long hug.

"Thank you, brother. This means a lot," Fin mumbled.

Tang Ping laughed. "Shit, man. Words. You know I got you. I love you so much, brother." He clapped Fin on the shoulder, waved warmly at Tara, and turned to go.

As Tang Ping walked from the parking lot and through a curtain of flowering vines that hung down from an intricately carved stone arch, Tara heard his maniacal laughter echoing between the walls. "Dude, yes! It's happening! *Finally!* This shit is exciting! Exciting!!"

Fin was still staring upward, lost in thought, seeming reluctant to move.

"What now?" Tara asked.

Wordlessly, he pointed at the tallest tower.

"Is there an elevator?" she said in all seriousness.

He almost smiled at that. "Come on. It's a pretty long climb."

They headed through the stone archway, then made a left up a long curving flight of brick steps. At first, they were broad enough to accommodate several people walking shoulder to shoulder, but after the third terrace, the path narrowed to only a yard or so wide and the stairs grew steeper.

By the sixth terrace, Tara had to stop, though Fin didn't appear to be out of breath. As they stood next to a tall flowering rhododendron, she asked him in annoyance why he wasn't winded, but he just shrugged and stared at his feet, waiting for her to catch her breath. She had never seen him look sad before. It was unnerving.

She followed him up the steps in silence, doing her best to keep her rest breaks to a minimum, but she was exhausted.

At one point she stopped and sat down on the brick railing, and was unsure she'd be able to stand back up.

"You can rest at the top. Up you get."

"Don't tell me what to do," she said, temper flaring. She had been through way more than the stupid eagle had, she nearly said. She felt drained, and the car sickness had only made it worse.

"We're nearly there. Come on. Just a bit farther and you can rest."

She glared at him, about to deliver some choice words, but the sadness in his eyes stopped her. Sighing, she stood and followed him up the stairs.

When they finally reached the top, her legs were about to give out again. This twelfth terrace was the broadest so far. Entire groves of trees and expertly manicured gardens meandered around to the left and right, replete with quaint little ponds and towering marble fountains. The sight reminded her of a botanical garden her father had once taken her to, although this one was much grander in scale.

"This is where that Xie person lives?" she panted. "He must be the richest *citta* in the whole Afterrealms."

"He has quite the share of tenacity, that's for sure," Fin nodded, his eyes squeezed shut as if angry or in pain. "He accumulates it. Relentlessly, mercilessly… he accumulates it, and keeps on accumulating it."

Tara took in the surroundings, marveling at the incredible variety of plant life, the color-coded plots of flowers, the harmoniously channeled streams and fountains. When she looked at Fin again, he had opened his eyes and was staring at a set of large double glass doors that stood open opposite them. On the other side of the doors, she could see the light of chandeliers gleaming from richly carved wooden furniture.

She looked at Fin again, but he seemed frozen in place. "Hey. You okay?"

He blinked, then gave a tight nod.

Tara thought she knew why he was acting sad. "You're mom's in there, isn't she."

He glanced back down the way they'd come and shook his head. "I don't know if I can go through with it. I just don't."

"Through with what?" Tara frowned, feeling suddenly very uneasy.

A tear rolled from Fin's eye. He wiped at it absently. "Sorry. Being stupid. I have to do this. It's been a long time coming. Come on, I need you," he said, and walked with sudden determination toward the glass door.

Tara hastened to catch up. Inside, they strode past the most magnificent staircase she had ever seen. The corridor they followed had a very tall ceiling and wound past room after room, each decorated more ornately than the one before and full of antique-looking furniture and gilded paneling. One chamber was easily three times as large as Tara's entire house. As they hurried along, she thought she glimpsed billiard tables on the far side of it, as well as something that looked like an ice rink with crimson and gold tapestries lining the walls.

They passed under the last of the chandeliers, and another set of enormous glass doors opened onto a grass-covered terrace. She could hear piano music coming from the left, and as she walked through the doors, what she saw in that direction made her stop.

At the top of the gently sloping grass yard was a huge, covered pavilion with solid crystal walls that extended from the main palace structure to the outside edge of a large balcony. The walls were tinged with pink and were very thick, almost to the point of opaqueness, and the slanting crystal lattices caused objects on the other side to appear indistinct and distorted. Tara could vaguely make out the shape someone seated at a grand piano. The notes rang out across the terrace, seemingly amplified by the crystal.

Fin continued up the yard, only stopping when he reached the wall. He turned to wait, fidgeting impatiently, as Tara trotted to catch up.

The piano-player stopped. "Hello?" The voice was muffled through the crystal walls. It sounded female.

Fin reached for Tara's hand as she came up beside him. "This is the wall I need you to break through. Are you ready?"

"Break through? Isn't there a door somewhere?"

"No. It's a prison. I can't get in without you, I told you. I've tried a thousand times."

"This is it. This is why I'm here," Tara realized out loud.

Fin pushed his left palm against the thick crystal wall and reached for Tara's hand. She gave it to him. He leaned in. "You might need to shield your eyes. This could hurt."

"Finlay?" The muffled voice said.

"Stand back, Mum," he said in a loud voice.

Tara felt his grip tighten. At first, nothing happened. Then the crystal wall began to emit a faint groaning sound. Fin pushed harder, grunting, and a crack shot out from where his palm was, spidering diagonally across the latticework. He grunted again, feet digging in, muscles straining.

Tara looked away just as the wall shattered outward and they were pelted by chunks of crystal. When it was over, she rubbed a spot on her neck where she had been struck by one, and her fingers came away with blood.

Fin had collapsed on the grass. Tara helped him up, and they stepped onto the platform together.

The woman was in shadow, crouching behind the piano, silhouetted against the bright blue sky. As they approached, she stood, and Tara saw with a fright that her entire body was blurred: her face, neck, forearms, bare feet, completely blurred. Only her clothing and hair were in focus. Tara faltered at the sight of her.

"Mum," Fin choked. "Mum." As the woman stood, he put his arms around her and broke down, sobbing like a baby into her shoulder.

Tara held back, heart breaking, an ache in her throat as she tried not to think of being embraced by her own mother.

"Finlay. I've missed you so much…." The woman sounded tired. In contrast to the bold strength of the piano notes she had been playing, her voice was thin and frail.

"I've missed you too," Fin sobbed.

They held each other in silence for a long while. Thinking she should give them their privacy, Tara walked over to stand by the fluted railing at the edge of the balcony. The view was tremendous and mind-boggling, but she absorbed it absently, not really seeing.

It took a moment for her to notice Fin and his mother were in intense conversation behind her.

"...what if, though, Mum? What if we could?"

"No, my son," she said, shaking her head solemnly.

"But if you would just listen, Mum, please. You can't imagine the tenacity that can be channeled from this girl. I feel sure—"

"No. I've made my decision. It's time."

"Yes, but Mum, what if we could make everything better? I feel sure we can defeat that bastard. You'd be free. Hell, we could take over his realms, starting with Prosperity. We could change all the rules, make the Afterrealms a better place. A place of freedom. We could completely outlaw draining, once and for all."

The woman broke away from Fin and lifted her chin proudly. "Yes, you can. You can do *all* of that, my son, and more. But Finlay, listen to me: I cannot."

"But Mum...."

"No. I *cannot*. I've made my decision. You must have known that, even before you got it in your head to go and do this. I'm sure you knew, son, that if I were ever released from this dreadful bondage, there would be only one place for me to go. And not any other."

Finlay hung his head, looking tense. Tara had a horrible feeling in her gut.

At length, he straightened. When he spoke again, his voice was clear, calm. He sounded resigned. "I'm sorry, Mum. You're right, of course. There was never any doubt in my mind you'd stick to your choice. I just…. And I want it for you, I really do, but I'm… I'm just… I'm…." He broke down again, sobbing uncontrollably.

"You're going to miss me. And I'll miss you, too, my son."

Tara felt tears leaking from the corners of her own eyes. She wiped her nose and looked at her feet, feeling suddenly very guilty, though she didn't understand why.

"But you'll be fine," the blurry-faced woman said. "You *will* make the world better. I know you will. You'll make it so that no one else has to endure what I've had to, ever again. You will succeed in that, because that's who you are."

"Yes, Mum," Fin said, recovering. "I will. I promise."

"Good. Hello, by the way," she said, gesturing for Tara to join them. "I'm Alice."

"Hi, ma'am," Tara murmured. "I'm Tara. Um, nice to meet you."

She could not see the woman's smile, but the blurred edges of her face had the shape of one.

"Now then. What say we have a great big fight so it's easier to say goodbye?" Alice chuckled.

Despite himself, Fin laughed through his sobs. "Yes, okay, let's do that." He put his arms around his mum and held her tight, swaying a little, eyes closed tightly.

After a minute, he let go and held a hand out to Tara. Tara took it, and Fin looked doubtfully at his mother.

"Now's as good a time as any, son. And the longer you wait, the harder this will be," Alice said.

"Just rip the bandage off, yeah?" Fin sniffed.

"Yes, son. I'm ready."

Tara felt Fin squeeze her hand, and she wanted to run. But she didn't want to abandon him, so she forced herself to stay.

He bowed his head. "I love you, Mum," he said simply.

"I love you too, Finlay. Your father would be proud of you."

He nodded and stood very still for a long minute, tears streaming down his cheeks. Then he let go of Tara's hand, placed all ten of his fingers just inside the back of his mother's blouse, touching them gently to the skin of her shoulders, and tensed.

There was no wail when she deflated. Right before she turned into a column of blue-black smoke, Tara thought she saw a smiling pair of eyes flicker into focus, just for a second. Then they were obscured, and Alice's essence rose up through the awning, light as gossamer.

They sat there for a long time, Fin against the tiled wall with his knees drawn up and Tara on the piano bench. At length, he got up and walked over to the balcony to gaze skyward for several seconds.

"Thank you, Tara. I couldn't have done that without you," he said, forcing a teary smile as he turned to her.

"It was a pretty sturdy prison, that's for sure," she said and walked over to him.

"So it was, but that's not what I meant," he said, taking her hand, and the smile he smiled then was not at all forced.

Tara did not know what to say. "Hey, a deal's a deal. So, um, what next?"

"Well I dunno, but a deal's a deal is right, so I guess next I get you home. But if you don't mind, we'll rest here for the night. I need to attend to a few affairs, not to mention recover, you understand. Alright?"

"Sure. I'm beat. Tomorrow morning then?"

Fin nodded. "Tomorrow morning. Promise. Come now, I'll take you to where you'll be staying. It's a grand digs, so it is. I think you'll like it."

They walked slowly down to the glass door and followed the chandeliered corridor back through the palace to the sculpted garden. At an intersection, they turned right along a cobblestone path. It wound past occasional benches and stone statues, ducking into a tunnel of branches hung with fragrant boughs of wisteria whose scent reminded Tara of her childhood. When they came out the other side, a flower garden opened up with blossoms of all the colors of the rainbow, brilliant in the sunshine. There was a man tending a rose bush growing next to an old stone wall.

Tara stopped, scuffing her shoe against one of the cobblestones and nearly losing her balance. The back of his head looked so familiar.

When the man turned, her knees gave way, and she sat down heavily on the wet path. "...Dad...?"

(To be continued in *Of Rain-Battered Vine*.)

Thank you for reading! Independent authors like me depend on reviews from readers like you to help get the word out and build an audience. If you like what you've read, please consider leaving a review by way of the QR code/link below. Thank you!

www.otherspect.com/books/OTCG#reviews

Acknowledgements

I am especially grateful for the wonderful support my partner Fiona Post has given me throughout this long process. Her patience, feedback, and inspiration have been invaluable.

In addition, I'd like to thank my brother, Gavin Post, for the amazing artwork he did for the cover.

Thanks also to my editor, Maxine Meyer, for catching so many typos and other mistakes I'd overlooked!

I also could not have written this book without the backing and encouragement of family and friends. Thank you all so much!

Special thanks must be given to those of you who pledged your financial support via the Kickstarter campaign, thus helping me fund this book's production. You have my eternal gratitude! You are, in alphabetical order:

Adam Blair, Amy & Andrew Trueblood, Andrew Banks & Umaporn Klangsang, Anne Brandt, Ben Atkinson, Ben Paul Owens, Carencia & Peter Harris, Carla Coleman, Charla Haas, Chris & Raquel Holland, Chris Williams, Christine and Adrian, Clare Sullivan, Clint Looney, Damian Stanley & Karen DiConcetto, Dori Anderson, Elizabeth Fischer, Ellie & Matt, Francesco Tehrani, Gaines Post Jr., Gary Deason, Gavin Post, Genji & Diem Terasaki, Geoff Bird, Hannah

Wesson, Heather Bellson, Hey You, Jason Krekel, Jay Sanders, Jenny & Morten Storaker, John & Carole Fearon, John Heath, Jon Wright, Joshua Guy, Kassie H., Kimberli Reese, Knut Mork Skagen, Larry Schultz, Lindsey Scruggs, Liz & Mike Berger, Margo Roby, Mark & Lesley O'Donohue, Matt, Matt Beins, the McWaters clan—Peter, Vicki, Marcus, & Jonathon, Melanie Stewart, Michael Hodges, Michael & Mary Trueblood, Molly O, Nancy MacLean, Nicholas Thurkettle, Pat Post, Paul Mueller, Perry Churchill, Peter & Gail Sefton, Rebecca McInnes, Rick Russell, Scott Casey, Shane Youl & May Ziade, Shawn Brown, Susan Bredensteiner, Tamara Mendelson, Tracy Parsons, Vikas O'Reilly-Shah, and last but certainly not least, Zeb Raft.

I also would like to express my gratitude to David Griffiths of On the Soul Side Café in Katoomba (NSW, Australia). Thank you, friend, for the help, encouragement, and support you've given me through my creative endeavours, and for all the great coffee as well!

Thank you!

About the Author

Born and raised in Nashville, Tennessee, GAINES POST transported himself to southeastern Australia in 2007, where he now spends his time dodging parrot droppings, racking his brain, and contemplating his navel. He loves the wilderness, spicy food, and good conversation, and keeps a blog at **www.otherspect.com**. There you can also find more information about his upcoming writing projects.